The Flipside of Here

A Novel

INKBLOT BOOKS

The Flipside of Here

Published by Inkblot Books
www.inkblotbooks.com

9781932461305

Printed in the United States of America

The Flipside of Here

A novel

K.A. Thompson

PART ONE

It seemed as if I blinked and was there; in one moment I was looking at the startled face of my husband, and the next I was sitting on a park bench, looking at the pond. Sunlight spilled across rippled water like shattered diamonds, the breeze teasing it over rocks that lined the shallow shoreline. I sucked in a slow, deep breath; don't panic, there has to be an explanation.

What just happened?

We had just finished breakfast and he was getting up, reaching for his plate. I had tried to push myself up and away from the table, but I couldn't move and couldn't speak. His plate clattered onto the table, and he lunged forward, his lips moving, hand reaching out.

Are you all—

All what?

Before he could finish the sentence, I was sitting on a bench by the pond, fighting to breathe easy, confused by the warmth of the sun and the feeling of the breeze whispering over my skin.

I'm dead, aren't I?

"No. You're not dead."

That voice was familiar; it was deep and smooth, hot chocolate comfort that should have been a shotgun fright. I didn't turn towards him; if he was there and I wasn't dead, then surely this was just a dream.

I closed my eyes and willed myself to wake up.

"You're not asleep, either."

I took a deep, uncertain breath and opened my eyes, and realized that the last time I had seen him was in this park; before he left me sitting there on the bench, he emptied a bag of popcorn into the pond, the kernels floating just above the water, hovering on wisps of air before falling in without so much as a drop of a splash. In my mind they hung there, suspended, as weightless as what was left of the aftermath of our divorce.

I was marrying someone else; I thought he should hear it from me.

Then the kernels dropped, and as they soaked up the water and sank, he crumpled the paper bag, shoved it into a trashcan, and then drove out of my life.

"If I'm not asleep and I'm not dead, then what is this?"

"I can't really say. It's yours, whatever it is."

"And you're here."

"Apparently so."

I leaned back, a thin sliver of cool air between us, and finally turned to look at him. Everything was the same; his jet-black hair in need of a trim, the shadow of a beard that he could never quite get rid of, and those bright green eyes that I had once gotten lost in. But the sorrow, the look of anguish that had rimmed those eyes in flecks of *I still love you*, was gone, and I could see the twinkle that had once drawn me in.

"You're a son of a bitch," I snapped. "What the hell? Of all the ways you could have died, you shoved a gun in your mouth and blew your own brains out. Do you have any idea what that did to the rest of us? To Chip?"

He gave a slight nod.

"I loved you, dammit. Just because I couldn't stay with you—it hurt like hell, Ron. It still does, because I never got past thinking I hurt you that much…"

"That wasn't it," he said simply.

"Then what?"

"It wasn't your fault. Is that enough to know?"

"Oh, bloody hell. You're not even real. I don't know why I'm asking you anything at all. It's not like you'll give me an answer I don't want."

One eyebrow arched, he tilted his head, considering carefully. Then tentatively, as if he wasn't sure it would be welcome, he set his hand on top of mine. His fingers were still rough and calloused, his palm sticky with sweat and warm as he laced his fingers through mine.

"I'm real," he said. "I don't exactly know why I'm here. I do know that you're not dead, and that you're not asleep. I don't know why you chose this particular spot, but I'm real."

"I chose this?"

"Oddly enough, I chose the same spot. But you weren't here. No one was."

"You chose this place, when?"

"In that last moment, before my heart finished beating. I came here and waited. It felt like I sat here for hours, but in linear time, it was probably only a fraction of a second. Once I accepted what I'd done and that it was all right, I moved on."

"I'm not dead but I'm dying?"

"Maybe not."

"Then…?"

"Waiting."

"For?

"To see what happens next, perhaps? I'm not really sure. The only thing I know is that you wanted me to be here, and here I am."

"In the same spot you chose when you decided to opt out of life."

"The very same."

"A spot where no one was waiting for you."

"The only person I would have wanted was in no position to be here."

The one person I thought he would want more than anything died nearly a decade before he did; I didn't understand why he would blink out of his life and wind up here alone.

"You were still very much alive and in that moment the only person I wanted to see was you."

"So this isn't some holding space where you get to reunite with the love of your life?"

"It can be, I suppose. But again, you were alive, and for that I was grateful."

"Pat—"

"She was not the love of my life, Kris. And don't panic thinking I'm here because I was the love of yours. Right now the love of your life is screaming into a telephone, trying to get paramedics and an ambulance to come save you because he knows he can't."

"But I just blinked—and you said I'm not dead."

"You're not. But you did have a stroke. What happens next, that's up to you."

~

"Purgatory," I guessed.

"No," he said flatly, but then added when I sighed hard, "I'm fairly sure you would have to be dead for that. You're not dead."

"Yet."

He shrugged lightly.

"I could die, right?"

"We all die sooner or later, angel. And once you're here, neither sooner nor later matter. How long do you think you've been here?"

It felt like we'd been talking for an hour.

"Doug hasn't even hung up the phone yet."

"What?"

"When I waited here, I thought it was for hours, nearly an entire day. Hoping. Wanting to see you. But in reality—your reality—it was less than half a heartbeat."

"You mean time drags on here that much?"

"No. I mean time doesn't matter here at all. A minute is an hour is a second is a year. You could turn around, and find Doug standing here, all bent over with age, cue ball bald except for a fringe of white hair, and he might ask you where you've been for the last thirty years. But to you, now, it might only be the time it took to inhale once and not quite exhale."

"You're screwing with me."

Ron leaned in close, his head touching mine. "Angel, you're the last person I'd ever want to screw with."

I couldn't stop the slip of a laugh that bubbled up.

"You know what I mean."

"Yes, but when you and I were in synch…that was very good."

"It was."

"How could Pat not be the love of your life, Ron? How could you pop up here where she wouldn't be waiting for you?"

"For one…I came *here*, to where I last saw you. This isn't a place where Pat would have waited for me. She wouldn't have waited for me at all, unless I had wanted her to. If Doug was not very much alive, I think you would have chosen another place and moved on quickly. He *is* the love of your life, Kris."

"But she—"

"She was the love of Grant's life. I knew that then, but I never quite knew how to make you believe that. If I'd done a better job…"

"Don't go there."

"It's all right. I don't mind being where I am. But truthfully, if I'd made you feel as loved as you thought she was, I wouldn't have chosen to leave when I did. I'd have waited for it to just happen."

"You didn't just leave, Ron. You killed yourself."

"I know. But things might have been different if I'd been a better husband to you."

"Or if I'd been a better wife."

"I was happy with the wife I had."

"You're either being very kind, or this is all in my head."

"I loved you. I still do. But no matter what might have been, what had to be, that's what happened."

"No, it didn't. You didn't have to die."

"I didn't see any other way."

"But *why?* All these years, that's what I've wanted to know. Why the hell you blew your own head off, down the hall from Alex Barstow's office."

"Because," he sighed, "Barstow wanted you dead, and I didn't want to be the one who pulled the trigger."

~

"Dead. The Secretary General of the agency wanted me *dead?*"

"You know what I was doing for them in the end, don't you?"

"Protecting your son," I snapped. "He wanted you to kill me?"

Ron spent his final days with the agency working—and there was no other way to think of it—as their assassin. He'd been handed a computer-generated list of names that included their offenses, and he methodically worked his way down the list. Officially his job didn't exist, though the rumor mill spun hard and nearly every agent that had been active for more than two or three years heard about the mythical Renegade Maverick agents. There were never more than three of them in any given time span, and they worked on their own timetables, using their own weapons of choice, and backing them were the resources of the entire intelligence field. Anything they needed, cash from the CIA, drugs from the FBI, firepower from the OSI, it was theirs for the asking.

I'd been introduced to the concept of the Maverick by my father, who worried that one day I would find myself tapped with an assignment to fly whomever the agency was using as their current kill boy; it would be a job in which I could ask no questions and in which my participation would be limited to flying the RM in or out of a particular location. Yet, if something went wrong, I would be as complicit on whatever the RM had done as he would be.

There would have been no rescue, no last minute savior swooping in; the RM didn't exist, and as his pilot, I wouldn't have existed, either.

My father had never been that pilot and he had no real confirmation that the rumors were true, but the fact that he had been hearing them for almost as long as he had been flying for the agency—nearly from its beginning—made him believe in most of the things he had heard.

"There are field agents," he said, gesturing to me, "and their team leaders. There are a few renegade agents who work in concert without a team leader, no more than three together, and there are nomad agents who work alone, but they all exist in an official capacity. The RM is a job that can't officially exist because the U.S. has a no-assassination policy. It's a job no sane person wants because the stress of it…could be fatal. And most of us don't work this job because we want to kill people. We work it because we believe in our country."

Ron took the job to keep his son from being sucked into the

agency machination so hard that there would never be a way out. I knew that; I had known all along that Chip had to be his only reason for crafting a crossbow by hand and then using it to pick people off one by one.

I felt as if Ron had punched me in the chest, forcing all the air from my lungs.

The Secretary General of the agency wanted me dead?

What the hell did I ever do to him, other than show up for one assignment too fatigued to safely fly?

"I thought he did," Ron said. "In hindsight? I just wasn't paying close enough attention. It was someone else's name on the list, but I saw it and thought it was you and there was no way in hell I was finishing that assignment. And if I wasn't going to finish it— one way or another I was a dead man."

It took a moment for that to sink in. "You freaking moron."

"Come on. I know you want a word much stronger than 'freaking.'"

"It's not funny!"

"It's also not tragic. I did what I thought I had to do, and if it meant you getting the life you did, I'd do it again. The life you've had with Doug? That was worth risking hell."

The idea of hell had completely escaped me. Why *wasn't* he in hell? He'd killed more people than I suspected we knew about. He killed himself; wasn't that reason enough to burn for eternity?

"Let me ask you this," he said. "Look at Chip. Do you think he deserves eternal damnation?"

"Of course not."

"He was barely sixteen years old the first time he killed someone, and then he took out two people in a fifteen minute time span. He tapped into something dark and vicious inside himself, and he didn't think twice about doing the things he did. He used women for his own horny gains and then tossed them aside like trash. He broke more laws than most people even know exist. So why wouldn't *he* wind up in hell?"

"I didn't say he wouldn't. I just said he didn't deserve it. I don't think you deserve it either, Ron. But I—"

"You make assumptions based on the rules of play you were

taught as a child. And that's all right. But what we grow up with, and what really happens? Those are very different things."

"Where are you then, when you're not here?"

He shrugged.

"You don't know or can't say?"

"I can't explain," he said.

"Damn, don't they teach you anything here?"

"Well, right now this is your place," he reminded me. "You can teach me whatever you think I need to know."

"Somehow, I think you already know it all."

Again, he nodded thoughtfully. "Something you accused me of many, many times. And at times I think I did believe I knew it all. Now I know better."

"What don't you know now?"

"Why you wanted me here. I'm glad that I am, but I still don't know why I'm here with you."

~

"What *do* you know?" I asked him.

Ron's eyebrows furled, as if he were giving considerable weight to how he answered. "I know that you've had a wonderful life with Doug. I know you had a son, that he married Chip's daughter. I know that you loved Doug enough to develop an amazing capacity for forgiveness. This morning you made plans to go to Chip and Terry's for dinner, and you were planning on baking a checkerboard chocolate cake to take over. I know that you've been happy. And I know that still matters to me."

"How? How can you know all that?"

"I just know things. I can tell you why cats purr, why water is wet. I could explain nuclear fission. But I don't really know how I know. I just do."

"And about the loose ends you left behind?"

"Chip wasn't my son after all." He stated it as fact, not something that was tearing him apart to admit.

"We were all a little bit relieved that you never found out,"

"It wouldn't have mattered. I loved him, and that was enough."

"Son of your heart."

He nodded. "Still. Always."

"He has four kids, you know."

"And grandchildren. I know every minute of their lives that matter, Kris. Minus any horny details. I'm not spying on all of you."

"You just know."

Another nod.

"Could you spy, if you wanted?"

"Not the way you think of it."

"Then how?"

He stared out at the water, his head just barely cocked to one side as he considered. "Chip is speeding down the Interstate, trying to follow the ambulance, muttering under his breath that they're too damned slow and his dead mother could drive faster. Terry is in the car with him, trying to call Eileen and Spider. Her hands are shaking, so she's having trouble dialing the number and wishes she had programmed it for one-key dialing. Chip is telling her to calm down, that you're far too stubborn to die. But he's terrified, and it would only take a stray thought about the possibilities to make him cry."

"Stop."

"They love you," he said simply. "And the love Chip has for you is very nearly equal to how much Doug loves you."

"Nonsense. He loves Terry that much."

Ron grinned, amused. "It's not a finite kind of thing, you know. Chip loved you when he was a teenager, and if he had been older and if you'd been a little younger?"

"Don't go there," I warned, remembering slivers of a conversation I'd had with Doug thirty-five years ago. "Don't."

He went on as if I hadn't said a thing. "But he is very grateful that you were just out of reach. Because you were, he has the life he wanted, with the woman he was meant to be with. He knows he wouldn't have that if he'd been willing to barge into and destroy our marriage."

"He has what he has because of himself. He made a decision to change and he did it. He learned to respect—"

"You're going to argue with me just to argue, aren't you?"

"I think I missed being able to, Ron. That's something else we did quite well."

"Fighting."

"We were spectacular at it, and you know it."

~

"All those people," I mused. "Dan, Grant, Pat…are they here?"

"Conceptually, in this space, no. But they're here."

"Do you ever see them? Hang out, talk?"

"I see the people I want to see. The people who want to see me, they see me."

"That's one hell of a non-answer, Ron. If I wanted to see them, could I?"

"Sure."

"And wherever it is they are, they'd be aware of it?"

He nodded.

"All right. You're here; I wanted you to be here. Are you somewhere else, too?"

He inhaled deeply, breath I was surprised he needed to take, but it was an expected affectation. If he didn't suck air in sharply every now and then, I would know for sure that he wasn't real. "In every moment, here or there, where I'm wanted or needed, I'm there. It's not linear, Kris. I can't explain it any better than that."

"So while you're sitting here talking to me, you could be hanging with Dan *and* banging the celestial brains out of Pat?"

He couldn't hold back the laugh. "You at least can wrap your head around the concept of non-linear existence."

"Well, no, I can't, but I'm trying."

"And I'm not banging the celestial brains out of Pat Davis."

"But you could."

"I don't stick my nose into your bedroom, woman."

"Not even a little bit?"

"I'm not a voyeur."

"But," I pressed, "you could."

"Why would I want to witness what nasty things you do to Doug?"

"Not that. Pat."

He hesitated. "I have no earthly idea," he admitted. "Until now, it didn't occur to me."

"Wonderful. Then you have the rest of your non-linear existence to contemplate the possibility."

"Yeah. Thank you for that."

~

"Do you remember when we met?"

"No. Not at all," he said dryly. His eyebrow arched, just barely, mouth turned up at the corners, and I realized how much I missed that mischievous elfin look of his.

"It was…electric."

"Dan knew having me there when you signed in was a mistake less than a minute after you got there. You were young and I was… smitten."

"Smitten. You were horny."

"No, smitten is a good word. I didn't just want to be with you, I want to be with you. Friends or more, I just wanted to be with you."

"Then what happened to us?"

"I was an idiot."

"You weren't—"

"I was. And I'm all right with that. My mistakes began long before we met, Kris. I derailed when I abandoned one life in favor of another, when I let my common sense fly out the window and let a friendship change the course of my life."

"When you and Grant left the priesthood and joined the agency."

"It seemed like a good idea at the time."

"And there was Pat."

He nodded.

"She did love you, Ron."

"Yes, she did. She loved Grant, too. Nothing in her life had ever given her the tools she needed to make a decision that would leave one of us behind. We both knew that, and we both used that. Chip was the casualty."

"You've forgiven her?"

"There's nothing to forgive. It happened, we tried to create lives around the mistakes, and we moved on. Someday I'll turn around and Chip will be here, and he'll understand. People do stupid, selfish things because they're human, and it's fine."

"He says he is who he is because of it all."

"And of all of us, he learned to make the better decisions before it was too late."

"So there is no hell," I said, thinking of the horrors of the things we had all done in the name of patriotism and love of country.

"I never said that."

"Then there is."

That eyebrow arched again. "I never said that, either."

"Fine. Where are you in all of this, Ron? Heaven or hell?"

"I'm on a park bench, soaking up the sun. With you. That sounds like my idea of heaven."

~

"If I die, what happens? Do I stay here? Do you?"

"That's up to you."

"You would just sit here with me."

"If that's what you wanted."

"What about what you want?"

"Kris," he breathed. "I'm doing what I want. And I think that if you wanted me here, it would only be until that moment when you felt that Doug needed you elsewhere."

"I thought this wasn't linear. I could be there and here?"

"I don't think you would want to be."

"Well. That would be rude, holding you hostage to my wishes and then running off like that."

"I would not be offended. In fact, I would want to see Doug, when he was in a moment where he wanted to see me, too."

"You don't think he would?"

Carefully, he said, "I think, that when Doug dies, whether or not you die first, what he'll want more than anything is you."

"Then what I wanted more than anything is you?"

"You're not dead."

"All right. If I'd died on the spot, would we still be here?"

"I can't say."

"Can't or won't? Don't know, don't want to share?"

"You are just full of questions. Whatever happened to just talking?"

"I'm sitting here with my dead ex-husband. That just inspires questions. Think about it, if you were in my shoes and popped into some existence and, say, Chip was there, out of context and very likely dead, wouldn't you have questions?"

"Of course."

"And what would you ask him?"

He thought for a moment. "I'd want to know, was it worth the pain?"

"He'd say yes."

"Still. I'd have to ask."

"Wouldn't you know the answer before you even asked?"

"I'm not omniscient."

"But you 'know' things."

"I know this. You haven't changed over the last thirty years. Still a mouthy little thing."

~

"They're giving you a drug to bust the clot in your brain," Ron said, sounding unconcerned. "Doug is in the emergency room with you, quietly pleading under his breath, trying to not get in everyone's way. Chip and Terry are in the waiting room…waiting. Spider and Eileen are on their way, and the rest of the kids will be there as soon as they can find babysitters."

"So they can sit there and wait? Why?"

"It's what you would do, too," he pointed out. "They all feel like they need to do something, and waiting is something they can do."

"They could wait at home, and keep their minds off the grim possibilities by playing with the kids or just mindlessly watching TV."

"Or they could feel proactive, keep the kids away from the

stress they radiate, and go wait with Chip and Terry, where they can keep each other company. And pray. They all believe in the power of prayer. They will do what they can, even if what they can do is send out the most powerful *die-and-we'll-disown* you vibes."

"I'm not ready to die, Ron."

"Then don't."

"How do I keep from it?"

He couldn't—or wouldn't—answer.

"Spider and Eileen have finally reached the point where they want kids. I can't miss that. I want to be around to see my grandchildren, and I want to babysit and bake cookies and—"

He started to say something, but I waved him off.

"Don't you dare tell me. If you know how many kids they'll have and when, I don't want to know. I want the joy of being surprised."

"All right."

"You were going to tell me, right?"

"Actually, I was going to muse over the idea of you baking anything. Still using the amount of smoke seeping out of the oven as a timer?"

"Shut up," I laughed. "I've gotten pretty good in the kitchen in my old age. Which explains my weight these days."

"You look fine."

"You have to say that. I got old and fat, but honestly, I didn't care about the fat part, not once I realized..."

When I couldn't go on he finished for me. "Once you realized that Doug not only didn't mind the few extra pounds, he didn't even see them. Why would he?"

"How could he not?"

"Because he always sees *you*, Kris. Not the shell. You."

"That's not always so easy to believe, you know."

"I know."

For the first time since blinking myself onto the bench next to him, I felt restlessness and anxiety bite at me, and stood up. I wanted to move, to walk, and to see what was just past the park, if there was anything at all.

"What do you want to be there?" Ron asked as he rose from the bench.

"It's not a matter of want. I just want to see what's there."

"It will be whatever you expect it to be."

I sighed hard, gazing up at the top of the gentle slope leading out of the park. "This can't be all up to me. Show me what you want to see, Ron. Where is it you hang out? What do you do? Who do you see? Is it even possible to show me?"

"It is." He reached for my hand, a mostly automatic gesture, and I felt him almost immediately begin to pull his hand back. His fingers laced through mine felt comfortable, though, and I grasped his hand just tight enough that he couldn't let go.

"This is fine," I said.

"But is it appropriate?"

"Doug would not mind."

"All right then." He turned just slightly and we began walking towards the hill; it felt almost flat under my feet, the effort to climb it no more than walking across an empty room. I marveled at the feeling, and opened my mouth to tell him how wonderful that was, to be able to move without pain winding its fiery fingers through my back and hips, but then we were cresting the hill and I was too surprised by where we were to speak.

Ron's favorite place to hang out.

San Francisco.

~

I turned to look back; the hill we'd walked up so effortlessly was gone, and the city skyline replaced the park. Behind us, just past Marina Green, was the path that cut through Fort Mason to Fisherman's Wharf and the Embarcadero; ahead was Crissy Field and a view of the Golden Gate Bridge, fog enveloping the upper towers.

The skyline was modern. Ron wasn't hanging out in the San Francisco of his life; he was hanging out in the here and now, and that surprised me.

"I enjoy the eclecticism of it," he said to my unasked question. "When I was alive, the city wasn't as crowded, but it also wasn't as nearly as interesting. I can come here and walk around downtown and be surrounded by all the energy, or I wander around Golden

Gate Park and enjoy the quiet. Sometimes I walk up the coast and listen to the waves crash onto the beach."

All things he was used to, things he did with Chip, and later—when we had time—with me.

"Are you tethered to the familiar?"

"No. If it suited me I could perch on top of a mushroom on the moon. This suits me. The people that come here have all the energy they did when they were alive. The performers who loved what they did still perform. People who never had the time to be tourists get to walk the streets and see everything they missed in life. The cable cars run, the traffic is horrible and loud, and it's all quite wonderful."

Ron's adult life had been lived in chaos; as middle age closed in he had begun to crave a normal family life, life in suburbia with a wife, a house, and a dog. What he had was a thin impersonation of his ideal: a wife who thought nothing of wandering into hostile foreign territory to steal prototype aircraft, an apartment he only saw on the rare occasions when work allowed him to be at home, and a son who despised life so much that his purpose seemed to be to end it.

It made sense to me that he would want to surround himself by the chaos of the city; here he could have bits and pieces of the things he was used to and the things he enjoyed, the noise and abruption of downtown crowds and the choice to be a part of it or apart from it, and when he had enough he could simply walk away and find quiet. He'd lived a life punctuated by adrenaline-pumping energy; why wouldn't he gravitate towards a more civilized form of it in death?

We walked toward the beach at Crissy Field; the biting cold that often rode in on wind across the Bay was absent, though water lapped onto the sand in a regular drumbeat of thin, soft waves. As we neared the sand, I noticed a golden retriever sitting patiently just outside of the range of the lapping water; his head turned and he looked at us, barked gently once, and went back to watching the bay.

"I want to see this," Ron said quietly. He took a few steps back, until we were off the beach and onto the sidewalk that separated it from the parking lot. He gestured to a nearby bench and we sat down to wait.

I wanted to ask what we were waiting for, but the energy swirling around him told me I would get my answer soon enough.

He radiated a mixture of apprehension and joy, expectation playing across his face in the same excitement as a six year old at Christmas.

Santa's coming, I thought.

The golden scooted back a few inches, his tail wagging fast, and when a spray of water shot up twenty feet ahead, he stood up on all four legs, barking excitedly.

"Reunion," Ron whispered.

Had he been waiting there for years? A young man—I guessed only thirty or so—came up out of the water coughing, and stumbled towards the beach, dropping to his knees. He was dressed in cutoff jeans and a bright yellow t-shirt, and as he came out of the water his clothing and hair dried rapidly.

The dog began a barking frenzy, loud and explosive, complete joy that called out, *I'm here, I'm here*.

The young man blinked rapidly and finally looked at the dog, his eyes wide with surprise and recognition.

"Rusty?"

Bark.

"No. You can't—"

Bark.

His hand went to his chest and he took a deep breath, testing, trying to absorb the sight of his long-dead dog waiting for him on the beach. Ron gestured for me to stay put, and he got up, whispering as he trotted across the sand to stand next to the dog.

With Ron's hand gently ruffling his head, Rusty sat down again, but his tail twitched in delight, and, I guessed, hope that his master was as happy to see him as he was to have his master back.

I couldn't hear what Ron was saying, but the young man tensed, panic playing across his face, but he almost immediately relaxed as half a dozen other people jogged past me and headed towards them.

Family.

Ron had called out to his family, anyone familiar who could help him make the transition.

With a tilt of his head, Ron gestured for me to walk and meet him a little further down the beach.

"Rusty," he explained, "has checked the beach off and on since he died. He feels time as a linear thing, and in his head he's been waiting for over forty years. Patiently waiting, I might add."

"Forty? Ron, that man was barely thirty."

"He died at sixty-six years old, when he fell from his boat while testing a new motor. He only looks how he feels, Kris. He felt young, he will be young."

"Oh great. I'll be old and fat for eternity."

"Look at yourself. Look at your hands, your skin."

I held my hands out in front of me, knuckles up. Skin that had etched itself with fine lines and wrinkles over the years was now smooth, and my age spots were gone. I glanced down at my legs and my hips, and realized that in a literal blink of an eye I had lost a good eighty pounds.

"How old do I look?"

"You look exactly the same as you did the last time I saw you, Kris. You're as beautiful now as you were then."

If Doug had said that, I would have scoffed; I believed Ron.

The urge to look over my shoulder to see how Rusty's reunion was going was overwhelming, and I caved. If a dog could be said to smile, Rusty was grinning wildly, and his master seemed very much at ease.

"They're fine," Ron said without looking. "He was surprised that he died, but he's relieved to be here and not somewhere less pleasant."

"How did you know?"

"The dog told me."

I didn't ask; if I could be sitting at my kitchen table in one breath and sitting next to my very much alive dead ex-husband the next, there was no need.

~

We wandered the city with no particular destination; I wanted to see the things Ron still enjoyed, and he guided me to each as they occurred to him. It didn't take long before I felt completely turned around; he turned left and I expected to be walking up the street towards The Palace of Fine Arts, but we were instead headed into Golden Gate Park. He turned right and I expected to wind up at the coast and the Great Highway, but we were at the edge of Chinatown.

"We could walk the entire distance," Ron explained, "but why?"

Everywhere we went, there were crowds of people. And yet everywhere we went, they remained a safe distance, sometimes glancing our way, but no one made an effort to interact with either of us.

I wondered if he was intentionally distancing me from people he would normally at least wave to.

"Rhinestone cowboy," I said under my breath as we strolled down Kearny towards Market Street.

"Apt," he said. "I do frequently walk these streets alone."

"Why alone?" I pressed.

"Why not?"

"Aren't you ever lonely?"

"No," he said simply.

"Hungry? Thirsty? Tired? Horny?"

There was a very slight smile tugging at the corners of his mouth; I amused him, but he didn't want to make fun of me. Again, he said, "No."

"You don't eat or drink. Never sleep? Never—?"

"I think we already established the latter part of your thought had never occurred to me. I suppose it's possible. If I had someone I was that connected to, perhaps."

"Pat," I started.

"I was never really connected to her, Kris. I don't think she allowed herself to ever be truly connected to anyone when she was alive, and if she is now, it's to Grant."

"You don't know?"

"It would be impolite to ask. And manners still matter."

That made me laugh. "All right. What about food? And sleep? You don't need it at all?"

"No, I don't need it." He gestured to a restaurant on the corner. "Need doesn't preclude want, however. The things we enjoyed most in life, we still want occasionally. You, for instance, would probably find yourself at Ghiradelli Square every now and then. The chocolate would still remind you of a teenaged Chip, and you might even have the impulse to roll around in it."

"Roll in it. Funny. You were never a huge fan of anything chocolate, but you've had it here?"

"I indulge every now and then, when I want to feel close to someone."

"Ah, then there is somebody."

For the first time, his composure cracked and he looked mildly irritated. He swallowed hard—something I thought was for affect and not because he suddenly had a mouth full of spit—and reached for me, pulling me against him, holding tight.

His breath skipping across my cheek was light, and when I breathed in, it was sweet. His hands were on my back, holding me close, and when I looked up at him his eyes were closed. Within seconds, there was static warmth between us, a vibrating hum of electricity that made me wonder if everyone around us could see sparks and a bright blue-white glow.

"Whether a minute passes as a second or a year," he whispered, "I miss you in every moment. There is no one, because I haven't truly let go."

"Ron."

He took a step back. "It's all right. I'm not sorry about it. I don't dwell on it. But I will always love you, and until you're here for good, I will miss you."

And when I was truly dead, if I chose to wait somewhere else for Doug, would he miss me then? I didn't have the heart to mention that possibility.

"You're not as Zen as I thought," I murmured.

"But I am at peace. I can miss you and still be at peace."

"And all these people around us"—I gestured wide—"no one has come anywhere near us. They look, but they stay as far away as they can without being obvious. On the beach, you had me stay behind rather than get close to Rusty and his master. What gives? If you're so much at peace, why are you keeping your distance?"

"Where they are is not up to me."

"You're not giving off some steer-clear vibe?"

"I am not."

"No subtle messages that you want time alone with me?"

"Kris." His hands went to my shoulders, thumbs tracing along my jaw. "If any of those people knew you wanted them to approach, they would. They don't sense that. They know you're only here peripherally, that you haven't truly crossed over. No one wants to overwhelm you, or worse, influence you."

"Influence me how?"

"You're not dead yet. Not one among them would risk being the one who convinced you to turn in any direction. Live or die, it has to be up to you."

"And how's it going on that front?"

His hands slipped from my shoulders, but he reached for my hands, bare fingertips against bare fingertips. "The drug is working. Doug isn't holding his breath as often or as hard as he was. Spider is upset because he can't hear what's going on around him and Eileen can't sign fast enough to keep him up to speed. But he'll catch up soon."

"So you know what's going to happen?"

"I can sense from how he's feeling, the energy he gives off. No, I can't predict what your end result will be."

"Even though time is nonlinear and all that."

The corner of his mouth twitched upwards. "Even though."

"Can you at least tell me how much longer I have, either here or there?"

"No."

"Can't or won't?"

"Would it matter? There will come a moment when your decision will be made, and that will be that. You'll either stay here, find other places to explore while you wait for Doug, or you'll go home."

"Home."

"Life with Doug is where you consider home to be, is it not?"

"When did you get so formal, Ron? 'Is it not?' I see you right here, but half the time you don't sound like yourself. You sound... separate."

"You haven't had a conversation with me for thirty years. Perhaps you don't remember—?"

"Bullshit. This is another divide. You're distancing yourself from me, whether you know it or not."

His hands fell away from mine.

"Another case of trying to not influence me?"

"Something like that," he admitted.

"There's more."

"Kris," he breathed. "Of course there's more. I'm dead but I still have feelings, too. And I still don't know why out of all the people you could have wanted being there in the park, you wanted me."

~

The San Francisco of Ron's choosing was everything I knew; it wasn't just the sheer volume of people, the running cable cars and the traffic, it was also the people. We stood on Market Street, watching a cable car lurch its way up Powell, talking above the volume of the boom box being used by a tall, thin, incredibly flexible and energetic young man who danced for the amusement of the waiting crowd.

The only difference that I could see was the absence of a collection can. He performed for them, without the expectation that at the end of the day he'd have fifty or a hundred dollars. He danced because it was his joy, and it radiated from him.

Vendors dotted the street, offering everything from brightly colored belts to hand knit caps; I knew without asking that no money would exchange hands. If you wanted something, you asked for it. There would be a smile and a polite exchange, lasting anywhere from a few seconds to an hour.

Heaven, I was beginning to think, was a large socialist network.

It didn't occur to me for a long time that the things I saw were so normal to me that they were out of place in the most Christian views of the hereafter. I watched two men walk hand in hand up the slope of Powell in the same direction of the cable car, trying to figure out what was out of place with the image until Ron said simply, "You are who you are, no matter where you are."

I wanted to be there the next time a hard right-leaning fundamentalist found himself standing in the same spot, watching the same men.

"You presume that fundamentalist would have the same vision of here as you do. Or as I do."

"Not the place a staunch churchgoing Republican would hang?"

"Not one who died certain that Hell was the only place reserved for anyone different than himself. Someone who allowed for the possibility that there are truths other than his own? That person might choose to be here to see for himself, and accept it as wonderful."

Ron, even with his deeply Catholic childhood, his scant few years as a priest, and the times he had grown up in, had no issues with how other people saw the world. In an era of free love and if it feels good, do it, where the masses hiccupped hypocrisy and shunned same gender relationships, Chip could have announced to Ron that he was a flaming homosexual and it wouldn't have mattered one way or the other.

The only things he wanted for his son were stability and a sense of worth he couldn't seem to instill in him. He understood why Chip was restless and as hard-edged as he was, but he could never figure out how to help him change that. When life did it for him, when Chip had his selfishness shoved in his face in the form of a hooker he had promised a lifetime to dead on his apartment floor, Ron had no idea how to help him. We watched Chip sink into depression, guilt winding around him like a tight coil that was so close to choking him that we could hear the first gasps.

Through it all, though, he loved and accepted Chip for who he was, even when it was apparent that part of who he was happened to be a teenaged man-slut.

I reached for Ron's hand and gave it a slight tug. "Come on. Walk with me a little more. I've seen where you go when you want quiet and when you want to feel the energy of the people. Show me where you go when you want to just be."

~

"Sleep is an option," Ron said as he closed the door. "It's not a necessity. I never feel tired, but sometimes all I want is to curl up in bed and read, and this is where I feel mostly at peace."

I thought he always felt at peace, but I was beginning to understand that the minute degrees between calm and happy and joyous might be different for him than they were for me.

We had turned around and walked up Market Street a bit further, towards the Embarcadero, but when he turned left onto Battery
Street the entire world shifted and we were standing on a beach near
Bodega Bay. It was instantly familiar; Chip's empty beach house
was less than a quarter mile up the coastline, waiting for when he
was here and wanting his own slice of the hereafter.

Just behind us was a small cottage, out of place among the
playgrounds of the slightly better than middle class residents I was
used to seeing there. It would have been a perfectly normal sight
in Lake Tahoe, but this was Ron's place, and what he wanted was
a small, single room winter cottage on the beach near the place to
where his son would often run when life was overwhelming.

This was where he would look for Chip when the time came.
If Chip died before Terry did, the beach house was where he would
wait for her. It was where Ron would wait for the son of his heart,
and likely where Grant and Pat would come. It was where Chip
could finally embrace the younger brother he still quietly and desperately missed. The place his family would come together, finally
whole and finally happy.

I expected the inside to be a bit dark and dusty, but Ron's idea
of wonderful was bright and clean; there was a queen-sized bed on
the far wall with a half dozen pillows and a colorful striped com-
forter, and it faced a crystal clear picture window.

Ron could curl up there and read, or sit back and watch the
waves pound perfectly upon the sand. The wind would never whip,
the beach would never erode, and the seagulls would never dive
bomb the window, or worse, stealthily rip hot dogs from the hands
of unsuspecting children.

Instead of a kitchen there was a nook with floor to ceiling book-
cases extending wall to wall, every shelf filled with trade paperback
books; they were, Ron said, some of the books he had never gotten
around to reading when he was alive. He'd wanted to, but work and
real life sucked the time away from him.

"You wanted to see where I go to simply be. This is it."

I stood by the window, watching the waves and listening to
the gentle roll of the ocean. "Water seems to be an important thing

between you and me," I said. "You waited for me at the pond. The first place you took me to was the beach at Crissy Field, and now here."

"Water is a thing of beauty," he said. "In life, it sustains you. But there's joy in walking in the rain, jumping in puddles, even just scooping it into your hand and watching it drip through your fingers."

"But what does it mean to us?"

"To me? That we were a lot like the water. Even when it was getting away from me, we were a beautiful thing."

~

We sat on the beach, and I dug my toes into the cool sand, relishing the idea that everything here felt wonderful. The sand was wet and gritty and my heels created blunt divots in it, but I felt none of the discomfort that time spent sitting on the ground usually meant for me. I understood why this was where Ron went when he just wanted to be; the quiet had the comfortable weight of an old quilt, it was familiar and almost lyrical, soft music that drifted in on warm breezes. It felt almost like home, and it was probably where I would go, too, though I would be lounging a few houses down, closer to the jetty.

Still, I could get used to Ron's eclectic slice of Bodega Bay.

Dan, Ron explained, could typically be found at Lake Tahoe, sailing through the water on the boat he'd wanted but never had time for. I felt a brief impulse to ask Ron to take me to him, but then realized I didn't want that badly enough. For a reason neither of us could yet figure out I wanted to be with Ron, and I obviously wasn't ready to add anyone else to the mix.

"Explain this to me," I said, cutting through a lengthy silence. "Say there's a diehard fundamentalist who thinks all sin is equal, and that sinners go to Hell. He knows he's a sinner, so he thinks he's doomed. Does he wind up somewhere with fire and brimstone and a thousand different kinds of pain?"

"I thought I'd wind up in Hell," he said simply.

"So the worst of the worst, they still wind up somewhere comfortable?"

"I didn't say that. You're thinking in very mortal terms, colored by everything you were taught as a child, and everything your religion gave to you."

"The truth is the truth—" I started.

"You're presuming there's only one truth. Kris, I'm not dumping on you anything you don't need to know yet. Just enjoy the view and hopefully the company. You need to be more focused on what you ultimately want, not where some serial killer might be lurking in his death."

What neither of us would say: it would be easy to cast Ron in the role of a serial killer. After all, he had systematically hunted people down to end their lives, typically with a crossbow's bolt plowed between their eyes or into their hearts.

I was curious if the fact that it hadn't been some perverted desire on his part to kill people that allowed him to exist in this comfortable plane; if he had enjoyed it or embarked on a killing spree out of willful, bent joy, would he be fighting fire somewhere else?

I wanted to know; yet at the same time I also didn't.

If he was there keeping me company on some temporary parole plan, I really didn't want to know.

"I am enjoying the company," I told him. And I was; I'd forgotten how comfortable we could be together, how he listened to what I was saying even when I wasn't sure he'd even heard me. How he was often one thought ahead of me, and stayed there to protect me from myself.

I'd also forgotten most of the reasons I'd wanted out of our marriage. I used fights about Chip—and we argued endlessly about him—and I used the specter of Pat Davis's ghost hanging over our bed as an excuse. I allowed myself to get increasingly closer to Doug because of it, but the years had shown me that I was wrong about how tightly bound he was to her.

Now the proof was right next to me; if they had been that connected, she would be here with him.

"You and Doug have always been good together," he said, without a trace of the sadness I would have expected.

"You're reading my thoughts now?"

"Not exactly. It's a vibe you're giving off. I can't explain it any better than that."

"Doug didn't want to be the reason you and I split," I said. "He wanted me to make the effort to save our marriage. He'd been there at the beginning and—"

"He wanted that because he's a good man and never wanted you to look back with regrets. And you haven't."

"No, I haven't."

"You've been a good wife to him. He knows that. He treasures that. He feels like he should have lost you years ago and can't fathom why he didn't."

I knew that. He'd spent one drunken night with Terry and was sure I would shove him out the door and slam it behind him, changing the locks before he could even take two steps. But I'd been guilty of wanting what he'd done; when I was married to Ron, toward the end, I would have slept with Doug in a heartbeat.

I would have regretted it, but I know I would have done it if only Doug would have cooperated.

Where would we be now if he had?

"If I die," I asked Ron, "and then wait for Doug somewhere, does that automatically mean we'll spend the rest of forever together?"

He sucked in a deep breath, pondering. "It's not automatic. You might come together and part for a time while you seek out the things and people that mattered to you. Even those people who were meant for each other in life…that doesn't automatically mean they were meant for each other for eternity."

I took a moment to process that. "I may be meant for someone else here?"

"You may share a deeper bond with someone else."

A wave of sadness swept over me in the same motion as water on the sand.

"Kris," he said gently, "it won't hurt. It will just be what it is. You'll be together when you want, and apart when you want, and it will feel perfectly normal."

"I'm more concerned at the idea that I might be connected to someone other than him," I said in a near whisper.

He didn't answer that, and in another wave, more abrupt than the last, I wondered if the reason I had wanted Ron to be there for me at the park, the reason he was waiting with me while I decided whether to live or to die, was because he was the one I was most connected to.

I had no idea how I felt about that.

He was only a part of my life for six out of over sixty-five years. Yet, I thought about him frequently, enough that it almost embarrassed me. I'd always thought that he flitted around in my brain because of Chip, because of the living reminder that I'd spent some important years loving someone else. I'd never assumed that it meant anything other than that I'd loved him more than I realized at the time, and I never would have guessed it might mean that I should have fought for our marriage instead of walking away from it.

"Are you sure I'm not just having some wild, drug induced dream?"

He ran a finger down my arm, leaving a static trail. "Are you sure I'm not real?"

"I know you're real, Ron. Let's just say I'm indulging in some doubt."

"The flipside of doubt," he said quietly, pulling his finger away, the electric thread still crackling between us, "is faith."

"I don't want..." I couldn't finish the thought, because I wasn't sure just what it was that I didn't want.

"To betray Doug," he finished for me. "You could never do that. I would never ask you to."

I wondered what my answer would be if he asked me to.

~

"Why," I asked him quietly, "am I so tempted to stay here with you? You keep talking about connections, and every time you touch me it's like this electric thread pulls between us, and it's warm and I want more of it..."

"But you're not sure what it is about it that you want?" he guessed.

"When you used to touch me like that—I remember being weak kneed and wanting you so badly."

"But this"—he ran a finger along my arm again—"doesn't feel like sex, or even foreplay."

"I don't know *what* it feels like, just that I think it's part of why I'm tempted to stay."

He scooted closer to me, and slid his arm across my shoulders. The static was nearly unbearable, yet I wouldn't have asked him to move for anything. "It feels good," he said. "And after spending the last decade in varying degrees of pain, it's nice to not have anything hurt. Having something pleasurable shoot through you? Of course you want that."

A mental inventory of my usual aches and pains confirmed what he was saying: nothing hurt. The grinding pain that typically had a stranglehold on my hips was gone. My knees and back didn't ache. I could tilt my head back without wondering if my neck would crack, and if it did, how bad would it be and would I even be able to lift my head back up?

Yet, that wasn't all of it. I had been living with the pain just fine. There was something about Ron that was making me think staying was a good idea. "I can live with the pain," I murmured.

"Physical pain, sure. You're strong. But emotional?"

"Emotional."

"No worrying, no hurt feelings, no anger over misunderstandings. You're here and feeling everything from a completely different perspective. The things that ticked you off seem fairly small right now, don't they?"

"Including whatever it was that made me walk away from our marriage."

"You did what needed to be done."

"Did I?"

"I know you did. Think about it; we rushed into marriage, and to be honest, it started to fall apart from the very beginning. When we came back from our honeymoon and had to deal with Chip and getting him out from under Grant's roof…it started to fall apart then."

"How? I didn't mind him being there. He turned out to be a blessing, Ron. He and Terry are my family—"

"And that's how it was supposed to be. He needed you in his life, but you and I as a couple?"

"Marrying you wasn't a mistake."

"No, it wasn't."

"If you say something dorky like giving love a chance is never a mistake, I'll give you a wedgy."

"You would try, wouldn't you?"

I leaned my head against his shoulder. "Now you're going to tell me you don't wear underwear, right?"

"I'd invite you to check, but..."

"Dead Ron is too damned respectful. Live Ron would have shown me."

"Dead Ron thinks you just want the answer to that one question he hasn't been able to answer."

"I admit, I'm curious. Knowing what I know about you, I have a hard time imagining you not being with someone."

"What, like I slept around so much?" He laughed. "Angel, I can count the women I was with on both hands and not use every finger. I was never like Chip."

"I didn't mean that. Sex was important to you."

"When I was in a relationship, sure. The deeper I was into someone—"

"If you're going to say the better you were at it, then I'm really going to regret leaving you."

"I'll take that as a compliment."

"It was meant as one," I yawned. "You never get tired?"

"Nope."

"Then why am I so sleepy? Am I dying?"

"Your body is tired, Kris. You may need to sleep. You may get hungry, too, and if you do, we'll go find food." He got up, holding his hand out to help me up. "I'm not entirely clear on what to do if you feel like you need to pee, though."

"I'm resourceful," I said, letting him pull me up. "There's an entire beach here. I can dig a hole."

"You would, too."

He led me back into his cabin, which was cooler than it had been just a while ago; I had to think it was intentional, for my benefit. He knew I liked the room cool when I slept, because it made digging under the blankets so much nicer.

It made cuddling more fun.

This was familiar, climbing into bed with him. I shucked off most of my clothes and climbed into the bed, sighing at its overwhelming comfort.

"I know you don't sleep," I said, "but I would welcome the company."

"You just want to see if I'm wearing underwear," he teased as he kicked his shoes off. When he slid in next to me I realized we'd taken the same sides of the bed that we had when we were married. For the last thirty years I'd been sleeping on the right side of the bed, but here I was, comfortably on the left, while Ron curled up next to my right side.

"Boxer briefs," I mused. "Those didn't even exist for Live Ron."

"I wish they had. They're comfortable."

"As opposed to the massive discomfort you face in your current existence?"

"Exactly."

"You used to sleep naked," I mused.

"Since I don't sleep…"

"Fine. Killjoy."

He rolled his eyes with measured exaggeration, but he wiggled under the covers and then tossed the briefs onto the floor.

Without thinking about it, I pulled myself closer, resting my head between his chin and shoulder, and slipped my arm across him. He stiffened for a bare second, then relaxed and pulled me close.

"How bored will you get when I fall asleep?"

"I won't," he whispered. "If you'll be less self-conscious about it, I can sleep, too."

"You've seen me sleep before. It doesn't feel all weird. I just don't want my fatigue to mean you're bored or not doing something else you want to do."

"I'm doing exactly what I want to be doing. And I hope I'm not stepping over the line when I say this feels better than anything I've done since I died."

"Natural," I mumbled, feeling the pull of sleep; it was happening so fast that I wondered if he had some control over that, if he was pushing me let go.

"Just don't drool on me," he whispered, just before I fell.

~

I had the sensation of dreaming, yet I floated in darkness. I was surrounded by soft, muted voices, beeping and humming, and the smells that assaulted my senses were antiseptic and harsh. Everything was distant and disconnected, and I thought if I could just open my eyes I would be able to become a part of it.

No matter how hard I tried, I couldn't; even if I could squint, I thought, it would be a victory. But my eyelids felt weighted, and I could only listen to what was happening around me.

"You need to go home and rest. We'll call you when she wakes up."

"I have to be here when she does."

"She'll kick your ass if you wind up in the bed next to her."

"I'll be fine. I am fine."

"Dad, I'll stay with her, I promise. I won't leave even for a minute and if her eyes so much as flutter, I'll text you."

I jolted awake.

Dad?

"Oh my God. Is that what his voice would sound like?"

Ron was still there, still holding me. "Is it what you thought it would be?"

I wanted to cry. I hadn't heard more than a few sounds out of my son since he was a toddler, when he stopped crying for everything he wanted. As he learned to sign he vocalized less, until he was silent.

"I never thought his voice would be so deep. So...perfect."

"He could squeak like a mouse and it would be perfect."

"When he gets here"—I nearly choked on the idea—"will he be able to hear? And to speak?"

"If he chooses."

"How could he not—?"

"Spider is comfortable with who he is. Signing is how he communicates. That might not change."

"But I know he wants to hear. He wants so badly to hear Eileen play the piano, and he wants to hear the kids laughing while they play outside... Dammit, Ron, he wants to be able to lie there in the dark and whisper to her, tell her he loves her, and know that she's heard him."

His fingers moved across my back, gently tracing. "He has his ways," he murmured, one finger drawing a heart on my skin.

"He does that?"

"He and Eileen have their own language, something they use only with each other. He'd never want to give that up. It's as intimate as sex, and means much more to them."

"So color me selfish. If I could wish anything for him, it would be that he hadn't been deaf."

"That's not true," he said, breath warm against my head. "If you could wish something for him, it would be for him to be happy, and he is."

"He is." I felt a little selfish. "But his voice...it's beautiful."

"It is," he agreed. "But when the time comes, you'll be fine with whatever he wants."

"I can't even comprehend that someday my son will die."

"You're not supposed to."

"And Chip?" I asked. "How does it feel knowing that sooner rather than later, he'll be here?"

"It's different for me, Kris. I've had time here; I know what being here means. While I don't want his life to end anytime soon, I know this is someplace he'll want to be. I think he'll need linear time to adjust if he gets here before Terry does, but the idea that he'll eventually be here doesn't bother me."

"Time to adjust?"

"It's like Rusty," he said. "Rusty exists in linear time, because he can't conceive any other way. Right now, you exist in linear time. When Chip dies, if he dies first, he will mourn the idea that it could be years before he sees his other half again."

"Terry is his soul mate," I guessed.

"They are incredibly connected," he allowed.

"They'll be the people who spend eternity together," I decided, knowing he wouldn't answer it if I asked it as a question. "You would love them together, Ron. With her, he became the man you hoped he would be."

"He became more than I hoped. You had a lot to do with that, you know."

"Not quite."

"Chain of events, angel. You kept them from meeting when she was too young and he was a jerk, and when the time was right, you threw them together. And over the years, your meddling has pushed them together when they needed it."

"Meddling," I snorted. "Doug meddled. I was just a cheerleader."

"Then you cheered them together. You've been a key component of their relationship. Embrace it. What they are is a good thing."

"I wish you'd gotten what they have, Ron. You deserved that."

"I have no regrets about the quality of my life."

"But everything you were cheated out of..." I pulled away a bit and sat up on the bed. "You didn't get the childhood you could have had because your parents were so focused on getting you into the priesthood, and God forbid you look twice at some girl. When you finally did look, she used you and let you believe you had a son—your life would have been different if she hadn't lied to you."

"It wasn't a lie," he said, reaching for my hand. "She did think I was his father at first. And then she wasn't sure. But I wouldn't change any of that."

"But all the things you could have had."

"I had more than most. I loved my job, up until it sucked Chip in. I loved being his father, even though I didn't see him as much as I would have liked and the time we did have together was usually tense. He will always be my son, no matter what. I had friends who were like brothers, I loved a wonderful woman, and she loved me back. Those moments made everything worthwhile."

"And when you were a priest, was that worth it?"

"Indeed. It made me realize that you don't have to go to extremes to honor your God. That maybe doing the right thing is enough, and that sacrifice is sometimes the right thing to do, even when it's the last thing you want."

"Hence, you took the job you would never otherwise have to get Chip out of the middle of the agency."

"As much as was possible. I was fairly sure he would never completely let go of it."

"He did, eventually."

"And now there's Nicholas, trying to walk in his footsteps."

"That terrifies Chip," I sighed.

"Yet Nick did it with all the good intentions in the world. He wants to right injustice, but he made sure he had secured his siblings' freedom from it before he would commit to the job. Even if they were interested, the agency would never consider any of them, not now."

"How awful was it, Ron? All the things you had to do…"

"None of it was pretty," he said. "If we'd been speaking at the time, I probably would have told you I was certain that I was destined to be Satan's little bitch."

"We were all afraid of that. Chip is still afraid of that."

"He'll know better someday."

"Will it be awkward, when he pops up here and you and Grant and Pat are waiting for him?"

"No. If he wants us all there at the same time, we will be. There won't be anything awkward about it, we'll just all be happy to see him and to be able to touch him again."

"So seeing them—?"

"Is fine. Has been fine. There comes a moment when you realize that you've let go of all the mortal garbage, and whatever happened in your life were just things that happened. You embrace the good, and learn how the not so good was helpful. When I see them, the only thing I feel is peace."

"And when you saw me?"

"That was joy."

"Even though I may not stay."

His hand slipped from mine, and absently he caressed my leg. "Even though."

"You know, you keep that up, and I may just have to take direct action to get the answer to that one question."

"You wouldn't. Because of Doug."

"Does it count if I'm here but not here?"

"You are here."

"And yet, my body is in a hospital bed in Vacaville."

"Conundrum," he said with a grin.

I lifted his hand off my leg and pressed a kiss into his palm. "I could justify it," I said, only half in jest.

"I have no doubt."

"And it is something we were very, very good at."

"I seem to recall that."

"You're not giving an inch, are you?"

He chuckled, his laughter deep and rich, a hymn to which I'd forgotten the words. "Give or take six inches."

"Give."

He pulled his hand away from mine, trailing an electric finger over my lips, down my chin and neck, between my breasts, stopping right at my navel. "This would be so very real," he said quietly. "And it would count. I won't do that to you."

"If you actually can."

His eyes were liquid, twinkling in the dim light. "I've known for the past couple of minutes that it's very possible. I never would have guessed that it would be, but it is."

"And you won't cave in to your baser instincts."

"You don't really want me to. Because you are still alive, and Doug is still alive, and you meant it when you said 'until death.'"

I slid back under the blankets, laying my head next to his on the pillow. "Doug would understand this much. I do still love you, Ron. It's not the same as it was, it's—"

"More mature," he said. "I get that. And once you're here for good, if you still feel the same way, I'll jump the fillings right out of your teeth now that I know I can."

He was trying to not smile, so filled with mischief that I couldn't help but laugh.

"You might want to test fire that thing first," I said, touching my forehead to his. "Just to be sure."

"Don't think I need to."

I lifted the blanket and peeked. "Just wanted to see what I might have forgotten."

"Fine. Do I pass inspection?"

"You do." I dropped the blanket. "Hard to believe I had a stroke just to come here and check out your junk, but whatever fate wants."

"Maybe fate wants you to see you've got better junk at home."

"Equitable junk," I allowed. I rolled onto my back, folding my arms across my chest. "Poor Doug. He's put up with a lot of my crap in that department. And I'm sure you don't want to talk about this."

"You've been married to him for thirty years, just about. I'm pretty sure you've had sex with him since Spider was conceived. That factoid doesn't bother me."

"But the details? I sure as hell wouldn't want to hear anything specific about anyone you were doing." I stopped to consider it. "Bullshit. Yeah, I kinda do."

"Since I just now figured out I could..."

"Before. What did Live Ron do after we split?"

"I worked. I stayed focused on not thinking too hard about what I was doing. And I avoided women."

"Ron, that's so sad."

"No. It was fine. I didn't want a relationship, and it would have been a bad idea under the circumstances."

"Well, hell, the occasional hooker..."

He laughed. "Didn't feel the need."

I felt his weight shift on the bed, and this time he sat up, his knees touching my side. "You're hungry. Doug can even hear your stomach growling, and it's the first thing that's made him come even close to a smile. He's warning everyone to be prepared for the demands of a freshly baked chocolate cake."

"Three layers," I said.

"And if that's the first thing you said to him, he would find a way to make it happen."

"Why am I not feeling everything my live self is feeling? Surely there's some discomfort in being in that hospital bed with all the tubes and wires. Why is everything I feel normal?"

"You're kind of in both places, Kris. The feelings that give you some kind of pleasure, like sleeping and eating, you're going to feel them over the things that are uncomfortable, I think. Why would you want to feel anything else?"

"Why now? I didn't feel them before. Why am I sleepy and hungry in such a short time span?"

He shrugged lightly, passing it off as something he wasn't sure about, but I knew then what he wasn't telling me: I was going to have to figure things out soon. Why I had wanted him there, and whether or not I wanted to live or die.

~

"Calories don't count," Ron said, guiding me across Union Square. "You can have a piece of chocolate cake as big as your head if you want. Post-indulgence barfing is optional."

"How about some real food first? What's the one thing you miss?"

He stopped to consider, as if he'd never thought about. "I don't really miss food," he said. "Other than trips to Ghiradelli every now and then? I think I've eaten something maybe four or five times. Twice was to be polite to a street vendor."

"You ate street food to make someone else happy?"

"Is there a better reason? She loved what she did when she was alive and wanted to keep doing it. Feeding others is a way to bring people together, share a few moments, and give something of one's self. It made her feel good to feed me, and it made me feel good to accept what on the surface seems so simple. We both understood she was giving me more than a taco, and that I was offering something in return by eating it. Call it...warm fuzzies."

That sounded a lot like life itself; how we socialized around the grill at home, with the court gate closed off to the rest of the world, our friends dancing in the street. It wasn't about the chicken or steak Doug and Chip were barbequing; it was about the laughter, the communion. I looked down the street, suddenly aware of how many people were working; in a place where they could simply exist, their choice was to do something that would bring them closer to others.

Warm fuzzies come with effort.

"I've never gotten a hot dog from one of the street carts," I told him. "I'm always afraid it'll kick back on me. Doug loves them, though. I don't think we've ever passed Union Square without him getting one."

"Then a hot dog it is. He's got giant soft pretzels, too, if you want one."

We headed towards Geary Street and the vendor on the corner. It was exactly as I remembered; bright stainless steel and Plexiglas, topped by a yellow and blue umbrella. There were even fat pigeons milling about, waiting for the crumbs that everyone inevitably dropped, intentionally in Doug's case.

He once fed half a hot dog bun to a pigeon that had practically marched up to him and demanded a fair share. "Little dude's got balls," he said with a shrug. "If you're that small and can shout me down, you get my bun."

The vendor was tossing bits and pieces of bread onto the sidewalk, watching with amusement as the birds almost politely—taking turns—jumped on them.

"Two," Ron said, holding up two fingers, as if he needed to illustrate the amount.

"Whatcha want on it, Bud? I got it all."

"Ketchup?" he asked me, remembering what I liked. "Ketchup on both."

"Drinks?"

"Diet," I said.

"Ah, you don't need diet," the vendor said with a slight wink. "Go for the gusto. Drink the sugar, babe. It's fat free, I swear."

I had to laugh. "Whatever you have is fine."

"She's used to the taste of diet," Ron said. "The sugar might be too sweet."

"You're not really here, are you?" he asked, handing over the hot dogs. "Lady, this will be the best hot dog you've ever had. If it's not, I'll refund your money."

"I want double back if she hates it," Ron said. "Triple if she spits it out."

It took me a moment to realize why they were both amused; Ron wasn't handing over any cash at all, and though I'd understood he wouldn't, it felt very odd. He exchanged pleasantries for a minute, I admitted it was a freakishly good hot dog, and we went on our way. I couldn't help but turn after a few steps and give a little wave, oddly thrilled when he smiled and waved back.

It hit me as we headed in the direction of Fisherman's Wharf: we never passed a doorway with someone huddled up, trying to sleep. There was no one standing on the corner, asking for spare change, begging for someone to buy them a hot dog. There were no urine streaked trees, no trash fluttering past in the breeze. No one grumbling, no one stammering expletives as we passed.

"Misery, if you're willing to let go of it, doesn't follow you here," Ron explained simply.

"What about uncertainty?" I asked, because I was still feeling it.

"Maybe at first, but once you adjust? It goes away."

"It would be nice if being here came with a few added brain cells."

"Still trying to figure out why?"

"Also trying to figure out why making a decision is so hard. I should just *know*, right? Go back and live out a life that might be a day or a week or a decade, or stay here and pester you for God knows how long."

"I think once you figure out why you're here, then you'll know."

"You're not helping."

"You're just still upset I wouldn't put out," he said.

"Live Ron would have," I countered, allowing him to lead me from becoming far too serious. "Live Ron thought I was hot."

"So does Dead Ron. Want to go see the seals on the pier?"

Distraction; something he was good at, and something he knew would work. "Seriously? The seals are here?"

"Where else would they be?"

"I don't know. In the ocean? Marine World heaven? I just didn't expect it."

"Animals are people, too," he smirked.

"They have souls?"

I wasn't sure he would answer that, not directly. But then he said, "You are the soul, angel. Your body? That's just a container. Animals are no different. I mean, you saw Rusty at Crissy Field. Tell me he had no soul."

"Apparently, he is one."

"Exactly."

"Chip's got a cat," I said absently. "He says Max is Satan wrapped in fur, but he's really very sweet."

"He'll be here for Chip."

"I can't picture him getting as excited as Rusty did, though. Chip could rise up out of the water, and Max would sit back, hitch his leg up, and start licking his nads."

Ron stopped walking, and looked at me as if he were considering something important.

"What?"

"When you die, if you want, I'll sit back, toss a leg up, and then lick myself if it'll amuse you."

"Oh God," I laughed. "If you're that limber now, I think I might stay."

~

"Just answer me without thinking about it: was it all a mistake after all?"

After walking along the Wharf, tossing slimy chunks of what I decided was pseudo-fish—because I couldn't fathom there being live fish to slaughter as feed—to the seals, and then a stop at Ghiradelli Square, I wanted to go back to his cabin. I loved the city and understood why it appealed to him, but what I craved was the peace of the beach, the solitude and absolute wonder of how perfect it felt there.

I hadn't put my finger on what grabbed me the most: that Ron created such a fish out of water type of place for himself there, or that it was so close to something familiar that had become a place of refuge.

Even without Terry and Chip, Doug and I spent a lot of time at their beach house; it had a cozy sense of home, something that surprised me, since I had initially been reluctant to ever visit it.

I decided it didn't matter; I just wanted to go back, climb into the bed with him, and stare out the window at the ocean as it teased waves onto the sand.

Ron might not have been tethered to the familiar, but I was. And familiar to me was a lost afternoon in bed with him, talking about anything and everything. It had nothing to do with sex, though that would have been familiar, too; cuddling up with him felt safe, and since I could make neither heads nor tails of why I was there and if I wanted to stay, I wanted to grab onto something safe.

But then I opened my mouth and asked him if we might have been a mistake after all, and after that, as pointed as the question had been, he wanted to do more than answer me.

He wanted to explore our relationship.

Unless I could pick my way through it, he didn't think he could answer. He propped himself up on pillows, let me snuggle in close, and then stayed there while I reached back as far as I could.

PART TWO

My father was a bit of a forward thinker; when other girls my age were playing house and having tea parties, he had me hanging around the airport, poking around his Cessna, learning what each of the controls were for, learning to not fear the idea of being in control of an airplane.

In junior high, he paid for lessons to learn to fly a glider; when I was sixteen, instead of fostering the typical excitement over getting a driver's license he whipped me into a frenzy over earning a pilot's license. I went into college fully capable of handling a small airplane, and along with my father dreamed about the day I'd own one of my own.

"I'll sell you mine," he'd say with a wink. "I want an excuse to buy a new one."

Then three weeks into my freshman year the agency stepped into my life with the offer of a full four years of paid tuition; the only thing they asked in return was that I continued to fly, spend my summers in training, and eventually become qualified to fly a passenger plane. After I graduated, I would only owe them four years of my time—service to my county, it was pointed out. My college years wouldn't be wasted plowing through to get a degree only to then have to wait for years of training before having the skills I was after; I'd be training all along. I would be flying. I would graduate with a degree in one hand and a license to fly whatever the hell thrilled me the most in the other.

I didn't jump on it; I had played around with the idea of joining the Air Force after college, and thought that was as viable an entry into commercial piloting as any. In exchange for the training I would owe Uncle Sam ten years of military service.

It should have been simple: four years over ten, but I knew about the Air Force; I had no idea about the generic U.S. Defense Agency.

It was a move I couldn't make without my dad's input; he drove up to spend a long afternoon with me on a warm Saturday afternoon, and after I had told him about the offer and my conflicting possible plans, he said bluntly, "You're a woman, Kristine. The Air Force isn't about to train you to fly anything. They may promise, but once they have you—you'll turn into nothing but a glorified secretary. And that might be fine, but that's not what you want."

"I should consider this?"

"You should consider this seriously," he said. "No more worries about paying for your education? A guaranteed job afterward that doesn't push you into someone else's idea of what a woman can or should do? The sky's the limit with this offer. You won't be trapped by stereotype, and you'll learn to do everything you've ever dreamed of."

"I've never even heard of this agency," I told him.

"I would imagine there are a lot of things about your country's inner workings you've never heard of."

He glanced away, suddenly uncomfortable.

"You knew about this?"

"That they might consider you as a viable candidate? I knew. That the offer would be this good? Not a clue."

I leaned a bit closer, studying my father's face carefully. His expression was a mix of embarrassment, guilt, hope, and expectation. Suddenly every long business trip he ever took made sense; he began flying cargo hops when I was fourteen or fifteen years old, the weeks he was gone explained away with, "I had an extra few deliveries to make," or "Sometimes I fly businessmen where they want to go, and I need to wait to bring them back."

He'd been with the Defense Agency from its early days, and whether he intended to or not, had been grooming me to step into his shoes.

"Does Mom know?" I asked.

"No, and we need to keep it that way. I fly cargo and people, and it pays the bills. That's all she needs to know. She doesn't need to worry."

How they would explain it if he died on assignment, I wasn't sure, but my mother was often emotionally fragile and I agreed: she didn't need to know that the cargo he delivered might not technically be legal, or that the people he shuttled were armed, dangerous, and likely had other people blasting away at them as he taxied down the runway.

"If I accept the offer," I wondered, "what do we tell her?"

"We tell her that you're already doing so well that you've been given a scholarship, and when you graduate we'll tell her you landed a job with a small airline as a charter pilot. She won't question it because she doesn't really want to know."

"How much danger am I looking at? I mean, how dangerous is it for you?"

"Sometimes, very dangerous, and don't think that because you're female you'll get any breaks. They know what you can do, and they know your potential. By the time you leave college you'll be flying passenger planes, and after your final training you'll be comfortable behind anything. Military cargo planes, small jets, prototypes...you'll be able to get into the cockpit of an aircraft you've never conceived was possible, and you'll be able to take off, fly, and land safely on the other end."

"But?"

"But, it's not for the squeamish. You'll have to fly under fire sometimes. You'll have to take off with your best friends stacked like logs in the back, bleeding and maybe dying. You may have to do more than fly, Kris. You'll probably have to do it all, including gathering intelligence and implementing the plans your team leader presents. You'll do more than just learn to fly...you'll learn to fight, to run like hell—"

"I may have to kill someone," I guessed was where he was heading.

"You may."

"And you? Have you?"

"Do you really want to know?"

I was about to commit myself to his life; I wanted to know, even though I knew the answer before he nodded.

"This agency is dangerous, and yet you want your little girl to join," I mused.

"I will be terrified every time I know you're on an assignment. But at some point I have to stop thinking of you as my little girl and start thinking of you as an important asset to this country."

He'd been thinking that from the moment he wrote that first check to pay for my glider lessons. He just didn't know it.

~

Eight years later, a useless degree in liberal arts under my belt, endless hours of flight training, months of hands-on agency training, and having survived my first lengthy assignment under a team leader who wanted more than anything to prove that women did not belong in the field in any capacity, I was standing outside of Dan Martin's office, waiting to meet my new boss.

"He requested you," my former team leader practically spat. He didn't want me on his team, but he hated the idea that anyone else might find me the least bit valuable. "He's a hard ass and doesn't take shit from anyone, so keep your head down and mouth shut. Watch your ass, because no one else will."

I know he was watching my ass as I walked out the door.

I hesitated outside Dan's door; I could hear voices coming from his office and wasn't sure that I should interrupt—he might have requested me but that didn't mean he wanted me hearing any strategic planning—but when I heard laughter, I knocked once and opened the door before he could tell me to come in.

Dan was instantly likable. He grinned when he saw me, offered his hand, and his enthusiasm in having me there won me over before I really had the chance to speak to him. He scrambled to get me a chair from the other side of his office—he might think I was as capable of any of the men but he still believed in manners—and was obviously happy to have me there.

It was a major change from my introduction to my first team;

they'd grumbled hello and barely looked at me, and the team leader waved me off as insignificant. I had to be there but he wasn't going to make the effort to include me.

"Kris Stevens," he said, gesturing across his desk, "Ron Gallery. We'll be working together for the next year at least, and I thought it would be best if we met formally before we get handed an assignment."

Dan, I would come to learn, believed in listening to his team members; he paid close attention to their gut feelings, and more than once it saved our lives. But at the moment, I was simply happy to feel like I was going to be taken seriously. I wasn't going to be the token female inserted into an available slot for the sake of appearances.

Ron reached out to shake my hand as well. "Sorry about your last team," he said with a little bit of a grin. "Harold Donnigan is a dick, but they keep him around because one way or the other he gets the job done."

I couldn't dispute that; we had successfully completed our assignment, and everyone came back mostly unscathed.

Half of what Dan said went through me like a whisper; I could barely keep my eyes off Ron, and knew he was working hard to not flirt. He wasn't exactly my type; I tended to lean toward the sweeter looking, blond haired boys that hinted they could be a little dangerous, if they wanted, but were also like puppy dogs, energetically happy and bouncing around life as if nothing really mattered.

There was no doubt that Ron was dangerous; he hinted that he could also be sweet if that's what I wanted. He wasn't much taller than I was, and unlike the blonde boys of my youth, his hair was jet black, so dark that it hinted of blue, and his eyes were a crisp green that bore right into me, inviting me to spend a day getting lost in them.

While Dan went on about the potential assignments, I tried to figure Ron out. Dan was talking about a potential job that would have us flying into an airstrip near the Colombian coast, and I was trying to decide if Ron was single or married, interested, or just the flirty type.

By the end of the meeting I still had no idea, but Dan called me back as Ron left and offered a gentle warning: "He's a flirt, Kris. He's also the walking wounded. Keep it professional, or you'll wind up a casualty."

Of course I would keep it professional, I assured him.

I heard his chuckle follow me down the hall. And at the door leading to the lobby, Ron was waiting for me.

~

"You're a pilot," Ron said, as if it was news to him. "Do you realize that you're the agency's first female pilot? You'd think that in twenty years there would have been at least one, but here you are. A trailblazer."

I knew I was the first; that slice of information had been thrown at me in the form of an insult from my first team leader; he left no illusions about his feelings on the matter: women belonged at home, baking bread and cookies and popping out babies, and only men belonged in the field.

Yet, the agency had a strong history of placing women in positions normally only offered to men. If there had never been another female pilot, it was only because of a lack of opportunity. They hired me because of my father, and because he had been making sure I would have what it takes to handle the job. If they'd found another woman who was both qualified and interested, I wouldn't have been the first, not by a long shot.

We were talking over a late lunch; it wasn't a date so much as it was curiosity on both our parts. He'd waited for me in the lobby with the expectation that I would want nothing more than a chance to see if the energy that had crackled between us was something worth exploring, or simply a momentary flash.

I didn't hold his arrogance against him.

"There have been women in the agency since the beginning, haven't there?" I asked. "In the field even."

He nodded. "We couldn't operate nearly as well if our only field agents were men. Women have ways of getting what they want, and there are some covers a man can maintain easier and better with a woman backing him up."

"Or him backing her up," I offered.

"I can't say for sure, but I think there were women among the first recruits. The President had incredible foresight—"

I stopped him. "The President?"

"Truman," he said. "This agency was created because of him. A little lacking on your employer's history?"

He had me there. I hadn't particularly cared about the agency's history; I only knew that my father had been with it from the first years, and that it had been around almost as long as I'd been alive.

"The conception phase began three years after he took office, I think," Ron said. "The U.S. had intelligence in place at every level you can think of; the new CIA and the FBI, not to mention military intelligence. The problem was that the most visible units of those agencies functioned with their hands tied, so to speak. He wanted to form what would eventually become the bastard son of the Intel community; the dirty, grubby kid who could go in and do whatever had to be done."

"The kid Uncle Sam could deny fathering."

"Exactly. We are the kid he can send in to do all the things the other kids can't because they've been taught to play by the rules. A CIA operative might score a wealth of information on the inner workings of the KGB and have detailed plans on new weaponry, but they can't necessarily get anything more than those plans. Us? We don't officially exist, so we can do whatever the hell needs to be done. If Uncle Sam doesn't want the KGB to play with its new toys, we just go in and take the toys away."

And then, I knew, we promptly turned them over to someone else, and those toys would eventually find their way back to the CIA.

"Someday you'll find yourself with orders in hand to slip into territory you'd rather not be in, and you'll be flying the toy out instead of smuggling it."

I already had, but didn't tell him that; I had no idea if he was fishing for my ability to keep my mouth shut, or if he was just making conversation. Either way, I wasn't telling him that I'd already swiped my fair share of the toys.

I wanted him to talk about something other than work.

"Come on," I said leaning forward, "we know what we each

do. And you probably already know more about me than I'd tell you yet. Tell me about you."

"Me?" He seemed taken aback a bit. "There's not much to tell."

"Ah, now see there? That means there's a lot to tell. Ever been married? Kids? Where were you born, or were you hatched in some agency lab under the White House?"

He smiled, amused. "No, I've never been married, but I do have a teenaged son."

"Your mother must be so proud."

He raised an eyebrow, not sure if he should be offended or not. "Trust me, I've given her far more reasons to not be proud. And that other question, I was born and raised in Chicago."

"Well, that's a start."

"I'm the oldest of seven," he went on, humoring me. "My parents are both still alive, and my father is a tough, stubborn son of a bitch who holds onto grudges so tight they explode. But no, they have no idea what I do for a living."

"And what is it they think you do?" I pressed.

He suddenly looked very uncomfortable. "Your father knows what you do," he ventured. "What about your mother?"

I decided to let it pass. "My mother thinks I'm a charter pilot, the same as my dad. You've worked with him?"

"A few times. He doesn't like me very much, you should know."

"He's going to like you even less when he finds out we had lunch together. He's progressive, but he's also very protective."

"I can outrun him," Ron assured me, his eyes crinkled with the effort to not smile. "No, he's a good guy and I'd trust him with my life anytime."

"And me?"

"We'll see. If you fly half as well as he does, I just might."

~

I had absolutely not intended to sleep with him. When I woke up the next morning and he was there, I had a flash of panic. First, it was a matter of *what the hell have I done*, which made an abrupt left turn into *I'll be damned...he stayed all night*.

The sweet but brainless boys I was used to usually crept out in the middle of the night, citing an early class or a job they needed to get to. I never cared; what was I going to do with them in the morning? Feed them? Feed them what? My refrigerator typically held a six-pack of Coke and a beer or two, and the pantry shelves were the foundation of a dust-bunny breeding program.

Ron was neither brainless nor a boy, which I supposed was evidenced by the fact that he hadn't tried to leave in the middle of the night with an excuse poised just so on his lips as he shoved his legs into a dirty pair of jeans. He also didn't drift off in a post-coital haze; while I fought sleep, waiting for him to mumble something about needing to be home to feed a cat he may or may not actually own, he curled around me and talked.

He was a cuddler, something else I wasn't expecting. I shouldn't have been surprised, though, because he also wasn't self-centered or clueless about what to do with a woman who had made it clear that he was welcome to kick off his shoes and anything else he was inclined to remove.

He took his time and paid attention; so why, I wondered as I watched him sleep, did it amaze me that he was still there?

Ron slept on his stomach, his face buried so far into the pillow that he seemed to be trying to suffocate himself. I put a hand on his back, feeling for the soft rise and fall from his breath, and when I was satisfied that he was just a quiet sleeper and not inexplicably dead, I glanced at the clock—we had a little over two hours before we were supposed to be at work—and then I slid as close to him as I could get and set my head next to his on the pillow.

A few minutes later he inhaled deeply and slowly opened his eyes, sleep practically dripping from his eyelashes. I leaned in and kissed the tip of his nose, whispering, "Good morning."

"A very good morning," he sighed, rolling onto his side. His hand went to my face, fingers tracing along my jaw, something that would soon become warmly familiar and later achingly irritating. "What did you do to me?"

"Which time?"

He grinned lazily. "You know if anyone at work catches wind about this…"

"Dan will spaz," I said.

His fingers slid down my neck, over my collarbone. "No. Officially Dan will bluster and huff, but only because he has to present some common sense. But those above him? This may piss a few people off."

"As if no one else is doing this."

"It's usually something to be avoided."

In spite of where his fingers were headed, the thought stabbed at me that I was about to be told this was a monumental mistake, and we needed to pretend it never happened.

"There's something about you, though," he went on, his voice barely above a whisper. "I told you things last night I just don't tell. So again, what did you do to me?"

"Flashed my boobs. What did you tell me that you typically don't?"

He replaced his fingers with his lips. "About my son, for one. I try to not complicate his life any more than it already is."

"I would have found out about him sooner or later. We are going to be working together."

Very gently, he pushed me onto my back. "But we don't need to talk about business right now."

"And yet, we have to be at work in about two hours," I said, trying to not let him distract me. "I can hear your stomach growling, and there's probably no food in this apartment. We—"

"I'll find something to eat," he said simply.

"Not exactly a nutritious start to the day."

"Mouthy," he chuckled. "You're going to argue with me on everything just to argue, aren't you?"

"I might. But don't stop."

He didn't stop, not until we realized we were already late for work, and even then he shrugged it off as nothing to worry about.

"They aren't going to fire me," he assured me as we got dressed. "I know too much."

That was fine for him, but I didn't know a damned thing, and it was only Day Two with the new team.

"Harold Donnigan," Ron said, rolling out my former team leader's name in syllables. We'd just pulled into the parking lot and he'd cut the engine on his car when he spotted Donnigan standing on the sidewalk, deep in conversation with someone in a black suit. "What are you up to?"

Donnigan speaking to someone wasn't instantly suspect in my book, but the fact that he was attentive was new to me.

"Who's the suit?" I asked.

Ron leaned forward, arms crossed on the top of the steering wheel. "CIA," he said.

"And you're sure about that?"

He nodded in Donnigan's direction. "That earpiece he's wearing isn't agency issue. Besides, the suit? That's CIA screaming 'I'm wearing a cheap off-the-rack black suit, so your argument is invalid.' Pushy bunch of pricks."

I had to laugh. "Don't we rely on them for money and information? And money?"

"Yes, we do. Not to mention, we rely on them for money." He grinned at me as he unbuckled his seatbelt. "Come on. If we get to Dan before Donnigan can get out of that conversation, we can probably get ahead of him on whatever the suit is here for. Could be a choice assignment."

"You'd yank one out from under him?"

"In a heartbeat. Besides," he added, getting out of the car, "wouldn't you love to screw him over just once?"

"For the way he treated me? Hell yes."

"That's my girl."

~

Half an hour later Dan rushed into Ron's office with a file folder in hand, slightly out of breath but looking ecstatic. "Got it," he said, kicking the door closed behind him. "Soviet pilot seeking asylum, CIA doesn't want to call attention to him until he's on U.S. soil. If we leave now, the assignment is ours."

"They gave it to us over Donnigan, why?" I asked.

"Because we have what Donnigan doesn't," Ron answered for Dan.

"What, clean underwear and pre-packed snacks?"

Dan handed the file folder to me. "Yes. Well, that and we have you. He's going to kick himself in the ass over losing you. Our Soviet friend just happened to take his plane with him. It's an off-the-line prototype, and it's yours."

I flipped the folder open for a cursory look. "South Korea? I'm flying us to South Korea, then flying us out in God knows what?"

"No," Dan said. "We're taking a company plane so you can rest up on the way, and then you're flying to Okinawa."

"Alone," I guessed.

"We'll meet you there," Ron said.

"When do we leave?" I asked.

Dan was reaching for the door. "We leave now."

"Well, now I want clean underwear," Ron grumbled as the door clicked behind us. "This is going to be a long flight."

~

Doug Stone waited for us on the tarmac at Travis Air Force Base; my first thought was that he was CIA, but his dirty blond hair was just a little too long and his sunglasses a little too non-issue, and he seemed a lot too nervous.

He had the cheap black suit, though.

First assignment jitters; his teeth were clenched, muscles near his jaw twitching—I knew he wanted to throw up and he was praying that he wouldn't do it in front of me.

Dan pointed at him as we boarded and grunted, "Doug Stone, Ron Gallery, Kris Stevens. Get in, take a seat and buckle up."

Confused, Doug scrambled up the ramp into the custom jet—the interior was plush, with first class grade seats that could be spun to face forward or to the side, with a private bunk in the rear—and took the first seat he came to; he hadn't said a word, but he was watching everyone apprehensively, and I thought I saw his hands shaking as he clipped the seat belt into place.

He radiated *Where are we going?*

"First time out?" Ron asked.

Doug nodded.

"Doug," Dan said, "will be joining us as our field physician. For now he's strictly observing, so if you don't absolutely need him, don't involve him."

Translation: cover the new guy's ass.

"You need to relax," Ron said, leaning back into his seat as the engines began to whine. "They don't come much easier than this one. You only need to survive the boredom of the flights there and back."

"Time to grab a book might have been nice," I agreed.

Dan pointed to the file folder I had resting in my lap. "You can pass the time memorizing that."

"Terrific. What do I do with the other ten hours?"

Ron spun his seat towards Doug. "We can play Grill the New Guy. You're what? Twelve years old and you're already a doctor?"

"Twenty five," Doug said softly.

"So we can at least get you drunk."

Doug almost smiled, but paled as the plane lifted off.

"Nervous flier?" I asked. "It really will stay in the air."

"Unless someone shoots us down," Dan mumbled.

They kept on poking at Doug, long enough that I wanted to tune them out. I opened the folder and began soaking in the details of the plane the Soviet pilot was turning over in exchange for a guarantee of his personal freedom. There were few details about the pilot, which didn't surprise me; what we wanted more than him was the plane. I knew what wasn't in the file: if all we managed to get was the plane, that was fine. The pilot was incidental. Dan and Ron likely had his personal details, and he had our protection, but he was not our priority.

Doctor Stone, I thought, glancing at him, he would be our biggest priority if anything hiccupped.

"This is a basic run," Ron was telling him. "We escort her in, she takes off, and we dump the pilot in Okinawa. He's protected, so there should be nothing between us and him."

"So I'm not really needed unless one of you get shot or stabbed."

"Would that make you happy, Doc?"

"It might."

"I'll jab Dan in the ear with my pen if nothing else pans out for you," Ron offered.

"Thanks for that," Dan sighed.

"I do what I can."

They weren't letting up on each other; it was high school all over again, though I got it—they wanted to make Doug relax and make him feel like he was a part of the team before he hit the ground.

Still, their voices were a buzz in the air that was becoming annoying, so I took the file into the rear bunk and stretched out, determined that by the time we landed I would have every available detail seared into my brain.

If I could visualize it before I ever set eyes on it, I could fly it.

Don't overthink it, my father would be telling me. If you can fly the big toys, you can fly them all, even if they are armed to explode.

"Ever helpful, Dad," I muttered to myself.

Just as the words were beginning to swim in front of me, there was a light rapping at the bunk entrance, and when I looked up, Ron was standing there. His head was slightly cocked to one side and he was almost smiling, slightly amused at having caught me talking to myself.

"Dan wants you to get some sleep if you can," he said, passing up the chance to verbally poke at me. "The rest of us can be wiped out, but you need to rest."

I waved the file at him. "I have important data to process."

He sat on the mattress next to me, taking the file and tossing it to the foot of the bed. "It's a plane. You're a pilot. You'll figure it out."

"It could be an airborne bomb. I need to make sure it doesn't go 'boom.'"

"Hm." He stretched out next to me. "Don't think about that. Think about something else."

"Such as?"

"I had a thought a little while ago, when you were headed back this way. You disappeared into here and I realized we've never walked down the street hand in hand."

"We've known each other for one day," I reminded him. "And I think we skipped the hand holding part."

"I don't think I want to skip that part," he said. "I think I'd like to go back to the very beginning, ask you out, pick you up and take you out to dinner. Maybe take a long walk somewhere, so that I can work up the nerve to hold your hand."

He sounded serious, yet amusement nearly crackled off him in sparks of swallowed laughter.

"I might let you hold a lot of things," I said.

"There's something about holding hands that means something. When we get back—"

He turned at the tapping at the bunk entrance; Dan was there, and he heaved a deep, almost disappointed sigh.

"This is a bad idea," he said.

"You're the one who wanted her to get some rest," Ron said.

"This"—Dan pointed at Ron and then me—"it's a bad idea."

"Dan, it's not like to going to rip her clothes off and jump her right here."

"You know what I mean." He turned, and as he walked away he was still muttering, "Bad, bad idea."

"He's probably right," I said. "I won't hold it against you if you get up and walk out and never try to hold my hand."

He reached up and jerked closed the curtain hanging limply across the narrow metal-stripped doorway, then rolled until his face was only an inch from mine. "I don't think I can do that. I think I need to find out what a long walk with you is like. I think we need to get caught outside in the rain, and not run to find someplace dry. I think I want to find out what the things that surprise you are, and what things can make you cry. I already know you're smart and have balls of steel, and I think I want to know what else there is."

"That's weirdly sweet, Ron. I think I want you to show me where I keep those balls of steel."

"Maybe after I've gotten the nerve to hold your hand." He leaned in and kissed me. "Dan was serious, though. You need to sleep. Word is, you were up most of the night."

"Had a hard time sleeping," I said against his lips. "The bed had these odd lumps and I was a little too sweaty to really rest."

"I'll get up if you think I'll keep you awake."

"No." I pulled one of the pillows I'd be leaning on out from under my head and slid it under his. "You were up most of the night, too. And I'm sure this won't be the first time you've slept on a plane with one of your co-workers."

"It would not," he agreed. "But you'd be the first woman."

"Good to know that about you," I snickered. "I'm not sure I can sleep, though."

He offered a back rub, very soft and gentle, to relax me, and while I practically melted under his deft touch, I found myself getting drowsy, and just let go.

~

When I woke, Ron was no longer next to me but the mattress was still warm. I could hear the buzzing of voices just beyond the bunker, and sat up, wondering how long I'd been asleep and how much longer we'd be in the air.

Sitting there in the bunk, leaning against the cold sidewall, I tried to feel for any slow sloping, a subtle change of direction, but all I could feel was the humming of the engines and the draft from the air exchange.

Was Ron out there trying to defend what Dan thought was a bad idea? I couldn't argue with him on that; it probably was three steps over the borderline into the realm of stupid and only having known him a day, walking away wouldn't be too painful. Yet, I wanted to get this assignment over with, just to prove to Dan that we could work together, and then to get onto the next thing.

It felt absurd, but I wanted to take that walk with Ron, and wait for him to hold my hand.

He gently pulled the curtain back, and smiled when he saw I was awake. "Nice hair," he teased as he slid back onto the mattress. "It's like part New York chic, part rat terrier."

"Jackass." I pulled my fingers through my hair, trying to pull as many tangles from it as I could. "How long was I asleep?"

"Seven hours or so. So was I. So were Dan and Doug, for that matter. I woke up and they were both leaned back in their seats, drooling."

"You'd think they'd put another rack back here."

"They might, if this plane was used for ops more often. It's the SG's air limo, mostly. He didn't need it, so here we are."

"Seven hours," I mused. "So we're still a long ways from landing."

He nodded. "We have time to kill. But once you get out of this bunk, you're back on the clock."

"Meaning?"

He shrugged.

"Didn't you tell Dan you weren't going to rip my clothes off and jump me in here?"

"True, I did say that. And I did mean it. But that doesn't mean we have to go out there right now. We can stay here and talk."

"With your tongue down my throat."

"Not that the impulse hasn't hit me, but no. I really do mean talk. Get to know each other."

"I'd say I already know quite a bit about you. Did you know you have a freckle right—?"

"I know where my freakish freckle is. I know you're wickedly fun in bed, too, but that's not what I meant, either."

"You want to know what kinds of things make me cry, what surprises me?"

"Yep."

"I don't really know," I said. "Hurt my feelings and I might cry, though it might also take a lot to hurt them. I was surprised at how attracted I was to you and how fast things happened. I don't remember the last time I was really surprised, though."

He crawled across the mattress and sat next to me, leaning against the wall, our shoulders touching.

"I think I can surprise you."

"How's that?"

He took a deep breath, and as he exhaled he said, "I was a priest."

"Yep," I said. "That'll do it."

~

The choice to become a priest wasn't Ron's. His parents were devout Catholics, and in the implosion of the Great Depression they did better than survive; they were comfortable, and the responsibility of having seven children was less a burden than it was a blessing.

Friends would joke about their proliferation, but they welcomed each child as a gift, and as payment for that gift there was no question: God was getting their firstborn in return. Ron never questioned it as he grew up; he was the chosen one, their Golden Boy, the son who would honor God and family by happily entrenching himself into his religion, by attending parochial schools, and by entering a seminary prep high school at the end of junior high.

He felt elevated to it; it was less expectation that drove him towards fulfilling his parents' promise than it was feeling that he was entitled to it. His brothers were expected to work hard in order to secure jobs that would mean they would work harder to provide for the families they would surely have. His sisters were expected to learn only what they needed to get by in the world; in them their parents fostered a love of reading, so that later they would be able to help their own sons grow into educated men. And in them their mother engendered a home work ethic: keep a clean house, have a happy husband.

Only Ron was meant for something better, and he reveled in it.

Then came high school, and the priests; the more time he spent trying to not squirm in discomfort and boredom in their classrooms, the less he wanted to be like them. He was taught that he was less than nothing; he was the product of sinful parents, and that they were inferior because they had caved to their baser wants. Yes, the family was a reward from God, but it was merely a consolation prize. There could only be true dedication to God in suffering and doing without; there could only be worthiness in celibacy and shunning anything that remotely resembled desire.

After two years of feeling as if his head was being crammed full of half-truths and what he was sure were a few outright lies, Ron no longer wanted to be a priest, but there was nowhere for him to turn. The shame he would bring upon his family was too great to risk, so he remained in the school, treading water in a pool of rapidly rising misery. In his mind he promised himself he would find a way out, that before it was time to enter the seminary he would be shown the front door with a warning to get out and not look back, but he could never bring himself to do anything outrageous or public enough to warrant a dismissal.

It wasn't for lack of trying. There were incidents of drinking, but the priests turned a blind eye to it, brushing it off as "boys will be boys." There were the girls, which earned him lengthy lecture upon lecture and punishments that seemed wholly halfhearted, and Ron was sure that the priests never believed that he had slept with any of them.

He lost his virginity in a quick and awkward encounter with a girl two years older when he was sixteen; over the next two years there were other girls, with whom he felt more comfortable than the boys he was forced to spend endless hours with in study and prayer. He thought he was in love once or twice, but always walked away from them because he knew he was in so deep that there was no honorable way out and not walking away would eventually break their hearts.

After a lifetime of being told that his very existence was solely to honor God, he could find no honor in anything else.

So he stayed; he entered the seminary, and just before his 25th birthday he found himself headed for Ireland, where he would exist to serve the whims of the nuns in charge of a parish school.

The sisters made it clear that he and his fellow priest-in-residence, Michael Brennan, were only there because the boys needed someone to look up to, and by God he and Father Brennan would set good examples for them.

Ron had no problem being that when he was at the school; on his own time, he took great exception to it, and found himself most afternoons warming a barstool at Frank's Pub. It was one place he and Mickey could be certain that there would be no nuns glaring daggers of disapproval at them, one place where they could be men and not "those priests."

After three years, he decided enough was enough; honor or not, he would find a way out, and his family would have to live with the

crushing disappointment of their offering to God turning his back
and walking away.

~

George, the bartender at Frank's was, Ron guessed, no more
than three or four years older than he was; he was a curious person,
very inquisitive and sharply observant. There wasn't much that got
past him; if someone walked into the bar, turned around and walked
out, George could describe him down to the color of his eyes, even
if he'd had just a glimpse.

He fascinated Ron; he could speak about world politics as if
he was there in the middle of it all, and he could argue either side
of an issue with equal skill. He and Mickey struggled to find news
worthy items that George didn't know about and couldn't dissect in
great detail.

And there was the accent; George swore he'd been born and
raised in Dublin, but every so often Ron could hear something else
simmering under the brogue, something almost New Jersey. When
he pointed it out, George brushed it off as something he'd picked up
on a lengthy stay in the United States.

"Aye, you'll see. Even now I hear a bit of the Irish roll off your
tongue, ya know."

Ron thought that was complete and utter bullshit, but he didn't
press. Where George had come from didn't matter. All that mattered
was his presence behind the bar every afternoon. He was a pleasant
diversion from the tedium of loud kids, angry nuns, and religion that
he found increasingly difficult to both swallow and spit out.

With George and with Mickey, he was honest. He wanted out,
and once he figured out what he wanted to do, he'd find a way. He
knew he wanted to go home, but it didn't have to be to Chicago,
where he'd grown up; he just wanted to be back in the U.S.

"Find a good woman and raise ten kids?" Mickey laughed. "I
wouldn't be opposed to that, myself, but I'm happy enough here."

Whether "here" meant Ireland, the priesthood, or the bar, Ron
didn't know, and he didn't ask. "I don't see myself with kids," he
said. "With a woman, surely."

"Aye, and who would have you?" George pressed, slightly winking.

"There were a few who wanted me, a long time ago," Ron sighed.

"And being the vow less heathen ya were, you took them up on their charms, did'n ya?" Mickey laughed.

"I was a teenager, not dead. Of course I did."

"Shame on ya, ya godless pagan."

"Oh, and you didn't?"

"No nerve," Mickey declared.

Ron doubted that Mick lacked the nerve; he had charm and women seemed to be drawn to him. What he had that Ron didn't was determination and a belief that he was in it for all the right reasons. He allowed himself to look at all the women who passed by, but he never allowed himself to entertain the idea that doing anything about them might be all right.

Mickey Brennan's journey to the priesthood was completely different than Ron's. He'd grown up in abject poverty; his father left home in search of work before he was even a toddler and rarely sent money. His mother struggled to put food on the table and his clothing was either his older brother's outgrown castoffs, or scavenged from neighbors' discards.

There were nights he knew that his mother had to decide who would eat and who would do without, and more often than not she did without, splitting what little she had between her two sons. They slept in the cold, bathed in the same water for days on end, and battled the rodents that scurried without any fear across their floor.

When he was twelve, the head of the parish school knocked on their door; Father McAdams had an offer, one he expected their mother to seriously consider. The school could take one of her sons, but only one, in residence. He would be fed, clothed, and educated, and with any grace, he would discover within himself a vocation.

Mickey's brother was insistent: the only one who should even be considered was Mickey. Sean was sixteen and wanted to leave school behind for work; if Mickey went, then all Sean needed to worry about was supporting their mother. He was sure he could find a job, sure he could put food on the table, but he wasn't sure he could do that for a boy who was about to start growing fast and who would need more than he was certain he could provide.

It was a gift and Mickey knew that. His brother wasn't trying to get rid of him; his brother was trying to protect him. He was content with the promise that they would see each other frequently; the school was a mile away, and Mickey would be free to walk home to visit often.

Sean found work just two weeks after Mickey left; he started in the city stables cleaning up after the horses, and by the time Mickey was entering the priesthood Sean was a city manager. He'd kept his promise to support their mother, and eventually moved her from the rat infested single room home he'd grown up in to a house with heat, water, and the comfort he thought she deserved.

Mickey was grateful; his brother had given him years of security he wouldn't have had, and he cared for their mother with more respect than Mickey's absent father had ever considered.

That gift, he guessed, was also what whispered to him that he did indeed have a vocation. He owed the priests for saving his life as much as he owed Sean for stepping aside and letting him take the lone spot available in the school.

So Michael Brennan had no issues with the idea that he would be a priest forever, though he did grapple with the idea that he might be missing out on having a family. What he hadn't considered, though, was testing the waters, finding out what being with a woman was like.

"If God wanted that for me, we wouldn't be celibate, aye?"

"I wasn't a priest when I wasn't celibate," Ron pointed out.

"True, but I had made promises."

"You're both worthless," George proclaimed. "Both pathetic. Neither of ya truly want to be where ya are. Get the fock out while you're young."

How? Ron wondered. *How do you fix a mistake this big?*

~

Mickey Brennan was three pints into the evening; the day had been long, trying to stretch food meant for fifty children into enough to feed twenty more, and he hated dealing with the nuns who felt compelled to bark orders and push the young priests into work other than what they had been assigned to do.

It wasn't the extra work he minded; it was the attitude, that he should be grateful that he wasn't one of the students, barely clothed for the bite of late winter cold and frequently hungry on top of it. None of them would care that he had once been one of those students, and that his youth had been spent scrabbling for anything his family could use, from others' cast out, worn out clothing to scraps of food intended for family pets.

"Aye, they do God's work," he mumbled over his ale, "but the mouths on those women…"

"Hypercritical," Ron said. "You know if any of them walked in here we'd be nailed to the proverbial crosses for daring to spend money on alcohol when we should be spending it on the children."

"Every damned t'ing on the children," Mickey sighed. "Remind me, brother. Did we take a vow of poverty along with them? 'Twas no attention I paid to the particulars, to be sure."

"Makes two of us. I might have declined if I knew I was supposed to be poor for the rest of my life."

"Aye, I've been poor. I may still be poor, who knows?"

George slid a pint across the bar towards Ron, waving off Mickey, whom he thought had had enough. "I don't care, not as long as you pay your tab."

Mickey and Ron turned toward the door as it opened, drawn by the sudden rush of cold air. Neither could turn away from the sight of the teenaged blonde scurrying in, trying to pull the door closed, her hair wind whipped and cheeks reddened from the cold air.

"Both of ya," George said, "I don't care if you wear those ugly collars, keep away from the girl. She's new, and I need her help here. Her *attentive* help."

Mickey wasn't paying attention to him; he slid off the barstool and met her halfway across the floor, helping her take off her coat. "And who might ya be?" he asked as he hung it near the door.

"I would be Patricia Cagney," she replied with a grin. "And you?"

"Michael Brennan."

"*Father* Michael Brennan," Ron added.

"Ah, 'tis a shame. And you?"

"Ron Gallery."

"*Father* Ron," Michael added.

Pat shrugged. "'Tis not going to be my night, now."

"Aye, but you've made ours," Mickey said as he slid back onto his barstool. "The priesthood did not blind us to your beauty and your charms."

"I'm warning ya," George prodded.

"Y'said to keep my hands off, and I will. But my eyes? I cannot."

"I won't have a problem with poking the damn t'ings out."

"Bastid," Mickey snickered.

"Aye. And you," he said to Ron, "I'll take yours as well. She's young and doesn't need to be distracted by the likes of either of ya."

"By the likes of the good fathers?" Patricia asked. "Assuming the good."

"My heart is as pure as driven snow," Mickey sighed melodramatically.

"Mine's not," Ron said. "I have no problem admitting that you'll be in more than one of my dirtier dreams."

"Father, really now."

Ron leaned over the bar. "We're just boys at heart, Patricia. And boys will dream what boys will dream, no matter how tight the collars they wear."

She leaned across the bar to meet him, their noses a bare fraction apart. "And how tight would your collar be?"

"Not so tight that I don't notice a beautiful woman when I see her, and not too tight to keep the blood from rushing from my head."

"And where," she whispered, "would it go?"

"Maybe someday I'll show you," he countered, and was struck by the thought that sooner or later, that's exactly what would happen.

~

Patricia Cagney was a student; Ron felt a stab of panic at the idea that the girl he was flirting so outrageously with was much younger than he supposed, but after a few minutes of pointed conversation he realized that she was a university student, studying history.

She had a particular fascination with American history, and was immediately taken with the idea that Ron was a potential font of information about the history of Irish American politics in Chicago; he was more taken with the idea that what little he did know would be enough to create a valid reason to spend time alone with her. She could pick his brains while he figured out a way to get closer without completely disgusting her.

He knew she was also leaning on Mickey Brennan for his knowledge of church history and European history in general, but Mickey was dedicated to the idea that he would cling to the priesthood with every shred of his personal integrity, so Ron never worried that there might be anything more between them.

He spent nearly six months boning up on the particulars of the Irish in Chicago so that he would be able to carry on coherent conversations with her, and most of those six months he worked at convincing himself that he wasn't falling for her. He waited in the bar nearly every afternoon for her shift to begin, sometimes with Mickey, but as often as possible without.

He also took that time to pry more conversation out of George; the bar had been there barely any longer than Ron had been in Ireland, and after some pointedly direct questions, he'd gotten George to admit that he wasn't all he seemed. He'd spent many more years in the United States than he wanted anyone to know, and he had his reasons for being vague.

George leaned over the bar, speaking only to Ron. "Y'want out of that collar. I may be able t'help, but push me too hard, and I'll not tell ya a t'ing."

Ron didn't push. He spent his free time soaking in as much American history as he could, either in the bar where he could watch George—paying close attention to the people he seemed to speak with the most, especially those he seemed to prefer to not be associated with—and in a back room of the bar, where he could be alone with Patricia Cagney.

George allowed them use of the room under the pretense that Ron was helping Pat research Irish immigration into the United States, but Ron noted from the start that what had once been a storage room was almost comfortable; there was a sofa against the far wall, a coffee table, and a floor lamp. And, he noted, the door locked from the inside.

He doubted George had decorated the room with Ron and Pat in mind—he suspected it was George's own hiding place and wondered exactly what and whom George might need to hide from—but he wasn't going to take issue with it. Many afternoons they locked themselves in the room and dutifully went over the work Pat was doing in school; for the first few months he forced himself to stay on topic, but the longer it went on, the less time they spent on history. He peppered her with questions about her life, her family, and the dreams she had for herself. She dragged the truth from him, that more than anything he wanted out of the priesthood; he wanted to pick up and run, head back to the United States and start over.

The first time he kissed her was on a cold snap of a day in early October; he warned her that if he did, he might not be able to keeps his hands off her from then on, and was pleasantly surprised when she lifted onto her toes to make it easier for him. She left her books on the coffee table and melted into him, sighing when he pushed her gently back onto the sofa, but making it clear that whatever his intentions, it would go no further than this.

A first kiss, she told him, followed by a hundred more, that's enough firsts for one night.

Evenings spent in the bar's back room no longer had anything to do with picking through history; he made his way to the room through the back door, not wanting anyone to see where he was headed, and he waited for her to finish her shift. Over and over he told himself he wasn't falling for her; he was leaving sooner or later, and she would still be here, trying to balance working in the bar with school.

Six weeks later Ron left Mickey in charge of the boys who lived in the dorms, giving them a break from the watchful eyes of the nuns; he took with him a stack of letters from his brother, chronicles of his experiences in World War II, with the excuse that Pat would find them interesting and perhaps useful.

He didn't care if Mickey believed him, but he also didn't think Mick had any reason to doubt him. Mickey often took books and newspapers to Pat, slices of their shared history that he thought she would appreciate. He would have no reason to think twice about Ron taking something he knew she would enjoy.

He had a dozen reasons to doubt himself; he was leaving, he knew that. He could feel himself being pulled away from the parish school in accelerated degrees, and he knew that he loved Pat, but not enough to take her with him. He wanted a life of his own, and he was pinning having that on George, who was gradually becoming more open with him.

But that evening, with Mickey stuck at the school trying to keep amused and in line a dozen boys and young men, Ron grabbed the stack of letters and headed for Frank's. He spent an hour sitting at the bar, nursing his drink, and waiting.

Just before Pat's shift was over, he said his goodnights to a few of the pub's regulars and left through the front door; a minute later Pat let him in through the back, and they quietly made their way to the back room. Ron locked the door behind him and leaned against it, watching as she moved George's mess of papers from the sofa to the floor. She kicked off her shoes and sat down, smoothing the folds of her dress, and when she looked up at him and smiled, he felt all reason leave him in one breath.

He forgot about the letters he had stashed in his coat pocket as he pushed away from the door, and when his lips met hers he had the thought that he didn't have to leave her; there was no reason she couldn't go with him. She wanted to see more of the world than her pocket of Ireland; he could show her his favorite parts of America, and they could see new things together.

When they tired of each other—and he was certain they would at some point—she could go her way and he could go his.

It seemed simple enough.

And she wanted him; her shy explorations over the last few weeks convinced him of that. He'd always stopped himself with the dull thought that he had made a vow and he was only willing to break it so much, but now that he was sure he was leaving? There was nothing to stop him, nothing other than the word 'no.'

He hesitated once, when her eyes went wide with surprise as his clothes came off, and he slapped away the notion that he hadn't done this in ten years and was likely no good at it, but she wasn't pulling back and he counted on her complete lack of experience to cover his own ineptitude.

Patricia Cagney surrendered her virginity to Ron on the dingy sofa of the former storeroom in Frank's Pub, and when it was over she held her hands to his face and said lightly, "I didn't enjoy that one bit, but I will. Give me time and I'll get better."

Ron had enjoyed it quite a bit, and in the absence of the guilt he thought he'd be fighting, felt downright triumphant.

He was no longer a priest; he knew that as surely as he knew he would take every opportunity he could to make sure she learned to enjoy his body as much as he did hers. And when the details were settled, he'd offer to take her with him. If she didn't want to leave, that was fine, but if she did, he wouldn't mind the company, not one bit.

~

"Person who just came in," George said. "Take a look, but for no more than a moment. Then turn back around."

Ron and Mickey both glanced and then turned back to George.

"Now. Every detail. Tell me."

Mickey shrugged. "Woman with brown hair. Not so unusual, my friend."

"Aye, yer pathetic," George sighed.

"Woman with brown hair," Ron repeated. "Parted on the right side. She's about five feet eight inches, a hundred and twenty pounds. She's somewhere in her early thirties, is wearing no makeup, but she does have a natural flush to her face. White sweater, brown skirt, brown leather boots. Wedding ring. Necklace with a small red gem, not sure if it's real or not."

"Eyes?"

"Two," he chuckled. "Hazel."

Mickey leaned away from him. "What the fock? How didja see all o'that with just a look?"

"I always notice women."

"He's observant," George said. "And the devil is in the details. Pay closer attention, Mick."

"Aye, I see enough."

"See the clock?" Ron said. "Don't you have a cafeteria to supervise?"

With a heavy sigh, Mickey slid off the barstool. "Ya'd think the little bastids could eat without me there."

George waited until Mick was out the door, then poured two pints and nodded towards the woman that was now seated at a table in the corner. "Come on," he said. "Time for you to meet her."

He set the mugs on the table, and sat in a chair across from her, pointing to the lone free chair for Ron. "Father Ron Gallery," he said, "Linda Jackson."

She barely looked at him. "A priest? You're recruiting a priest? Has all the Irish whiskey you've inhaled over the last three years made you stupid? The last thing we need is the Catholic church pissing about how we're trolling their waters."

"He's hardly a priest," George said. "Unless it's normal for the local priest to be fucking the barmaid at every turn."

Ron swallowed the bite of surprise; that George knew what was really going on in his back room only mildly surprised him, but that his brogue completely vanished did.

"I was wrong," Ron said. "Not New Jersey. Brooklyn."

"He guessed you weren't native," Linda mused.

George nodded. "This isn't sudden. He's been on my radar since I got here. He notes the small details, and he has a memory like a steel trap. He also thinks highly enough of himself that he'll have the ego he'll need to get the job done."

"Ego," she snorted. "That's one way of putting it. And the other one, the man who left?"

"Michael Brennan," George answered. "I'm less certain about him. He's bright, but he doesn't give enough weight to the things that don't matter to understand how important they might be. For instance, he has no clue that his buddy here is screwing the woman he's fallen in love with."

At that, Ron almost balked, but decided he was better off keeping his mouth shut.

"No use to us?"

"I think he could be very useful behind a desk," George said. "He's bright and curious. Probably not a lifer, but useful."

Linda turned toward Ron. "So tell me, Father, where do your loyalties lie? God or country?"

"God has pretty much fucked me over," Ron said.

Her eyebrows rose in surprise.

"Don't get me wrong. I'll always have that part of my life looking over my shoulder, but if you question whether I would choose my church over my country?" He leaned forward, elbows on the table. "My brother is in the army. He fought in the war. He'll fight again, if his country asks him to. I would trade places with him in a heartbeat."

"You'd die for the United States."

"I would."

She leaned forward to match him. "Would you kill for the United States?"

He didn't think about it before he opened his mouth. "I would."

Linda Jackson stood up and nodded towards George. "Get him ready."

"And Brennan?"

She nodded. "Don't make me regret this, Barron. If either one of them screws up, it's your ass I'll go after."

~

Three days before Christmas Ron and Mickey were in their usual spots at Frank's; the school was closed for the holidays, leaving Ron with little to do and Mickey bouncing between family and friends, but for the afternoon they intended to plaster themselves to the bar stools and wait for George to return with information on when they could expect to leave.

While Ron was simply waiting until he could leave Ireland behind, Mickey was grappling with what he would tell his family. They would understand if he'd come to realize that being a priest was not what he wanted after all, but to leave home to work in America?

He doubted his mother could accept that.

"You can't tell her what you'll be doing," Ron reminded him.

"Aye," he breathed out.

"Hell, why tell her much at all? You don't have to say you're moving away. Just tell her you're taking some time to go see the states. Once you're there you can send word you're staying. Then bring her over to visit every now and then."

"Aye," Mickey said again.

"Chicken shit," Ron laughed. "It'll be fine."

Mick opened his mouth to speak—Ron was sure it would just be to say "Aye" again—when the door opened and they both turned, expectantly. George took his time, making sure it closed behind him, hanging up his coat and scarf, knowing they were waiting for him. He was deliberate in making them wait, intentionally wandering past the bar to the office, puttering until he'd decided they'd been patient long enough.

"You," he said to Ron as he took his place behind the bar, "Two weeks, and I'll be going with you. Mick, you'll go in February. Linda Jackson will come back and accompany you to the U.S."

Two weeks, Ron thought. *Right after New Years*.

"Where will we be going?" Mickey asked.

"Does it matter? You'll go where you'll go."

"Aye," Mickey sighed.

"California," George said after a time. "Ron will begin training near San Francisco, but you'll be in Los Angeles. Chances are you'll eventually wind up in the same place but I can't guarantee it."

Mick allowed his disappointment to show; Ron, on the other hand, had never pinned any hopes on working near or with Mickey. Friends, yes, but he wasn't attached at the hip, and didn't think it mattered where they wound up, as long as they got the hell out of Ireland.

Unlike Mick, Ron didn't worry about telling his family. He intended to wait until after the fact, when it was a deed done and not something they could try to talk him out of or guilt him over. He already knew the end result: the moment he walked away from the church, he would be disowned.

He'd given his entire life to it and admired those who felt an honest vocation, but he couldn't find that anywhere inside; it was time to get something for himself.

He only half listened as George spoon fed small details to Mickey; how his training would differ from Ron's, the jobs they would hold. All he cared about was that he had two weeks, and then he was free.

When the door banged open, he made note of that. Pat stormed in and pulled it closed behind her loudly, stomping her way across the bar. He hoped it was just a product of being cold, but when he saw that her eyes were rimmed with red, he felt his stomach drop.

What if she didn't want to leave?

He'd miss her, but he was going either way.

George stopped talking; he set about puttering behind the bar, trying to ignore Pat's distress. It took Mick longer to notice, but when he did, Ron noted the look of longing and concern on his face.

Ron ran through a mental checklist: anger, fear, sadness. He could see them all in her, and waited for her to turn around and look at him before deciding if he should ask.

When she did, she spun on her heel and faced him, eyes filled with tears.

"You fockin' idjit!" She leaned across the bar and hissed, "I'm pregnant, you fool."

Without her raising a hand, he felt the punch to the center of his face all the same; there was no way possible he'd heard her correctly. While he felt his head spinning, he realized Mick had stumbled off his own bar stool and taken a step back, his hand to his chest as he gasped out, "But we were only together twice..."

And now, a kick to the crotch, Ron thought, wincing.

Pat was about to spit out something else, but caught herself when she realized what Mick had said. It was enough time for Ron to take in a deep breath and begin chewing through the anger.

"You were with Mick," he said evenly. "When?"

Pat stepped back, confused by having her fury snuffed out by this turn. "Didja not hear me?" she asked in a small voice.

"I heard. You're pregnant. Now whose is it?"

Mick stepped back to the bar but didn't sit; he grasped the edge of it, fingernails turning white under the strain. "Whose?"

"It can't be Mick's," she cried.

"But you slept with him."

She blinked the tears over her lashes. "Aye. But I never thought—"

"Never thought we would find out? We're *roommates*, Pat. We're friends. We live together. Didn't you think that at some point one of us would admit to the other what we were doing? And with whom?"

"Ronny."

He didn't want to give up his irritation. He could see her folding in front of him, the fear bubbling up over the sadness, but he didn't want to give in yet.

Mick was still holding onto the bar, pale, looking very much like he was about to pass out. "A baby," he murmured. "And it's not mine? It's his?"

"So she says," Ron sighed.

"Pat?" Mick was pleading as much as he was asking. "It's not mine?"

"It can't be," she answered, barely a whisper.

"Can't be because it's not possible or because you don't want it to be?" Ron pressed. "Can't be because he had no clue what he was doing and shot his wad all over the—what, the sofa? The bed?—or it can't be because the timing is all wrong. Why," he asked loudly, "can't this be Mick's child?"

Mick let go of the bar and grabbed Ron's arm. "It doesn't matter, brother. It's a child, and not its fault that we're all weak."

"'Tis yours, Ronny. I don't see how—"

He sucked in a deep breath, watching her crumble in front of him, and let the anger out when he exhaled. "All right."

"But you don't want this."

"No, I don't."

Mick let go of Ron's arm. "How could you not want your child?"

"You're the one with dreams of a wife and family," Ron reminded him. "And I'm leaving in two weeks."

"You're what?" Pat reached across the bar for him and he leaned back, not sure if she only wanted to touch him or hurt him. "You're leaving?"

"You knew I wanted out."

"Mickey, sit down," she said when it looked as if he really might fall over. "I'm sorry. I am truly sorry. Hurting you…"

"Yeah, we wouldn't want that now, would we?" Ron took a sip of his beer and turned on the stool as Mick slowly sat back down. "No one meant to hurt you, Mick. I had no idea, really."

"Aye," he managed to squeak out.

"I won't abandon my kid," Ron said to Pat. "Come to America with me. I'll make sure you're both taken care of."

"Taken care of," she said dully.

"As best as I can, Pat, I promise you that."

"Promises. D'ya even love me, Ronny? Even a bit?"

"Of course I do. But I never expected this."

"Never wanted this," she murmured.

"No, I don't want this."

"*I* love ya, Pat," Mick said, finally finding his voice. "I can do more than just take care of ya. I'd marry ya as easily as I breathe, and be happier for it, too."

Ron glared at him, but waited to see what Pat would say.

They both watched her, and waited.

"Good God," she cried. "I love ya both, and I am so stupid."

With that, she ran for the door and out of the pub, leaving her coat behind.

~

"Seriously. She just told me she's pregnant with my kid, and you pretty much ask her to marry you?"

"Ya don't want a family," Mickey pointed out. "I do."

"But it's *my* kid."

"And she would be *my* wife. I love her, brother, I love her enough to be a father to your baby."

Ron watched as George filled shot glasses and set them on the bar in a neat line. "What makes you think I wouldn't want to be my own kid's father?"

"You don't want to *marry* her. What kind of father can y'be if you won't marry the mother?"

"An absent one," George offered. "You're offering to take her to the states and basically leave her alone most of the time. Alone with a baby to raise. All you're offering her is money and a place to stay."

"Whose fucking side are you on?" Ron seethed.

"Do you love her?" Mick pressed. "At all?"

"I love her enough."

"Shite, man, if ya did, she wouldn'ta run out the door, cryin'. I love her enough to tell this focker"—he nodded toward George—"that I'll pass on the job and stay here with her."

"I want my kid born in the states," Ron started.

"Y'idjit! Ya can't have it all. Ya either marry the girl and make an honest woman out of her, or you step aside and let me be the father."

Ron picked up a shot glass and slugged back the whiskey, grimacing against the burn as it tore down his throat.

He didn't want Mick to marry her just as much as he didn't want to tie himself down to a family.

He was perfectly willing to support her and his son or daughter.

Yet, he wanted more.

"You're both idiots," George said, refilling the glasses. "None of this is up to you. Let the girl decide whom she wants. And whoever she picks, the other, you walk away."

~

She believed him when he promised he would take care of her and be as much of a father as he could; she also believed that he wanted none of it. Without coming right out and saying it, he would never marry her and would be a father in name only. She believed that he loved her, but thought that wasn't enough.

Mickey loved her openly and offered her everything; she loved him, too, though without the consuming passion she felt for Ron. Mick would be a good father; he would be the better father, wanting brothers and sisters for the baby she was carrying. He would never resent her for wanting to be loved and wanting a man who was happy to stay home.

Ron's hard edges could be softened over time, but she wanted something safe; she wanted a man who wanted her completely, and she wanted that man to love her child as much as he loved her.

With her hands protectively covering her belly, whispering a prayer of forgiveness, she told Michael Brennan that she did indeed love him and wanted to be his wife, and with tears swallowed whole she asked Ron to step aside and let her have her family.

Twenty minutes later he walked out of Frank's pub just behind George Barron, and she was sure she would never see him again.

~

Ten months after walking out of the bar Ron found himself sharing an office on the third floor of a nondescript building that had been built in the middle of Nowhere, California. Headquarters was, inexplicably, in an unincorporated section of Solano County, roughly halfway between Sacramento and San Francisco.

The agency was small; he was one of only thirty active field agents, and one of two hundred employees overall. He'd slid into position early in the game; he'd learned that the formation of the agency began near the end of World War Two, but that it had only recently begun to take shape. Still, in the time since he had completed his training, he'd been sent out twice, and both times had come back successful.

Barron was right, he thought as he poked through his final report. *I have the ego for this.*

He was vaguely aware that someone else had entered the office but he didn't look up, not until the chair that had been pulled away from another desk bumped up against his. As he looked up, Mickey Brennan was sitting down, looking at him with a foolish grin plastered to his face.

"Aye, lookit ya. As if y'truly know how to work."

"I've gotten good at faking it," Ron said, shoving the report aside. A dozen questions thundered into his head—*how's Pat? How's the baby? Hell, did I have a son or a daughter?*—but he swallowed hard and added, "How've you been, Mick?"

"Ah, y'don't give a damn about me, brother," he snorted, amused. "It's the wee one yer wantin' t'know about."

Ron nodded. "And Pat. I'd like to know how she's doing."

"Ah, well. Firstly, ya should know I haven't married her yet. I will, but the deed hasn't been done."

"Is she all right?"

"Aye. But after ya left, we spent many a night talkin' and decided we want t'do this right. And it won't be right until we can wed in the church—"

"How in the hell will you manage that?"

"Some paperwork here, some paperwork there. I'll be changin' my name to help hide my trail, and the agency will give me a new background."

Ron understood that; he'd considered it, briefly, until he realized he didn't care if anyone from the church could track him down, and he knew no one in his family would ever try. He didn't need a fresh start, other than the one he had given himself.

"Somet'ing else," Mickey said. "Pat and I agreed much from the moment ya left. We want you to meet your child. I don't expect anyt'ing more from ya than that, but I expect ya to be man enough to meet him."

"Him," Ron breathed out.

"Aye. Y'have a son. He's a beautiful boy—thank God he looks like his mother."

"When?"

"A few weeks ago," Mick said. "And I'll warn ya straight out, I had no hand in naming him, but when I change mine, we'll change his as well."

"Pat named him," Ron guessed. "No input from you?"

"Aye, well, I thought we had agreed. And she calls him by the name we chose."

"But?"

"But," Mick said, hesitating, "she named him after me."

Michael Brennan, the third, Ron mused. There were worse things she could have named him. "What is it you call him?"

"Jeremy."

Ron smiled, and then said, "I almost prefer your name."

"In my heart," Mick sighed. "Now, would y'be wanting to meet him, or do I tell Pat ya don't have the stones?"

"Of course I do."

Mick stood up. "All right then. Come on."

Ron followed him out of the office and down the long hall that led past the Secretary General's office to the elevators, and struggled to find anything to say on the ride down.

What the hell do you say to an infant? Nice to meet you? Sorry I suck as a father?

When they turned the corner from the elevators to the lobby, he spotted Pat seated in the corner, holding the baby close as she whispered to him. He could feel his heart begin to beat faster, and the thought that he never should have left her clapped in his head like thunder.

She smiled when she saw him and slowly rose from the chair, and laughed when he had no idea how to hold his newborn son.

"My God," he breathed.

Mick kissed Pat, a quick brush of lips, and quietly said he would give them some time; Ron was staring so intently at his son's face that he barely noted that Mick had left, he barely noted anything until he felt Pat's hand brush against his as she reached over to touch the baby's face.

"I knew you'd love him," she whispered. "And ya do, I can see it in your eyes."

"I do love you," Ron whispered to his son. "I can't believe..." The sudden rush of tears that filled his eyes caught him by surprise, and he inhaled sharply, blinking hard, trying to push them back.

I can't believe I didn't want you, he thought.

"No matter how much ya do love him, though," Pat said gently, "I will marry Mick soon. I still believe he'll be the better father."

"I know," Ron said, not ready to look away from that tiny face.

"But we both agree, that if ya want to be a part of his life, we won't stand in the way. Mick asked to be assigned here, so that ya might have a chance to know your son."

He finally looked up at her. "Thank you."

"I take it that means ya want him in your life?"

"You knew I would," Ron said. "You knew I'd take one look and fall hopelessly in love with him."

"Aye. Ya mind?"

"Not one bit." Carefully, still holding the baby close, he sat in the closest chair, and whispering a kiss against his son's forehead promised, "I will be the best father I can be for you. I swear."

~

"You deserve to know what you might be getting into," Ron murmured, cutting into a streak of silence that settled between us after he'd poured out his history. "I have a complicated life and I'm dedicated to this job, but along with that comes a kid I try to keep protected from all of it."

"And a love lost," I mused.

"His mother is gone," he said. "And as shitty as it is to say, I loved her but I was never in love with her. But I love my son."

"And he comes first."

"He should come first," he said, though I wasn't clear on what he meant. Of course he should come first? He should come first but he doesn't? I wanted to know, and yet I didn't. "You didn't owe me any of this, Ron."

Lips pursed thoughtfully, he inhaled deeply—something I would soon realize was a habit of his any time he needed to take a beat to think—and then nodded. "I have never," he said slowly, looking at me, "been this attracted this quickly to anyone. What happened last night? That doesn't happen, Kris. Ever. I am usually far more careful and far more jaded, but..."

"I can come on a little strong," I admitted.

"No," he said, though his eyes twinkled with a touch of amusement. "With you? I wanted you to peek over the wall. If you can do that to me just by breathing near me, I want to see what else you can do to me. I want to really know you. But you have to know what kind of baggage I come with."

"Bags that were packed for you when you were just a boy," I pointed out. "Unpack them. Relax. You were a priest, but now you're not."

"Well."

"Well?"

"Technically...I walked away. I didn't exactly go through the

necessary motions to be dispensed. I may have been excommuni-
cated, but I don't really know. Neither Mick nor I did. We just left."

"And that was sixteen years ago? I don't feel like I'm screwing
the parish priest, Ron. And I'm into this job, too."

"I'm invested in it," he stressed. "I don't know how committed
you are, but I can't imagine doing anything else and I don't want to.
This is it for me."

By comparison, I was still wet behind the ears; I wasn't sure
how dedicated I was to the job itself, but I was sure that I would
enjoy it during the time I was required to give them in exchange for
my college education. Beyond that? I could see myself flying charter for some company, or even as an independent charter-for-hire. I
loved to fly, but I didn't need the adrenaline rush that came with the
agency, and I hated the body count.

But, I could live with the idea that he was neck deep into it,
even if I was not.

"It won't be a problem," I assured him.

"A year from now," he ventured, his hand sliding absently
across my thigh, "when you know me inside out, when we've been
together and had fights loud enough to cave the roof in, and when
we've seen each other in every imaginable way? We're on an assignment and I tell you to do something you would never consider
doing, will you be able to set everything else aside and do it without
question? Because there's got to be a sharp divide—"

"Why don't we get to the place where you work up the nerve
to hold my hand first," I said. "A year from now I might be assigned
to another team and you might be feeling up some twenty-year-old
blonde Barbie doll that can spin her tassels in two different directions."

"Now that I might like to see," he allowed. "But a relationship
with Barbie would not be my thing."

"You see us in a relationship."

"I'd like to see where this goes. Because the woman I met yesterday? She got into places no one else ever has, and I'd be an idiot
to let her just walk away."

"She'd be walking slowly and slightly bowlegged after last
night."

"I'll take that as a compliment. But to be fair, if you want me to be really serious, I'll keep my hands off you for a while. Until you're sure…"

"Are you insane? If that wasn't a one night stand and you want to keep seeing me, I better keep seeing more of you."

"I—"

He stopped when Doug knocked on the door trim. He shrugged apologetically and stammered, "Dan, he um…we're landing soon and he…well…"

"We're back on the clock," Ron sighed. He shooed Doug away with the wave his hand and turned to look at me again, leaning in for a kiss. "Once we go out there…"

"I got it," I said, kissing him back. "It's all business, and if you shove me towards a flying bomb, I ride it to the end."

~

The plane was painted flat black, small enough that it could almost be mistaken for a drone, and so simple that I could have flown it before I turned twenty. All my internal red flags went off; there was nothing special about this plane, or—as far as I could tell—its pilot, so why did we want it so badly?

"Stealth capabilities," Dan said. "If this is their newest, we get to pull it apart and find out how far behind or ahead of them we are."

Ron had one hand on the nose cone. "Ahead, I'd guess, if this is as simple as she says." He cocked his head toward the Soviet pilot who stood nearby, handcuffed and with an army guard right behind him. He looked grim and wrapped in layers of exhaustion; I guessed him to be around my age, but the fatigue coiled around him could have been deceiving. "How forthcoming has he been about what he knows?"

"Everything he knows about the plane, Kris had in her file," Dan said.

"I'd like more information on the fuel range," I said, mostly to myself.

Ron turned to the pilot, and began questioning him; I wasn't surprised he could speak the language, yet at the same time it impressed me. To my untrained ear he sounded fluent, as if he'd been speaking Russian from birth.

"You can make it to Okinawa," Ron finally said in English. "And his name is Gregori Rostanov, if anyone cares."

Rostanov stepped a little closer, nearly squinting as he looked at me, and then said in stilted English, "You cannot be pilot."

"She fucking can!" Doug spat out, surprising us all. He took a protective step toward me, getting close enough to Rostanov to make Ron twitch. Ron didn't want to get between them, but if the Soviet so much as breathed wrong, he would.

Rostanov kept his eyes focused on me. "This plane. You need"—he stopped to think for a moment—"strong. You need to be strong."

"I can handle it," I assured him.

"She is the bitch," he added.

That's when Doug struck, jabbing Rostanov in the nose, a quick punch that came so fast no one else could react. "Shut the fuck up."

Rostanov snorted, first to clear the blood from his nose, and then in near-amusement. "The plane, she is the bitch."

Dan had his hand on Doug's shoulder, pulling him back and away from me. "No one doubts Kris's ability as a pilot. He doubts her physical strength, and it's a legitimate concern. Make another move, and I'll happily let him head butt you right in the face."

"I appreciate the backup, though, Doc," I said to him. To Rostanov's guard I said, "Nice job you're doing there, bud."

The soldier half-shrugged. "I'm just here to keep him from blowing shit up, ma'am. If you people want to poke at him, no one told me you couldn't."

"How thoroughly has it been checked?" I asked Dan. "I can fly this, but I'd really prefer to not wind up in a million little pieces over the East China Sea."

"Is not wired," Rostanov offered. "Is...spying."

"No munitions?"

He shook his head.

"Doesn't mean you didn't arm something in there," Doug grumbled.

"Yes," Rostanov droned. "That would make sense. Kill one

American. Then I die. We keep doing til one person is left. I give plane to Uncle Alex, not to kill you." His eyebrows knotted together. "Uncle Sam. Is right?"

Ron gestured for the guard to take Rostanov back into the flight office. "Doc, if he were using this plane as a bomb, it would have gone off when there were forty airmen combing over it."

"So we just trust him?"

"He's been vetted," Dan said. "The CIA knows why he's seeking asylum and why they're giving it to him. We're just the errand boys." He turned towards the flight office, and Doug started to follow. He looked back once, expecting Ron and I to be right behind him, shrugging it off when we stayed in the hangar.

"This really is nothing special," I told Ron again. "So we're doing this, why?"

"Because it's nothing special. And because we wanted to stick it to Donnigan."

"Really."

"We're a new team, Kris. This is a throwaway assignment that the CIA didn't want to bother with because it's not worth their resources."

"But?"

"But...aside from sticking it to Donnigan, the CIA does want this plane because it's a one-off. They want the pilot. And what seems so not special right now will look very good on paper. On paper? We're not yanking the rug out from under Donnigan, we're a new team volunteering to leave on short notice to extract a defecting Soviet officer. Doug didn't lose his cool and pop a handcuffed pilot in the face; he intervened and ended a potentially volatile situation between a Soviet defector and one of his team members. And you're not taking a nothing-special plane out for a pleasant flight; you're commandeering potentially new technology and turning it over to the United States."

"And you knew this from the start."

"Not when we saw Donnigan talking to the suit, but as soon as Dan contacted his friends in the CIA and got the basic details, yes. Donnigan wanted this because of how it would look on paper, but he had no chance—we co-opted his pilot."

"So now we get to look good on paper."

"It'll get us the next assignment, Kris. Half of this team has never worked together, and one of us? Doug is useless right now. But we need to make it all look good, or we'll spend months trying to get anything better than this."

"New team," I mused. "Is this Dan's first lead position?"

He nodded.

"What happened to your last team?"

"Our team leader was promoted to the Assistant SG's position. Two others took it as a chance to retire. Dan was offered a team and his choice in who he wanted working with him. He chose you, and he's gambling on Doug. Over the next year, he'll probably add one or two more. We'll see how it goes."

"Apparently right now it goes to Okinawa in a bitchy little black number that its original pilot doesn't think I can handle."

"Out-bitch it," he said, grinning.

"No problem there." I started to head for the flight office; I wanted one more look at the details and I needed my flight suit, but Ron reached for my arm and stopped me.

"When we get back," he started, glancing towards the office door. "I meant what I said earlier, Kris. I'd really like to see you."

I waited; I knew what he meant but he was damn well going to actually ask.

"Bad timing?"

"No, not at all. I'm half an hour from takeoff and you're standing here making statements."

"Ah. You're a picky little thing, aren't you?"

"A picky little thing that can out-bitch more than an airplane."

"All right. There's a funky little cafe downtown. The food is good and there's live music. I'd like to take you there when we get home."

I raised an eyebrow.

"Damn, woman. Fine. Kris, will you, please, go out with me? Day after tomorrow, dinner at the very least, dancing if you can stand to have your toes stepped on?"

"Sure," I said, grinning at his annoyance. "See how easy that was?"

"Yeah, you're not going to have any problems getting that plane to go where you want."

~

It was like riding a rocket; I felt like I was wrapping my entire body around that plane and using pure determination to keep it in the air and in a straight line. Rostanov wasn't kidding – she was a bitch. She'd draw a man in close to hear what she was whispering, then slap him in the face for daring to get near, and then reach out and grab him by the balls just for the hell of it.

She wanted to buck me out of the cockpit, just because she could. I held on tight, pointed her towards Okinawa, and prayed I wouldn't end up in fragments littering the East China Sea.

I landed two hours before Ron and the rest of the team and by the time they walked into the flight lounge at the airstrip, my blood pressure and heart rate had finally dropped enough that I could string together a coherent sentence.

"Well?" Dan asked as he walked in.

"The plane. She is a bitch."

"Want to fly it again?"

"Seriously? Hell, yes. But I would imagine it's headed stateside on a boat."

"Or in the belly of a C-five," Ron said.

Dan nodded. "Hit the chow hall while you can, folks. As soon as we have a fresh pilot, we're on our way home to rub Donnigan's nose in it."

They'd turned Rostanov over to the OSI at Kadena Air Base; from there he would be sent to Washington, debriefed, and then—I guessed—released into the wild like a captured wolf.

On the ride back I fully intended to sit in the cabin with the rest of the team; I still knew next to nothing about Dan and nothing at all about Doug, and was determined to be sociable for as many of the next ten hours as I could, but as soon as we'd taken off Dan grunted, "Kris has the bunk, since she's the only one who did any real work."

I held out as long as I could, trying to make small talk, until Ron unbuckled his seat belt and reached for my hand. "Come on," he said. "Your eyes are spinning around in your head so hard I can hear them clicking."

As I dropped onto the mattress, I pulled him with me and he muttered, "This doesn't count."

"What doesn't?"

He pressed a kiss against my fingertips. "As holding your hand. This was just guiding you back here so you could get some rest."

"I can rest out there just as easily, you know. Not that I'm complaining, but I don't need to be coddled."

"You heard Dan. You did the work, you get the bunk."

"And escorting Rostanov? That wasn't work?"

"That," he said, grabbing one of the pillows, "was a cakewalk. He's an interesting guy, talked a lot on the flight to Kadena. He's been working towards this defection since he was a teenager, trying to get to family in the states."

"And that family has been verified?"

"They're in Canada now, but they exist." He shrugged. "It's not our problem now, in any case. We go home and wait for the next assignment."

"Something we can yank out from under Donnigan?"

"If possible," he chuckled. "You were pretty amazing, Kris. If getting into that plane bothered you, no one could tell. It was like you had ice running through your veins."

"I only worried it would go 'boom' in the air. Other than that, simple as pie."

"I tried to make a pie once. It was not that easy. My son asked me to never repeat the experiment."

I almost offered to make him one, but managed to swallow the thought before it got out; he made it clear, he kept his son compartmentalized, and it could be a very long time before I met him, if ever.

"I should let you get some sleep," he said when I buried my face against the pillow, yet he sounded like he really didn't want to leave.

"Dan didn't say I had to have the rack to myself," I said, grabbing his belt to pull him closer. "You need to rest up, big night tomorrow."

"Oh, yeah?"

"Yep," I mumbled, feeling the fatigue slipping over me like a soft, warm cloud. "You have a date to hold my hand."

~

He knocked on my door at 6:30, flowers in one hand and a split of wine in the other. It was the first time I'd seen him dressed in anything other than dress slacks and a white button-down shirt, and it struck me just how well he could wear jeans and a t-shirt. I knew what he looked like shirtless, but that didn't stop me from appreciating the cut of his bright red shirt and the way it pulled across his chest.

"It's hot as hell out there," he said as he poured the wine, "but... should be quite a bit cooler downtown by the time we get there."

"The one good thing about this apartment is the balcony," I said, pulling the door open. "There's always a nice breeze out here. Granted, sometimes you can smell the exhaust from cars billowing off the freeway, but still, it's a breeze."

"You make it sound so appealing." He settled into one of the cheap lawn chairs I'd found on sale at K-Mart, ignoring how it creaked and groaned under his weight. "How awful is the noise to deal with?"

"Not bad. I'm not home enough to let it bother me."

"What, you mean you don't stay home every night reading trashy novels and knitting booties or scarves or whatever?"

"Domestic I'm not. I also don't cook well at all, so don't ever expect to be invited over for a home cooked meal. I wouldn't do that to you."

"Good to know. I'll make a mental note of it, and the next time we need to incapacitate someone, we'll just have you whip up a quiche and cut you loose on the perp."

"Ha. Funnyman. Where is it you're taking me tonight? Culinary academy?"

"I might have," he snorted, taking a sip, "if I'd known it was necessary."

"Hey. I can pick up a phone and order take-out and delivery. No one starves around here."

"That can't be healthy. If you're nice to me, I'll cook for you."

"You cook."

"I cook. I was determined to not be the dad taking my kid out for fast food every time I had a weekend with him. So I learned to cook, and I make him actually sit at the table and talk to me every night he's with me. He hates it, but he'll get over it."

"He might say he hates it..."

"He's fifteen. He's supposed to hate everything, his parents included." Ron set his wine glass on the unbalanced plastic table that sat precariously between our chairs. "But come on. This is our first date. We're not spending it talking about my kid. We're going downtown, having dinner at Sierra Coast Cafe, where I might let you talk me into one dance during which you will discover that you never want that to happen again, and then if it cools down, maybe put the top down on my car and go for a drive."

I presumed he was exaggerating, but half a minute into the first time I danced with him, I realized he wasn't; he refused anything but a slow dance, because—as he put it—no one wants to see an old guy out there being all spastic with a white-boy-overbite, but his slow dance wasn't much better. He was stiff, awkward, and apologetic, but shrugged it off, saying, "This is something else you have to know about me. I can't dance for shit, but I'll always try."

He had a sense of humor about it; hell, I realized he had a very subtle sense of humor about most things. The Sierra Coast Cafe was smack in the middle of the downtown strip, which itself was little more than a mesh of fifty oddly matched business fronts, from a battered thrift store to a sparkling new fine-arts theater. It was nowhere near the Sierra Mountains, which were a good three hours away, and less a cafe as it was the home-cooking of someone's grandmother, the type of grandmother who would take some serious offense to anyone leaving her table before ingesting huge quantities of stick-to-your-ribs food.

The walls, however, were a mural of snowcapped mountain ranges, complete with tiny skiers tumbling through hand-sketched trees. It was bizarre, and it made me laugh, and I was sure that's exactly what he intended.

"Alaska," he said when I asked him where in the world he'd been sent for work that he'd love to go back to. "There's nothing like seeing the Northern Lights while seated on a freezing cold tree stump in subzero weather, watching that light show play out right in front of you. It's truly awesome. You?"

We were walking down West Texas Street, taking advantage of the breeze that had kicked up and was chipping away the suffocating edge of the summer heat. After having my toes stepped on more times than I could count and then passing up dessert, we decided to walk the short length of downtown; we dodged other couples who were out doing the same thing, and were nearly run over by teenagers clattering past on skateboards.

"New York, I think. I love the energy there. Mostly I'd like the chance to see it instead working there."

"Energy is why I like San Francisco. But still...nothing beats Alaska."

"Hell, you could go to Minnesota or North Dakota to see the lights."

"True," he agreed, "and I've been and seen them there, too. It's not even close. I keep thinking I'll take some time off and go back, but I never seem to manage."

"No time to take time off?"

"A few days here and there. I suspect I haven't made it happen because if I go back, I may be tempted to not come home."

Not coming home was not an option, I knew that without asking; his job was based here, and his son lived here. He'd already said his life was complicated, and running off to Alaska would only make that worse.

"Won't even let yourself visit?" I asked.

"I might, if the right person wants to tag along," he replied, deliberately bumping his shoulder to mine. "It's one of those things you just have to show someone else. Like the Eiffel Tower or the Grand Canyon. They're incredible, but I imagine a whole lot better with someone else right there being blown away, too."

"And your theoretical someone else," I said. "Suppose the idea of the freezing Alaska cold is just too much to contemplate."

"I'll keep you warm," he chuckled.

"Presumptuous offer from a guy who hasn't even worked up the nerve to hold my hand."

"I was waiting," he said simply.

"For what? The second Tuesday of next week?"

"I was waiting to be sure there was no one else you wanted holding your hand while you walked down the street on a warm summer night," he said. "I'd hate to get my hopes up, only to find out I'm third or fourth in line."

"No worries there," I said. "Maybe second."

He stopped and turned toward me. "I'm mostly serious, Kris. I don't do the serial dating thing. If you're seeing someone else, fine, I'll bust my ass to make you think I'm the better choice, but…"

I stretched up on my toes to kiss him. "Ron, you are one bizarre little man. You'll sleep with me even wondering if I'm seeing someone else, too, but you can't hold my hand?"

"I won't even do that. I typically *don't* do that. I'm not that guy."

"There's no one else in line," I assured him. "And don't think that I tumble into bed with every man I meet just a few hours after meeting him. I'm a firm believer in doing what you want when you want as long as no one gets hurt, but I have my limits."

"I didn't think—"

"I'm betting it crossed your mind. Seven or eight hours after we met we were doing some pretty nasty things to each other. You had to wonder if it was the norm for me."

"No," he said. "I never thought that. But whatever this is between us, that doesn't mean you're not casually dating someone else, too."

"I'm not. I haven't been involved with anyone for almost a year and even that wasn't serious enough to be terribly upset over when it ended. And I could be asking the same of you, mister. Dan tried to warn me you were the walking wounded. Who broke your heart?"

"Dan," he said, turning to walk back the way we had come, "is under the mistaken impression that I haven't recovered from Pat's death. It's been a year and a half, and I came to grips with it a long time ago. I've dated since then, but nothing remotely serious."

"So maybe that's why he thinks you're still wounded."

"Maybe. I've never done serious very well. I'm sure he thinks she's the reason."

"And is she?"

"A few times she was," he allowed. "It was hard to let myself get close to someone else when she was always right there practically dangling my son in front of me. For the most part I've never gotten that serious with anyone because either the timing was wrong or the woman wasn't right."

"And you're leaning towards the idea that I might be the right one at the right time?"

He reached for my hand, slipping his fingers between mine, grasping my hand gently. "You know what I do. You know what I was. And you didn't flinch when I told you that I come weighted down with a fifteen-year-old son. Most women do. I tend to wait a long time before mentioning him, but even once they know me, they flinch."

"Perhaps because you wait so long to mention him? That's the kind of thing women like to know up front, Ron. You could save yourself a lot of time and effort by weeding out the women who can't handle the idea that you have someone else as a priority."

"Funny, Dan's been telling me that for years."

"You should listen."

"To you, maybe. To Dan? The man hasn't had a successful relationship since he was in college. But he does know my son, and thinks I need to foist him upon women just to see who runs screaming."

"Well, that would be rude. The screaming, I mean."

"It might have worked a few years ago. Now? Chip has already figured out how to charm women, at least the ones closer to his age. I gave up trying to keep track of the girls in his life."

"Jealous?"

"Maybe a little," he laughed. "All right, fine, my son is better with women than I am. What about you?"

"I don't bat for that team. I thought you noticed that already."

"Ha. I mean more like do you have kids you might want to mention now? Irate ex-boyfriends I might have to run from? And at what point are you mentioning me to your father, because I'll want to requisition body armor first."

"I'm willing to bet you already know the answers to those questions. Aside from my father."

"How's that?"

"You have access to my files, mister, and don't deny it. You know everything from my birth date right down to identifiable marks on my body. And I'm betting that somewhere in the file is a list of every person I've ever been involved with."

"Well, maybe not every one of them," he said sheepishly.

"The important ones."

"Nothing in that file can tell me how you felt about them, or who broke your heart, or even whose heart you might have broken. Your file is nothing but data points. I know you're thirteen years older than my son, when you learned to fly, when you graduated from college, and that you kicked a professor in the groin your junior year."

"That's in my file?"

"Apparently you were set on sending his testicles on an upward trajectory through his chest, his throat, and out through his nose."

"Where I would have tied them into a knot."

"What I don't know is why."

"He offered me an easy A."

"Ah. Good for you then. And I'll be careful to not offend you. I like mine right where they are, thank you."

I did, too, but I wasn't saying so. We kept walking, up and down the short strip of downtown, his hand clasping mine, until the breeze picked up and turned the night from pleasant to chilly. When I was shivering against him, we headed for his car and he drove to the backside of the air force base, where we could watch the cargo jets take off and land.

He asked me about each one of them, how heavy they were, what types of cargo they could carry. He didn't give a damn about any of it, but he knew I did, and that was all the reason he needed to sit there and watch with me.

We stayed there until he was asked to move by a military policeman, long enough that my interest in the planes had waned and we were both sucked back into being seventeen again, wrapped around each other in the back seat of his car, wanting to see how much we could get away with. How far could we go without going anywhere at all, really.

~

He wanted to go back to his apartment; he had wine chilled and fruit waiting, candles lined up in his fireplace, and music to which he would allow me to make fun of him if I wanted a slow dance or two.

You've probably got clean sheets, too, I thought, amused.

His apartment was a two-bedroom garden flat nestled in a quiet area of town; it was one of the first gated communities, and the first condos to go up for sale. Inside, it was immaculate, another reminder that he wasn't a finally-on-my-own post-graduation fling. His tastes ran toward traditional; it was less a bachelor pad than it was the home of an average nuclear family, though he warned me against going into the bedroom to the left.

"Teenager," he explained. "As long as there's nothing decaying to the point that it takes on life of its own, and as long as it doesn't spill out the door, I leave it alone."

"Progressive," I murmured.

He was lighting the candles in the fireplace, nodding towards the sofa. "I grew up in an oppressively Catholic family. The rules were so tight...I wanted him to have space of his own. I'm not sure how much of that he gets at home."

"And this isn't home."

He blew the match out and then went over to the stereo set on a bookcase next to the fireplace. "I'm a weekend dad, Kris. I'm pretty sure his mother drilled into him that this is not his real home."

"That's a shame."

Soft music lifted into the air, and he sat next to me on the sofa. "Maybe. And how is it we keep winding up talking about my kid? There are a thousand other things we could talk about."

"We talk about him," I said, setting my hand on his leg, "because he's important to you. And because I don't know Dan and Doug well enough to gossip about people at work."

"Fair enough. I can tell you about them. Dan will act like everything is incredibly important even when he knows it's not, but he's a good guy and a decent friend. Doug is scared to death about what he's gotten himself into, but they paid for medical school and he's got no way out yet. He was pretty talkative on the ride between Korea and Kadena. You kind of frighten him."

"Good, he should be frightened. Is he a legacy?"

"His dad retired a couple of years ago."

"And Daddy didn't prepare him for the job?"

"Did yours?"

"In his own way."

He slid closer to me, wrapping his arm around my shoulders. "I'm guessing he was set on raising you to be a hell of a lot more independent than the average daughter. I guarantee you none of my sisters ever considered being anything other than a housewife."

"Is that a bad thing?"

"Not if it makes them happy. But they were never presented with anything resembling a choice, and I wonder if deep down any of them resent it."

"Sometimes we make the choices when we're older."

He shook his head. "You can see that because you had a choice. If any of them wandered off that path our parents set?" He sucked in a deep breath. "They saw what happened when I did. It was very apparent that sides had to be taken, and if they took the wrong one, they might as well turn around and walk away and never look back."

"And did you?" I asked, setting my head on his shoulder. "Have you ever gone back?"

"Once. I took Chip to see them when he was eight or nine, thinking they might want to get to know their grandson. My mother was polite and my father tried to ignore that we were even there. My brothers and sisters welcomed him well enough, but there was no getting around the fact that we were not wanted there."

"They shoved that into a little boy's face?"

"Not overtly. Like I said, my mother was polite, but she was in no way acting like anyone's grandmother. Chip had no way of knowing any different, since his experience with grandparents was exactly zero. But my father? I got damned tired of him walking out of any room Chip walked into so I finally cornered him and called him on it. He came straight out with it. 'You're my biggest disappointment in life, and I don't need your bastard running around here reminding me of it.'"

"Holy shit."

"I turned around, and there Chip was. He'd heard the whole thing. I stopped dead in my tracks trying to figure out what to say to him but he shrugged it off, said he didn't know my dad was such a prick and that he wanted to leave. So we packed our stuff and left. I still had almost a week left to spend with him, so we headed for southern California to hit up every place he wanted, and I just enjoyed the hell out of the time with him. I never went back to Chicago, and I only hear of news about my parents when one of my sisters or brothers lets me know. Once in a while I get a fairly formal letter from my mother. But that's it."

"I am so sorry," I said quietly.

"It's all right," he said, and he meant it. "It's better to know where I stand with them. I wish Chip hadn't heard any of it, but it's all right."

"Still, I can't imagine either of my parents saying something like that to me. I know some of the choices I've made would disappoint them if they knew, but they'd get over it."

"You parents never intended you to be some kind of offering to God."

"If anything, they've always treated me like I was a gift from God."

"And you're their only one?"

I nodded. "And that may be why. I know they wanted more, but I don't know why they didn't have any."

"Would be kind of tacky to ask," he mused. "And while I'm thinking of it…there are only a couple of people in the agency who know what I did before signing on. It's not a matter of record and I'd like to keep it that way."

"All right," I said, not sure why it mattered.

"My son doesn't know, either. Not about me, and not about his stepfather. We agreed a long time ago that he was better off not knowing, just in case he felt guilty about potentially being the reason we both left the priesthood."

"He wasn't, though."

"Definitely not in my case, but that doesn't mean he wouldn't believe it. I don't ever want him thinking he's kept me from anything. He's got enough on his plate without having to choke that down, too."

I wondered how big that plate was, and how much a teenaged boy was expected to pile on it. "And the people at work?"

"It's just none of their business. I don't want to be saddled with being called 'Padre' or 'Father Ron.' And you know half those jokers would do just that."

"What makes you think I won't?"

He raised one eyebrow. "And here I thought you were nicer than that."

"I'm not nice, Ron," I snorted, pushing him back on the sofa, straddling him. "Nice girls don't do half the things I'm pretty sure I'm going to do to you tonight."

"Just be nice enough to keep my secrets, and you can do whatever you want to me."

"I could take that as a challenge, you know."

"Game on, then."

~

Two assignments later, a scant three months, and I knew I was falling hard for him. I was less sure about his emotional past; he was tangled in the mess of trying to be there for his teenaged son in the long-flowing wake of his mother's death, and he had strongly hinted that it would not be smooth sailing if I stayed in his personal life.

I was foolish enough to not care. How bad could a teenaged boy be, especially one living with his stepfather? Ron tried to make it clear that his son was surly, angry, temperamental, and did not treat women well at all, but as far as I was concerned, that wasn't my problem.

After all, I would only have to deal with him every other weekend. That was how it worked, right?

"His name is Jeremy," Ron said. We were standing in the parking lot of his apartment building, and I was three minutes away from meeting his son. "He prefers to be called Chip. In fact, if you call him by his given name, he'll ignore you even if you're half an inch from his face shouting it at him."

And you put up with this? I wondered.

Ron hadn't intended for me to meet Chip yet; our plans for the weekend had included a drive through Napa and then down to San Francisco, spending a night or two at a hotel on the Wharf, and walking through China Town and Union Square. The plans certainly hadn't included a surly fifteen-year-old boy who had hitchhiked his way from Fairfield to Bodega Bay without leaving a note to tell anyone where he would be and why.

"He takes off sometimes," Ron offered as a half-assed explanation. "He always has, even before his mother died. He's...restless."

He's a jerk, not restless, I thought, but knew better than to say it. I understood that Ron never had control over how his son was raised and he was just grateful for the time he got to spend with him, even when that meant cleaning up the boy's messes and keeping him away long enough for his stepfather to cool down.

I was prepared to meet the Asshole of the Year. I braced myself before Ron opened the door to his apartment, picturing the complete destruction of his living room, with a hairy, dirty, and utterly rude runt of a teenager splayed out on the couch, one who wouldn't even grunt so much as hello.

Chip was on the couch, all right, the TV on but the sound turned down so low I wasn't sure how he could hear it, and when he realized we'd come in he immediately jumped up to turn it off, and crossed the room to greet me.

He was not what I expected. The little hairy grease-ball of my imagination was almost six feet tall, hair neatly trimmed, clean shaven although he was sporting an early five o'clock shadow, and his eyes were an incredible piercing green.

Like his father, I mused.

He was reaching for my hand, and I only realized I needed to reciprocate after Ron gently nudged me.

This boy is absolutely gorgeous. And he doesn't look anything like a teenager. No wonder he's out of control, he looks old enough to get away with anything.

His smile was electric, something else I thought he'd gotten from his father. But the oozing charm? I thought Ron was a flirt and had charm to spare, but Chip exuded it. That one smile, as he shook my hand and said how happy he was to finally meet me, pushed aside every ill thought I'd had about him, and I began to quickly rewrite my stunted opinion.

"I'm sorry I blew your weekend," he said. "I told Ron I'd stay here and out of trouble, but—"

"Not a snowball's chance in hell," Ron grunted.

Ron, it hit me. *He calls his father by his first name.*

"I'm a fuck up but not a liar," Chip protested. "I said I'd stay here in the apartment, so you know I will."

"You and how many other people?" Ron countered.

Chip's eyebrow arched just a little bit, and he gnashed his teeth together to keep from grinning. "Come on. I feel bad about screwing it up."

I sat with Chip on the couch and Ron dropped into the recliner a few feet away. Instead of taking the far end of the sofa, Chip sat close to me, which I found odd yet not as unsettling as I normally would have. He and Ron dickered back and forth about leaving Chip in the apartment while Ron and I took off anyway, and while they talked I could feel the idea brewing in the back of my head and spat it out before I could examine it too closely and decide it was stupid.

"Why don't we all go?" I asked.

They both looked dumbfounded.

"You think I screwed it up *now?*" Chip asked. "You don't want me on your romantic weekend with the wine and view of the Bay Area's shopping mecca. You want me sitting here watching crap on a TV that he really needed to replace about five years ago."

"That TV works fine," Ron grumbled. I expected him to sigh hard and say it would be a better idea if we all just found something at home to do, or that he would understand if I wanted to bail and go off on my own, but instead he nodded. "Fine, you're coming with us. You can be the designated driver between Napa and San Francisco, and you can carry all of Kris's shopping bags while she drags us around the Square."

"That's kind of sexist of you," Chip said. "We all know you're the one who's dying to check out the latest fashions and fuck-me shoes."

"Well. I do enjoy my shoes," Ron said lightly.

"How about we skip the shopping and you two can show me the tourist sights? I've never seen the Golden Gate Bridge, there are museums there I've never been to—the only thing I really know about San Francisco is that driving through it used to make my dad swear like a drunken sailor, so we stayed away."

"You've seriously never scoped out the city?" Chip asked.

"Not yet."

"Ghiradelli Square," Chip said to Ron. "We'll turn her into a chocolate slut."

"The pier, too," Ron added.

"Ride a cable car."

"The Great Highway."

"We may need more than two days," Chip said.

"You have school, and you're not missing any more of it. We can always take her back another time."

"That school is a fucking waste of time and you know it," Chip argued. "You know what they have me doing most of the day? Working in the damned teachers' lounge. I don't get to go to half my classes because a group of frigid old women want me organizing their freaking files instead of, you know, actually learning anything."

"It's called in-school suspension, Chip, and you're only missing PE and study hall."

"Yeah, well, I could actually use study hall to *study*, you know."

"You could, but you won't."

"What the hell else is there to do in study hall?"

"Andrea Gladner? Is that her name? Or how about Becky Stiffler? Aren't they what you *do* when you're supposed to be in study hall?"

Chip shrugged, again trying hard to not grin.

"Suck it up. You'll reorganize and redecorate the damned teachers' lounge and every other office until they decide you've done enough."

"I could really use the study time—"

Ron got up, cutting him off. "Fine. I'll start dinner; you start catching up on your homework now. And if you argue with me, so help me God I'll ground your ass for the next month."

It was an empty threat and Chip knew it, but an hour later when dinner was ready he was still at the table working on a history assignment, and after he helped clear dishes away later he went back, mumbling that *algeblah* awaited him.

~

Half of Chip's problem, Ron said, was that he grew up with a sense of entitlement and neither Pat nor Grant had done anything to quell that in him. Grant made several keen business investments when Chip was barely more than a toddler, and because of that, Chip lacked for nothing. He didn't put any effort into school because he knew he had a future waiting for him; school was easy when he tried, but he rarely put forth concentrated effort because there was a career in real estate waiting for him, a series of investments insuring that no matter how hard he worked or didn't work, he would always have money.

He could get the grades if he wanted; he didn't want.

That sense of entitlement carried over into how he related to women as well, Ron thought. He hadn't come to the realization that what he wanted wasn't necessarily a good idea for the girls he used and tossed aside. They'd get over it eventually; he either didn't see or didn't care that he might be doing them irreparable harm.

The Chip I met that weekend was polite and entertaining, and I had a difficult time blending the image I had with the picture Ron painted. Chip navigated our way through the San Francisco public transit system without complaint when I kept changing my mind about where I wanted to go; there was no whining about the distances we walked getting from one place to the next. He was a font of information about the sites we visited, rattling off trivia about the Golden Gate Bridge, from its length to the sheer volume of time it took to paint it from one end to the other, to the price of tolls to get into the city in the forties.

He was anything but surly, and I was beginning to think Ron's opinion of his son was tinged with the bitterness of not having raised him, and from not having custody of him after Pat's death.

I wanted to know why he didn't claim custody of his son, and when Chip was kicking his way through wet sand at the edge of the beach running along The Great Highway, I asked Ron. Why wouldn't he want his son?

"I'm often gone for weeks at a time," he reminded me. "Grant knows that and he knows why. It would be pointless to pull Chip out of the only home he's ever known when I'm not there full time for him."

"You've never considered quitting?"

"No," he said flatly.

"Not even—?"

"It wouldn't be the best thing for him, Kris. If I'd ever thought that it was, I'd resign without thinking twice. His mother picked Grant to be his father for a reason, and even if I hate it, I'll respect it."

"As long as you're both all right with the arrangement," I said, not sure I meant it.

"Grant loves him. And I don't mean he tolerates having Chip there, I mean he loves the kid like he's his own. Chip doesn't see it and doesn't believe it."

"He's just a kid. He's not supposed to see it."

There was more, I could feel Ron working up towards telling me, but Chip had turned from the ocean and was walking back toward us.

"Man, I didn't sit down on that sand once but I still have it crawling up my ass," he said, tugging at his pants leg.

"Crabs," Ron grunted.

Chip snorted a laugh through his nose. "What's next on the agenda?"

"You tell us, cowboy," Ron said. "Since you seem to know the city so well."

We caught the next bus and wound up near Ghiradelli Square; from our vantage point we had the Bay behind us with the Golden Gate Bridge to the left and Alcatraz Island in full view to the right, and the Square in front of us. This, Chip said, is where I would become a chocolate slut. When I started to protest he added, "Really. You're going to try it, and by the end of today you'll want to roll around naked in it."

"If it's that good, maybe we should have dinner first? I'd hate to have to walk into a restaurant naked and covered in a mixture of milk and dark chocolate."

"But—"

"Keep that thought to yourself," Ron warned.

"Damn, what kind of a sick freak do you think I am? I was just going to say that she could take it with her and roll around in it later."

"Sure you were."

"Dinner," I repeated. "Come on, we're this close to the Wharf. You like fish, right?"

It took me the entire walk there to realize why Chip had laughed.

~

When we got back to the hotel Ron and I were reminded that in spite of how well behaved Chip had been for the most part, he was still a teenager. From the moment we walked through the door until Ron finally caved in with a sigh, we were pestered about going down to the pool. Ron tried to send him alone, but Chip was insistent: the rules were clearly posted; no one under sixteen was allowed to use the pool without adult supervision.

"No one is going to think you're not sixteen," Ron said. "Just go."

But no. The rules were the rules and what kind of person would he be if he didn't respect the hotel's rules?

With grumbling on a scale I expected from a fifteen year old and not a forty year old, Ron relented.

"Why are you picking now to respect rules?" he asked, shaking his head when Chip shrugged, with a quick glance at me.

I was slowly getting the message: Chip was determined he would not be the reason I ran screaming from a weekend spent with them both.

Still, it nearly happened, and from nothing that he did or said.

For the first fifteen minutes Chip was in the pool, swimming laps—which frankly surprised me—I hadn't noticed anything really different about him. He was a tall, thin kid, well-muscled, but still just another kid hanging out in the water, trying to catch the attention of girls who were lounging on the far side of the pool.

I got it; he liked to flirt. I didn't think he was going to do anything more than flirt, so I tried to ignore it for the most part. After a while the girls were flirting back, and I found it amusing because I'd been one of those girls, giggling stupidly over something some boy said or did, and when they jumped into the water with him, I had to bite back the grin and a laugh.

But then one of the girls looked closely at Chip, and cocking her head as if in deep consideration, she ran a finger across his chest, and that's when I realized he had an angry and reddish-white scar running nearly nipple-to-nipple.

"What happened to him?" I asked Ron quietly.

I could feel him stiffen beside me, instantly uncomfortable; the long breath he drew in was a loud delay tactic designed to make me think he was considering what to say. I knew him well enough to know he was trying to figure out how to not answer.

His son had been slashed open; there was no avoiding that.

"Grant," he finally said. "The night Pat died... I'm not terribly clear on exactly how it happened, but he took a swing at Chip with a knife in hand..."

He was squirming and I was instantly furious, not caring if Chip and the girls he was flirting with could hear.

"His *stepfather* did that to him? And you let him live with that son of a bitch?"

"Kris—"

"How the hell, Ron? He's *your* son."

"I know that."

I got up. "What the hell is wrong with you?"

I left before he had a chance to answer, and was in the elevator and headed upstairs to pack my bag and leave before he had a chance to follow.

~

"I have a little brother," Chip said. He stood near the hotel room door in wet shorts, dripping onto the carpet. I was shoving the clothes I had unpacked only that morning back into my bag, and was reaching for my room key.

"I know you do," I said, trying to be gentle with him, hoping he didn't blame himself for this.

"I can't leave him there alone. I hate my stepfather, Kris, but I can't leave David there alone. He needs me."

"You can't risk your life—"

"Yes, I can. He's ten years old. He's a freak with a huge brain and I think Grant is kind of afraid of him...but he's afraid of me now, too, I mean, I'm bigger than he is now, and I can protect my brother."

"Chip," I sighed. "You shouldn't have to."

"Ron wanted me," Chip explained, sure I had no idea. "When my mom died he wanted me to come live with him but he gets why it's better for me to stay with David. And you know, with his job Ron is never around, so I'd probably wind up being picked up by CPS because I really am a royal fuck-up, and this was just the best way all the way around. Ron doesn't *want* me to live with Grant, but right now it's the best thing."

"Your stepfather tried to kill you."

"I dunno if he wanted me dead, but still, he'll never get another chance, I swear. I don't get that close to him, and when I take off for a day or two he has time to regroup, so when I am home he's better about everything."

"What kind of life is that? You're fifteen years old. You need—"

"It's the life I've got. Come on, it's not what Ron wants, but it's not like he has any choice, either."

"He could fight for custody of you, Chip."

"I doubt it. Legally, Grant is my father. He's on my birth certificate. I'm lucky they even let me know that Ron is my real father. And this"—his hand went to his chest—"no one ever really knew how I got this. We sure as hell didn't tell the ER doc that my stepfather had tried to kill me. Since my mom had just died, like, that day, and they knew it, no one really tried to find out. So if Ron tried to get custody...he doesn't have a case. I'm pretty sure that's how my Mom wanted it."

"No mother wants her son to suffer like that."

"No, but she was different, anyway. She didn't want to see me hating my stepfather, so she just didn't see it, you know?"

"And the running away, she didn't see that either?"

He shook his head.

"And all the girls, unless Ron is exaggerating."

"I dunno. Depends on what he said."

"Pretty much that you're nailing anything that moves."

"I like sex," he said simply.

Not my place, I decided.

"This wasn't Ron's fault," Chip said, again gesturing to his chest. "He would have taken me home with him that night, but I wouldn't let him. He doesn't like it, Kris, he hates it, but I have to stay with my brother."

"Chip."

"It's complicated. It really is just complicated. But don't blame Ron because I'm still living with my stepfather. There's nothing he can do except what he already does. I know I have some place to go if I need it, and sometimes I bring David and he's okay with that. He doesn't owe my brother anything but he *always* lets him stay. He just calls Grant and tells him where we are and that he'll make sure we're all right. He takes care of us the best ways he can, even though he doesn't have to."

Chip was still wet and now shivering, and I was hearing what he wanted me to hear: *don't walk out on Ron because of me. Don't leave him. Give him a chance. Give me a chance.*

I tossed the bag back onto the bed and shoved the room key into my pocket. "You need to dry off and get some clothes on. I'm going downstairs to find your dad, and don't worry, I'm not going anywhere."

He reached into the bathroom for a towel and had wrapped it around his shoulders by the time I made it to the door.

"Do you love him?" Chip asked.

That was an odd question, I thought, and really none of his business, but it seemed to matter to him, so I answered, "Yes, I think I do."

"Does he know that?"

"I haven't said it in so many words, but I'm sure he has the general idea."

"He's never let me meet a girlfriend before, you know."

I didn't want to tell him that Ron hadn't intended for us to meet yet, but the circumstances had forced us together.

"Just so you know that," he added. "So it must mean a lot."

It meant a lot, but what I wasn't clear about was whether or not it would be enough.

~

I found Ron in the hotel's bar, sitting alone at a table in the corner where he would be able to see me if I came in. I was fairly sure he could also see if I walked past the bar's entrance and headed toward the street, and was glad I had been certain he would be there. If I'd hesitated, even a little, he might have braced himself against any conversation I wanted to have with him and gone on the defensive.

"I don't get it," I said before he could start explaining, "but I'll allow that I don't know enough about your relationship with Chip or his mother, and especially his stepfather. Just know that from where I stand it's so screwed up that it's unhealthy and borderline criminal, but it's what Chip seems to want."

As wrong as I thought it was, what Chip wanted was what Ron gave the most weight to. It was true, he had no legal ties to his own son, but Grant never tried to stand between them.

"For a while we were good friends," Ron mused. "Best friends, even, until Pat came along. But he knew when he married her that Chip was mine, and he accepted everything that came with it. I know what that scar looks like and I know what Chip thinks, but I don't think Grant tried to kill him and I know Grant doesn't hate him."

"Funny way of showing that."

"I've never been able to get all the details, Kris. But I *know* Grant, and I know that Pat had only been gone for a few hours. Something happened that neither will tell anyone else, but I know he wasn't trying to kill my son. If I thought he did? He'd be buried next to Pat."

"It's not fair to Chip to leave him with someone he hates, though."

"He thinks he hates Grant," Ron said. "And he thinks he's staying there for David. When he's a little older, he'll know better."

"You don't think he understands feeling hate?"

"I think," he said carefully, "that Chip doesn't yet understand the concept of projection, and when he does he'll have a better understanding of where his anger comes from, and why he doesn't hate Grant at all."

I let it go. I didn't know any of them well enough to interject or interfere in their relationships.

I thought Ron was a bit of an idiot where his son was concerned, but that didn't change how I felt about him.

~

The room was eerily quiet when we got back; Ron opened the door and we both expected Chip to be splayed out on his bed with the TV on, but it was off and he wasn't there. He'd left his wet shorts in a heap on the bathroom floor, a wadded up towel next to the sink, and his gym bag was on a chair and open, clothes spilling out onto the floor.

"So," I wondered out loud, "do we go look for him, or what?"

Ron's jaw clenched as he ground his teeth together and it took him a moment to be able to speak. "Unless you want to pound on every door in this hotel, I don't think we'll find him."

"The girls in the pool?"

"Who knows? It could be one of them or all of them, or he might be out wandering around the city looking for a hooker."

"A hooker."

"I wouldn't put it past him."

I wasn't about to point out that Chip was good looking enough and charming enough that he probably didn't need to pay for it. I suspected he was pretty good at getting what he wanted from any girl he was interested in, and he wasn't going to be interested in the girls who would obviously shut him down.

"You don't seem too surprised," Ron said.

"We don't even know if he's actually gone anywhere. He might be out scrounging for food. I swear, that boy has hollow legs.

I didn't know it was possible for anyone to eat that much and still be hungry."

"Well, there's another reason for him to live with Grant. I'm not sure I could afford to feed him."

"So it's possible he'll be back in a little while with a bag of burgers in one hand and a pizza in the other."

It was possible, Ron said, but not likely. If he'd specifically told Chip to stay put, he might have, but since he didn't, Chip would take that as permission to roam. And to him, roaming meant finding someone to hook up with.

"He's not completely selfish," Ron added. "He'll be here in the morning because he doesn't want to screw up this weekend for us."

I didn't think Chip was being intentionally selfish; I thought he was being a fifteen-year-old boy who lived with so few boundaries that he didn't always know when he was crossing a line.

We went to bed, curled around each other but with no other intentions on the off chance that Chip would come stumbling into the room at the wrong moment.

"Seven in the morning," Ron mumbled sleepily. "He'll creep in here around seven."

He didn't seem worried, so I pushed any concerns I had aside and tried to sleep, too.

~

The door creaked open at 4:30, and Chip tiptoed in, stumbling towards the bathroom. I slid out of bed, not sure what I'd say to him or even if I had a right to say anything, but I wanted to make sure he was all right.

He reeked of whiskey and drugstore perfume, and swayed horribly as he tried to focus on me.

"*Sssssh*," he hissed. "It's not morning. Morning. Morning."

"Shush yourself," I whispered harshly. "You're drunk."

"No. *Really?*"

"Where the hell have you been?"

He grinned. "Two floors down, that's all. It was a *parrr*-tee."

"You and who else?"

"Me and"—he ticked off on his fingers—"seven other peoples. But *ssshhh* don't tell them how old I am or they'll kick me out."

I sighed hard. "You're already out. How the hell did you find a party here?"

"The redhead from the pool," he said, leaning so close to me that his breath made my eyes water. "She's a redhead *all* over, you know. And she's very freaky. Free-key."

"I don't need to hear about it."

"Ah. Ok. Yes, that would be rude."

I put one hand on his chest to steady him. "Please tell me you used a condom, Chip."

"Always. Always, always, always. The clap ain't just applause, you know."

I turned him towards the bathroom, pushing gently. "Pee. Then go to bed. You can manage without passing out or falling over?"

"I'm fine. Finefinefinetyfine."

When I crawled back into bed Ron rolled over and mumbled, "Good thing we didn't bet on it, or I'd have lost."

"He's going to be all kinds of fun in the morning."

"Good. I'll wake him up at eight. And we'll spend the rest of the day torturing his hung-over little ass. Maybe he'll learn something."

~

The lesson learned was that Chip doesn't get hangovers. Ron threw the curtains open right at eight and turned the bedside radio on, music blaring close to Chip's head; Chip stretched and squinted, but he was fully awake in less than a minute and ready to get dressed, wanting to know where we wanted to go for breakfast.

Ron didn't say anything to him about his disappearing act; part of me wanted to put Chip's feet to the fire but another part of me realized that this was nothing new to Ron and he'd learned there wasn't much he could do about it.

I had a hard time grasping the idea that one's fifteen-year-old son could wander around on a whim and not suffer the repercussions.

While Ron was in the shower, Chip turned the TV on and dropped onto his bed to watch the morning news; I dropped right next to him, leaning up against the headboard, looking at the TV and not him.

"You could have left us a note," I said after a few minutes. "You know, 'hey, I'm going to see if I can find those girls, be back soon.'"

He didn't look away from the TV. "It was kind of obvious that I wasn't here."

"It would have been nice to know you were still in the hotel and not wandering around the city."

"Would it have mattered?" He turned to look at me, eyebrows knotted together. "Besides, I figured you guys wanted some time alone."

"Bullshit. You didn't think about either of us at all. We had no way of knowing if you were out for an hour, out for the night, or if you'd decided to just leave."

I saw the flicker of surprise in his eyes—maybe a note would have been a good idea—but he shrugged it off and went back to staring at the TV.

"Why do you do it, Chip? Why do you just wander off and leave them hanging?"

"They don't give a damn," he sighed. "They're relieved when I take off and they know I can take care of myself."

I wondered if he really believed that or if it was something he told himself to justify caving into his impulses. "I don't doubt that they know you can take care of yourself. That doesn't mean they don't worry, because they have no idea where you are."

"I don't expect you to get it."

"I don't give a damn what you expect right now. Ron at least needs to know where you are and that you're all right. He worries."

"No, he doesn't. He gets pissed but he's not worried."

"He's your father, he worries. It comes with the territory. Hell, my dad still worries and I'm pushing thirty years old."

"Thirty," he snorted. "Ron's a damned cradle robber. You know he's like forty five or forty six or something old like that, right?"

I didn't know Ron's exact age, no, but I wasn't going to let him change the subject.

"My point," I said sternly, "is that a little consideration goes a long way. I'm going to be in your father's life for a long time, at least I hope so. If you won't extend a little courtesy for him, do it for me. I *did* worry last night."

"You worried about me or that Ron would spaz out on you when he realized I was gone?"

"I can handle Ron. I was worried about you. You're only fifteen—"

"I know how old I am and it's almost sixteen. I've been handling myself since I was about eight years old. Trust me, you'll get used to not having to deal with my shit and you'll be grateful for it."

"No, I won't."

"Everyone does, sweetheart. You'll fall into line easy enough."

"Hey." I grabbed his forearm and squeezed, making him look at me. "You don't get to treat me like crap, Chip. You're not the little asshole you want everyone to think you are. I'm just asking for a little consideration here. I was worried about you last night, at first not knowing where you were and then when you came back drunk as hell."

He blinked, a bit puzzled.

"I care. Get used to it mister."

"Shit, my own mother never dogged me like this."

"I'm not your mother and I don't pretend I'll ever be even your stepmother. I want to be your friend. And friends care."

"You want to be friends. With a sixteen year old. That's kinda pervy, you know."

"Shut up. You know what I mean."

"So if you marry Ron, you're not going to get all maternal on me?"

"Let's not get ahead of ourselves. I've only been seeing him for a few months."

"Well, don't wait too long. He's getting really old, you know. He might only have a few good years left."

He tried hard to look serious, but I saw the corner of his mouth twitch with the effort to not smile. So much like Ron. "Just promise me you'll think a little before wandering off again."

"When I'm staying with Ron, I will make sure I leave a note or something," he conceded. "For you. He won't care."

"He cares," I sighed.

"Don't get me wrong. I know he cares about me, but he doesn't care if I take off for the beach house or spend the night with a friend."

"Beach house?"

"Grant bought my mom a house on the beach in Bodega Bay," he explained. "I go there a lot. It's quiet and I can just lie on the sand in the sun and not have to deal with everyone else's shit for a while. You and Ron should go there, you'd like it."

"The beach, maybe."

"Eh, Ron's been to the house. Probably more than Grant, and Grant doesn't mind if he uses it."

"Why do you do that?" I asked. "Call them by their first names."

"Neither of them has ever exactly acted like a dad."

"You called your mother by her first name, too?"

"Sometimes," he said. "Usually when I wanted to piss her off. She really hated it, but Grant said it didn't bother him. I think I called him 'Pop' when I was really little, though."

"And Ron?"

"I don't remember. Probably whatever my mom told me to call him."

We were both startled by Ron's voice cutting into the conversation. "Da," he said. "When you were a toddler, you called me 'Da.'"

"Da," Chip repeated, as if it felt familiar.

"The Irish in you, I suppose," Ron told him. "It's how your mother referred to me, and you called me 'Da' until you were four or five."

"Why'd I stop?"

"Who knows? You started called everyone by their first names, and Grant thought that you should be allowed to. I went with it—"

"Why? Because I was such a little shit that I was going to no matter what?"

"I went with it because I didn't want to rock the boat. I didn't get to spend much time with you and it wasn't worth fighting over. You had enough of that to deal with."

I wanted to know about the turmoil Chip grew up in, but he

didn't go in that direction. Instead, he asked Ron quietly, "Does it bother you? I mean, I can try to get used to calling you something else again."

"It doesn't matter now, Chip."

"Well, I will if you want me to. But not 'Da.'"

"Why not?"

"Because I'll freaking screw up and call you 'Dada' once, and you'll never let me live it down."

"Probably."

"I'm pretty sure that's why I started calling Grant by his first name," he said. "I think I called him 'Poppa' and Mom about lost her shit over it. I mean, like she thought it was funny, she wasn't pissed or anything. Still, I think that's when I started calling him by his name and he fired back by always calling me by mine."

Chip looked at me, as if he just remembered I was still there. "Grant hates nicknames. I call my little brother 'Davy' sometimes and it drives Grant freaking nuts."

"Which is why you do it," Ron said.

Chip shrugged.

"You know your life would be a lot calmer if you'd stop deliberately pushing his buttons."

I wondered if Ron was saying that for Chip, or for me.

Again, Chip shrugged.

"Come on, let's go get breakfast," Ron said, letting Chip off the hook. "I can hear your innards protesting from here."

They were so close to a real conversation, and I wondered why Ron just let it go.

~

We went down to the hotel's breakfast buffet instead of a restaurant. Chip insisted he didn't care where we ate, and I frankly wanted to see just how much he could eat in one sitting with no waiter in his way.

It was impressive.

"He turns sixteen next week," Ron said during breakfast. "Won't tell anyone what he might like as a gift, though."

"I have too much crap," Chip insisted.

"And there's nothing you would really like," Ron pushed.

"Sixteen is a major birthday," I added.

"It's a number," Chip said.

I could see it poised right there, ready to tumble out if Ron pushed, but Chip wasn't going to ask for anything. I gestured to Ron's empty juice glass and then slid mine toward him. "Would you?"

When he was far enough away I asked Chip, "You want a car, don't you?"

Another shrug.

"Every sixteen year old wants a car. I didn't even want a driver's license, but I wanted a car."

He glanced toward Ron. "If I tell them I want a car, I'll get a car. Only Grant will insist on buying it because he has something to prove, and I really don't want anything from him. I mean, he would get me a *great* car, probably an out-the-ass expensive sports car, but I seriously don't want anything from him. It would just be easier all the way around if they just ignored the whole thing."

"Ron won't want to ignore it, Chip. It's your birthday, he's your father."

"Yeah, no shit. I got that memo years ago." He sighed. "Sorry. I didn't mean to be a dick."

"He wants to get you something. Just cough up an idea."

"I dunno. A couple of records, maybe. But not that crap he likes to listen to."

"Not a standards fan?"

"Holy fuck, I just want someone to shoot me when he starts playing Sinatra. You'd think a little rock would make his balls fall off."

"So, hard rock, pop rock?"

"You like rock?"

"I suspect you and I have more in common musically than Ron and I do."

"Sweet. What do you like?"

"Jimi, Janis."

"Awesome. The Animals? Rolling Stones?"

"Definitely."

"Well, if he asks again, I wouldn't mind one of their albums."

"And if Grant asks him for ideas?"

"Fuck. Clothes. If I have to get something from Grant, clothes."

"For your sixteenth birthday."

"I don't want a car from him, Kris. I swear, I don't. A pair of jeans and a t-shirt, maybe. But he can't buy me and I don't want him to try."

"All right. I'll pass the word along."

He picked up his plate to head back to the buffet. "You want anything?"

"Oh my God, Chip, how can you possibly have room for more?"

"It's like free food. Who can pass up free food?"

He walked past Ron, deliberately bumping shoulders with him, feigning being knocked off balance. It made Ron smile, and for that I was just a little bit grateful.

"That looked deep," Ron said. "I pondered juice choices to give you a minute."

"Not too deep," I said, "but I know what he wants for his birthday."

~

Chip showed up at Ron's apartment early on the afternoon of his birthday; on the phone the day before he'd seemed relieved that Grant didn't expect to spend the entire day with him, and he seemed happy that Ron wanted to spend the afternoon with him and take him to dinner. I was happy when Ron told me that Chip had asked if I'd be there and stressed that he hoped I would.

I might not ever be his *friend*, but I felt like we were going to be friends.

He walked into the apartment dressed in new jeans and a bright red t-shirt with a giant multi-colored peace sign on the front. "Grant," he explained, gesturing to the peace sign. "He said it looked 'groovy.'"

I bit back the laugh I felt bubbling up over Chip's pained expression.

"You wanted clothes," I reminded him.

"Looks good, too," Ron chimed in.

"Oh, it's okay, but 'groovy'?"

"He's trying," Ron said.

"It's cool. He also gave me a new record player. He figured I might want once since David took my old one apart."

"He did this...why?" I asked.

"David takes everything apart. He wants to see how things work but he can never get that shit back together."

"And he doesn't get in trouble for it?"

"Naw. Grant actually helps him sometimes. He says it's how David learns. He's all hands on and stuff. If he breaks something of mine, Grant usually replaces it. I mean, he would have replaced the record player anyway, but he said this was an excuse to get me a better one."

"And what if David takes this one apart?" Ron asked.

"He won't. He already knows what the guts look like and he mostly figured it all out, so he'll leave the new one alone."

"Tell him if he ever takes my shit apart, I'll string him up by his size five toes," Ron said, getting up from the sofa. "All right, this is going to be lame, but Kris said you wanted records, and I know you hate my taste in music, so we're going to the music store and you're picking out what you want."

He ignored the wave of both surprise and mild disappointment that crossed Chip's face; I could see it: *what, you couldn't make the effort to go buy a damned album?*

"Seriously, I cannot understand why you don't like Bing Crosby or Frank Sinatra."

"Because I have taste."

"Questionable taste," Ron said as he locked the door. "Did Grant take you to the DMV today? If he didn't, I'll take you tomorrow."

Chip grinned broadly and pulled his wallet out of his back pocket, whipping out his new license. "I'm legal now. He even let me take the road test in his Jaguar. Man, you should have seen the look on the face of the DMV dork. I don't think he even paid attention to my driving, he was just blown away by the car."

"Did he let you drive it over here?" Ron asked.

"Shit, I didn't even ask. He might have if I had. I walked."

"It's hot as hell and you walked what, three miles?"

"It's not that hot. I walk everywhere, Ron, it's no big deal."

"That's because you're young," Ron sighed. "Fine, mister new driver. You can be our chauffeur."

"Nice." He headed towards Ron's parking slot, and stopped short when he realized Ron's convertible wasn't there. "Hell, where's your car?"

"I had to park in the visitor's lot."

"What, some douche took your space?" He stopped, suddenly contrite. "I'm sorry. That's your car, isn't it, Kris?"

I leaned against the ugly green-gray Mustang taking up Ron's parking slot. "I hate the paint job," I said. "It needs a better color."

"It's *fine*," Ron said. "It runs, that's what matters."

Chip shrugged. "It doesn't seem girly enough for you, but it's pretty sweet. I mean, you got a *Mustang*."

"Want to drive it?" I asked.

"Really?"

Ron slipped the key to me behind my back. "I would guess that one of us has to sit up front, because you're going to need to put the seat all the way back."

"Or Kris could sit in your lap," Chip teased.

When he was behind the wheel, with me in the back and Ron next to him up front, Chip ran his hands over the steering wheel and said, "Are you sure you want me to drive it, Kris? This is, like, kind of awesome and I don't want to wad it up. I mean, I'm a decent driver and I haven't even created any road kill, but you never know."

I leaned forward and poked Ron's shoulder.

"It's not Kris's car, Chip," he said.

"Yeah, right. So whose car am I about to steal, then?"

"Yours. Happy birthday, son."

I could see Chip's face in the rearview mirror, and his eyes went wide. "Are you fucking serious?"

"It's yours," Ron said again. "But I swear to God, if you commit a felony in it, I'll shove the whole thing up your ass."

"No armed robberies," Chip promised.

"No fourteen year old girls in the back seat, either."

"Ugh, that's gross."

"You get my point, right?"

"I got it." He fired the engine up and started to back out. "There's not enough room to get laid back there anyway."

Ron sucked in a deep breath. "I don't need to know that. Take us to music hell, Chip."

"No way. You're not buying me anything else."

I leaned forward. "But I am." I pointed to the cassette player. "We need tunes, kiddo. Music to piss your father off. Let's get something really loud and obnoxious, and then take him for a long ride up toward the lake."

Ron turned in his seat. "I thought you liked me."

"She *loves* you," Chip laughed.

"But not his taste in music," I said.

Chip was still laughing, but Ron gaped at me. I left that hanging in the air, the one thing neither of us had said yet.

We spared Ron a torturous ride to the lake with the car swelling to hard rock and went to shoot pool instead, and then went to dinner. After that, Chip drove us back to Ron's apartment, and begged off, saying he knew we wanted to spend some time alone.

We both knew he just wanted to go show off his car to his friends, and Ron was all right with that.

That one unsaid thing was still hanging there between, us, though, and I think it scared the hell out of him.

~

At two in the morning, when I thought he'd been long asleep, Ron rolled onto his side, facing me, and said quietly, "I'm sorry the last couple of weeks have been mostly about Chip. I hadn't intended to throw you two together for a couple more months at least."

"Why not? I think I wish you'd let us meet sooner. I like him."

"He could use an attitude adjustment."

"Find me a sixteen year old boy who doesn't need one," I snickered. "He's fine. He's funny and most of the time doesn't have his head up his ass."

"You've only gotten a small taste of it, Kris," he said. "He's been on his best behavior for you. His little disappearing act in San Francisco? The norm would have been taking off for two days and then acting surprised that it mattered."

"He's under the impression that it doesn't."

"He knows it does. But I also don't think he knows any other way to get the attention he needs."

Acting out was the quickest way to get his mother to stop dwelling on her own self-absorbed misery and to take a moment to remember that she had kids, he explained. She hated her life, so she paid as little attention to the details of it as she could. The end result was Chip trying to fend for himself, and doing whatever he could to make up for her apparent lack of concern.

"Don't get me wrong," he added. "She loved him and she wanted him. Hell, she married Grant because she knew he'd be the better father. But she didn't have her entire self locked into her own life and he paid the price for it."

"And now that she's gone?"

"Habit, I guess. It's become part of his personality. I really hesitated on the car, Kris. He doesn't deserve it, and I know he'll just use it to take himself further away than he already does."

"Then why get it?"

"Because as much as he didn't want Grant getting him one out of feeling like the car was being given to buy his affection…I'm just as guilty of that. I don't have many opportunities to be the good guy. And I admit, just once I'd like to have the upper hand. I wanted to be the one to give him the one thing he really wanted but didn't feel like he could ask for."

"Nothing wrong with that."

"Oh, hell, there's everything wrong with that. And I almost didn't buy the car because of it. But then I started thinking about how he runs away all the time, and that he hitchhikes through some of the worst places."

"The car gives him a margin of safety."

"Chip is a tough son of a bitch and I almost feel sorry for anyone who thinks he'd be an easy target, but definitely, the car gives him an out. He's going to take off no matter what we want, but at least now he's not at the mercy of random strangers he meets on the road."

"There's no way you and Grant can tag team his little ass and convince him to stop running away?"

"Trust me, we've tried to think to ways to convince him that we want him here, and safe."

"So you two aren't so much at odds that you don't talk about him."

"We're mostly on the same page when it comes to Chip. We're mostly both angry that we didn't do enough when he was little to keep him protected from his mother's..." He sighed hard. "His mother."

"His mother's mental illness?" I prompted. "Or am I treading where I shouldn't?"

"She was sweet and wonderful most of the time, Kris. But yeah, she was a little nuts the rest of the time. She could never make up her mind where she wanted to be or with whom, and I think Chip sensed it. I think it made him feel like he was an intruder in his own life, and he hasn't gotten over that."

"He doesn't feel loved," I guessed.

"Intellectually, he knows I love him. I hope someday he'll understand that Grant loves him. But deep down I suspect he thinks Pat resented him and that she felt like she had to stay with Grant because of him. He was fairly sharp as a little kid...he knew that my relationship with her was ongoing and he's not certain when it ended."

"That's a lot for a kid to carry," I mused. "If it's not being too nosy, when did your relationship with her end?"

"It was an on and off thing, Kris. The last off switch was probably flipped about eight months before she died. I had enough. I couldn't take her chaotic little whims anymore."

"But?"

"But, she was still my son's mother, and it didn't change how I felt. I still had to see her in order to get to him, and Chip could feel every bit of the tension."

"And being as sharp as he is, he probably knew that you still loved her," I said.

"Something like that."

"And that you resented the fact that for all those years she stayed with Grant."

"I'm not sure about that," he said. "The truth is that she made the right decision marrying him, because God knows I had no intention of it."

That surprised me. "Even though she was pregnant."

Even though, he said. He was so close to getting out of the priesthood and into a life closer to what he had wanted all along, and what he didn't want was to start that new life tied down to a distraction. A wife and kids, heading into the agency, he knew that would be a distraction and likely would cause him to wind up behind a desk instead of being out in the field.

Grant, on the other hand, wanted the wife and family, and he didn't care if it meant he'd be pushing papers for the rest of his career. He loved her, and even knowing how she'd played them both, he wanted to marry her.

"He was good with kids," Ron said. "He doted on the school kids, even when the nuns threatened him for it. They kept saying he was spoiling them; he didn't care. He said the kids deserved a little spoiling. I know it was completely selfish, but I wanted to run full bore with the agency, and he wanted a life with Pat."

"What changed?"

"I left Ireland and honestly thought I'd never see either one of them again. But ten months later Grant had finished his training and they popped up here, with this beautiful baby boy. There was no avoiding it then. The first time I saw Chip I fell in love with him, and realized I wanted to be his father."

"But not married to his mother."

"No. I never wanted to marry her, Kris. I had a hard time walking away from her, and I loved her, but marriage and this job didn't make sense, at least not then."

"The job hasn't changed, Ron. If anything, you're in deeper."

"But the woman has changed," he said in a near whisper. "Just because I felt that way a long time ago, that doesn't mean I feel that way now. The woman in my life now"—he brushed his hand over my shoulder—"knows the worst parts of my life and hasn't run. She knows the job as well as I do, and she's pretty damned good at it herself."

"So you're seeing someone on the side," I said lightly. "I can take her, you know. I have a mean left hook."

"I'm sure you do." His fingers were trailing along my jaw now, making me shiver. "About what Chip said earlier in the car. Hating my taste in music."

"Well, he has a point."

"You didn't correct him."

"Because your taste in music really is…old."

"You know what I'm talking about."

I grabbed his hand to stop him from distracting me. "I know what you're talking about. And no matter what I didn't say, I'm not pushing you. I do love you. I don't expect to hear it back. Yet."

"Yet," he laughed.

"One day you just won't be able to help yourself. I'm that adorable, I know."

"I do know. I knew you were that adorable the first time I saw you. I think I knew then this was inevitable."

"This. Just what is this? Aside from all the things my father would shoot you for."

"Your father wouldn't stop at shooting me if he knew what I'd been doing to you."

"He still thinks I'm innocent."

"I'm sure that's what he wants you to think."

"What is this to you, Ron?" I pressed. "If you're just in it for my kinky side, I can live with that, but I'd appreciate knowing."

"You have a kinky side? I'd like to see it sometime."

"I will pull sensitive hairs, mister."

"I don't want this to just be *this*," he said. "I want this to be it. For good."

"And how long have you been taking tap dance lessons? Because you're very good."

"Make an honest man out of me, Kris. And sooner rather than later."

"Ah. You really are afraid of what my father will do to you. I'm pretty sure you can outrun him, though. No worries there."

"Kris."

"Chip did say I should get whatever use out of you I can while

I can, seeing as that you're older than dirt and everything might stop working soon."

"This is not going how I thought it would," he mumbled.

"Should I ask how much older you are?"

He sighed. "I'm a good fifteen years older, if it matters. And I suppose it should matter, though I honestly don't feel like I'm about to turn into a giant wrinkle and die."

"I'm not worried about you dying. I'm worried about parts shriveling up and falling off."

"Funny." He rolled onto his back. "I suppose I should have considered the age difference. When I really am old, you'll still be young enough to resent it."

"No, I won't."

"Well, something's holding you back."

"Because saying 'make an honest man out of me' is not a proposal. And honestly, before you do that I *do* want to hear you say you love me. It matters. I'm not going to push for it, but it matters."

"That seems fair." He sat up, pulling me with him. "Kris. Kristine? Kristin? Kristophina?"

"Marge," I said.

"Marge. I love you. I seriously love you. I love you even though 'Marge' is a really horrible name. Will you marry me?"

"Ron. Ronald? Ronny? Ronatisimo?"

"Horatio."

"Horatio. You betcha."

"'You betcha' isn't an answer. I want to hear 'yes.'"

"Fine, you little prick. Yes."

"It's not that little."

"Dan is going to have a stroke," I said.

"What, because it's not that little? It's not like we compare, Marge."

"Two of his team members? He's not happy about us as it is, when he hears we're actually taking the next step? His stuffed shirt is going to explode."

~

We threw the wedding together in less than a month. It was either that, we realized, or wait until the next summer, when we knew we could force our work schedules to lighten up a bit. We spent an evening staring at the calendar, trying to figure out how we could squeeze in a wedding that wouldn't make my parents feel as if we were excluding them, and came to the conclusion that the only way to avoid waiting or eloping was to rush it.

Neither of us wanted to wait nearly a year. We picked the first open day, a week before a scheduled overseas assignment, booked a chapel for the wedding and a restaurant for a small reception, and mailed out store-bought invitations, all done within a weekend.

A few days later I was picking out a wedding dress with my mother and cousin-in-law Sheila's help, while Ron dragged Chip to be fitted for a tuxedo.

Almost apologetically, Ron told me he was asking his son to be his best man.

I couldn't see a more appropriate choice.

The wedding was simple and quiet, save for my mother's muted sniffling from one of the front pews; it was also short and sweet, something we both wanted. There would be no wedding mass; I worried that would offend my parents, but neither was particularly religious and didn't care. The relief was in not having to explain to them why; they didn't need to know that the man I was marrying had walked away from the priesthood without so much as a "Hey it was fun, sorry to bail!" note.

In contrast, the reception was obnoxiously loud, music pulsating hard enough that we could feel the beat through the soles of our shoes. Even though Ron did not dance well he thought it wouldn't be much of a party if no one else did, so half of the floor had been cleared out, and half the guests were out there, stumbling along to songs Ron swore he couldn't make heads or tails of.

"I might like it," he said, "if I could understand a damn word of it."

He'd allowed me to drag him around on the dance floor for a while, but after the last slow song he begged off, promising we'd go back out later, when he didn't feel like the oldest person to walk the earth. Dan Martin was dancing with my mother; I didn't think Ron could do any worse, but I also didn't mind sitting down and watching everyone else for a while.

Chip bounced from girl to girl, as if it was his mission to dance with every female in the room, save my thirteen-year-old cousin.

"If he goes anywhere near her," Ron grumbled, "I will whip out my service gun and shoot his kneecaps off. I'd aim higher, but I would like grandkids someday."

"He wouldn't," I assured him. "He's more interested in figuring out which one he has the best chance with, and a girl barely into puberty does not qualify."

"One would hope."

"Shut up," I laughed, jabbing him with my elbow.

Ron gestured toward Chip, who was now across the room at the bar, sitting next to Doug Stone; they were overtly watching women on the dance floor, and whatever Chip had said Doug found it wildly amusing.

"Does he know not to say anything to Chip?"

Ron nodded. "I made sure he knows. Those two are becoming friends...let's just say a reminder was in order."

I wasn't even sure when or how they'd met, but the idea that Chip could be influenced by someone older and hopefully more nature was one I embraced.

I should have considered that it would work both ways.

"What's your official cover, Ron?" I asked. "What do you tell Chip? I get mine. I'm the charter pilot. What's yours and what's Dan's?"

"Sales," he said, still watching Chip. "Pharmaceuticals. Haven't you paid attention to the giant 'Wymouth' on the front of the building? Ideally, it's a drug research facility and that's all Chip knows. Ostensibly, Dan and I sell prescription medications on the international market. You fly us there. As far as Chip knows, Doug is interested in medical research."

I'd never given any thought to the building or the name slapped across it in ten-foot tall letters. I'd only thought it was an odd place for a government agency, plopped out in the middle of undeveloped county land, wedged inexplicably between the tiny towns of Fairfield and Vacaville.

Over the years the name on the building would change a few times, but by the time it ceased being Wymouth Pharmaceuticals, we were no longer hiding anything from Chip.

Chip was pointing at a brunette seated down the bar from him and from Doug; neither Ron nor I could place her, and assumed she was just a customer of the restaurant.

"Target acquired," Ron mumbled.

"He may have to fight Doug for her," I said. "They're both looking."

"I don't think Doug has the nerve to hit on someone he doesn't know," Ron said. "He strikes me as a little bit shy."

"Could be his M.O.," I said. "Women like the shy, quiet type."

"Wanna bet on it?"

"You don't want to lose a bet to me on our wedding day," I said lightly.

"I'm not that invested in who Doug goes home with," he said, reaching for my hand. "Come on; let's go run interference for the poor girl who has no idea what she'd be getting into by merely speaking to my son."

"You're cock blocking your own kid?"

"Damn right. Think you can keep Doug company for a few minutes while I lay some ground rules for Chip? I think I can get him to promise to not use the apartment while we're gone, and if I'm lucky, he'll promise to stay home and not wander up and down California."

"Good luck with that."

Chip's annoyance at being dragged off was obvious; he was probably within a minute or two of making his move and he couldn't help but look at her one more time before going off with Ron.

"She's all yours now," I said to Doug.

He glanced at her, and then shrugged. "No point. I have rounds in about two hours."

"And you need more than two hours."

He shifted uncomfortably on his barstool, and his ears flushed red. "That's not my thing."

"Girls?"

"Oh, God. I meant I'm not like Chip," he said. "I don't hone in on the one I'm going to use for the night."

"He's young. He'll learn."

"Maybe."

"He doesn't know anything about what we do, Doug. I know Ron has probably—"

"I know."

"Chip sometimes seems older than he is," I said. "It would just be too easy to slip up and tell him things he's better off not knowing."

"Kris, we hang out and shoot pool. We don't exactly talk about anything...deep."

"You mean girly?" I laughed.

"Well, yeah. I mean, you might want to get all touchy feely, but all I want is to crack a beer open and lose a game or two of nine ball."

"He's sixteen," I reminded Doug. "If you're getting beer for him, Ron will eviscerate you."

"Chip's never asked me to, and I wouldn't."

We were both quiet for a few minutes, pretending to watch people out on the dance floor. I think we both were hoping for the same thing: for Ron to be done with Chip and for them to both rescue us from the discomfort of forced conversation.

"I saw the intelligence folder for next week," he said after a while, very quietly. "Amsterdam. Who does business in Amsterdam?"

"We do," I answered simply.

"It's not exactly a hot bed—"

"It's a meeting place. And not exactly something we should talk about here."

He nodded.

"Come on; tell me about your rounds tonight. I thought you were done with your residency."

"I'm on an ER rotation," he said. "And I still have patients to see."

"And leaving next week won't screw anything up?"

"Not unless *I* screw something up this week and kill someone. I'm off schedule by Thursday, though, so as long as I keep my head out of what could happen in Amsterdam, I should be fine."

"Nervous?"

"I still don't know what's expected out of me," he admitted. "So far my training has consisted of learning to shoot without screaming like a little girl when the gun kicks back, how to theoretically kick someone else's ass, and being told to just do what I'm told. I follow you around or I follow Ron around. Nothing has any context."

"You'll get context as you go along."

"You're not scared?"

I shook my head. "I feel cautious, but I'm not scared. And don't think you're wrong if you are. I was terrified the first few times out. If you're scared a year from now, then worry. But always, always keep that sense of caution going. You never want to get jaded."

"So Dan and Ron, they don't just do it? They feel that same sense of caution?"

"I would hope so. Not being cautious is a good way to get yourself killed."

"Cautious about what?" I heard Chip say from behind me.

"Flying," Doug said without missing a beat. "She's a pilot, for Pete's sake. How can someone get into a cockpit with all those controls and knobs and not want to piss themselves?"

"Dorkoff, she can do it because she has bigger balls than you do."

Doug pretended to regard me coolly. "No shit."

Chip glanced toward the end of the bar. "Man, you let the chick get away."

"The chick," I sighed.

"She was hot, too."

Ron stepped up next to me. "You're going home tonight," Ron reminded him. "Alone."

"Doesn't mean I can't talk to her."

Ron looked at Doug. "Will you take him home before you go to work? And make sure he actually goes into the house?"

"Will do," Doug said with a slip of a laugh.

Ron reached over for Chip and pulled him close, kissing Chip's forehead. "We're taking off now. You'll leave with Doug?"

"He's not exactly my type, but if it'll make you happy."

I looked back one more time before we walked out the door; Doug and Chip were focused on someone else, but they were laughing wildly.

Doug might have agreed to take Chip home before he went to work, but I had some serious doubts about what Chip might get into between now and then. Or even that Doug would make it to work.

"Stop," Ron said, tugging on my hand. "He said he'd go home, and he will. Don't let him get into your head, not now."

I didn't know how Ron could just turn it off, but I decided I'd try.

He wasn't my kid, after all. Not mine to worry about.

~

We spent four days on a beach just south of the California and Oregon border, intentional quiet time away from anything too touristy, knowing that we'd be on a plane headed for Europe in a week. We wanted to be alone, to walk along the water—though barefoot was not an option with the temperatures barely reaching 50 during the day—and to curl up in front of a fire in the evening.

The hotel room had a nearly floor to ceiling window facing the ocean, and as the sun went down we curled up in front of the fireplace and watched the diehards playing on the beach with the light dimming behind them. We purposely avoided talking about work, and Ron avoided talking about Chip.

With talk of Chip often came talk of Pat, it seemed, and he didn't want to go there. That was fine; I'd just married the man, and didn't want to explore his last great love, either.

That worked both ways; I avoided his questions about my pre-Ron love life, too. I didn't want to explain the sweet but basically brainless boys I usually drifted toward, and I really didn't want him asking about my love life. There was no Great Love looming in my past, but still; I'd had my heart broken and didn't want to tell him about it when all I really wanted at the time was for us to be wrapped around each other, not talking at all.

More than once he asked if I minded not wandering much past the hotel, if I didn't really want to explore the area. He was content to for us be alone, but didn't want to bore me. We only had a few days, I had to keep pointing out, and once we reported for our next assignment there was no telling how long it would be before we'd have any time alone together again.

By the end of the fourth day, however, we were ready to head home. Ron wanted to see Chip before we left, and I wanted to pack up what was left in my apartment. The where-will-we-live discussion had been short: I rented a small one room second story apartment off of one of the busiest streets in town, and Ron owned a spacious two bedroom garden flat in a quiet neighborhood.

He had Chip; we needed the second bedroom.

Within half an hour after we got home the phone rang, but I was pulling clothes out of the suitcase and didn't pay any attention to what Ron was saying until just before he hung up, when he sighed, "Send him over."

He stood in the bedroom doorway, looking at me apologetically. "I'm sorry. I don't know how ugly this is going to be."

"What'd he do?"

A deep breath in, slowly let out. "He managed to get himself expelled from school."

"What?" I dropped the shirt I'd had in hand back into the suitcase. "What the hell did he do?"

"Grant said Chip could tell me himself. Dammit, we don't need this right now. We have to leave in a couple of days."

"Does he know that?"

"He knows."

"Should I leave? I can head over and get a few more of my things."

He shook his head. "If you leave every time he screws up, I'll never see you."

"Not prone to a little hyperbole there, are you?"

"Maybe a little. But you don't need to leave."

I kind of wanted to. I didn't want to see Ron explode or Chip have to stand there and take it.

~

"Your teacher," Ron seethed. "You were having sex with your teacher."

Chip was wholly unapologetic, and just shrugged. "Her idea, not mine."

"She was your *teacher*, Chip."

'Was' being the operative word, I thought.

"Yeah. And?"

"In the teachers' lounge. You got caught having sex with her in the damned teachers' lounge."

"I know. I was there. That sucked, but what're you gonna do? The teacher says drop your pants, you drop your pants."

Ron's fingers went to his forehead, pressing as if he was trying to shove back in the headache that was trying to worm its way out. "How can you not see how wrong this is?"

"If it's so fucking wrong, why aren't you yelling at her instead, Ron? She's the authority figure, she's in charge, and she came on to me, not the other way around."

"And you're fully capable of saying the word 'no.'"

"Well, yeah, but why would I?"

"How about for the exercise of self-control, Chip?"

"You're kidding, right?"

"Do I look like I'm kidding?"

Frankly, he looked like he was a half second away from leaping across the room and grabbing Chip by the front of his shirt, and shaking until his son's fillings went flying in every direction.

"What the hell do you do about school now?" Ron pressed. "Is Grant supposed to pack up and move so that you can go to another high school?"

"No point," Chip said. "It's not like there are a dozen around here to choose from and I'm pretty sure my invitation out the door extended to the other high school across town."

"Private school?" I offered. "The church has one."

Ron didn't look at me; instead he exhaled sharply and then said, "You want to explain that one to her?"

Chip half shrugged. "They don't exactly want me there, either. I mean, that's where David goes, but they were pretty clear about not wanting me there."

"Anymore," Ron added.

"I wasn't enrolled there."

"No, you didn't get that far, did you? Grant was sitting in the office, checkbook in hand and you what—?"

"Before or after I kicked the nun?"

"You kicked a nun?" I asked. "Seriously?"

"She started it."

"Grant wanted to get him into the junior high," Ron said. "He was supposed to be on the playground staying out of trouble, but instead he got into a fight with two other boys. One of the nuns tried to break it up, pulled Chip off one of them—"

"She slapped me," Chip said.

"—and he kicked her. Hard. Two broken ribs, a major donation to the school with a promise that he would never be a student there, and here we are."

"That's it?" I asked. "He reacted to someone slapping him and he's banned from the school?"

"What else was there that day, Chip?"

"I dunno."

"You spit in the holy water," Ron said. "Flipped off one of the teachers. Commented on the size of another teacher's breasts. Told a priest to fuck off. All in about an hour's time. I'm willing to bet they haven't forgotten. So tell me, what the hell do we do now about your education?"

"Not your problem," Chip grumbled.

"How? How is this not my problem?"

Chip stood up. "You abdicated the role before I was born. Grant gets to figure it out, lucky you."

"Where the hell do you think you're going?"

"He wanted me to come over and tell you what happened, and I told you. There's nothing you can do or say to fix it, so don't even try."

"Chip."

"I get it. I disappointed you again. It sucks, but here we are. You should be used to it."

"Sit down, Chip."

"For what? So you can tell me again how fucked up I am and

what I loser I turned out to be? No thank you."

"I wasn't—"

"Yeah, you were. Maybe not straight out, but that's exactly it. I'm sorry I'm not the son you wanted, but I'm the son you've got."

Chip headed for the door, and Ron turned away, not even trying to stop him.

"Chip, wait," I said.

I thought he was going to keep going, but he turned around, looking at me expectantly.

"The fight on the church playground. What started it?"

"Does it matter?" Ron asked.

Chip's face softened. "There was a third kid," he said. "Really little, maybe a sixth grader, the other two were a lot older. Or bigger. Whatever. They were shoving him around, so I started walking over…just before I got there one of the other guys shoved a handful of dirt into his mouth and called him a faggot. He was crying so hard I thought he was going to choke, so I told him to run for it, and when they tried to close in on me, I beat the shit out of them."

"And the nun?"

"I didn't mean to hurt her, she just surprised me. She was like a freaking ninja nun, suddenly there out of nowhere."

"Why didn't you ever tell me this?" Ron asked.

"Why didn't you ever ask?"

Ron couldn't answer fast enough. I could see him trying to cough out the exact right thing to say, but he hesitated for a fraction of a second, and Chip was out the door before I could stop him.

~

In the tense silence that followed the click of the door closing, I knew that listening to Ron defend himself was not something I wanted to do. I wanted to go after Chip but I doubted I could catch up to him, and to avoid the fight I could feel bubbling up, I decided to get out for a little while. I sent Ron to the office to get our final assignment information, and I made the excuse of needing to go to the grocery store to avoid going with him.

When I got back an hour later Ron's car was still gone—I was actually grateful for that because I was still ticked off—but when I opened the apartment door I could hear the washing machine chugging along in the laundry room, and music coming from Chip's bedroom.

I dropped the grocery bags onto the kitchen counter and then headed for the room. Chip was stretched out on the bed with his arms folded behind his head, and he was staring up at the ceiling. I lingered in the door for a moment, until he cleared his throat and said softly, "I needed clean clothes. I hope it's all right."

"Of course it's all right. I wasn't expecting to see you so soon, though."

"I should have been straight when I was here earlier," he said, still not looking at me. "Grant told me to stay here for a couple of days. He's too pissed off to even look at me."

"Scoot over," I said, moving to sit on the bed with him. I sat leaning on the headboard, and he slid on the bed until he was sitting beside me, my shoulder pressing into his arm. "You can stay here as long as you want."

"Until you and Ron leave on your business trip."

"We won't be gone long."

"I'm really sorry, Kris. You don't deserve having to deal with my crap."

"It's not crap, Chip, it's your life. And I think you might need a fresh perspective, someone who hasn't been invested all along."

"Invested," he snorted. "They're not invested. They're just waiting until I'm old enough to be shoved out the front door."

"Chip."

"No, seriously. I know I was a shitty little kid, but now? They hate me."

"No, they don't. I know Ron doesn't. He loves you."

"Maybe, but he'd be happier if he didn't have to deal with me. When my mom died..." His breath caught, and from the corner of my eye I could see his fingers clench at the bedspread. "That changed everything."

"How?"

"It was my fault," he whispered. "She's dead because of me."

"She had a heart attack. That wasn't your fault."

"She and Grant went out that afternoon and I thought they were going to be gone until late at night. I mean, David was spending the night with his friend across the street and usually when he did that, they stayed out because they could. I mean, you know, Grant was at least trying with her. Anyway. I thought they would be out late, so I brought a friend over."

"Girlfriend?"

He nodded. "My mom never completely believed anything Grant said about me. He tried to tell her some of the things I was doing but she always said he was exaggerating and that I was just strong willed. But then they walked in and she got to see everything she didn't believe, and she freaked out. I mean, like screaming and crying and shit.

"Grant yelled at me to get that girl the hell out of his house, so we scrambled...I took her home and when I got back home the ambulance was in front of the house. She made it to the hospital but that was it. She was dead before Ron could get there so he never got to say goodbye. After Grant went home, I mean, I wanted to stay there at the hospital with Ron for a while but then he took me home, and when I got there—" His hand went to his chest. "He did this."

I reached for his hand, pulling it away from the scar, and slipped my fingers between his. "None of that makes it your fault, Chip. She didn't have a heart attack because of anything you did. She would have—"

"I broke her heart," he choked out.

"She was upset," I pointed out. "People get over being upset. She would have had a heart attack even if she'd come home and found you in the kitchen baking cookies."

He slid on the bed, letting go of my hand, curling up on his side. "I miss my mom, Kris."

"I know you do. No one stops very long to think about that, do they?"

"I don't know," he sniffed. "But they blame me."

I didn't think Ron did, but Chip was fighting tears that he didn't want me to see and I didn't know what to say to convince him otherwise. I reached over to push a strand of hair that was sticking straight up behind his ear, just to touch him, hoping he'd feel some kind of connection. "I can't speak for Grant because I don't know him," I said gently, "but Ron loves you, Chip."

"You can love someone and hate them at the same time."

"He doesn't hate you at all."

"Then he doesn't like me and I know he doesn't understand me. That's okay, I learned to deal with it a long time ago. I just... right now..."

"Right now you need your mom, and what you've got is your dad's new wife trying to tell you what to feel."

"But I'm glad you're here," he sighed. "Ron really needs you."

"Feeling a little sleepy?" I asked, knowing that all he really wanted was for me to get up and leave so that he could cry and not worry about how it looked. "You've had a hard day."

"My own fault."

"Not your fault entirely," I said, "but still hard. Take a nap, and I'll wake you in time for dinner."

"You don't have to feed me. I can go out and get a burger or something."

"Trust me," I said, ruffling his hair before I got up, "you'll probably wish I hadn't bothered to go anywhere near the kitchen. But you're not going out. Hell, we have to eat, too."

I quietly closed the door behind me, hoping he really would fall asleep for a while; if he was asleep, there was half a chance that he wouldn't lie there mentally beating himself up.

When, I wondered, was the last time anyone paid him any real attention, other than to tell him how wrong he was or how out of line he was acting. Ron praised him to me, but I couldn't remember hearing him do it in front of Chip. They took verbal potshots at each other all the time, half in jest, but the tension that simmered just under the surface was impossible to ignore.

Ron came home while I was starting dinner and wandered into the kitchen, a file folder in hand. He tossed it onto the table, but before he could tell me anything about the assignment I said, "Try to keep it down a little. Chip came back and I think he's asleep."

"Must be nice to be able to just stop and take a nap when you feel like it," he grumbled.

"Hey. That's not fair. Maybe you don't see it, but he's stressed out so hard he doesn't know what to do."

"He could go home, apologize to Grant."

"Apologize for what? For being sixteen and getting caught in an embarrassing situation?"

"A situation he brought on himself."

"No, a situation that he was pulled into. He's right, Ron, why aren't you going after the teacher? The adult in this?"

"Not saying I won't. But he knew better."

"No. He didn't. You're expecting adult behavior out of a boy. He may look grown up, but in here"—I poked Ron in the forehead— "he's still a boy. He hasn't developed his full ability to make leaps of logic and no matter how badly you want him to, he can't. He's not there yet."

"He knows right from wrong."

"He also knows that he's a horny kid and there was someone who wanted to have sex with him. Right or wrong didn't matter. What mattered is how both you and Grant reacted to it. Be pissed off, sure, but stand up for your kid."

"I do stand up for him."

"Really? When? I haven't seen much of it yet. What I've seen is you putting him down for things you probably don't have the whole story on. Like the nun. And I see you expecting him to think like a thirty year old and make those leaps of logic that he shouldn't have to yet. Expecting that is like shoving a batch of cookies into the oven, turning it up high, and then being surprised when they come out burnt. He's not done growing up, and it seems to me that you and Grant are both pushing him to it before he's ready."

"Kris, we've had years of this. It gets a little tiring."

"Try living it from Chip's side."

"I do remember what being sixteen feels like."

"You were never a sixteen year old being pushed and pulled between two fathers, your mother is still alive, and you never thought that the people who are supposed to care about you hated you instead."

He blanched at that. "Chip doesn't think we hate him."

"He's pretty sure Grant does. And he's pretty sure at the very least you don't like him very much."

"He said that?"

I didn't have to answer.

"He said that," Ron sighed.

"Today, I think he feels a little beaten up. No one stood up for him and everyone blamed him. But when you get down to it, it wasn't really his fault. He was just doing what most teenaged boys would have done, and don't lie—if you'd been in his shoes at sixteen, you'd have been all over that teacher."

"When I was sixteen, I was in an all-boys school, including the teachers," he said, knowing it sounded lame as it came out. "All right, I get it."

"He usually runs away when he's this stressed out doesn't he?"

"To the beach house, if we're lucky."

"But this time…Ron, he came here. Grant kicked him out, and he came here. He didn't run."

Ron took a step back. "Grant kicked him out?"

"Grant told him to stay here for a few days. That's the same thing in my book. But he came back, Ron. When he could have taken off, he came *here*, and we can't blow it now."

"I can't blow it. This isn't your problem."

"Chip is not a *problem* and I refuse to think of him as one. He's your son. And frankly, I like him and I care about him, and I want him here with us, not just trying to survive with his stepfather until he's eighteen."

We both turned at the sound of feet on the linoleum.

"Thank you for that," Chip said softly. "Whatever you're cooking, it smells good."

"Just spaghetti, but I made enough to fill your completely hollow self."

He glanced at Ron, but couldn't meet his gaze. "I know you have a business trip coming up. I'll be gone before then."

"The timing could be better," Ron said. "If we could push it back we would."

"S'okay."

"We'll be back in three or four days. If you can promise to stick to the rules, you can stay here while we're gone."

"And you'll worry about what I'm really doing the entire time.

I can go home. Grant will have cooled off by then."

"One would hope."

Everything flooded into my brain at once. "Chip, when we get back, your entire living situation has to change."

They both looked at me.

"This has to stop. You can't keep feeling...*this*. When we get back, you're moving in here. Grant will have to deal with it."

"Kris," Ron started.

"You guys travel a lot," Chip pointed out. "You're going to be okay with leaving me alone?"

"We'll figure it out," I said, though I wasn't sure how.

"And school?" Ron pressed.

Chip's face flushed, and his jaw clenched with the effort of not saying anything.

"How were your grades?" I asked.

"When he made an effort, he was a good student," Ron said. "He's bright, I'll give him that."

"I get bored a lot," Chip allowed.

"He can test out," I told Ron. "The state has an equivalency exam, if he can pass it, he technically graduates."

"Then what? A job? Who will hire him? He's sixteen. And frankly I don't see him standing behind a counter asking 'You want fries with that?'"

"Community college," I said evenly. "You won't be as bored there, Chip. You can pick the classes you want and take some time to figure out what you might want to do."

"How long have you been thinking this out?" Ron asked.

"Since I hit the door and found him here. He can't go back to living the way he does. He's not comfortable at home and he needs a place he can be." I turned to him when he opened his mouth to speak. "You can't stay just because of your brother. He's not your responsibility, and he's safe with his father. It's time for you to get your own life on track."

"But David's not going to understand. He's still little—"

"You'll still see him," Ron said, and in that moment I knew he was on board with the idea. "I'll make sure of it."

"But..."

"No buts." He leaned over and kissed me. "I might as well go set it in motion now. This is probably a good time to tell Grant I want my son now and I'm not taking no for an answer."

"Dinner?"

"I'll make a sandwich when I get back." He knocked shoulders with Chip as he passed. "You get to do the dishes, cowboy. I'll try to grab some of your stuff when I'm there."

Chip stood there in the kitchen, blinking, not quite sure what to do.

"Set the table?" I suggested. "Looks like it's just me and you."

He hesitated, still absorbing, but then quickly got out plates and silverware.

"It's all right to be irritated with me, you know. Here I am sticking my nose in your business...especially after you'd explained why you were still living with Grant. I hope you're not too ticked off, though."

"I'm not."

"You understand, then?"

"I don't know. It's more than David. You just got married, like *just*. Why would you want me moving in now?"

"Why would I want you living with someone you're sure hates you?"

"If I stay you might wind up not liking me very much, either."

"That goes both ways, mister. I don't take crap from anyone. Sooner or later I'm going to tell you to do something you don't want to, and I'll expect you to do it regardless."

"All right."

"And sooner or later you'll do something that really pisses me off and I'll call you on it and probably try to ground you, and I don't ever want to hear 'fuck off, you're not my mother.'"

I expected one of two things out of him then: he would either grin and tell me that was fine—even though he wouldn't mean it—or that he would roll his eyes and sigh hard. Instead, he nodded and said seriously, "You're not anything like her. That's a good thing."

"Chip, don't."

"I'm not trying to be mean. She was just"—he winced, thinking hard—"unhappy, I guess. And scattered. Kind of a drama queen.

I don't think she wanted to be anyone's mother, but she tried. The problem is that if she got distracted, she stopped trying."

And Ron was one of those distractions, I presumed.

"I could do pretty much anything I wanted as long as I didn't shove it in her face," he went on. "That'll be a hard habit to break."

"I'll try to be patient. Just promise me a couple of things. No girls in this apartment when we're not home."

"Okay."

"I mean that. And no just taking off if things get uncomfortable. I'm not saying you won't be able to, because Ron seems all right with it, but I don't want to wonder where you are and if you're coming home."

"Leave a note."

"I'd be happier if you waited to leave until you could talk to one of us, but I'll take what I can get."

"I promise I'll try."

I took what I could get.

~

"He looked like I'd just kicked his puppy," Ron told me later, after Chip had gone to bed.

We were at the kitchen table, ready to go over the file, something we'd had to put off until we were sure Chip wouldn't hear anything. But first I wanted to know how it had gone with Grant. When Ron came home all he said was that it went all right; Chip would have to stay with Grant while we were gone this time, but after that he was here for good.

"Then to top it off," he added, "it was like after I'd kicked the puppy, I picked it up and he knew I was going to run off with it."

"No argument over it, though?"

"For about a minute, he was livid and threatened to take me to court. But I think he realized Chip is old enough to tell a judge who he wants to live with and why... Grant is hurt, but he caved."

"He's hurt. Seriously?"

"I would be, too."

But Ron would be a better father, I thought. Marginally, maybe, but with some prodding he would at least stick up for Chip.

Grant lost the right to be hurt when he whipped a knife across his stepson's chest.

"Once we get back"—he tapped a finger against one of the folders—"we have to figure out what we're going to do with him when the next assignment rolls around. I can't take Chip from Grant and then expect him to babysit every time we have to leave."

"There may be no 'we' in leaving after this, Ron. If it comes down to it, I'll quit my job. I don't owe the agency any more time."

"Quit. To take care of my son."

"Someone has to be here, and I know you don't want to give up your career. It's just a job to me. If it comes down to money, I can work as a charter pilot."

"But you shouldn't have to."

"I don't have to, but I will. He needs stability. He needs someone to be here when he needs someone, not when it's convenient."

"That doesn't have to be you. If either of us quits—"

"You would resent it, and he would feel that."

"Why would I resent it?"

"You said before you'd never considered quitting. You're invested in this job, but I'm not. For me it was a means to an end; it got me training I never would have otherwise, but I don't care about making a career out of it. I mean it. If it comes down to money, I can find something else. Hell, I can borrow my dad's plane and run day charters and tours over San Francisco."

"Money's not an issue. You can quit if you want, but only if it's what you want. I don't want you leaving a job you like because I'm dropping the ball where my son is concerned."

"And I don't want you quitting something you clearly need to be doing. I honestly don't care about working for the agency, Ron. But I do care about Chip."

He leaned across the table and kissed me. "You are amazing."

"Yes, I am. Don't forget that." I reached for the file folder. "So what's the gig? What exotic route am I taking to get us to Amsterdam?"

"We're flying commercially and the destination has changed."

"Seriously? That kind of blows for me."

"I think they want you rested. This is a get in and get out kind of thing, but as low key as possible."

"Where to and what?"

"Germany. We're extracting the son of a U.S. diplomat being held near Garmisch. There's a pre-operations team in place that has him located and they have a mole on the ground to make sure the kid is where we'll expect him to be. It should be a simple sweep in, grab the kid, and go."

"Should be."

"Ideally. There's only one person inside, and a whole lot of people around him."

"What's the delay? Why hasn't someone gone after him already?"

"Placement, for one," Ron said. "We needed to wait until he was in a place we could easily get to. And you know someone has already tried and failed, otherwise we wouldn't have had any advanced notice."

I flipped through the few papers in the file, looking for the details I'd need to know off the top of my head. "Jesus, Ron, he's Chip's age."

"And he was taken to prove a point. His father isn't a high ranking diplomat, there's nothing to be gained in this, other than proving they can get to our people."

"The kid is a message."

"And if we don't get him, he'll be a dead message. They want nothing in return for him, so they have no reason to keep him alive."

"How about the fact that, hey, he's *sixteen*."

"You need to get that out of your head, Kris. Right now, he's our objective. Don't project anything else onto him. This kid is not Chip. Don't let yourself head in that direction."

"That direction," I said, just coming to the realization, "is why I need to be the one to quit. Because now that Chip *is* in my life, that's exactly where my head and my heart is going to go every single time."

~

In the last minute scramble to clear security with firearms, we were the last to board the flight from San Francisco to New York, and the last to board from New York to Germany. Dan's initial irritation over the paperwork was only tempered by knowing we weren't going to have to stuff ourselves into coach seats; the agency forked out enough for first class seats for this trip.

Ron grumbled about it; he didn't think we should all be on the same plane, and he especially didn't think we should all be seated together. Dan waved it off; the only unknown in the group was Doug, and the rest of us traveled together regularly.

We landed at night and took two cars to two different hotels; ostensibly Ron and Dan were there for meetings with several physicians, and Doug was there for educational purposes. I didn't need a cover; I was Ron's wife, traveling with him would not be odd. And while Dan had no issues traveling as a team, he didn't want us all at the same hotel; we would approach our objective location separately, taking different routes, so that we could each scope out the terrain, danger zones, and possible escape avenues.

Ron and I had just gotten married; why wouldn't we want to be off on our own, away from the boss and the eager new guy?

The approach was straightforward: Dan would make the initial contact with the agency's man on the ground, Ron and I would follow, trailed by Doug, whose job was essentially to observe and learn, and if necessary, to provide medical care for the teenager we intended to grab and run with.

On paper, this was an easy case. The boy's location was already known, we had someone on the inside watching him, and we knew that there were only two other people between our guy and the boy. We had an approximation of where he would be in the building we were headed for, and three possible ways out.

"Pizza cake," Dan said before we separated at the airport, something that over the years would be a very tired and too often said joke that he knew had crossed the line from almost amusing to shut-up-already. "We grab the kid and head for the embassy. We'll be back on a plane home tomorrow night."

Ron and I had an early enough breakfast at the hotel to allow for plenty of time; he always opted for precision in timing, never wanting to leave or arrive at any set point with more than a minute's leeway. We left on foot, walking hand in hand, looking like nothing more than two tourists setting out to take in the city, and I knew that he would be able to gauge how much we either needed to slow down or speed up at any given point, so that we would be where Dan wanted us to be at the time he wanted us to be there.

There was no taking the time to enjoy any of the sights; any looking we did was observation, making sure we weren't being followed and making sure we didn't look like we were expecting to be followed. This was something Ron was good at; he couldn't tell you what he'd just eaten for breakfast, but he could tell you what the people behind him looked like, what they were wearing, and how close they were. A week later he would be able to recite, in excruciating detail, every element of the assignment that he was involved in, from the way some woman's hair moved in the breeze to who said what and to whom.

So, when we were within sight of the building we'd headed for, I wasn't caught off guard when his pace suddenly quickened, but I was surprised when he broke out into a run, getting thirty feet in front of me before my brain engaged and I followed.

I tried to take in what he had seen in a heartbeat: Dan Martin on the ground, scrambling to get up, the blood on the sidewalk, and a struggle between two men that ended when the one with his back to us struck the other with a punch to the throat so hard and swift that blood gushed from his nose and he dropped, eyes wide in surprise, to the ground.

Before he turned around, before Dan could get up, clutching his wounded leg, Ron stopped short, his feet skittering on the sidewalk.

I made it half a step further, but then came to the same abrupt stop as Ron had.

It wasn't possible.

It was Chip.

~

Dan struggled to get to his feet; he had one hand pressed into his thigh, blood seeping between his fingers. Chip was bouncing on his toes, ready to keep fighting, but when he saw Dan trying to get up, he reached for Dan's arm and pulled him upright before Ron could take another step.

Doug was running up from behind; he hadn't yet noted Chip's presence, he was too busy fumbling with his backpack, trying to get to the things he would need to help Dan.

Dan hobbled to the door and leaned against the wall, and as he sucked in breath he said, "Inside. Grab him and go."

Chip didn't hesitate; he reached down and grabbed him by the front of his shirt and lifted, dragging him through the door. Ron and Doug quickly followed, and by the time I got inside Chip had let go of the shirt, leaving him in a heap on the floor.

Doug was cutting Dan's slacks away from his leg before anyone could get a word out, shoving gauze into the gaping wound.

"What the fuck, Chip?" Ron managed.

Through gritted teeth Dan managed, "Not now. He just saved my ass. We've lost our contact, and we still have to find that boy."

"He's not here?" I asked, torn between wanting to know how and why Chip was there, Dan's oozing wound, and the job.

"Not sure."

Chip was looking around, slowly spinning on the balls of his feet as he took everything in. The building was an old warehouse, at one point used for heavy machinery manufacturing. Open from the ground up, there were walkways lining the upper levels, but in every place where there should have been stairs or ladders there was a gaping hole.

I followed Chip's gaze up to the ceiling, to the heavy chains dangling from bolt points above.

"Who are you looking for?" he asked.

"Sixteen year old boy," Ron answered, clicking back into the job. "Brown hair, brown eyes, roughly five feet six inches and a hundred five to a hundred fifteen pounds. Reported to be somewhat baby faced. Short hair. Favors ripped jeans and Converse basketball shoes. Stutters under stress and his voice still cracks."

"And that's the short version," Chip guessed. "Where's he supposed to be?"

"Here. Northwest corner office, but..." Ron gestured to the

emptiness around us. "Obviously there are no offices here."

"Not here." Chip pointed up. "Up there."

We looked in the direction he was gesturing to. In the dim light I could make out a line of dirty windows on one wall, the space between each punctuated by a door.

"No way up," Dan groaned through clenched teeth.

"There's always a way to get where you want to go," Chip said, still looking up and around. He reached for one of the chains anchored to the ceiling and gave it a tentative tug, testing it for movement. "It's on a pulley, but it's probably rusted into place." He looked over at Doug. "He patched up enough that you could spot me?"

"Chip, no," Ron started.

Doug had a grip on one of the chains and Chip had begun to climb. "Relax, Ron. Think of this as the gym class I'm no longer taking."

"Fucking, no!" Ron hissed.

Chip was steadily working his way up, however, and there was nothing Ron could do to stop him. While Doug held the other side of the chain steady, keeping it from moving in the pulley, we watched as Chip shimmied up the chain like a six foot tall monkey, the clinking links echoing all around us.

"How the hell did he get here?" Ron asked of no one in particular.

"Damned if I know," Dan said. "I approached the building from the opposite side of the street, thought I was seeing our guy, next thing I know I've got a knife at my throat and Chip is getting between us. I caught someone's elbow to my jaw and the knife dropped into my leg...you saw the rest. Chip took him down like he was fending off a toddler."

"He followed us," I said under my breath, watching as he swung the chain to get a grip on a railing three floor-heights up. "How the hell did he follow us?"

"How the hell did he follow *me*?" Dan wanted to know. "I never saw him, never guessed anyone was there."

"That was sloppy," Ron accused.

"No shit."

Doug was still hanging onto the chains, eyes locked on Chip's every movement. "Kris, do they always state the obvious?"

"Usually."

"And I have how many more years of it?"

Chip had grabbed the railing and peeled away from the chain, creeping along the outside edge of the walkway with only a toe-hold and handgrip keeping him there. Doug let go of the chain and walked towards the area where, if Chip fell, he would land.

"Rotted wood," Doug said. He's got nothing to walk on."

I glanced at Ron; he looked as if he wanted to throw up, and when Chip reached the end of the railing and lifted himself over it, carefully shuffling across the few bare boards that remained, he had to look away.

Chip paused there for a moment, gesturing for quiet, as he strained to listen for anything other sounds. With a slight hand gesture to his right, he slid carefully, barely raising his feet as he moved, until he was in front of a door.

In one smooth move he opened the door and slid in.

"Son of a bitch," Ron muttered. "What the hell does he think he's doing?"

There was no answer, but even if one of us had one, it would have been lost in the explosion of dirt-caked class, the man that flew through it with arms and legs flailing as he fell three flights, and the sickening thud as he slammed into the concrete floor.

As if there might be question, Doug kneeled down to check his pulse, but he didn't even bother telling us the result. He might have been alive on the way down, but he was dead on impact.

Ron was grasping for the chains, trying to figure out how Chip had scaled them so easily.

"Gym class rope climb," Doug said. "Good luck with that."

Ron tested his strength with a few heavy pulls, and realized he'd never make it even halfway up.

"Why are we all just standing here?" I finally asked. "Find a damned access point. We need to get up there and make sure Chip is all right and has a fast way down."

"Just not as fast as this guy, though," Doug mused.

I wanted to move, to find a back way up, stairs or a ladder or a ramp. But I was as rooted in place as Ron was, wanting nothing more than to see Chip come back out the way he had gone in. Alive. Unhurt.

Just when I thought I could finally move, he crept carefully back out the door, the thin arms and legs of a much smaller boy wrapped around his neck and his waist.

Chip reversed his way up, and every few sliding steps I could hear him say, "Hold on tight, don't look down. Just hold on tight."

I held my breath when he reached the chains; he didn't have an easy reach and Doug couldn't swing them all the way to Chip's outstretched hand. With a deep breath, Chip finally jumped for it, sliding quickly with the added weight pulling him down, until he could get his legs wrapped around it to control his descent.

The moment his feet hit the floor Doug was reaching for Chip's unhappy passenger, who was in tears and hiccupping with the effort to breathe.

He was short, with jet-black hair, and was no older than eight.

We had the wrong kid.

~

"He was the only one up there," Chip said, looking up and around. "I figured he had to be the one, since he was tied to a damned chair."

Doug was still holding the sobbing boy under the arms, not sure what to do with him. Before he could set him down I reached out; Doug didn't have to move—the little boy latched onto me, wrapping his arms and legs around me, faced buried against my shoulder.

"You're all right," I whispered against his hair. "We'll take care of you."

Chip was still scanning the levels above us, concentrating hard, and just as I as was about to ask Ron why his son was doing his job, Chip's head cocked just ever so slightly, and he shoved me towards the front door, hissing at Ron to grab Dan and go.

We ran, hitting the door at the same time as a hail of fuel soaked, fire-lit bottles smashed onto the floor, and we didn't stop running until we were several blocks away.

"Mother fucker," Chip blurted out when we stopped. "What the hell was that all about?"

Ron was wheezing and couldn't answer, and I just glared at him.

"Sorry, kid," Chip said to the boy still wrapped around me. "You'll hear worse."

He was past crying, breathing hard, and his fingers were clenching at my shirt, legs wrapped around my waist so hard I was sure I'd have bruises in the morning.

"Get me to a damned phone," Dan told Ron. Blood was oozing through the bandage on his leg, but he pushed Doug back when he went to look at it. "You two," he said, gesturing to Chip and Doug, "take them back to Kris's hotel, find the closest coffee shop or bistro, calm the kid down, and wait for us. See if you can get him to talk, find out who he is."

Ron was torn; if he could have, he would have shoved Dan toward Doug, grabbed Chip by his neck, and dragged him off to find out how the hell and why the hell he was there.

We fell into line and headed back toward the hotel. I wanted to hand the boy off to one of them—he was starting to feel like an anchor—but I doubted he would go to either of them and I didn't want him to panic. By the time we reached the hotel he had stopped crying and had lessened his death grip on me, enough that I could get him to lean back and look at me.

His face was red and puffy from the strain of crying so hard, his upper lip slick with snot, wet eyelashes lumped together. He flinched when Chip put a hand on his back, but he didn't try to pull away and he looked at Chip, relief flooding his face when he realized that it was just the guy who had saved him.

"You hungry, kid? When was the last time you had something to eat?"

He shrugged in response.

"Gonna tell us your name?"

This time he nodded.

"I'm Chip. The lady you're with is my stepmom, her name is Kris. And this guy"—he gestured to Doug—"is my friend Doug. Those other guys you saw? One's my Dad and the other is his friend

Dan. They went to see if they could find someone who can help us."

"Nicky," he finally whispered.

"Nicky, do you think you can stand up by yourself now? I think Kris's arms are getting tired."

"I'm fine," I said, but Nicky nodded and wiggled out of my grasp and went straight for Chip.

"Hey, I'm not picking you up. You're a big guy. What are you, twelve or thirteen?"

"Seven."

"Seven," Chip repeated. "All right. If you were eight, I'd make you walk, but seven? Come on." He reached down and picked Nicky up as if it was something he did every day, and I was marveling at how calm he was with the boy until I remembered he had a lot of practice with his little brother.

"Food," Doug said, gesturing towards the café next to the hotel. "Get him a scone or donut or something."

"Well, that's nutritious," Chip deadpanned. "How about it, Nicky? Are you allowed to eat stuff like donuts?"

He nodded eagerly.

"You wouldn't lie to me, would you?"

He shook his head, but was beginning to relax, and he almost smiled.

The café was quiet and we took a table towards the back. Doug sat with his back to the wall, facing the door; without being reminded he knew he needed to focus on every person coming and going, making mental notes to relate back to Dan later.

Chip put Nicky onto a chair between him and Doug, the table between Nicky and the door. It was deliberate, almost instinctive, and I wondered if he realized how much he was getting right.

Once Nicky had food in front of him and a promise from Chip that he could have more if he wanted, I started asking questions, trying to find out who he was and why he was being held in that building, tied to a chair. He wasn't who we expected, but he was obviously who we needed to find. All he could tell me was his name—Nicky Lockhart—that he was seven years old, and his parents were Phillip and Bree Lockhart. He'd been taken from his school playground "a long, long time ago," which Chip determined to have been roughly two weeks, and that he didn't know where he was or who he had been with.

But, "they were really mean."

I wanted him to define "mean" but Chip went in another direction.

"Were you the only kid they had, Nicky? Was there anyone else?"

He nodded, a barely perceptible tilt of his head.

"Can you tell me about him?"

"His name is Jordan," Nicky said quietly. "He wouldn't let them hurt me, but I don't know where he is now. They made him leave me. Then I had to leave."

"Did they take you far? I mean, did it take a long time or short time to get from there to where I found you in the chair?"

"Short time," he replied, reaching for another scone. "Can I really have two?"

"Sure, knock yourself out. Did they take you in a car, or did you walk?"

"Car. But only for a minute."

Doug's eyes flicked from the front door to me and then back again. That split second said much: we'd been watched. They knew to expect us. Nicky was bait.

"So what school did you go to?" Chip asked. "Do you live near here?"

"Nuremburg elementary. I'm in the second grade."

Chip looked up at me. "I don't know German geography. Is Nuremburg far from here?"

"Not terribly far. There's an American school there, too."

"Nicky, did Jordan say what school he went to?"

"Munich, I think."

"Munich is closer," I said.

"Are you gonna help Jordan, too?" Nicky asked Chip.

"Yep, we're going to find him and help him, too. But first we have to get you back to your mom and dad." He looked to me for confirmation, and I nodded. "I think that's what my dad is doing. He's trying to find a way to get in touch with yours, and then someone will take you home."

"Will you take me home?"

I wanted him to say yes—if Chip escorted Nicky home, he'd be away from the rest of this assignment—but Chip shook his head and said carefully, "I think I need to stay here and try to help Jordan. But I promise you, my dad will make sure that whoever takes you home is nice."

For a moment, I thought Nicky was going to start crying again, but he sniffed once and then said, "Okay."

Chip peppered him with fairly innocent questions for the next fifteen minutes; I would have struggled to keep Nicky talking but Chip kept him going, even laughing, until Ron and Dan stepped through the door. I started to get up, but Nicky jumped up on his chair and shouted, "Did you call my dad? Is he coming?"

I couldn't tell if the pained look on Dan's face was because of the wound on his leg or that he didn't want Nicky drawing attention to us.

"We're going to take you to someone who will make sure you get home," Ron told him. His voice was even and calm, just reassuring enough to get Nicky to notch his sudden excitement down a level. "Can you walk? Were you hurt?"

"I'm okay." Nicky turned to Chip and asked, "But will you carry me?"

"Sure. Piggy back, ok? You're a big guy and you don't want me to carry you like a baby, right?"

"Right!"

Ron's jaw clenched; he hadn't intended for Chip to go any further.

"He'll feel safer with Chip," I whispered to him as we left the café. "He trusts him. The rest of us are a little too scary, I think."

Chip had Nicky on his back and was ahead of us by about ten feet, with Dan on one side of him and Doug on the other. He kept lifting up on the balls of his feet, making Nicky giggle, and Dan turned to look at them, the hard near-grimace he'd had softening.

"Did he tell you how he got here?" Ron asked.

"I didn't even try to go there. We were more concerned with calming Nicky down and getting some basic information from him."

"Nicky Lockhart," Ron said. "Dan's liaison was surprised to hear about him. They've been looking for him somewhere else."

"Whoever took him also has the other boy," I told him.

"The agency had two teams on them. They're aware of a connection but Intel had them in different locations."

"We were made, Ron," I told him. "That little boy was used as bait and now we can be fairly sure they've seen us and know who we are."

"We'll get recalled on this one," he guessed.

"No further information then?"

"Cold trail." He kept looking ahead, never at me, scanning the people ahead of Chip and Nicky. "Whoever they had on the inside..."

"Was he flipped or made?"

"Don't know. If I had to guess, I'd say he was made and is probably dead now."

"Wonderful. What's the end game then? Just kidnapping a couple of American kids for the hell of it?"

"They may have a point to prove. It could be a warning. If they can get to our kids, they can get to other people. It won't be our job this time to find out, we just have to find the kid unless they pull us back and send someone else."

"If we knew the reason, it would help—"

I stopped when I could feel him practically twitch beside me, and followed his gaze. He was looking at Chip's backside, and the spread of wetness down his shirt and onto his jeans. Nicky had started to squirm, squealing "Him, him, him!"

Without prompting, Chip did an about face and began trotting back toward the hotel, while Ron and Doug took off on foot. Dan pointed me in Chip's direction with the order to get them someplace safe, and he followed Ron, limping horribly.

Chip was running at a measured clip, one arm behind him as he braced Nicky's soaked bottom, his other hand clasping Nicky's arms. "Did you check out yet?" he asked easily, not minutely out of breath.

"Not yet."

"Then we're heading straight for your room. You go first and I'll follow."

One glance at his face and I could see him calculating: send

Kris in to make sure the room hasn't been messed with, err on the side of her experience, but get Nicky out from hundreds of prying eyes that might be watching our every move.

We ran past the front desk and up the stairs, two at a time, until we were in the hallway leading to Ron's and my room. Chip slowed to a walk and let me go ahead, allowing me the time I needed to check the entire room, and he didn't bring Nicky in until I told him it was all clear.

As I helped him peel Nicky off, I realized that by pushing me forward, Chip was taking control, and he did it as easily as tying his own shoes.

Nicky wasn't letting go easily; between terror and embarrassment, he wanted to stay glued to Chip's back with his face buried against his neck. He kept his fingers wound tightly around Chip's shirt until Chip finally said, "Man, let go. I'd have pissed myself, too. Hell, I almost did."

Nicky finally let go and squirmed away from me.

"Seriously," Chip said. "That was one ugly, freaky guy. He was one of them, wasn't he?"

Nicky nodded.

"You're allowed to be scared, man. You can even cry if you need to."

"I'm wet now," Nicky said, choking back the tears he was determined to not shed.

"So am I. We'll dry. We'll stink, but we'll dry."

"Hey," I said gently.

Nicky wasn't bothered by it. "Will your dad beat him up?"

"Something like that," Chip said. "Maybe he can find out where Jordan is, and then we can go back out and get you to your mom and dad."

"Can I call my mom?"

Before Chip could say anything, I answered, "Nicky, sweety, we're in a different city than your Mom and the phone number probably wouldn't work. We don't know what prefix to use."

Chip winked at him and said, "That means she's too cheap to pay for a long distance call."

"You sound like my mom," he said to me.

"I'm going to take that as a compliment." I went over to the window to see how much of the surrounding area we would be able to watch. The street was lined with shops and restaurants, and stretched too far for me to be able to see to either end.

Almost directly across the street, though, was a small department store. I pointed it out to Chip, and told him to run over there and get Nicky some dry clothes, anything he thought might fit. Chip started to protest; he didn't want to leave me alone, because who knows what might happen, and someone needed to be there to protect me.

"Protect me? Please tell me you didn't just say that."

"I'm bigger and stronger—"

"And I'm armed and quite good with a weapon. This is what I do, Chip, and I've never been on the losing end. Just go, and make it quick. I'll be able to watch from here."

He hesitated, and then held his hand out. "I'll need cash."

"Like you don't have any," I mused. "Nicky, do you know what sizes you wear?"

"Huh?"

"Your jeans, big guy," Chip said. "And your underwear. What size?"

Nicky shrugged.

I started to tell Chip to just guess, but he had Nicky back on his feet and folded back the waistband on his jeans.

"European sizes," I warned.

"I'll ask."

I watched from the window, and against my better judgment let Nicky watch with me. It was that, I thought, or push him from being nervous to frantic, and as long as he knew where Chip was, he was as close to being fine as I could expect.

"You're his stepmom," Nicky said as Chip ran across the street.

"Yes, I am." I hadn't thought of myself that way, but for Nicky's sake, it was the easiest way to explain what Chip was to me.

"Does he have any kids?"

"Chip? No, he's only sixteen. He's too young to have kids."

That we know of, anyway.

"Jordan is sixteen. Chip looks older than Jordan."

Up until Jordan was snatched, Chip probably had the harder life.

We stayed at the window for another twenty minutes, long enough for me to start to worry, until Chip was back out and running across the street again, bags in hand. It was another three minutes before he was at the room door, knocking gently, and before I opened he said, "Just me, Kris."

"Prove it," I said, just to annoy him.

"You own this killer purple lace teddy—"

I pulled the door open before he could go any further, and he was standing there, grinning like an idiot.

"I got you some sweatpants," he said to Nicky, "and a t-shirt and sweatshirt." He handed the bag to Nicky and thumbed toward the bathroom. "Take a shower, kiddo, you'll feel a lot better."

Nicky frowned. "A shower?"

"Or bath, your choice."

I had the feeling that any other time Nicky would have argued, but he was getting itchy in his wet clothing and there was no denying that he was starting to smell.

So was Chip, for that matter.

Once the shower was running, I pulled a chair up to the window so that I could still keep an eye on the street, and so that Chip could strip down and wash off, changing into clothes he had thought to get for himself, too. When he was done changing I pointed to another chair. I knew he wouldn't bolt, but talking to him would be easier if he wasn't pacing the room like a prisoner.

"Spill it, mister," I said. "How did you find us?"

"I followed you. Well, I followed you first, but wound up trailing Doug and Dan."

"Dammit, Chip, how? How did you even know where to start?"

He'd overheard Ron and me talking about the assignment, and after we went to bed he looked at the file we'd left on the table. From that he knew what flight we'd be on, where we'd connect to the next, even what seats we'd be in on both flights. In the end, he decided to trail Doug, thinking it would be easier and he'd be in a lot less trouble if he were caught.

"You're in so much trouble I don't even know where to begin."

"But you made it so easy," he said, as if that was a valid excuse. "I was right there in coach but none of you ever spotted me."

"But why? You were supposed to go back to Grant's."

"He wanted me to stay at Ron's while you were gone. Said you'd never know. And then I heard you guys talking and realized neither of you was doing what you said you were...I wanted to know. I wanted to see it for myself. I mean, Ron being a spy explains a lot."

"He's not a spy," I sighed. "Jesus, Chip, he's going to ground you for the rest of your life."

"If he's not a spy, then what is he?"

I wasn't sure I could, or even should explain it, but the fact that Chip was here—he needed some kind of answer. "Thief? Bounty hunter? Our jobs extend into several different directions. Sometimes we do what the other intelligence agencies won't because of politics. Sometimes we work alongside them. But we're not spies."

"So you're not like the CIA?"

"No, we're not."

"Military?"

"Sometimes we work with the military, but no. Chip, you can ask a hundred questions, but you've never heard of the agency, and you probably shouldn't know much more."

"Well, you guys can't be too good at it. I mean, I followed Dan and he never knew it, not until I was pulling that dipwad off him. He walked right up to the guy and was totally surprised by the attack."

"And you dropped him like he was nothing," I mused. "Where did you learn to fight like that?"

"I practiced on a nun."

"Funny. And the guy you sent crashing through the window?"

"Sidekick to his midsection. That was just simple physics. If we'd been on ground level he would have popped right back up to come at me again."

I wanted him to realize the enormity of what he'd done; two men dead in a fifteen-minute time span. In the years I'd worked for the agency, my kill rate was one, and that was with more reluctance than I cared to admit to.

I had a lot more I wanted to say to him, but the water had shut off and Nicky stumbled out of the bathroom in sweatpants that were just a little too big, and a t-shirt that was a lot too big.

"I didn't know what to do with my other stuff," he said, filled with uncertainty.

"I'll rinse your clothes out, don't worry about it."

He shuffled over to Chip, putting his hands on Chip's knees. "Can I sit on your lap?"

Before Chip had "Sure" completely out, Nicky was climbing onto him, where he curled up with his head resting on Chip's shoulder. He looked like he was only four or five in that moment, still terrified, and a stray thought away from sticking his thumb into his mouth.

"Tired?" Chip asked him. "I bet you've been sleeping like shit lately. You can take a nap if you want."

"I don't take naps. I'm seven."

"Come on. I'm sixteen and I would take a nap in a heartbeat if I could." He craned his neck to look at Nicky's face. "Real men sleep when they need it, Nicky. That way they're rested enough to take care of business when it's time."

"You would really take a nap?"

"Hell, yeah."

"So take one."

"It's your turn right now," Chip said softly. "Right now it's my turn to take care of you, and make sure nothing happens while you sleep. I'm going to make sure that those guys that had you don't get to you again. We'll just stay here where it's quiet, and I'll keep an eye on you. Okay?"

"Okay."

I thought Chip was going to get up and set him on the bed, but he tightened his arms around the little boy and let him drift off right there. I wondered how many times he'd done just that with David, but then realized David probably was too big for this, that the chances he'd ever curled up on Chip's lap were slim.

He was saying all the things to Nicky that he had wanted said to him. Every gentle word that came out of his mouth was a wish for the boy that he'd been.

I stared out the window, watching for Ron, and tried desperately not to cry.

~

An hour later Nicky was sound asleep, still curled up on Chip's lap, and Chip had barely moved. We spoke in whispers; Chip asked questions about the agency and I answered as best I could, without giving him too much information. He wanted to know how I got the job, surprised at the idea of legacy employment; I could only tell him that Ron had joined a few months before he was born, but Doug and I were brought into it, and that I didn't know what it would eventually mean for him.

He didn't ask the questions I know he wanted to — the danger, the kill rate, the specifics — in deference to the little boy he was holding, who might have his eyes closed even if he was starting to wake. I was touched by his sensitivity, and ready to forget and forgive that he wasn't supposed to be there in the first place.

"Is this why Ron left me with Grant?" Chip asked eventually. "To keep me out of it?"

I didn't know, and had to be as honest about that as I could. "I think his relationship with your mother and with Grant was a few steps beyond complicated. He's probably got a dozen reasons why, but he's starting to let go of those. We'll find a way to make it work, I promise."

"What happens to him now?" he asked, nodding toward Nicky. "We don't take him home, do we?"

"You could," I pointed out. "You could be his escort. He would feel safe with you and you could be the one to hand him over to his mother."

For a moment, I know Chip wanted to. But he sighed and said, "I told him I would help the other kid."

"That's not your job, Chip. And I don't know that you'll be given a choice. You could end up cuffed and stuffed until we get back."

"In English."

"Shoved into the back of another agent's car and held at the embassy until we've completed the assignment. Or shipped stateside right away. You should be sent home, you know."

"Am I in legal trouble?"

"I don't know. Ron has enough clout that even if you are he can probably get you out of it, but Chip...he's pissed off. I mean really angry."

"That's nothing new."

"It doesn't roll off you the way you want everyone to think," I said.

"It doesn't bother me as much as you think," he countered. He then nodded toward the window. "Ron's coming up the street."

I turned and looked in the direction he was gesturing. Ron was walking a few steps ahead of a still limping Dan; I know he was looking in every direction he could, but from where I sat he simply looked like a businessman heading towards his hotel.

Before he could knock on the door, though, I got up and opened it carefully, motioning for them to both be quiet.

"He's asleep," I said. "Let's keep it that way as long as we can."

Dan nodded; he just wanted to get inside and off his feet. The bandage Doug had slapped on his leg was bright red and blood had started to drip down his slacks. The agony of it was dancing in his eyes, and his face was beginning to pale.

"Where's Doug?"

"He'll be here in a minute. He'll come from the other way."

"Did you get the bastard?"

Ron glanced over at Chip and Nicky, who was obviously still deeply asleep. "He was useful," Ron said. "We know where to look now."

I didn't ask what they had done with him, because I didn't want the off chance that the boy would hear.

"We have backup coming," Dan said through clenched teeth. "And his parents are on their way."

"Chip's been very good with him," I told Dan, mostly for Ron's benefit. "I don't think I could have kept him as calm."

"He's good with little kids," Ron said absently, watching his son.

"Then he won't mind leaving with the kid's parents," Dan said.

Chip turned his head at that, but didn't say anything.

"He's staying with us," Ron said. "If we let him out of our

sight, there's no telling where he'll go. One of us with him, always."

"We're not goddamned babysitters, Gallery," Dan hissed.

"Apparently we are. We were sent here after a kid, after all."

I pointed at Dan, and then at Ron. "Don't start anything right now. I swear, if you wake him up…"

"How long until his parents get here?" Chip asked. "Will we be able to stay with him until they do?"

Ron shook his head. "We turn him over to the backup team, Chip. He'll be all right."

"But—"

Ron crossed the room and sat in the chair I'd been in, close enough to Chip that their knees touched. "We can't wait for them. As soon as the backup gets here, we hand him over, and they'll take him to the military base in Munich. His parents will meet him there. I promise, he'll be fine."

"How do you know you can trust them?"

"Because I know them, son. I specifically requested them. Their team leader is a female about my age and she's very good with small children. He'll feel like he's with someone's grandmother, and she'll earn his trust before they're five miles out. She knows what to do and what to say, and what to bring to distract him."

"He'll need to eat," Chip murmured.

"We'll make sure they know," Ron said.

"And don't tell them he peed all over me. He won't want anyone to know that."

I stepped up behind him and placed a kiss on the top of his head. "He's going home to his parents, Chip," I said quietly. "Once you tell him that, he'll be fine. And he'll never forget you, the person who saved his life, and then made him feel both important and safe. I promise."

"I just want to make sure he's okay, that's all."

"He will be. And you promised him you'd help Jordan. If you don't let him go with the backup team, he'll wonder why you didn't go help his other friend."

"He's just so little."

"From here on out he'll be safe every step of the way. You did that for him."

He craned his head back to try to look at me, and in that moment he seemed so young. "Will we ever know for sure that he gets home all right?"

"I'll ask them to notify me," Ron said.

Nicky stirred at the sudden rapping on the door; Ron got up quickly to let Doug in, but by the time he closed it the boy's eyes were open, and he was stretching against Chip. He was quiet for a minute, and no one moved in case we startled him.

Chip tightened his arms around Nicky and whispered, "Hey, guess what? You're gonna get to see your mom and dad soon."

"Are they here?" he asked sleepily.

"Not yet. But my dad talked to some of his friends, and they're going to come here and get you and take you to your parents in just a little bit."

"You're not going?"

"No. Remember, I said I'd go get Jordan?"

Nicky nodded.

"I have to go do that. But there's a really nice lady"—he looked to Ron for a visual conformation—"and she's going to come get you. My dad knows her and says that you'll like her."

"Is she your friend?" Nicky asked Ron.

"I've known her longer than Chip has been alive," Ron said, skirting the issue.

Nicky leaned back to get a better look at Chip's face. "Can we get something to eat first? I'm hungry."

"Tell you guys what," I said, patting Chip's shoulders. "Let's give Doctor Doug a chance to look at Dan's leg, and we can all go downstairs and get something to eat."

Nicky slid off Chip's lap. "I hafta pee first," he announced, his feet patting on the carpet as he walked past the bed where Dan was stretched out. "Are you a real doctor?" he asked Doug.

"Are you a real little boy?" Doug countered.

"I'm not little!"

"He's a doctor," Chip said. "But he's also a doofus. Go to the bathroom and we'll go eat in a minute."

Before we left the room, Dan lifted his head and said to Ron, "Send one of them up here before they take off with the kid. I think

I'll be going with them. I'm no use to you right now."

Ron was in charge from this point on.

In the coffee shop we sat quietly at the table while Chip and Nicky chattered on; I know Ron wanted to pump the boy for as much information as he could, but he instead listened carefully to the questions Chip was asking Nicky and the answers he was getting. Chip peppered Nicky with questions about the things he was interested in, what he did at school and the games he and his friends played when they were just hanging out.

They played baseball in the spacious yard that stretched between two military housing apartment buildings, but his favorite thing was when the downstairs neighbor was home and working on his motorcycle. It was a purple Norton Commando that he'd bought after a friend wrecked it and became too chicken to ride, so he was putting it back together, and on the days that it ran, Nicky and his friends got rides around the neighborhood.

Chip latched onto that. "I have a friend who has an old Triumph. We ride it all over the place. It's a ton of fun, isn't it?"

Nicky nodded, but some of the joy was sucked out of him.

"When was the last time you got to ride on one?"

"Couple days ago," Nicky said, now not all that interested.

"Really? Can you tell me what the bike looked like? Was it like the Norton?"

"Naw. It was a messed up bike. It was kinda brown and green but not like it was nice. Like it was old."

"Do you remember what kind it was?"

"I dunno. But it had a sidecar on it sometimes. And the guy who rode it didn't do it good. He made it jerk a lot, and he could hardly touch the ground with his feet."

"Eh, I don't like sidecars. They take the fun out of leaning a bike over."

Nicky leaned forward and said almost conspiratorially, "That part scares me sometimes."

"It used to scare me a little, but it's still fun. Did Jordon get to ride at all?"

"Yesterday, I think. He was in the sidecar and he wasn't happy about it."

"I wouldn't like it, either."

He had more to say, but turned toward the door when Ron did; two men came in followed by a middle-aged woman dressed in slacks and a bright red blazer. I didn't know her personally, but I knew who she was and how far up the agency ladder she'd climbed.

Linda Jackson, formidable and fierce, and Dan's equal in every way. She'd slid into a team leader position just before Ron joined the agency, and she held onto it with a tenacity that pushed people into two camps: those who still couldn't cope with having a woman in charge, and those who trusted her with their lives.

Ron was in the latter camp. He'd worked with her in the past, and would work with her again without hesitation.

That was good enough for me; the fact that she was taking time to sidetrack from her own assignment to escort a frightened little boy to his parents scored points with me.

Nicky's willingness to go with her waned quickly, though, and he spent the five minutes it took to for them to go get Dan trying to convince Chip to go with him and to just let Ron and me help Jordan. He stood near the table with Chip, his arms wrapped around Chip's waist, trying desperately to persuade him that Jordan would be all right without him, but he didn't want to go with those strange people.

Chip gently pulled him away, and crouched down to get to Nicky's eye level. "This morning I was a stranger, too, Nicky. These people just want to help you get home, and I know my dad wouldn't have called someone that you should be afraid of. Just go with them, and in an hour or two you'll be with your mom and dad."

"But why can't you go?"

"Because I have to stay with my dad and my stepmom, Nicky. I'm just a kid, too, you know."

Nicky saw a man in front of him; he had a hard time grasping that Chip wasn't another grown up.

"But I don't *know* her," Nicky whispered harshly.

Chip picked him up, and took a step toward her. "Nicky, this is Mrs—"

"Jackson," she said. "But, Nicky, you can call me Linda."

"You're also going with Dan, too," Chip pointed out. "He helped save you."

"Yeah, but he wasn't very good at it," Nicky murmured.

Neither Chip nor I missed the slight flash of a grin that came and went on Linda Jackson's face. When Dan was there and ready to go, she held her arms out, and Chip reluctantly handed Nicky over to her.

"He just ate but he's kind of a bottomless pit," Chip told her.

"It's all right," she said to him, gently. "We'll make sure he gets a snack if he wants one, and we have books and toys for him in the car. He'll be fine."

Deep down Chip knew he would be, but that didn't keep him from watching as she left with Nicky in her arms, and it didn't keep Nicky from crying out Chip's name when they were no longer in sight of each other.

~

I expected an inquisition. We waited for Doug in the restaurant; he was clearing out the room, making sure nothing had been left behind, no traces of Dan's blood or Nicky's urine soaked clothing. Ron took five minutes to check us out of the hotel, and when he sat down at the table I fully expected him to begin grilling Chip, but instead he poured himself a cup of coffee, and waited quietly.

Chip was fidgeting, waiting for the first shoe to drop. He looked at me, at the table, out the window, anything but look at his father.

Ron was certainly looking at Chip, though. He stirred sugar into his coffee slowly, deliberately, keeping his eyes on his son's face, knowing that he was making Chip squirm.

It wasn't until Doug sat down that Ron spoke.

"Where did you get a passport?" he asked Chip.

Still, Chip couldn't look at him.

"I know Grant didn't arrange for it. We decided a long time ago to not give you the means to get any further from home than you already had. So how'd you do it?"

"It wasn't difficult," Chip said, reaching for defiance but sounding more defeated than anything.

"Is it even legal?"

With a sigh, Chip reached into his back pocket and fished it out, reluctantly handing it over.

"Well, now. You're eighteen years old, who would have guessed?" He tossed it onto the table. "If you're going to get a damned fake, you don't use your own name."

"It's not fake," Chip said. "The passport is real enough."

"Then?"

"Altered birth certificate. Fake ID."

"And you needed a passport, why?"

Finally, Chip looked up. "Because I figured someday I really would want to run."

Ron didn't press him on that. Instead, he held out his hand and said, "Let me see the ID card."

With a grimace, Chip dug it out of his wallet and handed it over, with a subdued, "I didn't bring my real license, you know, because it didn't match."

Ron examined the card carefully, running his fingers over the edges, lifting at the corners, and he checked for a hologram. He raised one eyebrow slightly, and from that I knew he was impressed.

"Whoever you got it from does passable work," Ron said. "It's not perfect, but it would pass most cursory inspections."

"And you would know?" Chip asked, genuinely curious.

"I would know. And from the quality of the work, I'm guessing you were approached, not that you went looking for a fake ID." He turned to me. "This is agency work. They've already tapped into him."

In every clichéd sense, my gut clenched and heart hurt.

How early did they start working us all?

"I just..." Chip fumbled, reaching for his ID card. "I mean, I just thought it was funny at the time. He was just some squirrely guy offering me a fake ID. I could use it to get beer and stuff."

"And at some point in the transaction he pointed out all the things you could do with it. Get a passport, cross the borders to get wasted and laid. Right?"

Chip nodded.

"You think they set him up for something just like this?" Doug asked.

"Not this assignment specifically," Ron said. "But at some point he was sure to follow."

How, I wanted to know. Ron was usually careful, and he had never wanted Chip to know exactly what we were and what we were doing.

"Why now?" Doug asked Chip.

"Why not? I was just curious. I thought I'd just follow and you'd never know I was there."

"Well," Ron slid away from the table, "you're here. You do exactly what I tell you to when I tell you. There will be no arguments, no second-guessing me. If you're going to get a good look at what I do, then look. But don't make me worry that you might do something to get yourself killed. I don't want to be distracted."

"Are you insane?" I sputtered, following him to the door. I turned and pointed to Doug and Chip, telling them to stay put, and went outside. "You *will* be distracted, Ron. So will I, and so will Doug. You should be furious with him, and you should have shoved him into that car with Nicky and with Dan."

"I didn't say I wasn't furious. I'm mad as hell at him, Kris."

"Then why?"

He folded his arms, and looked at me as if he was debating whether I rated an explanation or not. He was straddling the fine line between work and marriage, and wasn't sure which side he should move toward.

"He's staying because Dan wants him to," he finally said.

"Dan? Dan doesn't get a vote in this! And what the hell was all that upstairs, Dan wanting him to go?"

"There was no vote, and that exchange was for Chip's benefit. Dan made a clear point, and I didn't completely disagree with it, though Chip doesn't need to know that. Eventually he was going to be dragged into this, and it's better that this is the assignment he decided to butt in on. What if he'd followed us on the last one? We dodged bullets the entire way from the end point to the airport, and you still barely got us off the ground. What if he tries to follow on the next one, which could be far worse? We're tapped for a possible trip to Vietnam, do I want him trying to find his way there? This is benign in the grand scheme of things."

"Benign? He killed two people, Ron!"

"And in doing that he saved Dan's life and he rescued the

Lockhart kid. This is one of the easier assignments I've had in years, and if he's going to butt into it, it's better that it's this one than any other. And truthfully, this is giving me a chance to judge his instincts and his ability to follow orders when it really matters."

"Fine, you saw that. He has good instincts; he's strong and fast and may someday make for a very fine operative, but not now. Send him home."

"I'm giving him a chance. If I send him home, he'll resent it—"

"So fucking what? Let him resent it!"

"—and I lose even more influence over him. If he sees he has this as a future option, we can get him to fall in line, and get him to go back to school. You and I will do the work on the rest of this case and Doug will keep an eye on Chip. But he'll get to see what happens, he'll get an idea of what to expect, and we'll earn a little more of his trust."

"He is sixteen goddamned years old."

"And I'd like him to see seventeen. And then eighteen. If he comes after us on the next assignment, he might not."

"If something happens to him, you'll never forgive yourself."

He nodded, and knew that I meant if something happened to Chip, I'd never forgive him, either.

~

We walked. Ron was not opposed to public transportation or a taxi, but Chip pointed out that we weren't exactly unknowns at that point, and being in a bus or car left us potentially cornered. Ron knew the odds against that, but he liked the way Chip was thinking and deferred to the slim chance that we might ride our way into death.

It was a little more than a mile, Ron said. The teenager had been at the machinery warehouse that morning, but they moved him on the word of a tip they thought was reliable, taking him out of the industrial area of town into the heart of the business and retail district. He and Dan had the approximate location and a description of the building; after that it was up to us to find him.

Doug still wanted to know what use a teenager was to them, and more importantly, who were they?

"His name is Jordan Kennedy," Ron said. "His father is post commander at McGraw Kasern in Munich, and taking him has the theoretical endgame of exposing security flaws. If kids go missing, they can see how tight the perimeter becomes and weigh the changes against security as they've observed in the past. The problem is that the post itself and the housing area where the schools are located are separate entities, so securing both at the same time is problematic."

"So they just want to see how much trouble they can cause?" Doug asked.

"No, they want to see what they could get away with if they wanted," Chip said. "Kidnapping the commander's kid is prelude to terrorism. It's a fishing expedition."

"Then why take Nicky, too?" Doug asked.

Ron looked to Chip, seeing what he would cough up.

"Diversion. Spread the worry, spread the security forces. See how thin they can pull the military police, and how many holes can be easily punched in their security."

Ron nodded. "We may be looking at preliminary work of what the Baader-Meinhof Group has become."

"Red Army." Chip stopped in his tracks. "They'll kill that kid once they have what they need to know."

"Most likely."

Doug put his hand on Chip's shoulder, sensing, as I did, that he wanted to start running, to get there ten minutes ago. "Did you or Dan get any idea of the time frame we have to work with?"

"We probably have until late tonight, or tomorrow morning at the outset."

"You think he knows?" Chip asked. "Does he have any idea how much trouble he's in?"

"I have no doubt he's been told repeatedly that if they don't get what they want, he's dead," Ron told him. "I doubt they've told him he's dead no matter what."

"Why keep him alive at all?" I asked.

"Because, with him alive, they have leverage if needed, and there's no body that might be found before they're ready to make their statement."

"His body would be the statement," Chip said.

"It would be one hell of a statement," Ron said, gesturing for him to start walking again. "And to them, this is minor, just a diversion."

"They blow a lot of shit up, don't they?" Chip asked, though I doubt he expected an answer. "That kind of absolves some guilt on my end."

"You did what you had to do in the moment, Chip," Ron said. "It was either Dan living or Dan dying, and you picked the right one. Between Nicky's life and that of someone who had duct taped him to a chair, you did what was necessary."

"Please don't make it sound right."

"Don't get caught up in morals here. Sometimes, in the name of what's right you have to do some fairly despicable things."

"Have you?" he asked.

"More than I care to think about."

"You killed someone."

"I have done whatever I needed to in order to get the job done, son. And I won't tell you any more than that."

"You're one brutal son of a bitch when you have to be, aren't you?"

"I always try to be fair," Ron said.

If Chip wanted to pursue anything more, it would have to wait. We were at the location Ron had directed us to, looking for a grey four-story building with a large glass door framed in brass.

It described nearly every building on the street.

"Fuck," Doug said under his breath.

Ron was nonplussed; he soaked in the details, looking at each one from the street level to the top, his eyes narrow as he focused.

Chip glanced up and down the street, shrugged, and pointed to the building two down from the one we were standing in front of. "That one."

"Based on what?"

"Based on the Ural," he said, nodding in the general direction.

I still didn't see what he was motioning toward, but Ron had a smile tugging at the corners of his mouth and I knew he at least had a clue what Chip meant.

"Messed up old bike with a sidecar," Ron mused.

"That's got to be it."

"Close," Ron said. "Without being obvious, look to the building across the street, second floor, third window to the left of center."

It took everything I had to not turn my head and stare.

"Window's blocked," Chip said, and I wondered how he could have noted that without even a bare turn of his head. "Every other window has the blinds up. And it's not like a curtain or anything, it's like someone put a bookcase or something in its way."

"Why would anyone do that?"

"They either needed floor space because the room is small, or they're hiding something."

"And why would someone need extra floor space here?"

"They wouldn't," Chip said. "This is retail space, right? Or is there residential over the retail?"

"Office space, I think, but given our situation, I'd say we can presume someone is hiding something."

"Or they want us to think they are," Chip mused.

"Don't overthink it, son." He reached for my hand and pulled me closer. "Kris and I are going to walk into the next store. You and Doug keep walking. Get a good look at that bike, and then keep going. When you're a good three blocks down, cross the street and come back up this way."

"Enter when we get there?" Doug asked.

"Find the stairs, don't take an elevator. Head up to the second floor, but don't go past the entry until you know we're on the other end of the hallway. We'll determine exactly which door to kick in."

"Kick in?" Chip uttered. "Seriously? Can't you just knock?"

"Go on," Ron said. "Just follow Doug's lead."

We headed towards the next storefront, but before we went in Ron grabbed my hand and pulled me close. To anyone else, he was taking a moment to laugh with his wife, to steal a kiss and a hug; I knew better. He was watching Chip as he moved past the bike and beyond, and we didn't go inside until he was sure that Chip would do exactly what he'd been told.

Ron's demeanor had definitely changed; it wasn't surprising, as he often had a sharp divide between his work self and his at-home self, but still, I was in the mood to argue with him at a time when it was neither appropriate nor welcome. What I wanted to do was grab him and loudly remind him that he was sending his son into an unknown, risking his life for the life of someone else's son, but he knew that. He didn't need me to point out the obvious. He only needed me to do my job, which was to do exactly what he ordered.

We wandered in and out of several stores in a halfhearted effort to make it look like we were shopping, not easing our way across the street. Ron wanted to blend in, but I felt like we stuck out in the crowd, two human neon signs that blinked *Coming to Get You* with a precise drumbeat in timing.

When we reached the door of the building, Chip and Doug were making their way toward us, but Ron slipped inside and I followed; he turned left where the stairwell was to the right, and on autopilot found the back way up. From there it was a scramble; we took the stairs two at a time, and once in the hallway he walked ahead of me slowly, listening as he passed each office door.

He moved silently, and when he was halfway down the hall he pointed to Doug, then the door, and then to me.

We had two seconds to get there; he'd chosen the most likely office, and was going to barrel his way in, whether it was locked or not. My heart began a hard, steady beat; he was going to be the first in, the first target.

This was Dan's job, Dan should be the first in, and Chip should be on his way to Munich.

The door was locked, and in one fluid movement between trying to turn the doorknob and it not moving, Ron pivoted, cocked his leg, and plowed through the wood door. Doug and I reached him at the moment of impact, side arms drawn, and we followed him in.

Chip did as he was told; he stayed in the hallway and listened, watching as much as he could from where he stood.

We had the element of surprise; Jordan was seated in a chair by the blocked window with two guards nearby and a third who came running from our right side. Doug immediately went for the guard to Jordan's left and I took the right, leaving Ron to deal with the guard bolting towards him with gun drawn.

It was too easy; they were all down in less time than it took to take the five steps across the room. Doug had nearly re-holstered his weapon when we all heard it, the sound of feet thundering toward us from the right.

Chip heard it, too, and ran in, heading straight for Jordan. He ripped the duct tape away from Jordan's wrists and was working on his ankles when the first shot rang out, and he flinched, protectively blocking Jordan from what could have been a bullet meant for him.

He spun around, and saw what Doug and I did: Ron being rushed by someone half a foot shorter, gun aimed directly at Ron's face. I scrambled to take in the details, and the first thing that pricked at me was, *Where's Ron's gun?*

And then I spotted it, on the floor.

Chip was moving, one near-leap across the room, and as he went into the air he shouted, "Hit the floor!" and without a second thought, Ron dropped as Chip's foot plowed cleanly into the man's face.

He went down in a splatter of blood and began to gurgle as he struggled to breathe; Chip bent over, grabbed the front of his shirt and growled, "Your keys, mother fucker."

Ron was back up on his feet, his gun in hand, as Chip grabbed keys from the bleeding man's pocket. Doug and I were still fighting, and Ron had more to deal with, but all I could think was that Chip was a heartbeat away from getting shot.

"I've got the kid," Chip shouted above the din. He grabbed a wild-eyed Jordan and ran towards the door yelling, "Gym class!" as he headed down the hall.

It wasn't until I heard the door at the end of the hall slam shut that I stopped dividing my attention, and pulled the trigger on my own gun.

~

Flecked in blood, we ran for it.

Once we hit the street I made a mental note that the motorcycle was gone, but that was all I had time for. We raced up the street until Ron spotted a taxi, and we piled in, with Ron yelling at him in fluent German to just go and we'd tell him where in a minute.

"How the hell do we find Chip?" I breathed.

"Hotel," Doug guessed. "The restaurant?"

That seemed as likely a place as any, so Ron told the driver to take us within half a mile and tipped him generously when we got out of the cab. We walked the rest of the way; I was certain everyone we passed could see how hard I was shaking, but outwardly Ron was still calm and collected, and if not for the streaks of red on his shirt, no one could guess that anything was wrong.

We walked quickly, at a near jog, until we were in the sightline of the hotel. We peeked into cafés along the way, and Ron sent Doug—who was the least bloodied of us all—to look in the restaurant.

He came out less than a minute later, shaking his head.

"He doesn't know the area at all," I said. "Where the hell would he have gone?"

"What was it he was yelling when he was on his way out?" Ron asked.

"Something about gym class."

Both Ron and Doug grinned.

"Gym class rope climb," Doug said. "He headed for the warehouse."

"Wouldn't that have burned down?" I asked Ron, falling into step beside him.

"Not likely. It was a concrete floor in a concrete building that had been stripped a long time ago. There was nothing there to burn, other than the fuel that was in those bottles. I suspect Chip is hedging his bets on them having abandoned it after we took Nicky."

"You'd better pray he's not wrong."

There was a veiled threat in there somewhere, but I wasn't sure what it was or even what I'd meant by it.

Chip had ditched the Ural a quarter mile from the warehouse, leaving us to wonder if he'd gone all the way there or stopped short, just in case. We kept a close watch around us, looking for anything that might suggest he was hiding in plain sight. Ron banked on Chip heading straight for the warehouse, opting to not, as he'd been told earlier, overthink things.

Ron trusted Chip's gut instinct; all I wanted was Chip away from all of this, and it kept pounding in my head.

We stopped when we reached the warehouse; I was itching to go in but Ron asked for one more look around. I wasn't sure what he was looking for, but I looked up and down the street, trying to see if there was anywhere else Chip might have gone. Doug, on the other hand, was staring at the door as if it was going to melt right in front of us.

"He's in here," Doug said after a minute. Very carefully, he ran a finger down the crack between the door and its frame, just above the latch. He pulled out a small piece of laminated paper and handed it to Ron.

"The corner of his ID card," Ron said, impressed.

We entered quietly; with the dimming outside light, the inside of the warehouse was even darker, and none of us could easily see more than a few feet ahead. We weren't going to call out to him, but instead rooted into place just inside the door, listening. The sounds of outside traffic were muted, and the smell inside was of burnt plastic, strong enough to make me want to go back outside just for a breath of fresh air.

Dead silence. Either Chip was that good, or he wasn't there. All I could hear was a car going by outside, and I listened, waiting to see if it stopped, and waiting for the sound of a car door closing.

The quiet stretched on for a good five minutes, until it was broken by a muffled sniff. We all turned toward it; it came from our collective left, around the corner from the entryway, pushed back into darkness we couldn't see into.

"Jeremy," Ron whispered. "Jeremy Dwight."

"Fuck you," he replied.

"Alone?"

"Jordan's here."

I could feel Ron relax next to me. "Find a phone," he told Doug. "Get our extraction team here as soon as possible, and for God's sake make sure you're not followed."

The accusation was obvious: he'd let Chip trail him, and he'd damn well better not let it happen again.

"Can you bring him out, Chip?" I asked.

"What's the magic word?"

"Grounded," Ron said. "Loss of car."

"Fine." He shuffled toward us, his arm around Jordan, who shirked back and tried to hide behind Chip. "For fuck's sake, it's my dad and my stepmom. They're here to help."

"Jordan Kennedy?" Ron asked.

Silence.

"He's being a little bitch," Chip said. "I haven't heard whining like this since David was like six years old."

"He's been through a lot," I reminded Chip. And to Jordan, "It's all right. You're going home."

"I don't know," he muttered.

"What, you don't want to go home?" Chip hissed.

"He doesn't know what's going on," I guessed. "Cut him the same slack you did Nicky. We don't know what's been done to him."

"I know."

Ron gestured for Chip to follow him, and they moved a few steps away, close enough that I could still hear.

"I was just busting his balls, Ron. He'd worry more if I didn't."

"I was your age once, I get it. Did he tell you anything?"

"They've been moving him around for over two weeks, and told him tonight was the last time. He knew what that meant."

"So he worries we're here to finish the job, or does he under-stand—?"

"He understands. But he's scared to death and exhausted."

"I want you to stick with him from here on out. Don't let him out of your sight, not until his parents have him."

"Damn, Ron, he has to pee sometime."

"And you'll be in there with him. There's no leeway on this,

Chip. Out of all of us he'll relate to you the best, and trust you the most. But after what he's been through and the stress…it might be too much."

"Fuck. You think after all this he'd off himself?"

"Just stick with him."

Chip never let Jordan out of his sight, not during the confusion of the building being swarmed by the extraction team, not when Jordan had a near breakdown at the sight of a dozen armed men storming in, and not in the confusion of getting them into the back of a military van.

He stuck to Jordan right up to the moment we arrived in Munich and handed him over to his father, and didn't flinch when he turned around to leave with us and found Linda Jackson standing there with handcuffs dangling from her fingertips.

"You'll see him at HQ," she told Ron as she cuffed Chip's hands behind his back. "Get there first and you can plead his case to the SG."

~

Ron made three phone calls, and within fifteen minutes we were on a military hop back to the U.S. The time frame he wanted would have allowed for taking a commercial flight, but he knew that if we landed on a military base, it was only one more phone call to get us a jet, and I could take us straight to Travis Air Force Base in California, and from there we could get to the agency in half an hour.

Linda Jackson was—intentionally—taking Chip back on a commercial flight; they would land in New York, suffer the lags from going through customs, wait for a layover, and then would have to change planes in Denver. It gave us a good two hours on them, enough time, he hoped, to get in to see Alex Barstow and convince him that in spite of how bad it looked, Chip had saved the assignment.

We scrambled; we landed at Langley Air Force Base and it took longer to secure the jet than Ron had thought it would, and as every minute ticked by he began to shed his composure and was visibly agitated. The delays were intentional, he was sure of it, and by the time we were in the air and headed for home he had just about convinced himself that Linda and Chip would get there first.

He had no idea what she intended to tell the Secretary General, but Ron wanted to be sure he had his version of events first.

When Doug asked him what the worst thing they could do to a sixteen year old was, Ron bit back a grimace and said, "I don't want to know."

"Come on, they can't do much. Maybe peg him for the fake ID—"

"What was his body count, Doug?" Ron snapped. "They have him dead to rights. Fake ID, a passport obtained under false pretenses, interference with a federal investigation, and murder. They can fucking nail him for *murder*."

"Self defense," I said.

"It won't matter, because in the end Jackson wouldn't have pulled him in without a direct order, and her orders come from pretty damned high up the chain."

"The SG?" Doug asked.

"Or his second. Either way, I have to get to Alex Barstow before Chip sets one foot through the agency door, and I'll have to pull a damned rabbit out of my ass to get him to listen."

~

We made it by twenty minutes. Doug drove and let Ron out of the car before he parked, and Ron bolted to the door. By the time we got upstairs to the SG's office, he was inside, the door closed and the clerk sitting outside at the administrative assistant's desk clearly indicated we were not invited to participate in the discussion.

We sat in hard metal chairs in the hallway and waited. I was exhausted and hungry and felt like I was teetering on the edge of a toddler-sized temper tantrum, and I doubted Doug was doing any better. That we couldn't even get into the more comfortable waiting area just inside the SG's office was a slap in the face, and I resented it.

"The outcome was good," Doug said, voice low. "We got the kid they wanted and another they thought was somewhere else. How can they hold this against Chip?"

"To prove a point? To test Ron? I don't know, but I'm honestly not surprised."

"I can't believe I never realized he was following me."

"He followed us, too, Doug. And that's a big part of the problem."

"Worse. He followed Dan." At the sound of the elevator doors sliding open, Doug got up, and we watched as Chip was marched down the hallway toward us, his hands still cuffed behind his back. He looked tired but not worried; Dan, on the other hand, was limping behind him and looked as if he wanted to paint the tile in whatever he'd last eaten.

I knew there was no chance of talking to Chip, so I stayed in my chair; he shrugged as he went past, and turned to wink at me before he was led into the SG's office.

Dan stopped long enough to tell us that Chip had refused to say a word on the entire flight other than to indicate when he needed to be led to the restroom, and to ask to have one hand free to eat with. Other than that, he was eerily quiet, refusing to answer any of Linda Jackson's questions, and refusing to engage in any small talk.

"For a kid that can hardly shut up," Doug said when Dan was gone, "that says a lot."

"You know him pretty well, don't you?"

He shrugged. "We hang out. Didn't we have this conversation already?"

"It's called small talk, Doug. Avoiding the elephant in the room. Distraction. Whatever."

"Fine. I know him well enough. But no, don't ask me why I'm friends with a teenager. I don't know."

"I don't need an explanation. If I wasn't married to his father, I'd probably want to be his friend, too."

Doug sighed hard. "Right now, he needs you for more than that. His mother... not saying that you need to step into those shoes, but he needs a maternal figure."

"I know. He needs me to ride a very fine line. I hope I'm up to it."

"Hell, I hope you get the chance."

An hour later, Doug was pacing.

Half an hour after that I was close to barging past the SG's glorified file clerk and into the office. When the door finally creaked open, we'd been waiting well over two hours; Linda and her team came out first, heading down the hall without so much as a glance our way.

That gave me a sliver of hope.

Dan came out after that, looking torn, but he at least gave a small shrug; when Chip came out he was rubbing his wrists, but he seemed happy enough.

Ron was slow in leaving the office, and when he did the anger was painted thickly across his face. He looked at Doug and barked, "Take him back to my apartment and sit on his ass until I get there," then gestured for me to follow him down the hall.

We wound up in Dan's office; I waited until the door was closed before asking carefully, "What happened?"

Dan shook his head, not willing to be the one to answer, and Ron was obviously struggling.

"They let him off, right? If Doug was taking him home—"

"They want him, Kris," Ron croaked.

"For?" It took a moment for it to sink in. "Come on, that's not possible. He's just a kid!"

"They don't care. He either takes the job, or he disappears."

"Disappears."

"Well, they're not exactly going to have a public trial now, are they? His choice was to take it...or not."

"Ron, there's got to be something."

"If you can think of it, I'm all ears."

"Dan?"

"We tried bargaining, Kris. Give him a few years to finish high school and a couple of years of college. Take him on part time as a paper pusher."

"They already knew he'd been expelled and the limitations that comes with," Ron said quietly. "And they offered him everything a kid that restless could want. Money, adventure, adrenaline-pumping training..."

"Funeral expenses?" I spat.

"He was eager, and he wanted it. I sat there and watched Alex

Barstow work my son, he used the goddamned passport and ID card as proof Chip was old enough to decide on his own, and nothing I said mattered. In the end Chip agreed to it, and the only concession I got was that after his training, he'd be assigned here.

"I just got him, Kris," he said miserably. "I just fucking got my son, and they're taking him away."

~

There was no grace period between Chip signing his name to the dotted line and the start of his training. I had assumed he'd follow the same path to the agency that Doug and I had: agree to the terms, sign your life away, and then wait for a report date to be sent in the mail, along with all the forms needed to begin medical insurance, get the ball rolling on W2 forms, and a list of acceptable items allowed while living in military dorms and crappy motel rooms.

Before Ron and I even left Dan's office it had been decided that the bulk of Chip's training would be done in-house after his initial introduction to the agency, and that he would report first thing in the morning. If he was suffering jet lag, it didn't matter: he was expected to be in Dan's office at eight in the morning, ready to be de-briefed about an assignment he never should have stumbled onto, and ready to begin training for a job that he shouldn't even know existed.

After two days of seemingly nonstop questions, an inquisition Ron was allowed to attend but at which he was not allowed to speak, Chip's composure never broke. He was, Ron told me later, unflappable. It was a series of questions coming at him with machine gun precision, and he had an answer for each one; he didn't fidget, and he never tried to make excuses for having followed his father halfway across the world and having butted into a fight that in which, by all rights, Dan should have had the upper hand.

An hour after the de-briefing ended, Chip was in a company car on his way to Travis Air Force Base for the first part of training. He spent a month confined to the base engaged in both physical conditioning and academic instruction; after that he was sent to San Diego to train with the Marines. He would have to survive the Crucible, and if he got that far, there was another six weeks in Washington, and then he would be sent home to finish on-site.

He left at six feet tall and a tightly muscled one hundred and seventy pounds; when he came home he was at least two inches taller, thirty pounds heavier, and his shirts strained against the size of his biceps.

His first assigned task was furthering his ability to ride a motor-cycle, which had Ron gritting his teeth hard.

Still, we wanted to see it.

"If he'd been military," Dan told us as we made our way across the parking lot of a racetrack just outside the county, "he'd have been booted out the first week."

We didn't need to ask if he'd had trouble with the materials he needed to memorize or the sheer amount of physical work; we knew what was getting him into trouble. Chip wandered from the dorms at every opportunity, and was found on more than one occasion with some random female base employee.

"He avoided military recruits," Dan said, as if it excused his behavior. "He apparently knew better than to risk getting someone else kicked out of the service."

We were at the track to witness a part of Chip's training that none of us had ever been offered. We'd all learned to drive under fire, but Chip was geared up in racing leathers, given a full-faced helmet, and pointed towards the track on a high-speed race-worthy motorcycle.

We stopped at the fence to watch.

"Crotch rocket," Ron sighed when he saw Chip swinging his leg over the seat. "Just what a kid with questionable impulse control needs to learn to ride."

"He already knew how to ride," Doug pointed out helpfully. "On the track he'll learn some control."

Before Ron could tell him to shut the fuck up because he didn't want his son anywhere near that bike, Dan was agreeing with Doug. "This will make him a better driver. He'll learn to see more of what's around him, he'll get a better sense of anticipation, and he'll learn to respect the speed."

"Sure," Ron grunted.

"At some point," Dan went on, "he'll be able to sense movement from another car simply by the slight turn of one wheel that he sees from the corner of his eye. He'll have less fear at speeds over one hundred, but he'll be able to see the flow of traffic around him as if he was going the speed limit. This is a good thing, Ron."

"If he doesn't crack up on the track and die."

We watched as Chip headed into a turn, his head cranked to see through it, his knee very nearly dragging across the asphalt.

"No fear there," Doug muttered.

Dan nodded. "That's what we want. Fast, fearless, and fierce."

With a heavy sigh, Ron backed away from the fence that separated us from the track and sat on the bleachers behind us. "He's being groomed to be our muscle?"

"For now. Face it, you and I are getting older and we've slowed down. Doug's specialties are not op related. And Kris"—he looked at me apologetically—"you'll never have the sheer strength that boy will. If the agency is going to stuff him into this job, then I want him in a position where he'll do the most good, and hopefully we can keep him somewhat safe."

"There is no safe," Ron grumbled.

"No, but his life will become decidedly less safe the more Intel he's allowed to process. His best bet to make it to an honest eighteen is if I keep him in a position where he has no choice but to follow either my orders or yours."

I heard Ron inhale sharply and turned quickly to look back to the track. Chip was on the ground, his body sliding one way, and the motorcycle the other. I held my breath until he popped up as if nothing was wrong, and then ran to upright the bike.

"Right there," Dan said. "If either you or I hit the ground like that, we wouldn't be moving. He's young and he's strong as hell. We need that."

I could see it in Ron's eyes: *what about what* he *needs?*

Dan and Doug left us to wander along the edge of the fence, to make their way to the gate where they would be able to watch from the field. Ron didn't budge from his spot on the bleacher, and while he was staring out at the track, I knew he was trying to not see.

Chip was back on the bike, speeding down a straightway, picking his line before entering the next turn.

I sat next to him, close enough to steal some of his warmth, setting my hand on his thigh; he would feel that even if he was trying to distance himself from everything around him at the moment.

"Christmas is in a few days," he said after a long stretch of silence. "It occurred to me this morning. He usually says something to remind me early."

I hadn't realized Ron would need a reminder, but then it wasn't glowing on my radar, either. I hadn't given it any thought beyond hoping I wasn't expected to cook a traditional dinner, because that would be cruel on more than one front.

"I used to get him every Christmas day around noon. Didn't matter where I was or what I was doing, I always made it home to pick him up on Christmas day. If I was home, I picked up a tree on Christmas Eve and we'd put it up together. If I wasn't getting back until that morning, I'd get one of the administrative assistants to get one and store it on my patio. I don't think Chip really cared one way or the other if there was a tree in the apartment or even presents."

"But you did," I guessed.

"Last year I made sure I had nothing on the schedule for at least a week before, and we broke with tradition and put the tree up early. Everything went in reverse; I had him for the entire time and it almost felt normal. He was actually excited, Kris. I took him shopping for presents for his brother and even Grant, and he suckered Dan into taking him shopping for me. We hung out, went to movies, shot pool. Right up until I drove him home on Christmas day so he could spend time with David, for the first time it felt normal."

"And this year?"

"I don't know. Last year he was a typical kid. This year he's not. I don't know what to make of it."

"So he's not a typical kid, but he is a kid. While he's picking up speed out there on the track, you and I are going to go shopping, and we're going to make sure that he has as close to a normal Christmas as we can give him."

He slid his arm around my shoulders. "As long as we remember that it's our first Christmas together, too. It can't all be about Chip."

"It can be mostly about him," I said, stretching to plant a kiss on his chin. "I don't mind, and it'll be fun. None of us have to go anywhere, and after he's done here today he's off until New Year's. We'll make him be a kid even if it kills us."

He winced as Chip sped past, and I could feel his muscles tighten as he leaned the bike hard into a sharp curve.

"Fine," he said with a heavy sigh, "I can't sit here and watch this anymore, anyway. Let's go buy the kid a bunch of crap and shoot for normal."

"You're a pretty good shot," I reminded him as we got up.

His eyebrow twitched up just a hair, and he fought against the grin that tugged at the corners of his mouth. "My aim might be a little off these days."

"Howso?"

"Got you in the chin last night. I was aiming for your boobs."

I shoved him towards the parking lot. "I'm living with two teenagers," I huffed as he stumbled a few steps before catching his balance. "And mister, Santa is bring you coal."

~

That first Christmas together was as normal as anyone could hope for. Chip came home that night, tired and aching and bruised, saw the tree on the back patio through the sliding glass door, and he lit up. For a few fleeting moments, he wasn't the trainee who had just spent the last three months learning to fight, learning to fire a number of weapons, and learning to take cars and motorcycles past lethal speeds without wetting himself. In those few moments, he was the kid we wanted him to be, excited that we'd remembered.

For the sole purpose of being obnoxious, he bounced into our room on Christmas morning and jumped butt-first onto the foot of the bed, sending me in an upward arch that very nearly launched me onto the floor. Ron threw a pillow at him and told him to get the hell out, but he sounded amused and not annoyed, and he was smiling sleepily as Chip shuffled out, feet deliberately scraping the floor in mock dejection.

It was also the last Christmas we had together that was anywhere near normal.

Three days into the New Year we crowded into Dan's stuffy little office, waiting for him to arrive with the information on our newest assignment. I hoped for something benign, something that was designed to ease Chip into the job, but what Dan handed over were pages upon pages of information gathered by a ground team in China. An hour after we knew where we were going, we were on a flight out of San Francisco, headed for a giant unknown.

~

"The objective," Dan said, tapping the first page in his file, "is to destroy the intelligence they've collected on U.S. and British troop movements, as well as U.S. weapons development. They're on the verge of building something new, and we're going to throw a wrench into those works."

"Is this a follow-up to the Vietnam job?" Ron asked.

Dan nodded; while Chip was safely ensconced in San Diego, at the mercy of the Marines, we were in Vietnam collecting information from informants who were feeding bits and pieces of intelligence to the CIA through every available back channel. We knew where the primary source of their information was located, and we now knew it was the repository for most of the data mining they were doing.

"The problem," Dan said as he spread a collection of photographs out on the small table that he'd set up between the military plane's seats, "is that they've embedded a good part of the data into the building itself."

"How's that?" Doug asked, craning his neck to get a better look at the windowless, drab gray building.

"Think caveman," Chip muttered.

"Exactly," Dan said. "Quite literally the writing on the wall. Code buried behind drywall. Code stored on rolls of reel-to-reel tape, buried behind walls and in vaults. Even computer punch cards, some stored opened, but a good chunk of them either vaulted or buried."

"Why?" I asked. "Why not just vault it all?"

"Where's the first place you would think to look?" he countered.

"I'd look in the most open places first, Dan. Hide in plain sight, that kind of thing. Then I'd presume to check every computer I could."

"You have access to those kinds of computers," Chip said. "I've seen that hallway in the basement. It's nothing but one long assed computer. If you didn't have that—?"

"Chip, I think they manufacture those. If they build it, they probably have access to it."

"Still."

"They've spread it out," Dan reiterated. "What we need to get rid of isn't in one spot."

Ron picked up one of the photos, turning it in his hands as he studied it from all angles that he could. "We blow the building up," he said quietly. "Get in, set explosives, get out."

"How the hell do we get in?" Doug wanted to know.

Ron put the photo back on the table, and tapped at a spot somewhere near the fifth floor of an eight-story building. "Venting access is through here," he said. "One of us scales up and goes in."

"Through a vent?" Doug shook his head. "How the hell does anyone get up there in the first place? And how do we know that it'll lead anywhere? And hell, that's a damned small grating to get through."

"Scale up," Dan said flatly.

"I'd never make it," Doug pointed out. "I'm not strong enough to get that far up. You'll never fit. Kris, well she would fit, but—"

"Kris doesn't have the physical strength to make it that far up," Dan said before Doug could finish the thought. "It's not just scaling the side of the building; it's scaling it with enough gear to do the job."

Enough fuse line and explosives, he meant.

I looked at Ron, presuming he would volunteer. I wasn't sure he was thin enough to fit through the opening and maneuver around, but he had a better shot of making it all the way up than either Doug or I did. He was still staring at the photographs, and I wasn't sure he was even listening.

When he did look up, it was at Chip.

I felt the anger bubbling before he even opened his mouth.

"You're the only one who can make it up that far and then get in," he said quietly. "You managed climbing those chains in Germany and you were able to get down with Nicky on your back. I think you can handle going a little higher. The difference is the weight load going up, and then actually getting in. You'll need to be able to get in deep and lower as much of the explosive as you can down as far as you can. And then you have to get your ass out of there."

I couldn't believe I was hearing this. "Ron—"

He finally turned toward me, my own anger reflected back in accelerated degrees. He didn't have to say it; I could feel it burning into me. *Not now. Shut up and do your job.*

It had been less than a year since I had assured him I could separate our private life from our work life; I shut up and listened to him take Chip step by step through everything he would need to know. I kept my mouth shut when we were on the ground, when Chip was climbing the side of the building in the cover of dark, and I didn't open it until he was back down, running as if his life depended on it.

The building came down in a series of loud pops, and we watched from a distance as Chip sprinted away from it as hard as he could, and as the building collapsed into itself.

Normal was off the table, and I didn't think we would ever see it again.

~

"Dan would have sent either one of us," I seethed. "All I had to do was say the word, that I knew I had the strength to make it that far, and goddammit we both know that I do. It wouldn't have been pretty but I could have done it. He wouldn't have blinked if you'd volunteered, either. I don't care how fucking old you think you are, but you damn well could have inched your way up that building. Either of us, Ron. Either goddamned one of us. Even Doug would have been a better choice, I don't care if he thinks he's not that strong."

Ron sat there and while we waited for the rest of the team to board, he let me wind up and watched me go on. The longer he listened to me vent, without offering any defense, the angrier I became, and the less sense I made even to myself.

"Observation," I hissed. "Holy shit, for the first three assignments with Doug the only thing we let him do was observe. That's all Chip should have been doing. Watching us, Ron, learning. Not *doing*."

He irritated me further by checking his watch and looking toward the door; I knew he was hoping for rescue, for Dan or Doug to step in and end my rant, but we both knew they were ten minutes from coming back, and I wasn't done, not by a long shot.

He let me go on, and when I hit the point of making little to no sense and there were only a scant few minutes until we wouldn't be alone, he asked, "Are you done yet?" as he huffed out a sigh.

"Not by a long shot, mister."

He held up a finger. "One, I don't think you could have made it, not weighed down by thirty pounds of gear. And it wouldn't have mattered if you could; we need you uninjured and ready to fly at any time. *Any* time, Kris. Whether we come and go commercially or on a military hop, you have to be able to fly."

A second finger went up. "Doug? Not a chance. We need his brain. We need his ability to take complex pieces of information and tie them together. We need him in case one of us gets hurt."

When he lifted a third finger, I wanted to reach out and snap it off at the joint. "I could have made it up the building, even with the gear, but I'm not flexible enough to maneuver in tight spaces. I might have gotten in, but I wouldn't have gotten out. You saw how hard Chip had to run to clear the explosion. I can't run that fast nor can I run that far in a dead sprint. Dan? He never would have gotten ten feet off the ground. Our job was to take out that intelligence, and the way to do it was to take that building down. The only one suited for it was Chip."

"And what if we hadn't had him with us?"

"We did have him with us. He did his job *without complaint*. You absolutely cannot think of him as anything other than another team member when we're on the clock. It doesn't matter how terrified you are for him, or how much you love him. When he's working, he is not my son and he is not your stepson, not unless the situation calls for exploiting that relationship."

"He's new, Ron. Brand spanking new. You wouldn't have done that to anyone else on their first assignment."

He leaned forward, elbows on his knees, and stared right at me, eyes going dark with anger. "I have done much, much worse to a new team member. Don't pretend you know my history on this job, Kris. I've made tougher decisions in less time, and at some point it might be you that I point in a direction no one will want to see you pushed toward. If you can't handle that, get out now."

Get out of what? The team, the job, or the marriage? I was tempted to ask, had it poised on my tongue, but Chip bounded in and blurted, "Are you two done fighting yet? I need to pee, and I really don't want to have to go all the way back to the hangar."

Ron waved him in, and when the bathroom door slammed shut he asked quietly, "Are we done?"

"With this argument," I said, my heart pounding hard, hoping he didn't mean more.

He glanced at his watch again, and then stood up, gesturing for me to get up as well. I felt unsteady on my feet, legs watery, and was filled with gnawing doubt that was mixed with dread.

"For the next minute, we're off the clock," he whispered, reaching for me. "I love you, you know that, right?"

His heart was pounding as hard as mine; I held on tight until he pulled back just enough to kiss me, and we stayed there until Chip was there making obnoxious smooching sounds, and Dan and Doug were on their way in.

~

A year and a dozen assignments later, the lack of normal in our lives had become, in its own absurd way, normal. Chip came and went when we were home, sometimes remembering to leave the promised note, but more often than not he would simply disappear for a few days, and would either show up for work requirements, or Doug and Ron would go looking for him.

I watched Chip turn hard; not just physically, which had happened in startling degrees until he was well over six feet tall and so muscular that his skin pulled tight, but emotionally as well. He had hopped from one bed to the next before, but now he seemed to do it for sport, because he could, and he didn't seem to care about the psychological detritus he was leaving behind.

With kids, he was gentle and sweet; with Doug he was funny and at ease, and I often saw glimpses of the sweet boy I had seen trying hard to not cry over missing his mother. He treated me with respect and as a treasured friend, but other women were nothing more to him than, Ron put it crudely but so aptly, "someplace warm and wet to stick it."

I couldn't argue with his instincts on the job; when we were "on the clock," as Ron always put it, Chip towed the line and followed orders without question. He was the muscle any other team would kill to have, and he carried out the worst of the orders he was given without regret. I admired his abilities, but I hated that he was there, and I often couldn't avoid saying something about it.

In the beginning, there were a few hiccups; he and Doug went missing in Amsterdam overnight, failing to report back in for an arbitrary curfew Dan had imposed. We were done with the job and had free time; Chip asked Ron if it was all right to go explore, to see what there was to do for the rest of the day. Ron pointedly told him to ask Dan; it wasn't up to him to say yes or no.

Dan shrugged it off and told them to be back no later than eleven; when they were gone he gave Ron a look of "what the hell?" and Ron said simply, "He needs to come to terms with the idea that when we're working, I don't get to give him permission to go or an order to stay."

"Job's over, Ron. When it's over he's your kid, not my minion."

I think Ron knew then that Chip, at least, would fail to show up on time, and wanted Dan to have a taste of what his newest team member could be like. By midnight we were out looking, and at ten the next morning we found them rolling out of a cheap hotel.

When Chip spotted Ron, he looked at his watch and said, "It's not eleven yet."

The week of Chip's seventeenth birthday was spent trying to get Doug out of an East German intelligence facility's security holding; when Dan and Ron failed to negotiate his release, Chip walked into the building, found where Doug was being help, disabled the guards, walked in, kicked out a window, and together with Doug ran for it.

They ran hard, but to give themselves a little leeway, Chip turned in mid-stride, pulled the pin on a grenade, and tossed it through the broken window. Blood came at them like drops of rain, but once he'd let go of it, Chip never looked back.

When he turned eighteen, he moved out. Two days after his birthday he sat at the kitchen table with a giant bowl of cereal, unshaven with wild bedhead, and announced that he'd rented an apartment and was moving his clothes and stereo out that afternoon.

I felt like he'd kicked me in the gut; Ron simply watched him over the edge of the newspaper for a long moment and then said, "You can take the bedroom furniture if you need to."

"Naw." Chip got up, rinsed his bowl out, and set it in the sink. "I bought a sofa bed and a TV. I'll figure the rest out later."

"Utilities? Phone?" Ron asked.

"Turned on. I'll call you with the number. I don't know it off the top of my head."

"Need help?"

"Yeah, sure," Chip said, as if he hadn't considered asking. "It's not that far away but an extra car load or two would cut down on the time."

It's not personal. He's eighteen; he's ready to move.

"What about sheets and towels?" I asked, trying to swallow the hurt whole. "Dishes, silverware, pots and pans?"

"Hm." He leaned against the counter, arms folded. "I'm not much of a cook but I suppose I need sheets and towels."

"Fine. You guys move your stuff and I'll go shopping."

"You don't have to."

You don't have to leave, either. "Do you really see yourself standing there trying to decide between two hundred and four hundred thread count sheets? Or figuring out which towels are going to hold up to a few dozen washes?"

He shrugged. "Hadn't thought about it. Sheets come in thread count?"

"Let her shop for you," Ron said. "She has good taste."

"Really now." Chip pushed away from the counter and headed towards the kitchen door. "And yet, she married you."

"Funny man." He tossed the newspaper onto the table and got up, crossing the kitchen to slip his arms around me, sensing my hurt. "He stayed longer than I ever thought he would, Kris. He'd stay longer if we asked, but it's time."

"But he's *just* eighteen. That's like being a practice grown-up."

"Come on. If it were anyone else, maybe. He's been headed out the door since he got here, and he's only stayed this long because we wanted him to."

"I still want him to."

"I know."

"Are you ready for him to leave?"

He shook his head sadly. "When he's not out wandering around, and when we're not working...I waited a lot of years to have my kid, Kris. I'm not sure I would have even had the last two years if not for you, but if he's ready to move on, we have to let him."

"Bribe him," I said against his shoulder.

"With what? He makes good money and he has a car. There's not a lot I can bribe him with."

"Then tell him he'll break my heart. I know I'm not his mother..."

He pulled back to look at me, absently pushing my hair behind my ear. "He didn't need you to be his mother. His mother was a train wreck. He needed you to be his friend and his confidant, and you did that. You can still be that, even if he's on his own."

"I kind of feel like I'm more than his friend."

"Because you are. And nothing says you can't be an obnoxious thorn in his side even if he's living somewhere else. We'll probably see as much of him as we've been seeing."

I put my hands on his face, gently scratching at his stubble.

"He leaves, and you and I will be living alone for the first time, you realize that?"

I did realize that, and as he bounded out of the kitchen to change and then help Chip gather up his things, I couldn't help but wonder if that was part of what bothered me.

Chip was a buffer; he was the cause of most of our arguments, but he also kept them from escalating out of control.

Without him there, I had no idea what we were in for.

~

The two weeks following Chip's move toward independence were pocketed with more stretches of silence than I realized two adults could generate. We tried to figure it out: was Chip so much of a presence that he filled the silences simply by being there, was he that noisy, or were we running out of things to say to each other without the inevitable interruptions that come with living with a teenager?

Ron filled the time not spent in his office sitting at the kitchen table or the desk in the bedroom, hunched over paperwork that was cloistered into file folders that he closed any time I walked into the room. I didn't take it personally, but it did pique my interest; whatever he was plodding through was important enough to be locked in the safe when he didn't have the folders in hand, and important enough for him to tell me that if anything happened to him I was to report to George Barron, the assistant Secretary General, and no one else. Tell him nothing more than that Ron was working on something, where it was, and then let him into the apartment to get it.

"Not Dan. Not Doug or Chip or even Barstow himself. The only one who needs to see that or know about it is Barron. Ever."

He trusted me with the combination to the safe, assuming I would be able to resist the urge to peek. It was like dangling a chocolate bar in front of a fourteen year old; sure, the kid would want it but would also try to be too mature to grab for it.

I wanted the damn chocolate, but not enough to lose any cool points by trying to snatch it from his hand.

While he worked—which seemed to be a lot of reading interrupted by the occasional scratching out of a note or two—I was either stretched out on the sofa with a book or I headed out to catch a joyride with my dad. I did anything I could think of to put off the inevitable need to clean Chip's bathroom; I'd managed to force myself into the bedroom to haul garbage out from under his bed and to clean the carpet, but I was almost afraid of what I'd find in the bathroom.

He might have thought of himself as an adult, but the odor wafting from in there had a decidedly sour teenage edge to it.

I was just about to cave in—once I finished the chapter I was on I'd tackle the damned bathroom and hope I wouldn't need to be decontaminated after—when Ron leaned over the sofa and told me we'd been tapped for a training assignment in London and needed to pack.

"Pack," I repeated dully, though inside I was relived to have an excuse to avoid the cleaning. "Now?"

"Now."

I closed my book and tossed it onto the end table, and followed him into the bedroom. "And you've known about this how long?"

"A few days. And before you get upset, lack of notice is part of the training aspect. We're giving everyone an hour to get to HQ, ready to go."

"I really thought I was done with all the little pop-quiz training exercises," I grumbled.

"Barstow's idea," Ron said. He pulled a backpack out from the closet and tossed it on the bed. "He wants to throw two or three teams at the same assignment and see how well everyone can play together."

"Teams have been cooperating all along, haven't they?"

"Cooperating, yes," he agreed. "But he sees the world stage getting bigger and along with it the agency getting deeper into territory usually covered by the CIA and OSI. When the assignments get harrier? Our agents need to be able to suck it up and take orders from someone other than their team leaders."

"I would think the teams could do that without practice."

"You'd think." He handed me three boxes of ammunition along with my passport, gesturing towards my pack. "It won't be so easy for some of the people sitting in the mayor's seats to take orders from someone else."

"Dan can handle that just fine."

"Dan doesn't have his ego wrapped around his job title. He listens to all of us, even Chip." He finished shoving his clothes into his backpack and slung it over his shoulder. "If everyone takes it for what it is, this could be a hell of a lot of fun."

A few days in London with nothing scheduled but training?

Fun wasn't what came to mind.

~

We waited in the parking lot; Dan and Ron leaned against the back of the truck we were taking to Travis AFB while Doug paced. We'd been there for fifteen minutes, and the only one missing was Chip.

"He's technically not late," Ron muttered, mostly to himself.

"He thinks he's late," Dan chuckled. "I gave him twenty minutes to make a fifteen minute drive, and I know he had to get rid of the girl he was with. I could hear her in the background bitching something like 'but *I'm* not done!'"

Doug stopped pacing, and he was biting back a grin. "That's kinda cold."

"Indeed," Ron said. "I kind of wish I'd done it."

"The perks of being me." Dan pointed to the far side of the parking lot, where Chip was scrambling out of his car. He raced across the lot, skittering between cars as he fumbled with a backpack that wouldn't stay on his shoulder.

He was apologizing before Dan could open his mouth. "I'm sorry, I'm sorry. I was going fast enough to get here on time but then I got pulled over—"

"Anyone ever tell you that you run like a little girl who just saw dick for the first time?"

Chip wasn't even out of breath. "You know that look? Man, you have to stop hanging out around the junior high. It's gone way past creepy."

Dan slapped the back of the truck. "Get in. We have a plane to catch."

"Isn't that, like, a prisoner transport truck?"

"It's what you deserve," Dan grunted.

"Can I drive it?"

Ron sighed, not half as annoyed as he sounded. "Get in, hotshot. And zip your pants up."

"What?" He grabbed for his zipper, which was closed. "Real mature, Ron."

"Just something I'd like you to practice more often," Ron sighed as he pulled himself into the back of the truck.

They both reached out and helped me up. The back of the truck was dirty and smelled, and we were seated on hard metal benches facing each other.

Chip was right; at one point it had probably been used to haul prisoners around.

"What's in London?" Chip asked Dan as the driver started the engine.

"Training assignment. We're going to see how well we can function working with two other teams, and how well the SG's new pet can play the game."

"His pet?" Doug asked.

"Cooper," Ron offered. "Barstow has a nomad operative that answers only to him. Previous coops have been the go-between for several teams in the field at once, and this new one? We get to test him."

"Is he, like, new-new, or just new to the job?" Chip asked.

"A little of both," Dan answered. "He was a desk jockey for five or six years and has spent the last two as a nomad. I don't think he's ever worked with a team."

"They do that? Take guys off the desk and toss them into the fire?"

Ron nodded. "When they have brains the size this kid has, yes. He's a genius when it comes to strategic planning; it's the implementation he needs to get a little more experience with."

"So basically a nerdling is getting his balls and going outside to play with the big boys. Can I fuck with him?"

I heard both Ron and Dan sigh hard, and Doug swallowed back a bubble of laughter.

"No," I said. "You're not screwing around with him. If he's that smart he can fling it right back at you, and you'd just wind up looking like a dick. Just...behave, all right?"

Doug leaned forward to look past Chip. "I suppose that means all of us."

"All of you. Especially from here to the base. I'm flying us on the first leg—anyone gets out of line, I fly the plane upside down."

"You wouldn't," Chip grumbled.

"No co-pilot. Who's going to stop me?"

"Gravity?"

"Do you really want to find out?"

"Fine," he sighed. "But all this behaving is sucking the fun out of this job."

~

Ron and Dan walked the length of the room, stepping carefully over the charred remains of desks and typewriters. On paper, this staged assignment was taking place in Germany, and the local police had already combed over the area, followed by a more thorough inspection by the Bundespolizei. Agents from the OSI had been there for a cursory inspection, a chance to see up close the damage being peppered across the country.

If no one had told me we were immersed in a training exercise, I would never have guessed that this wasn't real.

"It's supposed to be a fucking publishing company," Chip said quietly, watching as they headed back toward us. "What's the point?"

"Depends on who did it," Doug said.

"Some frustrated writer who couldn't get a book deal?" Chip asked, half in jest.

He was staring at the splintered shell of a desk, drawers blown out, the legs on one side nothing more than inch-high stubs; it left the desk listing to one side, a blotter that had surely been placed squarely in the center now hanging half off, its pages blackened and torn.

I could see what he was seeing; someone sitting there, blissfully unaware, hunched over his desk while he held the phone receiver to his ear as he assured his wife he wouldn't forget to stop on the way home for milk and bread. Laughing at something she said, eyes crinkled in amusement just before they widened in the horror of the explosion.

Those few minutes played out in his imagination as he tried to soak it in, horror etching itself in the lines around his eyes as he squinted against the image he didn't want to envision.

I was close to grabbing him by the arm and pulling him out the door when Ron stepped around the desk and looked just past us, his heavy sigh suggesting I wouldn't be happy about who was walking into the office.

"Donnigan," he said, a cursory greeting.

"Hell of a party you're throwing," Donnigan said.

"Did you bring beer?" Chip asked. "If this is a party, we need some damned beer."

Donnigan ignored him. "What the hell is going on, Dan? I was diverted from a damned good job to come here. If it's to poke through embers, I'm going to be pissed."

Ron shoved his hands into his pockets, stopping just short of snorting derisively. "I didn't realize you were above doing any of the grunt work."

"Yeah, well, some of us aspire to handle the more important aspects of the job."

"Like what?" Impatience snapped in Ron's voice. "I'm willing to bet you don't even know what the job is yet, Donnigan. I wouldn't start reaching for the glory until you have a clue what it is you're here for."

Smugly, Donnigan folded his arms across his chest. "I have as much clue as you do."

"Really." Ron turned toward Dan. "Are we the only ones who know?"

"Know what?" Donnigan demanded.

"What we're here for, sunshine," Chip said. "Even I know that much."

Donnigan ignored him.

"Not even curious about the condition of this office?" Ron asked him. "Not going to ask who did it, if anyone was hurt or killed?"

"Looks to be a civilian matter. Don't care."

"Isn't it your job to care?" Chip sputtered.

Donnigan spun on his heels towards him. "Isn't it your job to shut up and do what you're told? I'm telling you now. Shut up."

I glanced at Ron, expecting him to jump to Chip's defense, but he stood there with his hands shoved into his pockets, waiting to see what Chip would do.

"I'm pretty sure I don't take my orders from you. In fact, I'm pretty sure none of us are taking orders from you on this one. Especially not until we have everyone who's going to be doing this all in one spot."

"All right, Einstein," Donnigan sneered. "Who are we waiting for?"

Chip twitched toward the door, a fraction of movement that had me straining to hear what he obviously had. "We're waiting for whomever is in charge. Should be soon."

"Soon," he repeated dully.

We heard her before we saw her. "Listen to junior," Linda Jackson said. "He's right. You wait for the mayor in charge."

"So what, we're all here and he's not?"

Ron and Dan looked at each other; Ron's left eyebrow arched and Dan pressed his lips together so hard that they were a thin white line across his face.

"Seriously?" Chip asked.

"He can't comprehend the probabilities," I told him. "Our kind are supposed to be at home baking cookies and perfecting our swallowing techniques."

"God. If he's got some woman at home, she needs to snowball the bastard, not swallow."

Linda stepped up behind Chip and hugged him hard. "I think I love you."

"You are *not* in charge," Donnigan sputtered.

"What the hell is your problem, man? It bothers you that both these women have bigger balls that you or what?"

Donnigan took a quick step toward Chip, but when Ron cleared his throat, he stopped, thinking better of whatever he'd intended to do.

"What's the first step?" Ron asked Linda.

"Inspect the premises, get a good look at the damage," she said simply. "Then we'll all sit down and clarify the assignment."

The coffee shop Linda herded us towards was barely bigger than the break room at HQ, but other than the old woman behind the counter it was deserted. Ron bought her inattention with the purchase of two pots of coffee and two dozen sweet rolls, and we pulled tables together so that we could each get a look at what information was available to us.

Ron set the plate closest to Chip. "Anyone else wants one, I suggest they grab it before he inhales."

"Hey, I share," Chip protested.

"We've all seen you eat," Dan said. He turned to Linda. "What have you got?"

She tossed a short stack of photographs onto the table and spread them out. Cooper looked like he was twenty years old at the most, with dull brown hair, oddly violet eyes, and a crooked but playful smile. "Our nomad agent is Justin Ray. He's spent the last two years as Barstow's errand boy, but it's time for him to get a better taste of what his job will really entail."

"Which is?" Chip asked.

"Kid, you need to shut up and listen," Donnigan grunted.

"No, the kid needs to ask questions when he has them," Jackson said. "How else is he going to hone his job skills?" She looked at Chip. "Think of the agency as the hand controlling a yo-yo. Each team is on the string. Cooper is the spinning piece of plastic. He gathers information from different parts of the string—the various teams he works with—and reports back to the SG."

"The hand," Chip surmised.

"Exactly. And in this case, the only hand playing with the yo-yo is the Secretary General."

Chip took a long look at the photos spread out on the table, and then looked back at Jackson. "Why? Why only one hand guiding this yo-yo around? It can't be tradition. The agency isn't that old."

"It's a matter of trust," Ron answered. "The SG needs someone he can trust implicitly, and it has to be someone with both the brains and the brawn to not only understand the broader implications of what this agency does, but the ability to do what he needs to in order to make sure the jobs get done."

"And he can't trust more than once person?"

Donnigan was still grumbling. "Come on. Really?"

"He has a circle of trust," Linda said, ignoring Doonigan. "But he's also looking ahead to a potential future SG. That doesn't mean this Cooper"—she tapped a finger to the top photograph, her fingernail touching the image of this kid's mousy brown hair—"will ever be that person, but it means that Barstow thinks he's the most likely candidate right now."

"Right now. Does that mean he can lose the job?"

She nodded.

"How? I'm guessing he can't just quit."

"Natural selection, kid," Donnigan said. "He dies, he's done. He lives, he's got lifetime employment."

"Or he can become the Assistant SG," Ron said. "There are avenues other than dying as a way out, Chip. The last Cooper is now working with the President. The one before him? She's with Defense Intelligence and coordinates with the OSI."

"And before that?"

"George Barron," Linda replied.

"Barstow was never the Cooper?"

"He was the first one. And he set the bar pretty damned high for anyone who follows him."

Donnigan leaned back in his chair and snorted. "No worries on you getting tapped for it."

Dan stood up, leaning across the table, hands pressed into it so hard his fingernails went white. "Harold. This is a training assignment. A learning experience. He's making an effort to fill in any gaps he has, and I would think you would respect that and contribute to the discussion, not insult those who are participating in it."

"He's been on the job for two years, he should know this by now."

"Really? Like everyone normally sits around and discusses job descriptions that aren't officially on the books? How would he know?"

"He should know everything he needs to by now," Donnigan said flatly.

Chip grabbed another roll off the plate, ripping a piece of it off. "I know this much," he said, flattening the piece between his fingers. "You're a first class douchebag. And you're not stopping to consider that at some point on this gig, training or not, you just might need to rely on me to save your sorry ass. If you keep shoveling shit my way, I might let it slide back and smother you."

Donnigan turned to Dan, who was back in his seat, very slight smile playing on his lips. "You let your junior team members get away with this?"

"With being right? Hell, yes."

"And I will indulge any questions that help an operative better understand his job," Linda said. "Get a grip on your disappointment in having to answer to me, Donnigan. If this was your assignment and he was your team member, you'd be answering these questions willingly and you know it."

"Not to a kid. He shouldn't even be here."

"He's here at the request of the Secretary General. You, you're here because your name was next up on a list. What does that tell you?"

"It tells you," Ron said evenly, before Donnigan could answer, "to just shut up already." With a heavy sigh—he wasn't about to defend Chip's being there—he turned back to Linda. "We're here to play with Cooper. What's on the agenda?"

She slid one of the photos across the table toward him. "Justin Ray. The mock explosion is staged from one that occurred in Hamburg two years ago."

"But we already know—" Chip started.

She held up a hand to stop him. "We're not sharing information, Chip. Each of us needs to comb through that wreckage and get from it what we can, and then chase down whatever leads we can cough up. We'll feed the details to Ray, and see what he does with it."

He considered that for a moment. "Do we get any upfront information beyond that? Like, if I have questions, can I ask you?"

She nodded. "Direct them to your team leader first, but anything he can't answer, yes, you may ask me."

"Red Army," Chip said when Ron asked him what he'd been about to impart before Linda stopped him. "If this was based on a real bombing in Hamburg, we already know that it was the Red Army. They blew up a publishing company and seventeen people were injured. Two of them were arrested, I think. Red Army, not the injured."

We'd left Donnigan and Linda Jackson arguing in the coffee shop and headed back to the staging area. Chip was still looking at it as being very real, but he was processing the details, and as he did I noted that both Ron and Dan were watching him carefully, soaking in how he was connecting dots and how carefully he avoided contaminating the scene.

"Are we supposed to know this already?" Doug asked.

"Someone attentive to current events might have felt a little bell go off in his head." Ron glanced at Chip, who was leaned over the listing desk he'd been looking at earlier. "And one of us has been fixated on Red Army activities for the last two years. If he thinks this was modeled after a particular bombing, I would take his word for it."

Chip sighed hard, and turned away from the desk. "Yeah, but I don't think it is. They wouldn't make it that obvious."

"Reason?" Dan asked.

"Jackson said I was requested on this, right? It's no secret that I pull information on RA stuff all the time. So I'd think if this is a training exercise, they'd make it look like that to see if I go in that direction, but it's not."

"Then what is it?"

"Dunno. But they're telling Linda this is Hamburg, two years ago. Or telling her to tell us that. All we got is that this is staged. Donnigan didn't seem to know anything, but he was probably just blowing smoke up our asses. Hamburg might be intentional misinformation, and we need to figure out the more likely scenario. Then we dump it all on Cooper. Linda tells him it's Hamburg and the Red Army. Donnigan tells him it's a waste of his precious time. We tell him whatever we figure out, and then let him decide."

He moved through the office carefully, skirting around desks, squinting as he leaned closer to inspect desk drawers and chairs.

"First thing?" he said after a few quiet moments. "If this is all supposed to look real, then this place was bombed after hours."

"How so?" Ron asked.

"No blood. Anywhere. If it had been during office hours, there would be blood in places where people would normally be. Splatters on desks and the drawers, even on chairs. Floors. Agency stagers would have gotten that detail right, including the splatter patterns."

"Who blows up an empty office in a publishing house?" Dan pressed.

Chip shrugged. "Who blows one up in the first place?"

"Are we back to your frustrated writer theory?" Doug asked.

"Naw. Something about all of this just doesn't feel right. Like, why stage anything at all? Why not just have the principle players have the necessary information, feed it to Cooper, and let him do his job? In the field he wouldn't necessarily be on site, right? He'd be collecting information like a little kid collecting bugs. This"—he gestured wide—"feels like overkill. And we're not cops, we don't do crime scene investigations...what the hell are we supposed to take from all of this?"

"Staging is atypical," Ron admitted. "Go with your gut. What's it telling you?"

Chip squinted, focusing on a spot near the front door. "For one, that we're not in here alone. Pop lights on near that door and I think you'll find Mrs. Jackson in the corner watching us, very quietly."

We all turned, and she stepped out of the shadows, chuckling softly. "You're not half bad."

"You're wearing perfume," Chip explained.

"And you could smell it from there?"

He nodded.

"Duly noted. It was just a dab, but apparently a dab too much. Now go with Ron's question; what's your gut telling you?"

"Right now it's telling me to pay attention to the little things." He bent over and up righted a desk chair, ignoring Dan's sharp intake of air as he rolled it across the floor. "I could piss all over this place and still not contaminate the scene. I mean, it's good, it looks real, but it's missing too much. Blood. Ash. The smell of broken bodies and burned hair and paper and wood."

"After hours—" Dan started, but Chip was shaking his head, and Ron held out a hand to stop him from saying anything else.

"He's thinking out loud," Ron said quietly. "Let him go."

"That popped into my head a few minutes ago, yeah," Chip went on. "But the other things are missing. And if we're supposed to gather information meant to help another agent piece together a puzzle, the stagers would have made sure everything was perfect. We'd be gagging on the smell of the dead in here."

"I think you might be a bit ahead of Cooper on skills," Linda told him.

"I can't be that far ahead."

Doug snorted. "Your brain is more warped than the average person."

"Where's Donnigan's team?" Chip asked Linda. "Why did he report alone?"

She hesitated. "He no longer has a team."

Ron twitched; I saw the one eyebrow arch before he caught himself. "Is that part of internal restructuring or did he lose his team?"

"I can't really say. But it did make him extremely available for this assignment."

I saw the same thing in both Ron and Chips' eyes, a split second of muddled doubt and curiosity. Did she mean can't as in she didn't know, or can't as in she was not allowed to say? Or was she simply choosing to not share?

My brain went in one direction: his team quit. He might have been an effective team leader, but he was an insufferable bastard, and I was running with that thought, ready to cut loose with it, when Ron asked simply, "He went nomad, didn't he?"

Her discomfort was the only answer he needed. He turned to Chip instead. "What's your gut say about that, cowboy?"

"That Donnigan is a bigger douche than I thought," he grumbled, backing away to walk the perimeter of the room again.

He began opening and closing desk drawers, rifling through stacks of papers on desks that had been left upright, and he lifted notes and pictures tacked to a cork bulletin board.

He was less than careful about it all, but Linda never made a move to stop him. She spent another few minutes talking to Ron and then left after telling him we would all meet in the morning.

As soon as the door closed behind her, Chip stopped his bizarre inspection and made his way back to where the rest of us waited. "Meet for what? A new backstory?"

"What has your hackles up?" Ron asked.

"All of it. There's nothing here that offers any real training to anyone as far as I can tell. Fine, a staged explosion based on something that happened. But we have one complete team, one guy here on his own, and someone in the mayor's seat who is not only not telling us everything, she wants us to know she's not telling us everything."

"She can't," Dan said.

"Bullshit. She let me change a crime scene. She didn't even try to stop me. I really could have pissed all over everything and she wouldn't have done a thing."

"To what end?" Ron asked.

"To say loud and clear what she really can't. This thing doesn't matter, and we're not here to try to figure out what might have really happened. We're here on pretense, and I'd bet my left nut that Donnigan knows that."

"Are you still thinking out loud?"

Chip shook his head. "Maybe. Well, no. I'm positive. Donnigan knows what this is all about. So does Linda, and she doesn't like it."

"If this doesn't matter," Doug asked, "then why are we here?"

"We're bait. We're a reason to pull Cooper in out of the cold."

"Wait a minute." Dan stepped past Doug to get closer to Chip. "Out of the cold? That implies he's on the run."

"Not necessarily," Ron said. "It might only mean that someone high up wants him in a specific location."

"They'd call him in."

"Not necessarily."

"Come on, Ron. When they want you, they bring you home."

"Man, you don't get it," Chip sighed. "They don't want to bring him home. They want to lure him to Donnigan."

"Again, why?"

"Because you don't bring someone home when the end goal is to have them disappear. Donnigan isn't just a nomad. He's *the* nomad. Donnigan is here to kill the poor son of a bitch."

~

We hadn't been in our hotel room for a full minute when Ron picked up the phone and left a message for Linda to call him back; he wanted a meeting with her, and he wanted it before she connected with Dan and Donnigan, definitely before throwing everyone together in the morning.

There were too many questions hanging in the air, he told me, but more than that, he wasn't entirely sure what the questions should be.

He trusted Chip's gut instincts; he wasn't sure that Chip had both feet on the right track, but he believed in what Chip saw when he looked at the mock explosion remnants. On the surface it looked good, but the details were missing.

He chewed over those, but did it quietly, letting it all stew in the back of his head. If he'd figured it out, he wasn't going to say anything, not until he'd run it by Linda.

A little before midnight we were stretched out on the bed, and I'd given up on her calling back. I was close to telling him to either turn the lights out and let me sleep, or give me a reason to not mind being tired in the morning, when the phone finally rang. I reached for it but he grabbed my hand and said quietly, "Wait."

It stopped on the second ring and he let my hand go as he sat up and reached for his shoes. When it rang again, he snatched up the receiver before I could.

He listened quietly without saying even "Hello," but just before he hung up he said, "Ten minutes."

"There's a diner down the street. I don't know about you, but I'm actually a little hungry. Bet you could get a good spotted dick there."

"Oh my God."

"It's food," he chuckled. "Pudding. Come on. They've got to have pie or something else you like."

"You want me to go?"

"You've been quiet as hell all day, which means you're soaking everything in. I'd like you to be there to hear what I don't."

I debated it for about three seconds and then rolled off the bed. I doubted he needed me there, but he wanted me to go, and hell, I wasn't passing up late night junk food. "The only thing I've heard today is that I was right all along. Donnigan is a douche. Though I am curious about how he became a nomad. Did he volunteer or did his team quit on him and left him with nothing else to do?"

"Here's your chance to find out." The door locked behind me as it clicked shut, and Ron reached for my hand. "Damn, when was the last time we took a late night walk?"

"This is work related. I don't think it counts."

Gently, he squeezed my hand. "We're alone. It counts."

I thought it would count more if he'd get the urge to set all his paperwork aside and take a long break for an evening walk at home, but it didn't seem as if he had much of a choice. In between assignments he was handling more and more data analysis, and while he plundered through most of it at home, I wasn't privy to it and didn't feel as if I could ask him to set it aside.

It was enough to know that if I did ask him to stop for a while and pay attention to me, he would.

Still, a simple five minute walk with him in the middle of the night was nice, work related or not. We didn't talk as we made our way to the diner; he was surely mulling over work, but he was with me and happy about it, and before we went in he pulled me close so that he could steal a kiss.

Linda was already there, seated at a table across the room from the door. She was hunched over a tattered paperback book, and while she appeared oblivious, I knew that she not only realized we were there, she'd already taken note of Ron's non-work-attire faded jeans and t-shirt, that he had a thick brushing of whiskers across his face, and that he was making an effort to not lose physical contact with me.

I also knew she hadn't expected me to be with him, but she would never let me see that.

"Before you even think about making fun of my reading material," she said as she closed the book, "my daughter gave it to me. This is her favorite book, apparently *ever*, and if I don't read it and then gush about how wonderful it is, she'll be crushed."

I leaned forward to get a better look. "Kathleen Woodiwiss," I mumbled. "I can't make fun of you. I read that and enjoyed it."

"My girl says this writer will change the face of romance novels. Since this is the first one I've ever read, I'll take her word for it."

"It's got a thirty five year old man and a seventeen year old girl. Let's hear it for pedophilia."

Ron sighed audibly.

"Oh, fine," I grumbled. "Let's talk about things that go boom. That'll make you happy."

"Men," Linda snickered. "All right, Ron, let's hear it. What is so important that you wanted to see me in the middle of the night?"

"My kid has good instincts," he ventured.

"He does."

"If he says he smells bullshit, I'm not going to inhale extra hard to see if he's right and I'm not stomping around barefoot to figure out where it is."

"I haven't seen any cows wandering around here."

"This is the U.S. we're dealing with. We import the finest bullshit found anywhere in the world. This assignment reeks of it, and it didn't take Chip long to catch a whiff."

Linda's lips quirked in a squelched grin, and she turned her attention to the waitress who approached the table. She ordered scones and coffee for all of us, and after the waitress had left she warned that the coffee was horrible, but it was our best bet there.

"So the coffee sucks," Ron said. "Get back to the bullshit. Is Donnigan the new RM?"

"Wow, straight to the point."

"I don't tap dance, Linda."

"No, you don't." Her eyes flicked toward me briefly, and she tapped her fingernails on the tabletop as she considered.

"It's above my security grade," I guessed. "Give me your book and I'll go hide on the other side of the diner."

"Talk about bullshit," Linda cackled. "You have ears like a cat. And yes, it's above your security clearance grade, but what the hell."

"Chip's already guessed as much about Donnigan," Ron said.

"So everyone knows."

Ron leaned forward, folded arms resting on the table, and looked her in the eyes. "This isn't field training for Justin Ray. You want him here, but I can't figure out why you just don't recall him. He reports to the SG, so why isn't he just skipping home like a good little Cooper?"

"Is this thinking out loud trait genetic?" she asked me. "How nuts does it drive you?"

"Very," I sighed.

"It's the whole setup, Linda," he went on. "Chip is right, there's nothing to be gained in it. All the important details are missing."

"Are they?"

"Yet...it still is a training assignment, isn't it? Just not for Justin Ray."

I shifted on my seat to look at him. "Then for whom? Donnigan?"

He was still looking at Linda. "No, she wasn't lying when she said Chip was requested on this assignment. Give him something he's interested in, pepper it with just enough reality that he has a chance of figuring out what it's supposed to be, and then bring Cooper in on the pretense that he's training his potential future replacement."

"But Chip figured out the scenario a little too quickly," Linda said.

"It was incomplete."

"It should have been enough. Who knew that with just a handful of data he would connect the dots?"

"You knew."

The waitress interrupted them, sliding a loaded plate of scones across the table, then as she filled coffee cups. Linda was deliberate as she took the time to stir sugar and milk into her coffee, blowing carefully into the cup before she took a sip.

After a few minutes, when we all had coffee and scones in front of us, she said, "I had hopes, Ron. Some of the small details were left out, because I want Chip to get a step ahead of Cooper."

"Why?"

"You know why Donnigan is here. If you know what he is now, you know why he's here."

"To take out Ray."

"I won't officially confirm or deny that. But I will tell you that he's not intended to be the first in line to get that job finished."

"Chip," Ron said flatly.

"What the hell did Cooper do?" I asked.

"Well, there's the rub," she said. "Usually the RM has an idea of why he's doing what he's doing. He's under the direct order of Alex Barstow, and Barstow didn't give him a reason."

"You shouldn't know that," Ron said.

"No, I shouldn't. But Harold isn't comfortable with any of this. He doesn't like the way Chip is being tested or the way they're trying to get him to take out someone who is supposed to be in a serious position of trust. He doesn't like the scenario, and he doesn't want to kill this kid without having a solid reason behind it."

"So either Chip does his job, or finds him a reason for it."

"No, not quite. I believe the expectation is that Chip will figure out on his own whatever Ray has done that has the SG's shorts in a wad and do it on principle. I don't think the SG took into consideration that in spite of how quickly Chip seems to act and what his terminal rate is, he doesn't kill as a knee jerk reaction. Whatever Ray has done would have to be so big—"

"Chip knows why Donnigan is here. The reason won't matter; he's not killing Cooper. He's not the hothead everyone wants to believe."

"That's what Harold and I are hoping."

"To what end? If Chip doesn't do it, then Donnigan has to."

"It's a conundrum," she said as she sipped at her coffee.

"What happens if he doesn't?" I asked.

"It's never happened, as far as I know," Ron replied. "It's one of those 'do it or else' type things."

"Theoretically, if Donnigan doesn't finish the job, he's dead," Linda said. "One way or the other. He can't just walk away from the job, he knows too much."

"Well, the typical RM knows too much," Ron said. "This is his first assignment, right? If he's just ineffective?"

She shook her head. "Harold Donnigan acts like a jerk and is not exactly well liked, but he is an effective agent and he gets the job done. If he fails at this without Ray taking him out first, he'll wind up choking—literally—on a blanket of suspicion."

I felt like I was being covered in a blanket of stupid, and said so. "So Donnigan doesn't want this particular assignment because he doesn't have a valid reason. I get that. But how does Chip play into this?"

They both inhaled and exhaled loudly, and I almost laughed at their timing.

Ron was the one who answered. "It's playing both ends against the middle. Chip is supposed to think we're here to put Cooper through a few training exercises. Coop thinks he's coming to put Chip's feet to the fire. Throw them together, have them work with each other, and hope they click."

"As in hang-out-after-hours kind of click?"

"Chip's likeable," Linda explained. "Ray is still pretty young and probably won't mind letting Chip drag him along in his nightly quest to find women and alcohol. The closer they get, the more Ray lets his guard down."

"And Chip is sharp enough to see what Ray isn't showing him and to hear what he isn't saying."

"And based on that the SG thinks he would kill the guy?" I asked. "Unless Cooper has molested a kid or killed a string of women, that's not how Chip operates. Even then he'd torture the guy for a while and turn him over. He won't kill anyone unless he feels like he has to."

Ron agreed. "Chip would drop Ray without blinking if he was an immediate threat, but without something that solid? It'll never happen. Anyone who knows him knows that."

"I know that. Harold knows that."

"But Donnigan is counting on Chip getting to whatever reason Barstow has for wanting his most trusted agent killed."

"If the reason is good enough"—she gave a light shrug of her shoulders—"Harold will do his job."

The bigger picture was still slipping past me. "And if not, he lets Ray run?"

"Donnigan will give him a subtle warning," Ron said quietly. "He'll give Ray a running start, and then spend the next couple of years tracking him down."

"This smacks of being personal," Linda said, "and it's convoluted because of that...but you didn't hear that from me."

"But eventually Donnigan will have to take the guy down," I said. "So why wait?"

She took another long sip of her coffee.

"What's he got and how long does he have?" Ron asked.

I jerked with a spasm of surprise. "What?"

With a heavy sigh, Ron said, "The only way Donnigan can give this guy breathing room is if he's about to run out of his own. And I'm guessing Linda is the only other one who knows. It's not a matter of record yet, is it?"

She set the cup down, being very deliberate in how she slid it away from her, turning it until the handle pointed toward Ron, laying the spoon she'd used to stir it on a napkin. "I have known Harold Donnigan almost as long as I've known you, Ron. He can be abrasive, he's a throwback to the thirties where women are concerned and hates the idea of us in the field, and he can be a total jerk, but he's still my friend. On the job I will give him as hard a time as he gives everyone else, and I will chafe at his unfortunate sexist viewpoints, but..."

"But off the clock is different," Ron guessed.

"He's more open off the clock. You two," she said pointing to Ron and then me, "when you two got married, while everyone else was moaning behind your backs that it was a stupid move, he was telling them to shut up. Whether or not you personally were a good match, he thought it was a brilliant career move, giving you solid covers. And he honestly wished you well, that your relationship would be so much more than work. And you," she looked at me, "he may not have wanted you on his team, but he still fought like hell to keep you."

"Oh, come on."

"He thinks women should be in protected positions behind desks if they have to be involved at all. But he also knows how good a pilot you are and when Ron came bearing transfer papers, he balked. If you weren't going to be behind a desk, he wanted your skills right where he could make use of them. He tried to take it to Barron, he raised holy hell, but Dan had a new team and needed reliable players, and his second had incredible pull."

"He was not happy, no, but he did treat her like shit when he had her, Linda," Ron said.

"He treats everyone like shit. He's not about to get close to his subordinates because he thinks that will reduce their willingness to follow orders. That doesn't mean he doesn't recognize talent when he sees it. It also doesn't mean he won't take huge risks to protect someone from a job they shouldn't be doing."

She was looking at Ron as she said that.

"When I had to bring Chip in after his little German adventure a couple of years ago, Harold went a little nuts. Others grumbled about it, but he exploded. And none of it was 'Oh, Gallery's an idiot, letting his kid in on this.' It was all directed at the SG and how horribly he was using your son. As far as Harold is concerned, Chip getting one foot in the door is criminal."

"And you don't disagree with that."

"Hell, Ron, *you* don't disagree with that. Right now, it feels like Barstow has his sights set on Chip as the next Cooper. And we can't let that happen."

"No," Ron said quietly. "We can't."

"All we want right now — and this is from me, this is in no way official — is for Chip to glean a reason from Ray about why he's such a sudden target. Then let Harold decide what his next step is."

"How do you propose we help him?"

"Don't let any of this go any further than this table. Don't let Dan push Chip into anything that will complicate Harold's end game, and don't hint to him that this is anything more than what he was told it would be. Dan thinks this is pure training, so let him keep thinking that."

"With all the holes in it? He should probably be told that Chip is the one the whole bomb aftermath is meant for."

She nodded. "All right. When we meet in a few hours, I'll tell him that much. And because of that, keep your team members at bay. This should just be Dan, Harold, and me."

"I still can't picture Donnigan as the RM," Ron said.

"And he's dying?" I choked out.

"No. But his career will be over sooner rather than later. He's hoping that if he winds up letting Ray run, that sad fact will save his ass when the time comes."

"It would have to be as good as fatal," Ron said.

She nodded. "He noticed some uncontrollable twitching in his fingers a while back. It comes and goes, but happens enough that he thought he should see someone."

"Outside of the agency," Ron said.

"Absolutely. And when it gets bad enough, he'll pop into the clinic and let them re-diagnose him with the Parkinson's disease he already knows he has. He doesn't seem to think that will be in the too-distant future."

I didn't like the guy, but I wanted to take a moment to commiserate even if he wasn't there, but she went on.

"Harold is shadowing Chip, just so you know. Not knowing what Ray has done, he thought it would be the wiser move. Any idea how Chip will react if he realizes he has a tail?"

"When he realizes? If he were being tailed by an unknown, it would get physical. When he spots Donnigan, he'll probably allow his inner fourteen year old to come out and play and either give Donnigan a hard trail to follow or he'll confront him with a barrage of insults."

I voted on the latter. "I'm sure Chip has a list of names he hasn't used on Donnigan yet."

"And I'm sure he's tested every single one of them on me," Ron snorted.

"He's a good kid, Ron. It's a shame he got sucked into this, but he's still a good kid." With a sigh, she slid her book across the table toward me. "I hate to ask you now, but there are a few things I need to discuss with your husband."

"That's all right." I pushed away from the table and got up. "I'm just going to head back. One of us should get some sleep tonight."

Ron stretched up to meet me as I leaned over to kiss him. "I won't let her keep me too long. And be careful, all right?"

~

Later, I chalked up my inattention to the idea that as I walked back to the motel I was chewing over the notion that Harold Donnigan had wanted me on his team after all. His treatment of me was nothing special; he was an ass to everyone. He never needed me to know that he appreciated my job skills, he just needed me to do my job, and apparently I'd done it well enough that when Ron told him I was being reassigned, he fought it.

It wouldn't have mattered. I would have wanted out of Donnigan's team even if he'd lavished praises about me where I could hear him do it. I didn't need the aggravation of working under someone with a perpetual hard-on for bad moods, and the relief I felt at reassignment wouldn't have changed.

Still, while I didn't like the guy, I hated what he was facing.

I was in the motel parking lot, maybe fifty feet from the door to our room, thinking that I would find a way to ask Doug about what Donnigan had to look forward to—without letting him know why I wanted to know—when I finally heard soft footsteps behind me.

The moment of hesitation—a heartbeat or two that I took to decide if it was Ron trying to catch up to me or if I should run—was a moment too much. Before I could get a step further I felt the sickening crush of hands griping at my arm and neck, and watched my own feet flip into the air as I was turned upside down.

It took another heartbeat for the pain of being slammed into the asphalt to overwhelm me; it was just long enough to recognize deeply violet eyes that were hardened in anger and fear, and I tried to protest, but as he straddled me his hand went around my throat and he began to squeeze.

Fighting back was pointless; I could have flailed and clawed at him, but it would have been energy wasted. I wasn't going to out-muscle him, but I also wasn't about to let him crush my airway and kill me before I had a chance to throw him off me.

I stretched my neck, leaning my head back as I tried to loosen the hold he had on me, just enough to be able to keep breathing and to let blood flow to my brain.

"No," he barked. "Don't move. Don't speak. I swear to God I'll break your fucking neck. I'm not taking any of your shit. I'm not letting you follow me. You're not turning me over to your fucking Russian. I won't let it happen. I'll fuck you over until you can't blink, you stupid cow."

Suddenly, he let go of my throat and I sucked in a sharp breath, but before I could move, he jammed a thumb into the space just under my right ear near my jaw, and the pain of it exploded through my head.

"I will seriously, seriously fuck—" He pressed harder, causing tears to spring from my eyes. "Yeah, why the hell not? You're a goddamned traitor, it's what you deserve. I'll fuck you so hard you'll wish you would split in two."

"Fucking. Try," I wheezed.

He thrust his thumb as hard as he could, and in a flash of white heat I felt my skin split; he kept it there, covering half my face with his fingers and I felt him fumbling and heard the clatter of his belt buckle as he undid it, then as he unzipped his jeans.

Don't waste your energy. The bastard wants to play, he has to get off you and get between your legs, and you can rear up and snap his goddamned neck with a fast scissor.

I went slack; I wasn't going to fight him, not until he was in a position where I could whip both legs up and wrap them around his neck.

"Yeah. Don't fucking move, or I swear I'll—"

In that instance, he flew off me, and I heard his skull crack against the fender of a car five feet away.

Pain shattered through me as I rolled onto my side, trying to get up, and Chip was there, palming the guy's head in his hand as he bounced it into the pavement over and over.

Blood was already pooling on the ground.

I fell back, too drained to move, and not eager to stop him.

I closed my eyes and listened to the sick thud of a skull being crushed, and tried not to picture the carnage. I laid there until I heard someone else running across the parking lot and prayed it was Ron.

"Jesus, Chip! Stop. He's dead."

The noise stopped, and I forced my eyes open. Chip was

standing there, wiping his hands off on his jeans. As if nothing was out of sorts, he leaned over me and asked, "You all right?"

"I've been better," I croaked, hating the rasp that rumbled through the agony that was now boiling in my throat.

"Can you get up?"

"I think so."

He reached down and grabbed both of my hands, very carefully helping me sit up first, and then stand, and his hands lingered on mine as he considered me closely, doing his own assessment of the damage. "What the hell are you doing out here alone in the middle of the night?"

I was about to ask him the same thing.

"Don't look," he said, pulling me away. "Where's Ron?"

"Diner down the street," I managed.

"All right, we'll go there if you can walk."

"I think so."

He turned me in the direction of the diner, standing behind me in case I turned to see the damage he had inflicted.

"Donnigan. You coming?"

I heard Donnigan's feet crunching bits of gravel as he walked towards us and I almost turned, but Chip had his hand on my back and he wouldn't let me.

"No, I'll clean this up." He pointed to the thin ribbon of blood running down my neck. "And you'd be better off taking her to the doc instead of her husband."

I knew Chip didn't want to take me into the motel; it would mean walking past the carnage he'd left in the parking lot. But he also knew Donnigan was right, and said quietly to me, "Seriously, don't look."

"I'm sure I've seen worse."

"Hell, I know she has," Donnigan said. "She's a big girl, Davis. She probably would have killed the bastard if you hadn't."

I wasn't as sure about that; I'd wanted to break his neck and I was certain I could have inflicted enough damage to get away, but I didn't know if I would have kept the fight up until he was dead.

"Can you get Ron before you clean this up?" Chip asked.

"Yeah, sure. But Jesus, Chip. You just took out Cooper."

~

The first thing Doug told me to do was to take my shirt off, and I balked. I had a small puncture wound just behind my ear, I argued, and my throat was sore as hell, but that was it. I hadn't hit my head on the pavement—even as I was being slammed down I had the presence of mind to tuck my chin into my chest—and I was not taking my clothes off for whatever gawking he was inclined to do.

While he started digging through his bag for supplies Chip gently turned me so that I could see my back in the mirror; the shirt was pocked marked with holes and peppered with small spots of blood, and I realized then that I wasn't in pain because I was mostly numb.

Chip started to turn away as I began to peel the shirt off, but I only managed to get it halfway up before the first twinges set in. My right shoulder was tight and the simple act of trying to pull my shirt off sent a spray of agony through it, and I had to ask him to help.

I sat at the edge of one of the beds, and Doug handed me a pillow. "Clutch it," he said. "This might hurt and if you're hugging that, you're less likely to squirm."

I flinched once, when he pulled the first bits of gravel from my skin, but that was less the pain of it and more the surprise that I had a dozen or more tiny rocks embedded in my skin and he was going to pull them out one by one.

"It's not bad," he said as he dropped one into a glass. "Not deep. But you're going to be bruised and by this afternoon it'll feel like someone ran over you with a truck." He pointed towards his bag and asked Chip to get a pair of scissors out, and before I could ask what he wanted them for, he cut through my bra strap.

"What the hell, Doug?"

"The hooks are bent and I needed to get under the strap. Just keep the pillow in place and we won't be ogling you."

"Well, I'll certainly try," Chip teased.

"Like you haven't seen enough boobage in your lifetime," I sighed.

"Boobage?" He let out a short laugh and I thought he was going to say something else, but he was reaching for the door handle and pulled it open before I could tell him to give me a second to cover up a little more than what the pillow was hiding.

Ron bolted in, slightly out of breath, with Linda three steps behind him.

"I'm all right," I said before he could ask. "Minor road rash. Sore throat. I'm fine."

"I shouldn't have let you come back alone," he breathed. "Son of a bitch."

I sighed hard. "I'm not some teenage girl, Ron. I don't need an escort or a chaperone."

"But—"

"But nothing. This isn't your fault. I'm not even sure it's my fault."

"How could it be?" Linda asked.

Ron sat down on the bed next to me, very carefully, setting his hand on my leg. "All Donnigan could tell us was that Cooper attacked you in the parking lot. What did he do? Are you sure you're all right?"

"Doug says I'll be sore, but I'm fine."

Linda reached for a chair by the door and pulled it over to the bed. "Details," she said as she sat. "What did he do and what did he say?"

"Grabbed me and slammed me down onto my back," I told her. "He didn't say much of anything that made any kind of sense."

Chip snorted. "He didn't have to. The son of a bitch was trying to get his pants off. Barstow's favorite agent intended to rape her."

"Kris." Ron squeezed my thigh gently. "I'm sorry. I should have come with you."

"Maybe not," Linda said. "Clearly, Justin Ray had some issues. If you'd been with her there's no telling what he would have done. He might have shot first with no intention of asking questions."

"Is this why Donnigan is supposed to take the mother fucker out?" Chip asked. "He's a goddamned rapist?"

She didn't try to gloss over Donnigan's role in this training exercise. Instead she told him that neither she nor Donnigan had been given a reason he'd been sent to eliminate Cooper. They both wanted one; he didn't have a problem with the job if it was warranted, but he didn't want to do it without a clear reason.

"Yeah, well, now he doesn't have to worry about it."

As Doug finished picking tiny rocks out of my skin, Donnigan came in. He dropped a gun, wallet and passport onto the other bed, and then fished a small notebook out from his back pocket, adding it to the pile.

"I took all ID off him," he said. "It'll take too long for a cleanup team to get here, so I left him where he was. Give it two or three hours and someone will spot him and call the police."

"Should we bug out?" Doug asked.

"No," Ron sighed. "We stay put and if asked, we heard nothing, we saw nothing."

I tried to turn my head to look at him, but Doug held it still as he dabbed at the wound behind my ear. "That waitress can spot us as having been at the diner in the middle of the night," I reminded him. "And she'll surely remember Donnigan coming in to get you."

"Still."

"Whether we stay or go really doesn't matter," Linda said. She reached over and picked Ray's passport off the bed and began flipping through it. "I'm curious about him. He was obviously good enough for Barstow to tap him for the Cooper's job, so what changed? Why does the SG want him dead? And why did he attack Kris?"

Donnigan sat on the other bed, directly across from me. "He recognized her, most likely."

Ray's anger-laced voice cut through me. "He did say he wasn't going to let me follow him. He said he wasn't going to let me turn him over to my Russian. And that I was a traitor. Whether than meant just me or all of us, I don't know. I don't think his original intention was rape, though. It seemed like that was an afterthought."

"A message," Ron guessed.

"Or he was just fucking nuts," Chip said.

Linda turned to look at him. "Chip, I like you, and I appreciate your formidable skills, but if I hear you say the word 'fuck' again in any form for the next forty eight hours…"

"Sorry," he said, biting back a grin. "Didn't mean to offend."

"He comes by the mouth honestly." Ron looked up at Chip, his eyes rimmed with pain. "Just find a few new adjectives, all right?"

"Next move?" Donnigan asked.

"We report back. The job's done, Harold."

Ron's grip on my leg tightened a little. "I still want to know what the deal with this guy is. If he'd gone rogue, we'd have a shoot on sight order. If he was breaking laws left and right and calling attention to himself, Barstow would have just recalled him. You said it smacked of being personal? It has to be, and I want to know what pushed Ray over the edge."

Donnigan lifted the notebook off the bed and handed it to Ron; he finally let go of my leg, reluctantly, and reached out to take it. "He kept a record of his safe houses. It gives us places to start."

"More than one is local," Ron mused as he flipped through the notebook. To Chip he said, "On the off chance someone saw you... let Doug cut your hair. Go for short, mangle it if you have to, just make sure it's different. Ditch your clothes. Slash the underside of the mattress and bury them in deep, then remake the bed. And then I want you and Doug to take Kris back to our room and stay with her. Make sure she gets some sleep."

"I don't need a babysitter, Ron."

He ignored me. "One of you stays awake until I get back. One of you stays with her at all times. You got that?"

Chip nodded.

I wanted to argue with him, but he was—as it was beginning to annoy the hell out of me—on the clock. My input was not asked for nor required.

"We'll check out the closest addresses and report by the end of the day," he told Linda. "In the meantime you need to call Ray in as deceased and abandoned. Have you let Barstow know that Chip already shredded the exercise to hell and it was worthless?"

"No."

"Good. Buy Donnigan and me some time. Tell him that Chip is proceeding with it, that he knows it's an exercise for his benefit and not Cooper's. That might give us a day or two."

"Done."

He leaned over and kissed me, lingering for a moment. "I know, not exactly professional," he whispered before he got up. "We'll make this as fast as we can."

Linda followed Ron and Donnigan out; Doug was shoving supplies back into his bag, and Chip handed me my shirt.

"Turn around, you perv," I sighed. "You, too, Doug. I don't care how many other agent's boobs you've seen, you don't get to see mine."

Without complaint, they both turned around. I tossed the pillow back onto the bed and shrugged out of the remnants of my bra before gingerly pulling the shirt over my head, praying I wouldn't have to ask one of them to help.

Doug was right, I was going to ache, and it was going to be bad.

As I ran my fingers through my hair, trying to smooth it out, I looked over at them. They still had their backs to me, but Doug was looking down at the floor, and Chip was looking right into a mirror, grinning at me.

"You sons of bitches."

"You told us to turn around, not to not look," Chip said. "Thumbs up, by the way."

I wanted to be irritated, but between his unapologetic grin and my fatigue, it didn't seem to matter.

After Doug butchered Chip's hair, Chip quickly changed clothes and did as Ron said; he had Doug lift the edge of the mattress up so that he could slice into it and he jammed the blood stained clothes in as deeply as he could, the hair he'd had cut off wrapped into his t-shirt. When the bed was re-made they started gathering their things up, shoving clothes into backpacks and wallets into back pockets. Whether I liked it or not, I had two hairy babysitters for the duration.

Before he opened the door, Chip stopped and turned, an almost puzzled look on his face. "Man—no one woke Dan up. He has no clue what's going on. He's going to be pissed."

~

Just before dawn, when they thought I was asleep, I rolled over and tried to see them through the dark. They were sitting at the small table by the window, playing cards by the thin light that seeped in from the parking lot. Chip kept pulling the sheer curtain back an inch or two, looking for signs that Ray's body had been found.

Past the dull buzz of their hushed voices, I didn't hear anything; no one screaming at the discovery of a dead man with his head bashed in, no sirens in the distance.

"I can't believe Ron just left," Chip said, voice low.

"He's got a job to do."

"Fuck the job. His wife was attacked and damn near raped. He should have stayed here with her and sent one of us instead."

"Kris is why he went," Doug said. "It probably feels personal."

"Personal? Then send *me*. Send his son. But stay here with her when she needs him. And don't tell me she doesn't. As tough as she can be, after that, she needs him."

I wanted to speak up and tell them that it was fine; I understood what he was doing and why. I was fine with him taking off with Donnigan to chase after the secrets of a dead man. There were questions hanging in the air and we all wanted the answers, and he was the best one to get them.

I wanted to, but even with the truths buried there, I would have been lying.

As the soreness ramped up, and as every twitch was turning into misery, the only thing I wanted was Ron curled up in bed next to me, the warmth radiating off of him a quiet assurance that all was all right, and all would keep being all right.

~

"Scale of one to ten," Chip said as he looked across the coffee shop to where Dan and Linda were in a heated discussion, "how pissed off is he?"

"Twelve," Doug said.

I glanced over; Dan was gritting his teeth, his jaw working hard as he chewed and tried to swallow his anger. "It might have gone over better if he hadn't been woken up by sirens and people shouting. We should have gotten him last night."

We heard the first sirens around five o'clock and forty five minutes later police were pounding on the door. Chip gestured for me to stay in bed, dropped a pillow and blanket on the floor and told Doug to lie down and cover up as he whipped off his shirt and pants, tossing them to the far side of the bed.

When Chip opened the door he looked disheveled enough—his hair was wild and he hadn't shaved in two days—to have been pulled from sleep by all the noise. I sat up in bed, keeping the blanket pulled around me; we denied hearing anything during the night, gave the officer the names we had registered under, and when asked about our relationship—something which I was primed to refuse to answer because it didn't matter—Chip screwed up his face and said, "Man, she's my *mom*. Don't look at us like that."

When the cop looked at Doug, Chip sighed and said, "He's my boyfriend. Got any more questions?"

Twenty minutes later Dan was on the phone ordering us to meet him at the coffee shop; we stuffed everything we had brought with us into backpacks, knowing we wouldn't be going back to the motel, and set off on foot, hoping it looked like we were just heading out for the day.

Everything hurt; my neck felt wrenched, my back felt like it was on fire and it took effort to move my arms without groaning. Even my legs hurt. I tried to move as if everything was fine, hoping I didn't look as strained as I knew I was.

When we were around the block, out of sight of the motel, I caved to the discomfort and asked them to slow down. Chip let me lean into him, my hand gripped around his arm for balance, and we made our way to the coffee shop slowly.

Dan was there when we arrived and already mad as hell.

Chip gave him the abbreviated version of events, and when Linda walked in we stayed rooted to where we were; none of us wanted to follow them, and I especially didn't want to be a part of their discussion.

He was still tense as he made his way to our table, and Linda was right behind him, shrugging almost apologetically as Dan dropped heavily into the booth next to Doug. She pulled a chair from a nearby table and sat at the end of the booth, her arms folded and resting on the table.

Almost as soon as Dan looked at me, the irritation faded away.

"Are you sure you're all right?" he asked.

"Sore, but I'll live."

"And Chip got there in time?"

"My hero," I snorted. "Dan, I'm bruised and sore, but that's all."

"I want another look at your back later," Doug said. "Before you get a chance to shower, I want to check it. And your neck."

"You just want to get my shirt off again."

"I'll help," Chip offered. "You know, because you're so sore and all."

Linda sighed hard, less annoyed with him than she was amused. "We need to leave the area," she said. "I presume you're all prepared to go?"

She wanted us to head back to the faux publishing office to give Chip a chance to take one more long, hard look at it, and to take as many photographs as he thought he would need. From there we would head to another hotel and wait for Ron and Donnigan to report to her. What they found would determine where we went from there.

It was a long day of sifting through the carefully placed rubble; Chip had Doug taking photos of the damage from every conceivable angle while he searched for clues that would back up his Red Army theory. While he found no traces of blood, he found small blast marks on the underside of two desks and at juncture points along the wall, six bombs in all.

Nothing stood out as proof, but he said his report would reflect that he understood it was an exercise and that he would be unable to obtain definitive samples of residue, but based on his knowledge of the organization and its history, as well as being told to base his assumptions on this being Germany and not England, this was staged to be the work of the Red Army.

If he was wrong, so be it.

"You have at least forty eight hours to write the report in your head," Linda reminded him. "Scratch out notes on the ride home, but be sure you let us read them. We'll back up whatever you say."

Dan balked at this. "You want him to falsify a report."

"What I want," she said evenly, "is for him to give the Secretary General exactly what he expects."

It wasn't until late afternoon that we checked into a hotel fifteen miles from the last. Linda and Dan checked in together, causing

Chip to snort in amusement, and I checked the rest of us into the same room, telling the desk clerk that my husband would be joining us later.

I had no strong desire to share a room with them, but Chip was adamant—one of them was sticking with me until Ron returned.

"I do not want to share a bed with you," Doug grumbled on the elevator ride up.

"What? You don't want to be my boyfriend anymore?"

"You damn well better buy me a giant steak dinner before-hand."

"Hey, baby, you want the fancy dinner, you better put out a little something up front. We get upstairs, you can do a little dance for me. Shake your cha-chas."

"Cha-chas? What kind of freak are you?"

The bantering didn't stop until when we were in the room; it was stuffy and dim, but before I could get Chip to open the curtains and a window, Doug was gesturing for me to take my shirt off and let him look at my back.

"You can lift it and peek under," I said. "Your boyfriend will ogle otherwise."

"You," he said to Chip. "Find the ice bucket and go fill it. A plastic bag, too, in case I need to make an ice pack for her."

When the door had closed behind Chip, I reluctantly asked Doug to help me peel the shirt over my head and stood there with it clasped firmly to my chest while he very gently ran his fingers over the small tears and divots on my back. He gingerly touched a finger to spots on both shoulder blades and said, "You're starting to bruise and it's going to get much worse. By the day after tomorrow you'll be black and blue from one side to the other."

"Don't tell me it's going to hurt more."

"Unfortunately, it will. Before you go to bed I want to put an antibiotic cream on all the nicks and cuts. That's about the best I can do until we get stateside."

He helped me tug the shirt back down, and as he was probing the wound behind my ear Chip knocked on the door, waiting a few seconds before coming in.

"Ice in a bucket. A bag full of ice." He set them on the bath-room vanity. "Anything else?"

"Could you go down to the front desk for me? Doug asked. "See if they have any Paracetamol, and if they do, get an entire bottle if you can."

"Parawhat?"

"It's Tylenol. Paracetamol. If you forget it by the time you get there, ask the guy for something that's aspirin, but not. He'll know what you mean."

"Is that going to be strong enough?" Chip asked.

"I can't exactly fill a prescription for anything stronger here. Hopefully it'll be enough to take the edge off."

"I don't hurt that much," I said.

"Yet." Doug turned to Chip. "Paracetamol."

I crossed the room to the window, intending on pulling the curtain open, but as I raised my arm the pain shot across my back and I instead found myself fumbling for a chair nearby.

Doug scrambled to help me, letting me grab onto his hands as I slowly sat down. "How bad is it, really?" he asked. "No bullshit."

"The Tylenol isn't going to cut it, Doug."

"Scale of one to ten?"

"Seven." I sucked in a sharp breath between clenched teeth. "And a half."

"So, it's more like an eight." He sat in the other chair. "I don't think you broke anything, but I'd be happier if I could get you in for x-rays. At the very least I'd be happier if I had access to some better pain control for you."

I would have been happier, too. "I'll survive," I assured him. "I've felt worse. And this is all surface pain, nothing deep."

"Kris, your spine isn't exactly buried deep. Neither are your shoulder blades. I want a better look."

He wanted a better look, I wanted to cry. I didn't think either of us was getting what we wanted for a while. I also wanted to lie down, but that was going to hurt too much, and I damn well wasn't going to jack up the pain any higher than it already was.

Leaning forward and resting my arms on the table wasn't an option, either. I tried to move and fire ripped between my shoulders, effectively pinning me in place.

I was about to tell Doug I thought it was getting worse by the minute, but the phone rang and he got up to answer it. I closed my eyes and began breathing deeply, hoping that I could distract myself through the spasm.

When I heard him say, "Yeah, we'll be down in a minute," I groaned audibly.

"You want to get up," he said, holding a hand out to help me up. "Chip ran into Linda, she made a phone call, and you're getting some decent pain meds. Hydrocodone."

"I have to go downstairs for this?"

"You have to go down to the restaurant and eat something. You need food in your stomach when you take it, and she wants to see us all anyway."

Professionalism be damned; I leaned against him the entire way down, my head on his shoulder and hands gripping at his arm. He walked slowly across the lobby with me, and eased me into a chair at the table where Linda and Dan were waiting for us.

"Chip's outside waiting for the courier," Linda said, looking at me with sympathy.

I gave a bare nod of my head; I didn't care where Chip was, I didn't care that Doug wanted me to eat, I didn't care if Dan suddenly threw his clothes off and started dancing on the table. I was exhausted and wanted to sleep, and the nausea of fatigue was making the idea of food a horrible one.

I barely noticed when Chip came in and sat across from me, but I shook myself into enough awareness to order whatever the soup of the day was when Doug nudged me. I let their voices become a dull buzz while I went back to deep, slow breathing, my inner mantra a litany of *this sucks, this sucks, this sucks*.

When the waiter brought the food, Chip took half of one of the sandwiches he'd ordered and set it on a napkin, sliding it across the table toward me. "You need more than soup," he said. "And I'm not handing over the magic pills unless you eat."

Calling him a bastard was too much work.

When he did finally hand them over, it was to Doug.

I didn't care.

I dutifully ate the soup and turkey sandwich, and sat back to wait for Linda to be done with whatever she was talking about; I crawled into my own head, wishing she would get to the point and let us go.

When Doug got up, I started to follow, hoping he would offer to help, but he stepped aside. I clenched my teeth, steadying myself against how I knew it was going to feel as I pushed myself up, but before I could suck in a deep breath, Ron was sitting beside me, his hand warm on my arm.

"I know that look," he said softly. "How bad is it?"

Better than it was a minute ago, better now that I won't be getting through the night alone, better if we can get our own room so that if it does get the better of me I can cry and not worry about how it looks and how awful I'd feel if it was someone other than you comforting me.

"Tolerable," I lied.

"Doug's going to drug her to sleep tonight," Chip offered.

"And I still want you both with her tonight."

"One of us awake?"

"No, if you think you can wake easily, go ahead and sleep."

I set my hand on his. "Wait. You're not staying?"

When he took a long, deep breath, I felt my irritation begin to bubble. "We have a few more places we want to check. You'll be on a plane in the morning, though, so you'll be able to sleep in your own bed tomorrow night."

Our bed, dammit.

"I can go with Donnigan," Chip said. "Go home with her."

"Not your job, Chip. I need to get this done."

I tuned him out. If he wasn't staying, I didn't want to hear what he had to say. It wasn't his job, either; it was Dan's job. It was Donnigan's or Linda's, but clearly not his.

Half an hour later we were alone at the table; I hadn't noted where Dan and Linda went, but Chip and Doug were waiting by the door. Ron leaned close, sliding his arm behind my shoulders, very gently, trying to not jar me.

"This trail you're running on better be worth it," I said.

"It will be if we can get ahead of the SG."

"Ahead of him? Why?"

"He wanted the Cooper dead for a reason. We want to know what it is."

"And then? Become his next target?"

"There was more in Ray's notebook than addresses, Kris. He had specific notes about you, what you look like, and that you had a protracted conversation with a Soviet pilot two years ago. We know what that was—it was when you flew the stealth jet from South Korea to Okinawa—but his notes never mentioned the reason behind that. You said Ray mentioned a Russian...that makes me think the SG used you as bait to get Ray to do something stupid enough to get him killed. I need to find out more, and Donnigan wants to destroy anything and everything we find that even hints that Ray was there. If we bring proof of that back to Barstow, that we erased as many traces of Ray that we could, he'll accept it as us having cleaned up after Cooper. If we find the reason Barstow wanted him dead, he never has to know."

"And do what with that information?"

"Depends on what it is. But we're only taking forty-eight hours. More than that and he'll be suspicious. I'll be two days behind you, that's all. I'll make sure Chip takes care of anything you need."

Chip couldn't begin to take care of what I needed. I couldn't ask him to help me in and out of the hot shower I was dying to take. I didn't want to rely on him to help me change clothes. I wasn't going to be able to curl around him in the middle of the night, I refused to admit to him that I knew if I closed my eyes I'd see him pounding Justin Ray's head into the pavement, and I sure as hell wasn't go to break down in front of him, not with Doug there.

What I needed kissed me goodbye and walked out the door with Harold Donnigan.

~

Seventy-two hours later he crept into the apartment late at night, headed straight for his safe and quietly opened it, shoved something into it, and then kicked off his clothes and slid into bed. When I asked him if he'd gotten the information he wanted he said he had, but didn't offer anything beyond that.

He asked all the right questions—how was I feeling, did Doug get a chance to do a thorough exam, were there any residual problems— but he never did the one thing I wanted.

He never apologized for not staying with me when I needed him the most.

There was nothing broken, the small cuts and divots on my back were healing over, and the wound behind my ear was fine. I was still sore but didn't need the pain medication Linda had procured for me in England; Chip had helped me dress and undress until I got home, when I felt like I could finally manage on my own.

The visions of him killing Justin Ray were beginning to fade.

I told Ron I was fine, kissed him goodnight, and rolled over.

~

"Hawaii."

Chip was sitting in a squeaky metal chair, tipped back just far enough that with a bare nudge he would fall over. Doug was in the chair next to him, feet planted firmly on the floor, his elbows on his knees, and I had taken Ron's desk chair. Ron was seated on the edge of his desk, arms folded across his stomach, and he nodded to Chip's surprised repeat of where we were headed.

"I have a meeting at Hickam Air Force Base and they want Kris to deliver Barstow's jet to a team headed for Brazil. Since Kris is flying, we have the right to request Doug, and if he's going, you might as well, too."

"Where's Dan?" Doug asked.

"Taking a few personal days."

"What's her name?" Chip asked, finally setting the chair upright.

"I didn't ask and he didn't volunteer," Ron snorted, amused. "We can fly out tonight, leave the plane at Hickam, and take three days after my meeting. Free vacation, folks. After that clusterfuck in London last month? We need the down time and I think we should make the best of it."

"This isn't going to be like the time we went to Tahoe for the weekend is it?" Chip asked. "Because I really don't want to share another hotel room with you two. All the heavy breathing is really gross."

"Hey, we never—"

He winked at me, so fast I barely caught it.

"You'll room with Doug," Ron said. "Go home, grab some clothes, and be back here in two hours."

~

We arrived at Hickam mid-morning and turned Barstow's jet over to Linda Jackson, then took a taxi to the hotel. I was exhausted by then and only wanted to sleep, and Ron needed to head for his meeting with an OSI liaison; we checked in, he reminded Chip to at least let Doug know where he was going to be if they weren't hanging out together, and I crashed until late afternoon.

Sometime around four o'clock I forced myself to get up; I felt like I could sleep another five or six hours, but knew better. If I could put up with being tired, I'd be able to sleep at night; if not, I'd be tossing and turning and keeping Ron awake.

At some point, he'd come back to the room. Taped to the mirror over the sink was a note: *Be back around seven, don't wait for me to get dinner. Maybe drinks, walk the beach? Love you, Ron.*

He'd pulled the curtains closed; I'd left them open, hoping the light would wake me early, but all he probably saw was me with my head buried under a pillow, and closed them in hopes that it would help. That little bit of consideration tugged at me, and I smiled as I pulled them open.

The view was incredible. He'd gotten us rooms looking over the ocean, and I slid the door open, stepping out onto the balcony. The warm breeze washed over me and I stood there, holding onto the railing as I soaked it in, until I heard movement beside me.

Doug was on the balcony next to mine, elbows on the railing as he stared out at the water.

"Chip take off on you already?" I asked.

He snorted out a laugh as he nodded. "He zoned in on someone half an hour after we got here and within an hour had her offering to show him the sights."

"Kind of rude, just leaving you like that."

He looked over at me. "I would have done the same thing."

"I don't think so. You've never struck me as the type, Doctor Doug."

He turned, angling his body so that he was facing me, but still able to lean against the balcony rail. "How so?"

"You're a lot nicer than Chip."

"Aren't you supposed to be, you know, non-judgmental about him?"

"As has been pointed out many times over the last two years, I'm not his mother. I love him, but face it; he can be a little prick."

"That's probably a good thing," Doug mused. "That you don't think of yourself like his mother."

"How's that?"

"Nothing." He turned back to look at the ocean. "Ron's not back?"

I let it go for now. "Apparently he was here for a little while and I slept right through it. He left a note saying he'd be back around seven. Have you eaten yet? Because I'm starving and I wouldn't mind the company."

"I could eat."

We met in the hallway a few minutes later and rode the elevator down with half a dozen other people. We were pressed against the back wall and Doug stood there leaning back, hands stuffed into his pockets, while he pretended to stare down at his own feet, but with a glance I could see where his eyes were really aimed. He tried to soak in every detail of the young brunette just ahead and to his left, her sunburned skin and bikini that was about a half size too small, breasts threatening to spill out of the top.

"Doug," I whispered, leaning in closer so that only he would hear, "I swear to God, if you pop a boner in here, I'll point and laugh and make sure she knows."

"Just looking," he sighed. "Besides, she's got a ring on her left hand. That's as good as shoving ice cubes down my shorts."

That didn't keep him from looking, and even as she left the elevator he kept watching her.

Halfway through dinner, I realized that Doug "just looked" a lot. Any time a woman even close to his age walked by he took notice, and no matter what we were talking about his gaze followed her across the room.

"You could be a little less obvious," I finally said. "And go talk to one of them. It doesn't do you any good to sit here with me and mentally drool."

"Well, that would be rude," he said, turning his attention away from a twenty-something redhead who had just made her way to the bar. "And I am being rude. I'm sorry."

I waved it off. "My feelings won't be hurt if you want to trail after someone like a puppy dog."

"Not really interested," he said. "We're only going to be here a few days."

He took a sip of his beer, and I took a quick inventory of Doug Stone. Dirty blond hair, dark, brooding eyes; he was a little taller than I and fairly thin, though not in a way that suggested he was ever one of the kids picked on during gym class. He knew how to be polite and was always apologetic when he thought he'd crossed a line. His smile was bright, his hair usually a few days past needing a trim but never unkempt; even his fingernails were neatly trimmed and always free from dirt.

So, I wondered.

"Are you just looking to look like you're looking," I asked, "or are you just the shy type?"

"What?"

"I've never seen you flirt, Doug. You look, but that's it. So what is it? Are you just shy, or do we need to find you someone a little hairier?"

"Holy crap. I'm not gay. And that's not the first time you've hinted that."

"Just checking."

"I'm just not..."

"Chip," I finished for him.

He nodded. "I don't chase women the way he does. This taking off to 'see the sights'? I don't do that and I don't see the point. I might have, at one time, but that kind of thing gets old really fast."

I picked up my beer bottle, waving it in his general direction. "Does Doctor Doug have a girlfriend at home he's not interested in cheating on? Someone we just don't know about?"

He drained the beer and signaled to the waitress to bring him another.

"Sorry," I said. "Touched a nerve there, didn't I?"

"Barely. And don't let me order more than this last beer, or you'll be dragging me back upstairs and that would look really bad. But no, there's no one at home."

"But there was."

Lips pursed thoughtfully, he nodded. "I blew it, but at least I blew it early enough to keep it from hurting like hell."

"Bullshit. It hurts."

"Little bit. Like a ripped off bandage. My heart's not broken."

I didn't believe him; he'd stopped looking at the women around him and was looking at his beer bottle, but I let it go. "So. You're not interested right now. That doesn't mean you can't flirt a little."

"I'm not especially good at it, Kris. Not when I know that if I hit it off with someone I'll be leaving in a couple of days and it'll go nowhere."

"Ah, you're one of those guys. Looking for Mz. Right."

"Instead of Mz. Right Now, which Chip seems to favor."

"I keep hoping he'll grow up…"

"Some woman is going to have to knock him on his ass before that happens," he said. "And before that can happen, she's going to have to get his attention for more than two hours."

"And you don't think he'll let it happen."

"I think he's set the bar pretty high. He has his ideal woman, and he's deliberately not looking in the places he would find her."

"At least he has an ideal. What's she like?"

He hesitated. After a deliberately slow sip from the beer he said, "She's fierce. Strong. Tough when she needs to be. She doesn't take shit from anyone, but she's fair about it. Absolutely beautiful though she's less aware of it than are the men around her. And she won't give up on him, even when everyone else has."

"He could find that."

Doug was swirling the beer in the bottle, regarding me with measured consideration. "What makes you think he hasn't found that?"

"You said he wasn't looking."

"Well, there's the thing. You don't have to be looking to find something. Sometimes it's just *there*, but there's nothing you can do about it, and the circumstances pretty much make you not want to do anything. You just accept it, and move on, and hope that someday you find it again."

"Getting a little tipsy, Doc?"

"I'm an easy drunk," he agreed. "But I know I'm making sense."

"Talking in riddles. Chip's got some ideal woman in his sights, but the timing sucks?"

"Something like that. But...not."

"And he's just going to screw his way around the world until he finds another one just like her."

"Looks like it."

"That's a shame. I mean, I think he's too young to be tapping into the last relationship he'll ever have, but it would be nice if he would just stop long enough to consider what he's doing."

Doug leaned forward, setting the beer aside. "He's a good kid, but he doesn't think he's any good. What you want for him, he doesn't think he deserves that. Not yet. And I'm not sure it would be a good thing for him anyway. He's got such deep anger issues."

"He talks to you about this?"

"Not in so many words," he sighed. "But I'm pretty good at reading between the lines. He talks about his mother and stepfather a lot, and I know more about Ron than I probably should. It doesn't take a genius to put the puzzle pieces together."

"And yet, you are a genius, aren't you, Doug?"

"Not really."

"Hm." I signaled the waitress for another beer; she brought two, which made Doug sigh hard. "I was thinking about it a while back. Ron made a comment about you and me both being at UC Davis at the same time, and I thought he meant you were a freshman when I was a senior, but no. You were in your senior year when I got there, and you were done almost done with medical school when I graduated. You're four years younger than I am, so I figure you must be some kind of genius."

"Naw." He put two fingers closer together, squinting to look between the small space he'd left between them. "I may be a little bit smart. A little. If I was a genius, I wouldn't have taken the job I did."

"Regrets?"

"I have a few," he chuckled.

"But then again?"

"Too few...I'm a little drunk, you know that, don't you?"

"If you were female, you'd be Chip's dream girl, Doug."

"For one night anyway." He took a long sip from the beer and sighed hard. "You should know, that woman I described"—he tilted the bottle toward me—"he's looking for another you. That's why it's a good thing you've never been like a mother to him, because that would just fuck him up even more than he already is."

The room did a quick spin in my head, a moment of *oh holy hell* and *how could I not see that?* I was one of the few people who could corner Chip and not have him come out swinging, but to be an ideal for him? I didn't see how, and I said so.

"Why wouldn't you be? He's young but he's not blind. He's also not stupid. You have all the qualities he admires, and you're fucking beautiful on top of it. He's shallow enough to want that, a woman who can make him toe the line and who's hot as hell. Hell, if you weren't married to Ron, more than half the men wandering the agency's halls would be all over you."

"You really are drunk."

"Just stating the facts. You know, I'm glad you've become a friend, but I'd be lying if I didn't admit my shorts got in a wad when I found out you'd reported to Dan just one damned day before I did, and Ron had already managed to give you a major case of tunnel vision. You scared the hell out of me, but damn...one day. Just one lousy day."

I reached across the table and pulled the beer bottle from his hand. "I think you've had enough."

"True that."

"And I hope you know that I really do love my husband. It's a little more than he happened to be the one who met me first."

His shoulders rose and fell in either understanding or dejection; I really couldn't tell. "I wouldn't have had a chance then anyway. Somehow I don't think you'd have wanted to be—" He reached for the bottle again, but I pulled it out of his reach. "It wouldn't have worked then."

"Then it's better that we're friends, right? Because if anything between us wouldn't have worked, we'd probably hate each other by now."

"Probably. But I'm just sayin'… there's a reason Chip has put you up on a pedestal, and it'll be a while before he builds another one for someone else."

"You need coffee," I muttered, getting up and scooping up all the beer bottles. I told him to wait there, and headed for the bar with my arms loaded, removing the temptation for him to drink anything more and say something he might regret later.

That, I thought after I'd asked the waitress to bring us a pot of coffee, *came out of nowhere*. Doug was Chip's friend, and that's all I had ever presumed to think. I wasn't blind; he was cute and I had noticed that; he was smart and I had noticed that, too, but I never would have guessed he'd looked at me as anything but someone he worked with, and someone who occasionally nagged his young friend to stop being such an ass.

Loneliness and beer, I decided. Chip was off doing who knows what to whom, I had Ron, and Doug was stuck in a tropical paradise with nothing but a firm resolve to not follow his best friend's behaviors and chase down a one night stand.

I respected that, but still.

He was awfully cute.

I kept him talking for another hour, trying to keep the conversation revolving around work, and failing that, I prodded him to tell me about the patients he saw in between assignments. He sleepily obliged, telling me about the more gruesome of the injuries he saw as part of agents' post-assignment aftercare, and about the sheer volume of STDs running rampant amongst our co-workers.

I wanted to ask if he'd ever had to treat Chip for anything, but I knew he wouldn't tell me and I knew Chip was careful.

When the beer haze was starting to lift, he slapped his hands against the table and announced he wasn't going to waste an evening in Hawaii, and alone or not he was going to take a walk along the beach. If I was so inclined, he would welcome the company, but wouldn't be offended if I begged off, what with having an advanced case of marital tunnel vision and all.

Still a little tipsy, I thought, and probably not a good idea to let him wander around water alone. I left word at the front desk for Ron, letting him know where we were, and followed Doug out, trailing a few feet behind until we'd reached the sand.

"Ever been to Chip's beach house?" he asked as we walked along the water line. "Half the time it's too cold to sit out on the sand, but it's nice and quiet there."

"Haven't been. And it's not high on my list of places to go."

"Really now."

"I'm not keen on the idea of spending much time in a place where I'm pretty sure my husband was screwing his ex's brains out. And with my luck, I'd decide to give in and go, and then walk in on Chip and one of the choices from his thirty one flavors menu."

"No worries there," he snorted. "Chip doesn't take women there. Can't say who his mother was there with, though."

"I'd rather not spend a lot of time thinking about it."

"We've all got pasts, Kris. Some of us more than others, but still."

"Doesn't mean I want it shoved in my face."

"Your husband," he said, jamming his hands into his pockets, stopping to turn to me, "loved someone. It was hard, and he didn't walk away. That's not shoving it in your face, that's just proof of who he is."

Doug had Chip's abbreviated version of the story of his parents' great love; he couldn't know that Ron walked away before Chip was even born, or that he'd walked away a dozen times after finally meeting his son. Doug didn't realize that Ron had ended it eight months before Pat died, and I wasn't going to tell him. If Chip wanted to believe his parents had this great—even if difficult—love story, I wasn't taking that away from him, and if I told Doug the truth, eventually he would tell Chip.

"I know Ron loves me," I said quietly. "I don't need proof of who he is."

"But you'd like to forget the fact that Chip's mother did exist."

I didn't know how to explain it to Doug; no matter how much Ron loved me, Pat was still there. Even though he'd ended the relationship—or presumed it had reached its end—that didn't change the fact that she hovered nearby most of the time, slivers of her memory threading through his brain, stray thoughts that could surface in any moment, catching him by surprise.

"I love Chip," was all I could say to Doug.

"Can I ask you something?" He turned back towards the hotel and resumed walking. "It's personal."

As if he hadn't been tap dancing all over personal most of the evening. "Go for it."

"If not for Chip, do you think you would still be with Ron?"

This time, I stopped. "What the hell?"

He shrugged. "Seems to me you guys fight a lot, and half of it over Chip. You're pretty vocal about wanting him out of the job, and it pisses you off to no end that Ron doesn't seem to agree. We can all see how attached you are to Chip...I just wondered. If he hadn't been part of the package, do you think you'd still be with Ron?"

"What the hell kind of question is that?"

"An honest one."

"Oh, fuck off, Doug." I stomped off, hoping he'd get the hint and stay there, but half a minute later he was right there beside me. "You have no idea..."

"All right."

"Seriously. None."

We were at the hotel door and I grabbed the handle and pulled hard, half hoping he would run right into it. As we were coming in, Ron was on his way out, and when he saw us he smiled, his eyes lighting up, and before he said anything he leaned over and kissed me.

"You are one lucky bastard," Doug grunted, pushing past him to get to the elevator.

Ron watched him, confused. "What was that all about?"

"That was Doug getting his bitch panties in a wad. Chip took off with some girl this afternoon, I have you, and he's here alone. I don't think he wants to be alone, but he's too shy to do anything about it." I grabbed his hand. "Come on, I bet you're starving."

"Already ate."

I pulled him toward the door. "Then go out with me. My first night in Hawaii, I want to make out on the beach and get sand in places I normally would hate."

~

My mind was off on so many tangents that when Ron dropped next to me on the beach towel and asked me where I was, I had no idea. I started out watching him toss a Frisbee around with Chip and Doug, but after five minutes the boredom crept in and I let my brain take off on its own, and paid little attention to the directions it roamed.

He picked up a bottle of suntan oil and shook it at me, eyebrows arched in the question he didn't need to ask. I nodded, and he crawled up onto his knees, scooting behind me as I pulled my hair out of his way. He slathered the oil on gently, massaging with his fingers but avoiding the spots he knew were still sore, and I sighed, not wanting him to stop.

"Wherever it was that you were," he said, leaning in to place a kiss on my neck, "you were staring holes into Doug. And he was annoyed last night. What was really up?"

"He was drunk. Three beers, and he was nearly shitfaced."

"And?"

I turned my head look at him. "And nothing, really. I'm not sure if I'd be betraying a confidence if I told you what he said, anyway."

"Won't go any further than between you and me," he promised.

I doubted that; if I told him Doug had regrets about not meeting me first, Ron would have definite things to say to him. Instead I sighed and said, "The man has a slightly broken heart. He's a little pissed off right now."

"Ah. Wallowing in that state of not wanting anyone else to be happy? That would explain why he thinks I'm a lucky bastard."

"Well, you are. Lucky, anyway."

"You'll get no argument from me." He was working the oil into my shoulders, his fingers trailing just far forward enough to make me wonder if he was intentionally trying to torment me, or if he was not thinking about the fact that his son was right there.

I decided it was intentional; when I leaned into him he chuckled under his breath and then stopped, dropping back onto the towel. He propped himself up on one elbow, facing me and not Doug and

Chip, who had stopped throwing the Frisbee and were looking towards the hotel; Chip was pointing at something, but I wasn't inclined to turn to see what.

"What else is bugging you?" Ron asked. "You're too quiet to just be musing over Doug's lousy love life."

"Just one of those days?"

"I don't think so." He reached out, rubbing my leg gently. "Come on. You've been distracted since last night."

"Funny, I thought I was very undistracted last night."

"Well, you were something last night. I'm not complaining, but that was fairly angry sex, Kris. I almost didn't have to be there."

I winced, and he saw it.

"I'm not trying to be mean."

He wasn't; the way he looked at me was very tender, and I knew he was right. I'd used him for sex, and at the time he was a willing warm body with functioning parts in my bed.

"All right," I said after a moment. "But this might sound like it's coming out of left field."

"Okay."

"Do we fight too much?" I asked. "And I'm serious. Are we arguing more than should be normal?"

I expected him to shake his head, and to say no without thinking about it. Instead, he drew in a long breath and said, "We do tend to bicker."

"And it's mostly about Chip, isn't it?"

"Seems to be. But that's all right. I have a blind eye to what he needs a lot of the time and you're fighting for him. It's not like we're squabbling over stupid things."

Chip and Doug were heading toward us; I was suddenly angry, at Chip for his bad timing and at myself for not insisting we go elsewhere to talk. "The arguing has to stop," I said. "And dammit, we'll have to finish this later."

He craned his neck to look up at Chip. "Go away. I'm about to get lucky."

"Yeah, well, think cold thoughts," Chip said. "Linda Jackson is headed this way."

"That would do it," Ron muttered, getting up. I looked back

and Linda was slogging her way across the sand; she was dressed in slacks and a blazer, and she didn't look at all happy. "Somehow I don't think this is going to continue to be happy fun time, guys."

Linda smiled apologetically as she reached us.

"Are we being recalled for something?" Ron asked her.

"Not exactly," she said. She turned to Chip and asked, "Do you remember Nicky Lockhart? Little boy you extracted in Germany?"

"Yeah, sure." Chip said. "Not like I could forget. He peed all over me."

"He's stateside now, and he wants to see you."

Ron's hand went up, stopping Chip from saying yes or no. "Why are you delivering the message, Linda? An invitation could have waited until we checked back in at home. Any one of the administrative assistants could have told Chip this."

"I know." Her eyes fluttered closed for a moment, a deliberate pause as she tried to gather her thoughts. "Nicky is a sick little boy, and it doesn't look good. He kept asking to see you, so his father used a few connections...so I'm here on his father's behalf, asking you to go to Texas."

Chip looked like he wanted to melt into the sand. "What's wrong with him?"

"Leukemia, and that's all I know," she told him gently. "I do know that he's asked repeatedly over the last two years if he would ever see you again, but now..."

"You have to go, Chip," Doug said, putting his hand on Chip's shoulder. "I'll go with you. I can answer any questions, let you know what to expect."

"We'll all go," Ron said flatly. "If you want to go, that is."

"Of course I'm going," he said, nearly whispering.

"Any chance you're headed in the same direction?" Ron asked Linda. She was shaking her head before he could get the full question out.

"Sorry, guys. You'll have to go on a commercial flight."

As she walked away, Chip sank to the sand, sitting with the Frisbee clenched tight between his fingers. Ron watched Linda leave, and then said almost absently, "I'll go make flight arrangements. Let him sit here as long as he needs to."

I started to ask Chip if he was all right, but he waved me off, asking to be left alone. Doug nodded, gesturing for me to walk with him. We gave Chip some space, but stayed where we could see him.

"He'll be all right," Doug said, "but that's some rough news for him to handle."

"I hadn't thought about that boy in a long time," I said absently.

"Hell, I don't think I've thought about him since we finished that assignment. They kind of blur into each other after a while."

Most of my assignments, unless something specific poked up at me, were a blur. I knew what Doug meant, and I was fairly sure that most of what we'd done was a jumbled up line of events in Chip's head, but that one, the assignment that shouldn't have been, was the one I doubted he would ever be able to get out of his head.

I would never forget it, simply because it was what had pulled Chip in.

Chip was spinning the Frisbee between his hands, staring at it, lost in thought.

"Ever notice," Doug said carefully, "how Ron seems to take charge of everything?"

"What?" I looked toward the hotel, wondering if Doug had seen Ron coming out. "I don't follow."

"Like now. Normally we'd all just go in and pack and then decide who was going to call and get plane reservations. But Ron took charge. Seems to me he takes charge most of the time."

"Dan's not here," I reminded him.

"Wouldn't matter if Dan was. Think back, even all the way to the assignment that dropped both Chip and Nicky into our laps. Who made the most decisions? Who always makes the most decisions? In China, who sent Chip into that building? Last time in Germany, who had me sniffing around that female East German agent, which, by the way, I'm still a little embarrassed about."

"You got caught," I poked back. "You should be embarrassed. And what's the point?"

He was still looking at Chip. "Did you know that Ron was offered this team first? That he turned it down in favor of Dan being named team leader, but that he was the one who hand-picked you and me to be a part of it?"

"Ron is Dan's second," I reminded him. "Why would he have turned the leader's position down?"

"Good question. But on paper, he turned it down, yet if you dig deep enough, he's listed as being in the mayor's seat."

"Same difference," I said, waving him off.

"Normally. Team leader, mayor, same damn thing. But not in this case. Dan's our boss, but Ron? He's Dan's boss."

How in the hell he could know that, I wanted to ask, but I knew how. Doug was privy to nearly every bit of information on all of us. Where I used to tease Ron about knowing all my identifiable marks from reading my personnel file, Doug probably had a detailed illustrated guide.

"Why are you telling me this?"

"I just thought it was interesting, that's all," he said.

"If I was supposed to know, I would know. And you damn well don't say anything to Chip. If Ron is higher up the chain of command than Dan, Chip doesn't need to know."

"Hell, I don't think *Dan* knows."

"How would that even work, Doug? It's not like Ron could pull rank in the field."

"Dan defers to Ron because of experience, and because he's been told to give heavy weight to what Ron thinks. What I haven't figured out is why Ron didn't want to clearly be the one in charge."

"And I haven't figured out why you're really telling me this."

He nodded toward Chip. "Because someday the shit will hit the fan, and he's the one who'll get splattered on the most. He's here because of Ron, whether by choice or force. Either Ron wanted him involved, or the agency is using Chip to get something from Ron."

"Makes no sense."

"Nope," he agreed, "but my gut is telling me that. And even you think I'm freakishly smart."

"I also think you're an ass."

"I can live with that." He took a tentative step toward Chip, but stopped. "Don't think I'm telling you any of this because of what I said last night. I just think you should know. If Ron didn't tell you, it's because he can't, not because he's hiding anything. It's just part of his job."

He hand-picked me. Does that make me part of his job, too?

Doug walked over to Chip and held a hand out to him, helping him up.

Brothers.

It struck me then, Doug would do just about anything to protect Chip, even if that meant making me take a closer look at my marriage.

~

We'd been in the air for three hours, long enough for Chip to fall asleep out of sheer boredom, and long enough for Doug to get lost in the book he'd picked up at an airport newsstand. Ron looked drowsy, but he was awake, and since neither of us could get up and walk away or allow anger to escalate into a shouting match, I thought it was as good a time as any to finish what we'd started out on the beach.

"First class," I sighed, getting his attention. "Who's going to have a cow over this? Dan or someone higher up?"

"I'm not sure I want to tell you."

"What? You won't get fired over this, will you?"

"No. And I'm hoping I won't wind up divorced over it. This is a personal trip, Kris. The agency isn't paying for it."

It took a moment for that to sink in. "Holy hell, can we afford this?"

A bare nod of his head. "We're fine. Come on, we both work and it's not like we're out there spending money hand over fist. We still live in that small apartment and we're both driving cars that have to be a decade old each. You don't seem to have any weird shopping habits and I don't have any expensive hobbies." He reached over the armrest for my hand. "You should probably pay closer attention to our finances, angel. If something happens to me, you need to know where everything is."

"Before I married you it was all in one savings account," I mused. "I knew where everything was."

"And now you need to know where my savings accounts are, investments, life insurance policies, where my safe deposit boxes are, bonds…"

"You have investments."

"Small ones. If I'd listened to Grant fifteen years ago they'd be a hell of a lot bigger, but it was always enough to be able to leave Chip something. I upped my life insurance when we got married and poured a little more into savings to make sure you'd be comfortable, too."

"I really don't want to sit here and contemplate you being gone, Ron."

"Nope," he chuckled, "you just want to sit here and talk about how much we argue. There's nothing wrong with us, Kris. We argue when it's important, and sometimes you have to raise your voice to get me to hear. I might be annoyed in the moment but I actually appreciate it."

"But other people notice it. We have to stop fighting over Chip so much."

"Come on. If we argue about him it's because we both care about him."

"We should be able to talk, not fight. I'm done fighting, Ron. He's an adult now and I can't change all the things that have him bouncing around like he's got a giant spring in his ass, and I can't change the fact that whether I like it or not, he's been sucked into this job. I hate that, I hate it hard."

"I know."

"He wouldn't quit now even if the agency offered to terminate his contract. So I'm letting it go. He's been trained well and he knows what he's doing...no more bitching on my end when you send him off to do something that scares the hell out of me."

"You don't bitch about it. You're just trying to protect him."

"And I don't need to do that anymore. We can find other things to fight about."

As soon as that was out of my mouth I wondered—what else did we have to argue about? Or even talk about? Our lives revolved around work and Chip. I wasn't sure what else we had.

"We'll find something, I'm sure," he said as if he'd read my mind.

"Are you willing to take some time off?" I asked.

"For?"

"For me," I said. "I want time away from the job and away from Chip. Face it, the last time we went anywhere alone was when we got married. We've gone places, but..."

"We've always taken Chip."

And we had. In reaching for little bits and pieces of the sense of normal that real life wasn't going to give him, we centered short trips around Chip; weekends in Tahoe, overnight trips to San Francisco, even one weirdly wild road trip where we wound up at Disneyland, trying to unleash his inner eight year old.

"Alaska," I said after a moment. "Show me the northern lights."

"Alaska," he repeated, grinning. "You remembered. As soon as we get home, we'll put in a request for some time off. I'll take you to see the northern lights, and anything else that suits your whimsy."

~

It was late when we landed in San Antonio; too late, Ron pointed out to Chip, to head for the air force base hospital. Given the choice between checking into the hotel and showering up or heading straight for Wilford Hall, he would have gone to Wilford Hall, and after fifteen minutes of dickering about it, Ron finally put his foot down.

"You look like shit and need to sleep first," he said, cutting off one of Chip's protests. "Nicky definitely doesn't need to see you looking like death warmed over. We're going to the hotel, and you're going to stay there and sleep. No wandering off on your own."

"Fucking bad time to pull rank, *boss*," Chip huffed.

"This isn't a business trip. I'm not your boss right now."

"Then an order doesn't stick."

"Oh hell, yes, it does," Ron said. "I'm still your father."

Chip opened his mouth to retort, but then closed it just as quickly. I don't think I'd ever seen Ron play the father card, and judging by the look on his face, I don't think Chip had, either.

Doug took Chip by arm and steered him towards the luggage carousel. "Nicky is probably asleep now, anyway. And he needs his rest, Chip. He'll be there in the morning."

Chip flinched at that; *would* Nicky be there in the morning? Just how bad was it?

At the hotel Ron handed Chip his key and then watched, worried, as he disappeared into the room. Without being asked, Doug said quietly, "I'll keep an eye on him tonight. He won't go anywhere. He has too many questions he hasn't asked yet, and now's a good time to fill him in on what to expect."

"What can he expect?" I asked.

"Depending on where Nicky is in treatment? He'll either look normal but tired, or he'll be bald and stick thin. He could be mobile, but he could also be bedridden. I'll make sure Chip has a reasonable idea of what he's walking into."

"I appreciate it," Ron said, clapping him on the shoulder as he turned toward our room.

Of all the things Chip had seen in the last two years, the blood and gore and violence, I was sure this might be the worst of it. No matter how sick Nicky was, how bad or good he looked, Chip would know that the odds were against his young friend, and I wasn't sure how he would take that.

We arrived at Wilford Hall en masse; Doug wanted to be there to see Nicky for himself, for any quick visual assessment he could make, and to get any information he could in order to either relieve Chip's concerns or give him forewarning. I wanted to be there because I wanted to see Nicky, too; he'd been small and frightened when he left Germany in Linda Jackson's arms, and I hoped he'd had a chance to grow a little, and that he wasn't so scared.

Ron was there for Chip. He wasn't letting his son walk into Nicky's hospital room without knowing that his father was, at the very least, just down the hall.

I trailed half a step behind Ron as we made our way down the corridor that led to Nicky's room, watching him look at Chip; I felt a sudden and inexplicable stab of guilt, having wanted to grab Ron and run off without Chip.

You have every right to want time alone with your husband.

There were tight lines drawn on Ron's face, fatigue and sorrow; he might not have a problem sending Chip halfway up a building with a backpack filled with explosive putty, but he had serious issue with sending Chip in to see a little boy who would very likely wind up breaking his heart.

The realization smacked me in the face, hard: *there's the other half of his heartbeat, there's the reason he lives.*

I tried to swallow the thought, and with it the guilt over being upset that it wasn't me.

Nicky was seated on the edge of his bed when we walked into the hospital room, and he scrambled to his feet, rubber soles of his sneakers squeaking on the tile floor. He was dressed in jeans and a t-shirt, his black hair combed neatly, and other than the fact that he was incredibly pale, he looked like a slightly taller version of the little boy who had clung to Chip so hard just two years earlier.

He stopped in his tracks when he saw Chip, mouth gaped in surprise. "Oh, man, you got *big*," he blurted out.

"So did you," Chip pointed out. He grinned, motioning for Nicky to come closer, and when he did, Nicky took a running step and flew at Chip. "How old are you now? Fifteen? Sixteen?"

Nicky's arms were tight around Chip's neck. "Nine. And a half."

"Ah. That half is important."

"You're eighteen now, right? I remember your mom said you were sixteen. You look kinda old now."

"Thanks a lot." Chip set him back down, ruffling his hair. "You look pretty good, kiddo. I kind of expected you to be in bed with a tube up your nose or something. You feeling okay?"

"I get tired," Nicky said simply. "Hey! You want to see the playroom? They have a bunch of stuff for all the kids and even a color TV."

"Cool. Sure, take me to it."

Nicky grabbed Chip by the hand and led him out, turning at the door, as if he had just realized the rest of us were there. "Oh yeah. Hi!"

We watched them hurry down the hallway, and when Nicky pulled Chip into another room Ron turned to Doug. "How's he look to you?"

"Pale," Doug said. "Fatigued. I could only guess at anything else, at least until I know how long he's been in treatment and what his doctors think the outcome will be."

"Jackson said it didn't look good," I pointed out.

"Then we hope that someone exaggerated in order to get Chip here," Ron said.

Doug pointed to the waiting room and suggested we hang out there; he went to the nurses' station to let them know where we would be, so that we'd have a chance to speak to Nicky's parents when they arrived.

"The nurse at the desk said Nicky's dad just went down to the cafeteria and will be up soon," Doug said as he sat in a chair directly across from Ron and me.

"Did she give you any idea how he is?" Ron asked.

"He," Doug said pointedly, "did not. And I didn't ask."

"Ethics," Ron muttered.

"You want me to have a sense of ethics, Ron. It keeps me from spilling the things that I know."

I tuned them out. In the buzz of their conversation I heard moments of punctuated, but stifled, laughter; whatever Doug thought about my marriage, he wasn't taking it out on Ron. And whatever he knew about Ron's position within the agency, he wasn't letting Ron in on it. He was there as Chip's friend, as moral support. Ron could have sent him home and made this side trip a family affair, and I wondered if it still was—did he see in Chip and Doug's friendship what I did? Did it occur to him that Chip had found in the doctor a big brother?

Did it bother him?

I should know those things; I shouldn't have to sit here and wonder, and then wonder more if I should ask my own husband what he thought about it.

Ron's deep laugh punctuated the bubble I'd been trying to burrow into and I could feel it fall away. "I found him lying there on the sand, spread eagle, staring up at the sky," Doug was saying. "Half a dozen bottles were scattered around him and I was sure he was drunk off his ass and I'd have to drag him across the beach and into the house. I looked down at him and he squinted and groaned 'fucking seagull took my hot dog, Doug.'"

"Drunker than drunk?" Ron asked.

"Stone cold sober. He'd been drinking root beer. But he was mad as hell about that hot dog."

I started to ask when this was and where, but *Bodega Bay* popped into my head and before I could say anything, Ron was on his feet, his hand extended, saying, "Colonel Lockhart, it's a pleasure to meet you."

I got up without thinking about it. Nicky's father was a formidable presence, six feet of muscled discipline stuffed into a military service dress uniform. He stood ramrod straight, and I imagined Ron's hand would be sore for a day or two after that handshake.

The Colonel's ingrained resolve softened quickly, and he said, barely above a whisper, "Thank you. Not just for coming, but for saving my son's life."

"Your real hero is in the playroom with Nicky," Ron said. "We got here as soon as we received word…I am terribly sorry, Colonel."

"Phillip, please. And my wife extends her apologies for not being here. Our younger son is running a fever and couldn't go to school—"

"And he can't be around Nicky," Doug said quietly.

Ron introduced Doug and me to the Colonel, and suggested we give Nicky and Chip more time to play before interrupting them. Doug took the time to pepper him with questions: how long had Nicky been ill? What treatment had he undergone? What was the prognosis?

He grilled the man, but he did it gently, with the understanding that he only wanted the bigger picture, something he could use to drag through his own brain. He had access to government studies; he might know of something Nicky's military physicians didn't.

"They've done everything they can," the Colonel said. "He'll have more chemotherapy, but realistically he only has about a ten per cent chance."

"He looks so damned good, though," Ron said.

"Sheer determination. He refused to be in bed, in a hospital gown. Once he knew Chip was actually coming"—he smiled wanly—"he sucked everything up as hard as he could, and insisted on getting dressed and he refused to be in bed at all today. He didn't want Chip to see him like that." He leaned forward, elbows on his knees. "For nearly a year after he was kidnapped, he talked about Chip like he was some mythical superhuman who'd swept down and flown him out of hell and into Disneyland. I don't think a week went by that he didn't ask if I knew where Chip was and what he was doing, and if he'd ever get to see him again. So when we got the word..."

"That had to take effort, tracking him down," Ron said.

"It took effort to get anyone from your agency to admit that it even existed. One call to General Kennedy—his son Jordan was the other kidnap victim—and I had the information I needed, but until I had real names? Yes, it was an effort. And no, I won't tell you who tipped me off. All Nicky remembered was Chip, and finding someone with that name...it took some time. If I blew a cover, I apologize, but this is the only thing he's wanted. All year, seeing Chip again. That's it."

It was providence; until now Chip would have been nearly impossible to find. No one from the agency would have tracked him down while he was in the field, and we'd spent most of our time on one assignment after another.

How long had they known? How long had they waited to pass the message along to Chip?

As hard as Chip had become, he wasn't jaded enough to let a little boy's wish roll off his shoulders; if he'd been given that message in the middle of an assignment, he would have either bailed— stirring up more trouble than we'd be able to get him out of—or he'd have been so distracted that he would have gotten himself or one of us hurt.

I felt bad for Nicky and that he'd been asking for Chip all along, but I was grateful the Colonel's way to him had been blocked.

We sat in the waiting room for over two hours, staying out of Nicky and Chip's way. It was time that Ron used to answer all of the Colonel's questions; he'd only been given the official version of what had happened to his son in the weeks he'd been missing, and while we couldn't give him explicit details of what Nicky's life had been like in the hands of his kidnappers, we could give him exacting detail of his rescue. It was a stark reminder of Ron's steel-trap memory for details, and he was able to give the Colonel a clear picture of what those few hours had been like, and I was able to paint an image of how Nicky had bonded to Chip.

Wisely, he didn't ask how Chip happened to be there, he was only grateful that someone who could relate to his son had been such a major factor in sending the boy home.

When lunch time rolled around, the Colonel reluctantly got up; no matter what game he was torturing Chip with, he had to make Nicky eat something, anything, and he needed to nap.

"He'll fight me on it," he said as we headed down the hall, "but food is a battle I'll win."

"And the nap?" I asked.

"I know when to retreat," he said, sad laughter coating each word.

He stopped just short of going into the playroom and his face softened; I looked just past him, to where Chip was stuffed into a bean bag chair, Nicky on his lap sound asleep, much in the way he had slept on Chip's lap two years earlier.

"Lunch can wait," the Colonel whispered. He did a neat about-face and headed down the hall, away from the waiting room, past the nurses' station, and disappeared around the corner.

~

By the time the Colonel had composed himself, Nicky was awake. He woke slowly, his eyes fluttering open, but it took a moment before he was really seeing anything. He unfolded himself and stretched a bit without leaving Chip's lap.

"You're still here," he said, fighting a yawn.

"I told you I'd take care of you," Chip said softly. "Are you hungry, buddy?"

"Not really," Nicky whispered.

His father opened his mouth, but stopped when he realized Nicky was barely registering his presence.

"You kinda need to," Chip said.

"I just don't feel like eating."

Chip inhaled deeply through his nose, and Nicky's head bobbled against his chest as it expanded. "You remember a couple of years ago when you didn't want to take a nap? Do you remember what I said then?"

Nicky looked up at Chip's face, his eyebrows knotted together, when it came back to him. "Real men sleep when they need to."

"That's right. Because a man has to be rested in order to be ready to take care of business. You know what else real men do, even when they don't feel like it?"

"Take a bath?"

Colonel Lockhart smiled, sucking in the laugh that had bubbled up.

"Besides that," Chip said. "Real men, when they need food, they eat. Sometimes it's hard when you feel like crap, but man, it's just like being rested. You have to keep your strength up, so you have to eat."

"You got pretty strong."

"That's because he eats like a horse," Doug muttered.

"I'm pretty sure he ate an actual horse," Ron added.

Nicky laughed, but he rested his head against Chip's chest again. "Can I go downstairs?" he asked quietly. "I don't like the food they give me up here."

Chip looked to Nicky's father, who nodded his permission.

We trailed behind them; Chip carried Nicky on his back the same way he had before, bouncing lightly on his toes to make the little boy laugh. Nicky held on tight, resting his cheek on Chip's shoulder, until we were in the cafeteria.

The Colonel watched in fascination as Chip convinced Nicky to eat small bites of everything. His appetite was low and he ate slowly, but he followed Chip's lead and nibbled on baked chicken and, after seeing Chip happily wolf it down, ate the broccoli and carrots he swore he hated.

"Food is fuel," Chip told him. "The better the food, the better the fuel. Vegetables? Those are really good fuel."

"You eat them without your mom and dad making you?"

"I didn't get this big eating junk food, kid."

"But sometimes I can't," Nicky confessed, sounding defeated.

"You just do the best you can. Every time they bring you food, eat a little bit. Even if it's just a couple of bites." He leaned down, and whispered loudly, "I know it sucks, but you gotta do it to make your mom and dad feel better. They can't fix you and it scares them, so they try to make sure you get good food. Make them happy, and just try it."

"'Cause real men do that?"

"Yep, they do. And then they get a cookie or a chocolate pudding if they want."

After lunch, we left Chip there to spend the afternoon and went back to the hotel. Doug and I headed for the pool to soak up some sun while Ron checked in with Dan. We both hid behind books; I didn't want to say anything that would remind him of his beer-laden confessions, and I really didn't want him poking around my relationship with my husband.

Twenty minutes later Ron was pulling a lounge chair up to mine, and he sighed hard as he sat down.

"Not good news?" I asked.

"We have to head back tomorrow," he said. "You and I have a run to Washington, and Chip apparently has to show up for a language class."

"Language."

"Portuguese. Dan said Chip's been tapped for three different immersion classes, and this is the first one."

"Well, shit," Doug huffed. "If you two are going to Washington and Chip has school, that means I have to actually work."

"You have a tough life," Ron snorted with amusement.

"Tell me about it. There's nothing like standing there listening to someone's excuse about just how that soda bottle got wedged up his own ass."

"A soda bottle up the ass?" I asked.

"It's happened. Requires surgery, too, if the bottle goes in neck first. Creates this nice little vacuum—"

"Uh, I've heard enough, thanks."

Ron was laughing. "Tell me if it's true or not, but you don't have to tell me who…are the rumors true that someone pretty high up was carted off in an ambulance while still, um, in the saddle, so to speak?"

"Wasn't with his wife, either," Doug snorted. "Woman he was with had vaginal spasms and clamped right down on his pecker. By the time EMTs got him in, he was in a world of hurt and she was mortified. It took some heavy duty drugs to get her to relax enough for him to pull out."

I tossed my book at him. "Oh my God. You're making that up."

"Nope."

"I hope you get stuck looking at hemorrhoids the rest of the week." I looked over at Ron; he was laughing through his nose. "How long are we leaving Chip at the hospital?"

"I told him he could stay until lights out unless Nicky tires out sooner. He'll take a cab if he thinks he needs to leave before then."

"It's a shame he can't stay another day."

"We'll try to figure out how to get him back here if he wants."

"He's got personal time banked," Doug said.

"Doesn't mean they'll let him take it," I said. "If he's on the books for back to back assignments, he might not get back here in time."

"He will if I sign off on it. Hell, I can even force the SG into taking time off. If Chip needs me to exaggerate something to get him a few days, I'll do it."

Ron leaned forward, looking past me to Doug. "And I'll pretend I didn't hear that."

Doug waved him off. "What are they going to do, Ron? Fire me? I fudge some paperwork to get Chip time off, no one will care. It's done every day, no big deal."

"But you don't admit it to the people who are supposed to nail your ass to a wall for doing it."

"Be his dad, not his boss," Doug grumbled. "If he gets medical leave, let it go."

"What the hell do you think we're doing here now, Doug? I didn't bring him here because I'm his superior at work. I brought my *son* here because he wouldn't have been able to live with himself if Nicky died without having seen him. And I'll do what I can to get him back here if that's what he wants, but not on company time. He wanted the job; he'll do the job. If it cuts into something he wanted to do, it sucks, but that's life."

"He's a kid," Doug said.

"Not anymore."

"Don't bullshit yourself, Gallery. He follows orders well, but he's still a teenager, and he still thinks like one."

"I know that."

Doug turned on his lounge chair; I was between them, but I don't think either of them saw me there anymore. "I don't think you do. I don't think you know even half of what's going on in Chip's head and how completely distracted he is most of the time."

"Bull. He's focused."

"Focused. We were in Hawaii one night. Any idea what your kid was up to in that one night? Or who he was with?"

"I'm sure he found someone to kill a few hours with."

Doug held up three fingers. "Three girls, Ron. He's so focused that he hooked up with three different girls. Well, the last one turned out to be underage and he was smart enough to not lay a hand on her, but still. His brain isn't engaged into his own life most of the time, so he bounces all over the place. Don't tell me he's focused. He's a disaster waiting to happen."

"He engages when it matters," Ron said evenly.

"You mean when you need him to do something dangerous. He focuses on the job, which suits you well enough. But when he's not working do you have a clue what he's up to?"

Ron flinched at that; Doug hit a nerve, a tender one. I kept my mouth shut because he was getting Ron to listen where I never seemed to be able to.

"He's out of control," Doug went on. "He's only disciplined on the job. Off it? It's more than the sheer number of women he sleeps with. Do you have any idea how easy it is for him to get alcohol and how much he drinks? How many bars I've pulled him out of and how much he just roams around? When he's not working he has nothing to connect to, and sooner or later that's going to bite him in the ass. He's either going to wind up in jail or dead. So if I have to fudge some paperwork to give him official time off to come here and focus on a dying little boy, I'll fudge the fucking paperwork. Report me if you want. Fire my ass. But I'll give that kid something to really focus on, because no one else seems to want to."

Doug grabbed his book and got up.

"Instead of keeping him in line on the job, how about you step up and figure out a way to get him out of it and into school so that he has a chance to find out what he could really be, and not what you want him to be?"

He didn't wait for an answer; he walked away, leaving Ron to stew in his own anger and me to figure out if I wanted to stir the pot or turn the heat up.

I wanted Ron to hear what Doug was saying; he'd poured out in a few minutes what I had been trying to say for two years. If Ron could get past being pissed off and really hear Doug, maybe it would make a difference for Chip.

I was done fighting with him about his son, but that didn't change what I wanted for him.

I waited for him to say something, but he just grunted and slid back in the chair, closed his eyes, and shut off any chance I had to nudge him in the right direction.

~

Without making an issue of it, Doug signed off on medically required time off for Chip when the first part of his Portuguese class was over; he cited a spike in Chip's blood pressure as the cause, claimed it was due to work related stress, and took a few days for himself, accompanying Chip to Texas.

Ron didn't say anything about it; he had meetings in Washington and I presumed he shrugged it off, knowing the team had no upcoming assignments. Dan muddled through paperwork in his office, and as I passed his door on the way to Ron's office I wondered if Doug was more right than wrong; why was Ron the one always being sent to meet with liaisons from the CIA? And the internal goings-on—Dan and Ron spent hours locked behind closed doors with the assistant secretary general and sometimes the SG himself, the reasons for which the rest of us were never given an explanation.

They were working on something and I had a bad feeling about it.

When Chip and Doug returned from Texas the first time, he was assigned little more than physical training; his days were spent in the gym lifting weights or in combat training. While he worked on his fighting skills, Ron picked away at whatever project he and Dan had going, and I spent my time in the air, flying other agents to and from U.S. based assignments.

It was a welcome slice of boredom.

Ten days after Chip returned from his trip to Texas with Doug, I walked into the apartment, tired from a long day in the air, wanting nothing more than to jump into the shower and scrub the grime away. I'd passed Ron as he was coming out of Dan's office earlier and made plans to shove everything work-related aside for the evening and to go out to dinner, but I opened the door Chip was there. He was sitting on the sofa, staring at the TV, sound muted, and he didn't look up even though I was sure he had heard the door close.

"What's up?" I asked as I sat next to him.

"I still have a key," he muttered. "I hope this is okay."

"You know it's all right."

He barely nodded. "I came to ask a favor. You can say no. I know you've been flying all day."

"Won't hurt to ask me." I slid my arm behind him, rubbing his neck gently.

"Will you fly me to San Antonio?" He finally turned to look at me. "I talked to Colonel Lockhart this afternoon. If I want to see Nicky again, it has to be now." He swallowed hard. "He's got days, maybe a week. I have to be able to say goodbye, you know?"

He never got to say goodbye to his mother, and that ate at him.

"I'll call my dad," I said, pressing a kiss into the side of his head. "I'm sure he'll let me use his plane. Do you want Ron and Doug to go?"

"No. I don't want..." He inhaled sharply, his breath catching. "Nicky is just a byproduct of a job to Ron. And Doug, I dunno, I just don't need to hear more medical facts. If you're busy, I could go on a commercial flight."

He could, but he wanted someone with him, and he didn't want to make that return flight with two hundred other people around him. "Not a chance, mister," I said. "I'd like to see Nicky, too. Let me make a few phone calls, and we'll be on our way."

~

In the little more than three weeks since I'd last seen him, Nicky had lost a great deal of weight, and was weakened to the point of painful movement. Still, when Chip walked into his hospital room, he sat up and tried to swing his legs over the edge of the bed.

He was dressed in bright blue pajama pants and a t-shirt and his feet were bare; it struck me how small he looked then, out of the jeans and sneakers he'd insisted on during the first visit. His black hair and the dark circles under his eyes, the fatigue wrapped around him in so many layers that it had a sickening weight to it, accentuated his pale skin. If I could feel it, Chip was struggling against it.

"Get your ass back in bed," Chip ordered. "I can walk all the way across the room to you."

As Chip sat on the edge of the bed, pulling a blanket over Nicky, the little boy's eyes flicked toward me and he asked, "You're Chip's mom, right? I remember you from before."

"That's right," Chip said before I could correct him. "Her name is Kris." He looked up at me. "He can call you Kris, right?"

"Definitely."

"My dad said when you got here we could go to the playroom if you wanted to. And the nurse said he brought us some popsicles, and if you behave we can have some." Nicky tried to sit up again, but Chip put a hand on his chest to keep him in bed. "You're gonna behave, right?"

"I wouldn't screw up getting a Popsicle. But we need to wait for your mom or your dad before we go anywhere. I don't want to get in trouble for letting you get up if you're supposed to be asleep or something."

"I won't get in trouble. But you're gonna have to carry me."

"Getting lazy?"

"My legs are just tired," Nicky said.

"I bet you're tired all over." Chip was rubbing Nicky's chest, an absent-minded gesture that seemed to calm them both. "Are they still making you take a lot of pills and stuff?"

"My dad says I'm done with the pills. And I had this needle in my arm, but he made them take that out, too. I think maybe that means I get to go home soon."

"Could be, buddy," Chip murmured.

"I just wanna go outside again," Nicky told him, the bare edge of a whine in his voice. "It stinks in here."

"I know. I tell you what, if you close your eyes and try to take a short nap, I'll go ask your dad if it's okay if we go sit outside somewhere for a little while. I can't promise anything, but I'll ask. Okay?"

Nicky nodded and settled back into his pillows.

"Does the nurse know where your dad is right now?"

"I think so." He looked over at me. "Will you stay here?"

I got up and took Chip's place on the edge of Nicky's bed, and when Chip was out the door he reached for my hand.

"I'm not sleepy," he whispered. "Will he be mad if I don't take a nap?"

"I don't think Chip could ever be mad at you, Nicky."

"Do you remember when he saved me? I was really scared. He made me feel a whole lot better."

"Chip's a good guy to have around when you're scared. He's a pretty good guy to have around no matter what."

"Will he still come see me when I get better?"

His hand squeezed mine tighter; the question was there, the one I couldn't answer. "Chip is your friend, Nicky. He'll always come to see you when he can."

"He's my best friend."

"And that's what best friends do. They always come when you need them."

"When I grow up," Nicky whispered, drifting off into the sleep he said he didn't need, "I'll go see him. I'll have a job and I can get on a plane..."

"I'll come get you," I said softly. "You can ride in my plane."

He drifted off, his grip on my hand relaxing very slowly.

~

Two hours later Chip and Nicky were sitting on a blanket stretched out under a tree that had been planted in the middle of a small island of dirt and grass at the far end of the parking lot. It wasn't Nicky's ideal—he had in mind being out in a park, on the swings with Chip pushing him—but it was the best his nurse could come up with. His parents and I were perched on creaky metal folding chairs, and his nurse was close by, waiting in the wheelchair he had insisted on bringing.

Nicky refused to ride in it; he wanted Chip to carry him outside, and he didn't want a piggyback ride. Chip carried him on his hip like he would a toddler, and Nicky clung to him, resting his head on Chip's shoulder until the Colonel had spread the blanket out.

Even then, Nicky was half in Chip's lap, refusing to break contact.

I sat close enough to Chip to overhear his conversation with Nicky, but tried to not eavesdrop. I made small talk with his parents, muted chat that danced around their son's illness and the inevitable outcome of his disease. They had stopped treatment; it wasn't working, and they wanted what time he had left to be as drug free and comfortable as was feasible.

Bree Lockhart couldn't take her eyes off her son. He was clinging to someone else and she was as charitable about it as possible, but the longing in her eyes made me wonder if she resented it, at least a little bit. Yet, she said simply, "Your son gave us two years we wouldn't have had with ours, and I am so very grateful that he's been so willing to keep coming back."

Chip got that compassion from someone, and I had no clue who it was.

Nicky had climbed completely onto Chip's lap, using his arm as a pillow; I could hear them talking, very quietly, and strained to hear.

"I don't want you to ever forget me," Nicky whispered.

"I won't."

"You're gonna get old, though. You might. Old people forget things."

"Kiddo, your name is tattooed on my heart. I swear, I will never forget you."

Bree's eyes filled with tears and she turned away from Nicky, her hand shooting out for her husband's arm.

"I'm not gonna get to grow up, Chip."

"I know. It sucks and I hate that. I'd trade places with you if I could."

"No. I want you to get old. And there might be another kid you have to save."

"Maybe," Chip allowed. "But I guarantee you, you're always gonna be my favorite."

Bree stood up, wiping at her eyes with the back of her hand, and she turned toward the hospital, walking away. If Nicky noticed, he didn't say anything; the Colonel looked conflicted: go after her, or stay with their son.

"Go," I whispered. "We'll take him back up in a minute."

He hesitated, but seeing his wife stumble across the parking lot, wracked in sobs, he hurried after her. Nicky's nurse slowly rolled the wheelchair closer, and then sat near me, waiting.

"Do you know what's gonna happen to me?" Nicky asked Chip. "What happens after?"

"Did you ask your mom and dad?"

"When my grandma died, they said she was in heaven with grandpa and she was happy there and having fun. It'll be okay if I get to have fun."

"I think," Chip said carefully, "that your grandma and grandpa will be waiting there for you, and they'll take care of you as long as you need them to. And then you'll get to grow up."

"Will there be baseball? I wanted to play in Little League but I got sick and they wouldn't let me."

"It wouldn't be heaven without Little League," Chip assured him.

They grew quiet then, and I wondered if Nicky had fallen asleep, but Chip was making no move to get up, and the nurse was still seated quietly.

Then, like a kick to my teeth, "Am I gonna have a funeral?"

Please, God, don't let me start crying now.

"Sure," Chip said. "I think your parents will have one for you because it will help them. They'll get to say prayers, and tell everyone how awesome you were and how glad they are that you're their son. Someone might even sing. Hell, I'll sing if you want me to."

"Chip?"

"What, sport?"

"I don't want you to go."

"To your funeral?"

"Yeah. Because everyone there is gonna cry and stuff, and I don't want you to be sad. I want you to be happy."

"What if I promise to not cry?"

"No. Because I'll be in a box, right? I don't want you to see me in a box. Promise me?"

"All right. But I can send flowers, okay? A giant bunch of flowers, and maybe they'll make your mom smile."

Sleepily, "Purple ones? I like purple."

"The purplest of purple."

"Chip?"

"Yeah?"

"I think I peed on you again."

I glanced over at them, just as Chip pressed a kiss into Nicky's forehead. "It's all right, sport. We'll take you inside and get you cleaned up."

"Don't tell my dad. I peed on him and he cried."

Chip was struggling to his feet, holding onto Nicky as he got up. Nicky looped his arms around Chip's neck and buried his face against his chest, legs locked around Chip's waist. "I'm pretty good at keeping secrets, Nicky. I'll keep yours."

In the elevator, his face still hidden against Chip, Nicky whispered, "I'm really scared, Chip."

"So am I. It's all right to be scared."

"Real men don't get scared."

"Then you know what?" Chip pulled Nicky tighter against him. "I don't want to be a real man right now. Right now, we get to be kids, okay?"

"You're a grown up, though."

"Not really," Chip said, as if realizing it himself. The doors opened and he stepped out carefully. "I'm not a grown up yet. So we get to be kids, and we get to be scared, and we even get to cry."

I stopped at the door, not wanting to intrude; the nurse slipped past me and I could hear drawers opening and closing, and Chip asking Nicky if he wanted him to step outside while he got cleaned up.

Nicky wanted him nearby. I leaned on the wall just outside the door, arms wrapped around me like I was trying to hold myself together; I was, really, standing there trying to not give the lump forming in my throat another millimeter, blinking back any tears that threatened to spill.

"You look a little sleepy," Chip said.

"A little. If I take a nap, will you stay?"

"I'll stay until you fall asleep. When you wake up, I think your mom and your dad will want to spend some time with you without me here. I've kinda hogged you all afternoon."

"Will you come back tomorrow?"

"Yep. I have a couple of days off work, so I can come back. Maybe we'll go back outside."

"We didn't get popsicles."

"That's okay. When you get up from your nap, you go ahead and get one. Maybe your dad will have one with you, and you can make fun of him for being really old and eating a Popsicle like a little kid."

There was a stretch of quiet, and then, "I like your Mom, Chip."

"I do, too. She's one of my favorite people, right next to you."

Ten minutes later he tiptoed out of the room, whispering, "He'll be asleep for a good two hours. Let me tell his parents that we're leaving and that I'll come back tomorrow."

He was quiet the rest of the day; if I asked him something he answered, but he had disengaged and I knew his head was still at Wilford Hall. Conversation at dinner was forced, and afterward we sat in the hotel room on our beds, staring at the TV. When the news was over, just to spare him the awkwardness of the silence, I told him I was tired and going to bed, knowing he would turn the TV and lights off.

In the dark, when I couldn't see him, he said quietly, "Tomorrow is going to be hard, Kris. I'm never going to see him again."

"He won't know that," I said, hoping it would help.

"It's not fair."

"Not even close to being fair," I agreed.

I heard him roll over, and within an hour his breathing evened out and slowed, and I tried to relax, praying I would figure out how to help him get through the next day.

~

At three a.m., the phone rang.

Chip scrambled out of bed and grabbed it before I was awake enough to think clearly. I started to turn the light on but then thought better of it.

Good news does not come at three in the morning.

I barely listened to Chip's voice rumbling across the room in the dark, but I could hear his agony begin to leech through every word he said, and when he hung up the phone, I reached across the space between the beds and took it from him.

"He died in his sleep," Chip whispered. "Fuck it all."

I struggled to come up with something to say to him, but he crawled back into bed and rolled over, his back to me. I was still struggling when I heard his breath intake sharply, and I stepped over to his bed, slipped in beside him, and put my arms around him as best as I could, and listened quietly as he went from fighting the tears to gut wrenching sobs.

For two years I had wanted nothing more for him than to be allowed to be the boy I knew was buried somewhere deep inside; what he had become wasn't fair. He shouldn't have been pretending to be an adult, and the adults around him?

We were failing on every front.

He needed to be a kid.

But not like this.

Not ever, I thought as his sobbing gave way to hiccupped and then sinus-gurgling breathing, like this.

~

Spoiling for a fight, I cornered Ron in his office, blocking the door to keep him from walking away when I wanted to dump out every raw feeling I had into his lap. He'd been gone when Chip and I returned from Texas, and in the three weeks that followed we kept missing each other; either I was flying somewhere, or he was off with Dan.

It felt deliberate.

That wasn't rational and I knew it, but it felt like he was hiding from me, and hiding from his son's pain. So when I knew he was there, I stormed into his office and shut the door loudly, leaning against it just in case he invented an excuse to bail.

He looked up from the blueprints spread out across his desk, and my anger melted away in that smile. He practically jumped up and crossed the room in three steps, and had his arms around me before I could complain that he was ruining my bad mood.

I noted, too, that he wasn't scrambling to hide the blueprints on his desk; I was used to him closing whatever file he was reading when I came into his office, or shoving paperwork into a desk drawer.

On the priority list of need-to-know, I was near the bottom and he was near the top, so blueprints spread out where I could see them piqued my interest. After he'd kissed me and nearly hugged the breath out of me, I gestured to his desk and asked what he was working on so hard.

"Something for Chip." He unfolded a hidden part of the blueprint and ran his hand over it, smoothing out the creases. "He's hard to explain when it comes to this agency, so we thought it was time to create a cover for him."

"A cover."

"It gets him away from this building and limits his connection to it. If we get this off the ground, he'll look like just another businessman trying to get something going."

"And this is...?" I was looking at the plans, but had no idea exactly what I was looking at.

"A restaurant. Fairly high end, too." He was pointing to different spots, and I still couldn't follow him. "Fairly luxurious eat-in bar, a stage for live music, dance floor, dining room set up for private couples' dining, and a chef's kitchen."

"And Chip is supposed to run it."

"With help."

"He's eighteen."

"He'll be nineteen before this is ready."

"And does he know anything about it?"

"Not yet." He turned and sat against the desk, reaching out for my hands. "This isn't as out of the blue as it seems, Kris. When

Colonel Lockhart was able to track Chip down…I decided then he needed a buffer. And it's not going to hurt him to learn something besides this agency."

"But a restaurant?"

"It's something he can actively engage in, yet turn over to a manager when he's on assignment. And being a kid who does a fair amount of wandering, that won't look odd. He comes from money, so having the means to open a place like this isn't suspicious, and having the means to just pick up and travel won't be, either."

"His stepfather has money, Ron. Money Chip wouldn't touch."

"Yeah, well, he'll get over it. On paper, Grant is loaning him the startup costs. And on paper, Chip will pay him back every dime over the next three years."

"Does Grant know this?"

Ron nodded. "He's on board. He's also on board with the trust fund Chip supposedly has. Hell, he does have, if he'd actually take anything from Grant."

"So on paper, he's tapping into it."

"To explain how he has the money to address whatever whims he has."

"All this for a cover."

"We've all got them, Kris. You fly, Doug's a doctor, and I sell drugs."

"Funny." I leaned in for a kiss, wondering where in the hell my steam went. I wanted to be mad. "When are you coming home? Tonight, I hope."

He nodded. "I'll be late, but I'll be home."

"I'm getting a little tired of eating dinner alone, mister."

"Grab Chip and Doug. Take them out, and then make them pick up the check."

"You're so sweet." I stole another kiss, and headed for the door. "I'm waiting up, so you better not be too late."

"Should I be afraid?"

"Very. Hey, does Chip know anything about this?"

"Not yet. Kind of need to keep it that way for a bit, too. I need one final stamp of approval from the SG before I spring it on him."

Chip running a restaurant.

I gave it two years, tops. Three if they did, indeed, find him a good manager.

~

The fight I'd wanted to have faded to an all but a lingering want-but-don't-want, so I picked up the phone and called both Chip and Doug; I didn't want to drag them to a restaurant, but my fridge was stocked with plenty of beer and the closest pizza delivery served up a decent pepperoni, so I invited them over with a promise that I wouldn't go anywhere near the kitchen unless it was for plates and beer bottles.

Chip was reluctant; his mood was still bleary and he had spikes of anger that he barely controlled, but after a few assurances that we didn't care if he was depressing as hell, he agreed to come over and inhale as much pizza as he could. He looked tired and put up with Doug's concerned questions—yeah, I'm trying to sleep, yeah, I'm eating, and shut up, I'm not talking about *that* in front of Kris—and when I was satisfied that the only thing that was wrong was lingering grief, I popped open a bottle of beer and handed it to him.

"I know you drink, Chip," I said to his look of surprise. "You can drown it out if you want, but if you do, you're sleeping here tonight." Before Doug could offer to drive him home I cut him off. "If he's even a little bit buzzed, I'll feel better if he stays here."

"Then I won't drink that much," Chip said. "I know you and Ron have been on opposite schedules. You don't want me here tonight."

Don snorted out a laugh. "Ron might."

Chip nodded thoughtfully as he sipped at the beer. "True enough. He is getting awfully old now, and she's still young...ish."

"You can both bite me," I sighed.

"We're kinda related," Chip said. "I'm not sure that would be appropriate. But the doc here is fair game. If, you know, you just can't wait for the old man to get home."

"I don't do married women," Doug said. "Besides, Ron could hurt me. I might be able to outrun him, but he's a better shot and has good aim."

I nearly choked on my beer, wincing as it shot up into my sinuses.

"What?"

"Let's just say that sometimes his aim is a little off."

Chip's face screwed up in disgust. "Ew. I don't need to hear that."

"What's he up to anyway?" Doug asked. "I'm getting tired of slapping bandages on scrapes and burns and bullet holes. Why aren't we working?"

"We are working, just not together. I'm not really sure what he's up to right now. I'm not in the loop."

"And he doesn't share?"

"Don't do that, man," Chip said. "Ron wouldn't tell God himself anything unless all the paperwork was in order, in triplicate, and he produced the right security clearance. Don't make her feel like he shouldn't hold back just because she sleeps with him."

Before Doug could apologize, I said, "Don't think it doesn't annoy me. In the last, what, six weeks I've been flying crap jobs to kill time while he's off in meetings all over the country and he can't tell me what for or why. And yeah, sometimes it pisses me off. Half the time I don't know where he is."

The down time suited Chip. He was spending his days either in the gym or on the track, and had developed a serious want of his own motorcycle. The only thing holding him back was knowing that he'd never get away with running a bike at those speeds on the Interstate, and if he couldn't ride hard and fast, what's the point?

"Keep it on the track," Doug said. "At least there you're in racing leathers and it's controlled. I'd really hate to have to peel you off the road and have half your skin stay behind."

The minute sliver of happiness I thought I'd seen in Chip melted away. "Yeah," he said quietly, "I'd hate to do that to you."

"Enjoy the hell out of it on the track, though," Doug quickly added. "I'd have killed for that chance when I was your age. Instead, I was poking around cadavers in an anatomy lab."

That was probably around the same time I was puking my way across the parking lot at UC Davis, terrified of the first day of classes. "Were you given a choice?" I asked him. "I've wondered. Did you always want to be a doctor or were you steered toward it?"

He knew what I meant. "I knew what I wanted to be when I was ten or eleven, but there was never pressure. I didn't have an inkling about the agency until I was his age"—he gestured to Chip—"and they came sniffing around, offering to pay for medical school. All I could think of was getting through it debt free. I didn't see the bigger picture."

"Your old man didn't spell it out for you?" Chip asked.

"Not really. But I don't think he was ever as high up the chain as yours. He spent most of his time sitting behind a desk, shuffling paper from one side to the other. I'm sure he thought I would just work in family practice, or even be a hospital connection. He probably didn't have a lot to tell."

"Data analyst?" I asked.

"I think so."

"He must have been privy to some serious shit," Chip mused.

"Never thought of it that way," Doug said. "I just assumed he wasn't in the kind of physical shape he needed to be to work in the field."

"We need brains making decisions in the office," I pointed out. We needed them in the field, too, which is why Doug was assigned to an active team, but I wasn't telling him that. He knew he was smart; if he hadn't figured that out for himself, it was because he didn't want to know.

On any typical assignment, protecting Doug was a given. Without being told, even Chip understood that. Dan might technically be in charge, but when it came to assessing a situation, if Doug thought we needed a new tactic, Dan listened. If he dismissed Doug too easily, Ron backed Doug up.

Doug was right; it didn't matter what was on paper, whether Dan realized it or not, Ron was our team's final voice.

I wondered if Dan knew Ron had turned the leader's position down and that he was the second choice.

Chip drained his beer and he set the bottle on the end table, but didn't get up to get another nor ask if it was all right if he did. "When I was little," he said, leaning back, "I used to get pissed off that Ron was gone for a couple of weeks at a time and I couldn't figure it out.

He was a drug rep. He convinced doctors and hospitals to buy the medications he was selling. Why did he have to be gone so long?"

"International sales," I snickered.

"Yeah, well. He also would never talk about exactly what he was selling, like the latest cough syrup was super-secret."

"Probably couldn't bullshit his way through that," Doug said.

"Maybe. I was just pissed off because he was gone so much. I mean, it's not like he would have done the whole pee-wee football coach thing, but it would have been nice to have that option."

"He missed a lot," I guessed.

"He missed everything," Chip sighed, getting up. "I'm beat, I really am. Are you sure you don't mind me crashing here?"

"It's still your room," I told him.

And will be for as long as I'm here.

As soon as the bedroom door clicked shut, Doug picked up the beer bottles and said he should probably go, but I put a hand on his arm and told him to just stay for a little while. Ron wasn't going to be home for at least another hour, maybe two, and I honestly didn't want to be alone.

I'd had enough solitude over the last few weeks; I wanted company, even if we just sat there and stared at the TV.

"Does that thing even work?" Doug asked. "It's, like, well… older than I am."

"The very first time I met Chip he was complaining about how old that TV is. Ron never really watches it and it works, so he's never seen a point in replacing it. Now that Chip has moved out I only turn it on for the news."

"You're capable of replacing it yourself," he pointed out.

"I could have. But back then it was something they could poke each other with and I thought they both found it a little absurd, in a funny kind of way. Now I don't see a point."

Doug was looking around the living room; he'd been there before, but until then hadn't taken the time to pay any attention to it. "This place was Ron's before you got married, wasn't it?"

I nodded.

"So why haven't you put your own stamp on it?"

"What do you mean?"

He held his hand out, gesturing to the room in general. "This is all very… I don't know — it's generic, there's not much in the way of personal things on display. I don't see you in anything at all. Is there anything on the walls or on a shelf that you picked out?"

Surely there was. But I looked around and realized he was right; the apartment was almost exactly like it had been when I moved in; not a bachelor pad, but almost impersonal. A home staged for sale, not living.

"I bought a vacuum cleaner," I said.

"Well score one for women's rights," he kidded. "I don't mean anything by it; it's just surprising that you haven't changed anything. Most women would, right? Soften things up a little?"

"Most women aren't spending their days flying men out of strange little countries where people are shooting at them," I pointed out. "When we got married I put my stuff into storage. Ron already had everything we needed, so what was the point?"

"To have pieces of yourself here," he said. "Hell, at least sneak something bright and frilly in here just to yank on Ron's shorts."

"Says the bachelor," I retorted.

"Hey, I wouldn't mind in the least if you brought something bright and girly into my apartment."

"Ron might have something to say about that if I did."

"You know what I mean. A woman who's going to stick around in my life gets to bring her shit in. And I mean more than a tooth-brush."

"And how's that going? Still finding excuses to avoid asking women to dance?"

"I'm dating."

"Seriously dating?"

"Well, no. But I'm not above trolling for Chip's cast-offs. Hang around him, and a guy can get very lucky."

"I thought that wasn't your game."

"His game is not my game. But he brushes past some very nice women, and I'd be an idiot if I didn't at least try to make a move."

"There are lots of nice women at work," I pointed out.

"That would get too complicated," he said. "If it works for you, terrific, but I'd like to keep my convoluted work life separate from my love life."

"Come on. If the perfect woman was right there, blowing the gonads off of a paper target on the firing range, you wouldn't take a chance?"

"I'm not sure I'd want to be with someone who has enough accuracy to shoot my junk off."

"Bull. Your heart would go all gooey at the idea you not only found the right one, but she was bad ass as hell. You know it."

"Maybe," he allowed with a chuckle. "But I really think that I'll hold off on the whole serious relationship thing until my time is paid off and I can wander into civilian life and leave the agency behind. I want a family, and from everything I've seen, that's not the best idea on this job. I don't want to turn around when my kid is a teenager and worry that he'll become another Chip."

"Chip," I said, angry about it, "was not supposed to become this Chip. He was supposed to take the state equivalency test, go to community college, and find a real life for himself. This is not what we wanted for him."

"Not what you wanted," Doug corrected.

"Holy hell, Doug. We'd been married for all of five days when Grant shoved him out the door. And that was fine, I'd already decided it was stupid for Chip to be living there and I wanted him here with us. Ron and I had decided—I would quit so that Chip would have someone at home for him, he'd go to school, and for once he'd have a reasonably normal home life."

"You were going to quit? Why not Ron?"

"Because this job doesn't mean anything to me. It was a means to an end. I would have had no problem spending the last two years being Chip's stepmother and actually acting like it."

"Instead he followed us to Germany."

"And now here he is, back in his old bed, agonizing over what having followed us eventually ended in. He connected with that little boy, Doug. I saw a side of him back in Germany that I don't think anyone else other than maybe his little brother had up until then. And I saw it again a few weeks ago, when he was holding Nicky on his lap and soaking up as much of that boy's terror as he could."

"When you two got back I offered to get on the next plane back and go to Nicky's funeral with him."

"He promised Nicky he wouldn't go. And it's been chewing away at him. He thought he was going to have one more day to say goodbye—"

"It's better that he didn't have to," Doug said softly. "He never would have gotten out of Nicky's room without breaking down, and no matter what anyone wanted to believe, Nicky would have known that he'd never see Chip again. At least this way he died thinking that his best buddy would be back in the morning. And Chip didn't have to drag himself away."

"He never should have met Nicky in the first place."

"Ideally, no."

"We were so stupid. We left everything Chip needed to follow us right there on the damned kitchen table and never thought a thing about it."

"I can't picture Ron being that careless."

"He was distracted," I said. "I was distracted. Hell, I'd *just* decided to quit my job and be someone's mother." I reached for my now-warm beer and drained it. "When Chip and I were in Texas, Nicky kept referring to me as 'Chip's mom' and Chip never corrected him. Neither did I. Yet he's not my son and I don't think of him as my stepson, even though he is. What the hell?"

"Complicated," Doug said. "I know he doesn't think of you as his stepmother. Yet he's nearly Oedipal in how he feels."

"Oedipal."

"Oedipus Rex," he explained.

"I know what it means, Doug. And it's not the first time you've insinuated that he wants to do nasty things to me."

"That's not what I meant. He doesn't, not at all. He loves you, but it's all very complicated in his head. You're not his mother, not his step, he loves you but isn't *in* love—yet you are exactly what he wants in a woman. He had a piss poor imitation of a mother when he was growing up...and here you are, not his mother but loving him like you were, and you're more than a stepmother, if that makes sense."

"It makes sense."

"He needs role models. He never got that, not until you came along."

"What does that say for the kind of father he'll be someday?"

"I don't know. But it might be enough that he's had you in his life. If he winds up with the right woman, she might be able to ground him enough that he'll learn to be the father he always wanted."

"And his own was never quite that," I sighed. "I don't think he really wanted to be."

"Seriously."

I looked over at the closed bedroom door. "Ron loves Chip, Doug, don't ever think he doesn't. But right after we met, he made it pretty clear that he was so deep into this job that it came first. I was fine with that, because hell, we'd just met. We both thought it would go somewhere, but we'd *just* met. What I didn't realize then that it also came before Chip."

"And when you realized that?"

"We were already married. I can be so stupid and blind...he'd warned me, he really had. I came straight out and asked him if he'd ever considered quitting and he said no. He backtracked later and said that if it would have been the best thing for Chip he would have, but..."

"You don't think he would have."

"No, I don't. Ron's priority list is the job, Chip, then me, and that's pretty fucked up."

"But he was honest about it."

"He was, but I doubt I really believed that he would put his job before his own kid. I mean, who would?"

"What if you'd known how serious he was about that?"

I inhaled slowly, exhaled slowly, and let the truth punch me right in the face.

"I wouldn't have married him, Doug. I love him, and I mean I love him deeply, but I shouldn't have married him. I should have walked away the moment I found out he would leave his own son with a man who had tried to kill him. And if not for Chip, I would have."

"And yet, here you still are," he whispered.

"Here I still am. Because of Chip."

Chip stood in the middle of the dance floor, his hands jammed into his pockets, and he soaked it all in. From where we were standing we could see almost all of it; the dining room with muted mood lighting, small private booths meant for two, the few tables meant for larger parties. There was a stage just behind us, fronted by a heavy silk curtain, and the dance floor was a deep, beautiful oak. To our left, hidden behind a lattice wall was the bar; if anything spoke to Chip, it was the bar.

I almost asked how he managed to get a liquor license, but the answer would have been given in a shrug.

"Now what?" he muttered under his breath.

"For now you let Teddy take the reins," Ron said. "He's here to help you learn to run the place."

"Help me? He's going to have to do it all."

"For a while. You'll get the hang of it."

The sigh Chip heaved was peppered with doubt. "I had to hire people. What the hell? Tons of kids applying for jobs as waiters and waitresses, and I had to guess if they'd be any good at it." He looked over at me. "You want a part time job? I want someone to stand at the front door and tell people to go somewhere else. We only serve food poisoning here."

"You can do this," Ron assured him.

"I'd better be able to do this. Holy shit, Ron, this place screams sex. Once people get word of it, it'll be packed. I'm not even sure the food will have to be all that good."

"With the name you picked? Son, the food has to be outstanding to get over that hump. 'Charybdis.' What the hell?"

"Read something besides security reports," Chip muttered.

I thought the name lent something to the place. It was obscure enough to get people to notice, and it was memorable enough to make the restaurant stand out once word started circulating. If the food was good enough, the name would only make people remember, and would bring them back.

Still, Chip was less than certain about the whole thing. He celebrated his nineteenth birthday in a Tokyo bar with Doug, and when he came home, Ron dropped the restaurant into his lap.

Having a cover, Chip understood. But needing a cover, he wasn't quite as sure about. He was fine with letting people think he was the overindulged stepson of one of the city's wealthiest real estate moguls; he didn't care if the people who filtered in and out of his life thought he was lazy and worthless to boot. To Chip, that was cover enough.

While I hadn't quite agreed with this being something for him to hide behind, I was starting to see why it was a good thing. Sooner or later—and I hoped sooner—that woman Doug was sure would knock Chip on his ass was bound to come along, and in the grand scheme of things it was better if it looked like he was making something of himself, not living life as a trust fund baby.

As he gave us the grand tour I couldn't help but hope that eventually the restaurant would be his ticket out of the agency.

After Ron left, Chip took me into his office; the walls were paneled with rich, dark wood planks running floor to ceiling, capped by matching crown molding. On the far wall was a fireplace with a substantial hearth, and the wall above it was rock with a darkly stained oak mantel. He'd picked out an executive desk that practically disappeared into the wall behind it, and he'd had a custom sofa made that spanned the entire length of one wall.

It was long enough and deep enough, I mused, for two people to engage in some fairly horny gymnastics.

Over the next year, between assignments that were few and far between, Teddy taught Chip well. His uncertainty over understanding what he needed to do was gradually painted over with confidence; as the customer base exploded, Chip realized not only could he do it, he was damned good at it.

Women flocked to the bar and were, Teddy reported, crushed on the nights Chip wasn't there. Yet he knew better than to do anything more than flirt with his female customers; he flirted hard, and he seemed to offer more than he would ever give, but he never took any of them back into his office with the giant sofa, and never left with one of them.

But he still had a parade of women in and out of his life. Doug gave up trying to keep even a rough mental count. "He's with someone every night," he told me. "The only difference between now and a couple of years ago is that once in a while, he'll see the same girl two or three times."

"That's something."

"I guess. Once he has a normal conversation with one of them, though?" He stuck his thumb out and pointed backwards. "Maybe he's making forward progress, but he needs to stop intentionally picking boobs over brains."

Coincidentally or not—I leaned toward 'or not' because he knew I'd be there—Doug and I wound up at the restaurant at the same time, ostensibly to see if Chip was available to have lunch. I'd known there was only a slim chance he'd be there, and Doug had to know there was zero chance of him being there, but I often dropped by to see how my not-my-son was doing.

Frequently, Doug was there, too.

We had lunch together; there wasn't a reason not to. Chip was off trying to learn to speak Farsi and Ron was busy pushing Dan Martin's buttons, and since I had nothing on the schedule and Doug was off, why the hell not?

Doug listened; he made the effort to not just talk to me, he actually listened, and that was something I was finding less and less of at home.

"You're shutting Ron out," Doug kept telling me.

I didn't think so. I was just tired. Tired of coming in third, tired of either seeing nothing of Ron for weeks at a time and then being thrown together nonstop until I just wanted to shove him into traffic, tired of everything.

The one thing I kept coming back to, Ron's melting smile every time he'd come home, I saw less of as his workload increased. The sheer static that popped between us, the sex that was so good that just thinking about it turned my guts into jelly, had become so infrequent that I rarely considered it.

When he was home and wanted sex, more often than not I went along with it because, hell, he was still my husband and I wasn't getting it anywhere else. But I'd stop initiating anything physical, and he'd noticed.

Instead of trying to talk to him about it, I tuned him out.

You put me third in line; you don't get to be too picky about it.

"Maybe Chip will find some medium, someone with smaller boobs but bigger brains," I told Doug. "It would be a start."

"Maybe. Well, hell, there is someone he's mentioned more than once lately. Some girl he knew in high school that's been hanging around here. I get the feeling he's been spending some time with her."

"Really now. Have you met her?"

He shook his head. "I rarely meet the women he's with unless I'm there when he's trying to pick them up. It's not like he'd go out of his way to introduce me to someone when he's not even sure what her name is and he has no intention of calling again."

"We have to meet her," I decided. "I want to see what kind of woman can pin him down for more than five minutes."

"And we do this, how?"

"If she's hanging around here, so will we. Sooner or later we're bound to run into them together, right? Chip can be a jerk but he's not going to refuse an introduction."

"You sure about that?"

I wasn't, but honestly, it was something to do, and I was just bored enough to find the idea entertaining.

Stalking Chip.

What could go wrong?

~

"Skank."

Doug's eyes widened in surprise.

"Well, you asked me what I thought. That's the first thing that popped into my head. Skank. Did you see the track marks on her arm? What the hell is Chip thinking?"

"I have no idea," he said after another quick glance across the bar. We were sitting next to each other in a back booth, and Chip's so-called girlfriend was perched on a stool at the bar. "They know each other from high school. Maybe it's something left over from there."

"He was a little slut in high school, Doug. I'd be surprised if he even had any female friends, much less someone he had feelings for."

"He's still a little slut. But yeah, let's hope she's just a distraction. Because you're right, there's a whole lot of wrong swirling around that girl."

"Along with tobacco and marijuana smoke," I said as she sipped from her drink. "I know Chip drinks, but he's not doing anything else, is he?"

"I really doubt it. But if you're worried, I'll pay closer attention."

At that point I didn't know whether to worry or not. I was certain that I did not like this girl, and I wondered what the hell Chip was thinking, but I also knew better than to tell him that.

"I don't see him doing drugs," I said after a minute. "Doing her? Sure, but not getting close. I don't get it."

It was mean, but we sat there and dissected her, from her spiked hair to the thick makeup to the skintight clothes she was wearing. It was high school, but we kept at it, laughing until the absurdity of what we were doing occurred to both of us.

That was right about the time I realized Ron had come in and was two steps away from the booth.

"Move," I told Doug, waving Ron to sit by me. Doug scrambled to the other side of the booth and when Ron sat down I said, "Girl at the end of the bar."

He looked, then frowned. "The hooker?"

"Chip's girlfriend," Doug snorted.

"You're kidding." He looked at Doug, then at me, then back to the girl. "Girlfriend, as in someone he's not just screwing around with?"

"I'm not sure yet," I said. "But apparently they're hanging around together a lot."

"Is he high?"

"Hey, she might be really nice," Doug said.

"For fifty bucks, maybe," Ron countered. He blinked the image of her away and leaned toward me, brushing a kiss against my cheek. "I took a chance that you'd be here since you weren't at home."

"And I was just leaving," Doug said, sliding toward the end of the booth seat.

"Stay," Ron said. "Otherwise I'd just have to track you down, too. We've got an assignment, quick trip to escort the Secretary General to a meeting in Brazil."

"They need me for that?" Doug asked.

"You're on the orders."

"He has a personal physician."

Ron shrugged. "We're going whether we're needed or not." His eyes flicked toward the girl; Chip was now standing next to her, leaning against the bar so that his face was near hers, and he was listening closely to whatever she was saying. "I may need you there just to keep his ass in line."

"Your trust in my abilities is astounding," Doug deadpanned.

Chip finally looked over our way, and Ron beckoned him over. The girl, thankfully, stayed put.

"Brazil in the morning," Ron said as Chip slid in next to Doug.

"For?"

"Does it matter? Report at five a.m." He glanced towards the end of the bar. "And make sure you've actually gotten some rest. Don't be drunk or…whatever."

"Whatever."

"High, stoned, drunk, diseased. Take your pick."

"Have I ever reported drunk, high, or stoned?"

"Not that I'm aware of. Who is she, Chip?"

He glanced over his shoulder. "Brenda. Why?"

"Been seeing her long?"

"Six months or so. Again, why?"

"Six months?" I sputtered. "How the hell have you hidden a girlfriend from us for six months?"

All three of them looked at me like I'd just blurted out Ron's personal measurements. How could he? When had he ever introduced us to one of the women he was with? Or even one of his friends?

Hell, did he even have friends other than Doug?

Did I?

"She wandered in not long after we opened," Chip said. "I remembered her from high school, we started talking…" He shrugged. "She kept popping up in here and we kept talking. It just moved on from there."

"And if I ran her name through the system?" Ron asked.

"You wouldn't."

"If I think she might compromise your position, yes, I will. You don't need to draw attention to yourself, son."

"Like this restaurant doesn't? Did you know I've been dodging a reporter from The Chronicle? They want to do an article on Fairfield's newest dining gem. We're drawing customers from the Bay Area, and apparently that's news. It's also attention, and I can't avoid it much longer."

"That's different. It's business."

"It starts that way. But then they want to know about the person behind the business, his life, how he got where he is. Do we really want this reporter poking into my life?"

"The bases were covered, Chip."

"Business bases. And in any case, you don't get a vote in this. I'm seeing her. That's all you need to know."

I reached across the table, intended to touch his hand, but he pulled it back. "Don't get us wrong, Chip. If you're seeing someone we're happy for you, but come on. You have to see where we'd be a little concerned."

"You don't even know her."

"No, and we won't as long as you keep hiding her from everyone."

"Fair enough," he said, getting up. "You'll have plenty of time to get to know her after we get back from Brazil. I asked her to marry me."

~

We sat at the kitchen table for at least two hours, quiet, each pouring over paperwork from our finished assignments and Ron was boning up on the one we would report for in the morning. In between pockets of silence, Ron gave me basic details: we were escorting Alex Barstow to a meeting in Brazil, at which Ron would be present, but during which Doug and I had nothing scheduled. Chip, on the other hand, had been tapped to courier documents to a nearby embassy. My presence was required only because the SG wanted me to pilot his jet from HQ to Langley and again on the return trip, and Doug was going because of Chip; while the SG would

not require Doug's medical expertise, it went without officially saying that Chip, being Chip, very well might.

"You two can go with Chip if you want," Ron said, "Or take the
day to be tourists. Whichever you feel like."

He wasn't going to fill me in on why the SG needed him for this
meeting, and I knew better than to ask. I wondered why Ron hadn't
mentioned Dan at all, but with the words on paper in front of me
beginning to blur, I passed on pressing him for further details.

If he wanted me to know, he'd tell me.

If he wanted to talk about Chip's announcement, he would.

We got little from Chip. Her name was Brenda Webb. She was
nineteen years old. They met in high school; she was a year behind
him, but they were never friends, only aware of each other. She suited him, and anything else was not up for discussion.

Ron brushed it off, reminded Chip what time he wanted him
ready to go, and got up. Without him asking whether or not I was
headed for home, I followed, leaving Doug sitting in the bar alone.

Before getting into our separate cars, Ron said he'd pick something up for dinner on his way; he was sparing us both from any
domestic impulses I might have to feed him, but I felt a few pangs of
guilt. He'd been working long hours and it felt like the least I could
do was feed him. There were a few things I didn't mutilate or burn
beyond recognition, but after nearly five years he was tired of them,
so while he stopped to pick something up, I changed the sheets on
the bed and vacuumed.

If I can't feed him, I can clean for him.

It made sense in my head.

Ron was still scratching out notes when I closed my file folder
and pushed away from the table, unable to focus any longer on what
I was reading. I'd hit the point of wanting to fill out every report I
needed with *I flew the plane. It didn't crash. Mission accomplished.*
While that worked when reporting back to Dan, I didn't think it
would fly with desk jockeys in charge of pushing paper around.

Without looking up from what he was doing Ron asked, "Heading for bed?"

I hadn't been sure what I was going to do, but standing there
I could see our dinner plates in the sink and glasses that needed to

be washed, and it had to be done before we left unless we wanted to come home to a flourishing science experiment. "I'll do the dishes first," I said.

"You're tired," he said, tossing his pen to the table, "and I'm just about done. Go soak in the tub. I'll do them. It'll take me five minutes."

"You're tired, too," I pointed out.

"Not that tired." He got up and brushed a quick kiss on my lips, then pointed me toward the door. "Go. Soak. I have no idea what our accommodations will be for the next few nights and you might be stuck with a tiny shower with no hot water."

"Brazil is not in the sticks," I snorted. "We'll have hot water."

"Still. Go."

The lure of soaking in hot water won over the need to leave a clean apartment behind. I filled the tub and slid in down to my chin, and closed my eyes. He was right, I was tired, but it wasn't necessarily fatigue. I couldn't put my finger on it, but I was drained and it had nothing to do with needing sleep.

I had no idea what I needed.

Twenty minutes later Ron knocked softly on the bathroom door and then pushed it open. He was carrying two beer bottles and handed one to me, then he sat on the floor near the tub, leaning against the far wall where he could face me. "I think we'll only be gone three or four days," he said absently, swirling the beer in his bottle. "And I know it's a crap assignment, but...at least it's something."

Better than the nothing we'd been getting.

"I've been getting flight hours in," I reminded him.

"Is it enough? I know it's a lot of bullshit taxiing other teams around and it's not exactly worthy of your skill level."

"I'm not getting shot at. That's something."

He took a long draw from the beer and was quiet, sitting there with his knees up and arms dangling over them as he stared down at the floor. I was thinking of flinging water at him to see if he had drifted off when he said very softly, "Chip is making the biggest mistake of his life."

"I know. But it's his mistake to make."

"I can't think of anything to say to him that won't push him toward her even harder. If I warn him off of her, he'll marry her as soon as he can. If I don't, he'll assume I approve."

"Maybe we should suck it up and try to get to know her. If we make an effort, at the very least we might be able to get him to make it a long engagement."

He barely nodded.

"Come on," I said, "give me an idea of what you're going to be doing while I'm doing nothing in Brazil. What is it you've been doing that doesn't include the team?"

He couldn't tell me, and we both knew it; I saw the corner of his mouth twitch up, trying to not smile. "Porn."

"Really now. Hard core, soft core?"

"Truth?"

"Of course."

"I wouldn't know."

This time, I did flick water at him. "Oh, come on."

"Nope. I have never watched porn. At this point, I'm not sure I want to."

"I'm not buying it, mister. You're a little too good at a whole lot of things to have never seen an example."

He raised an eyebrow and sipped at the beer.

"When was the last time we had sex?" I asked.

"You mean when we both wanted to?" I flinched at that, and he saw. "It's not a criticism, Kris. But it's been a long time since we've been on the same page as far as that goes. Don't think I don't appreciate that you don't push me the hell away when you're just off a long string of flights and having me paw at you is the last thing you want...but it's been a long time since I was sure you were totally into it."

I wasn't going to lie to him and proclaim my undying desire for him; he'd know better and I'd feel like a fraud. But part of the truth, that would go a long way into making him feel better.

"You're hardly ever here, Ron. And I admit, sometimes it pisses me off. It's hard to want something when you're perpetually annoyed."

"I'm sorry," he said softly.

"You're here now, though. And I'm not pissed off. I'm anything but pissed off."

"And you're tired. I know that."

"Ron. Take your clothes off. Help me out of the tub, and take me into the bedroom. We don't have to have sex but it's been a long time since we've just *been* together. Kiss me until my toes curl."

"That might take a while," he mused.

"Not as long as you think. Now, strip."

He set the bottle down and got up. "I'm nothing if not obedient," he said as he began to unbutton his shirt. I watched as his clothes came off, slowly, deliberately, knowing he was staring at me, and that he could see every change in me I was barely aware of: how deeply I was beginning to breathe, the speed of my pulse where he could see it on my neck.

When he kicked off his pants, I climbed out of the tub, reaching for my towel; he took it from my hands and wrapped it around me, and began to slowly dry me off. His breath skipped across my skin as he worked his way down, until he dropped the towel and began tracing with his fingertips, drawing fine lines with his lips.

"God, I can hardly think," I breathed.

"Don't think." His lips were on my neck, then at my ear, trailing hot kisses along my jaw until his mouth was on mine, greedy and full of want. I pulled myself tighter to him, feeling how hard he was, and God, the want was drowning me, wrapped like thick humidity around us both.

He lifted me up and I wrapped my legs around his waist; his strength always surprised me a little, how effortlessly he could carry me into the bedroom, but before he could put me on the bed I tangled my hands into his hair, pulling his mouth to me, arching my back dangerously against the wetness of his tongue.

I needed him, and in a flash of surprise, wanted him as much as I ever had; I could not get enough of him and pushed him back onto the bed, pinning him under my weight.

"Not yet," he said roughly, and before I could reach for him, he rolled over. "Slowly. Slowly."

His kisses became deeper, softer, hands moving softly over my body, teasing feather soft promises onto my skin, until I was squirming against him. Even when I reached between us, pushing him into me, he was deliberate, moving slowly, until I was arching against him, my fingers digging sharply into his back, his name slipping from my lips like a prayer.

~

Neither of us slept. We stayed wrapped around each other through the night, drowsy whispers pulling us toward morning; at three o'clock he sighed hard, muttering that it was too late to bother trying to get any sleep, not when we would just have to pry ourselves up in an hour.

"You have to fly," he sighed, just remembering.

I tried to assure him I'd be fine—it was only a flight across the country and not across an ocean—but I was exhausted and my eyes burned with the need for sleep. He started to roll out of bed to make coffee, but I held him back, my hand on his chest.

"Three or four days stuck with Chip and Doug," I said. "Like you said, who knows what our accommodations will be? And you might be stuck with Barstow the whole time."

"We've had worse times in the field."

I slid my hand the rest of the way across his chest, leaning against him, melting my lips against his. "We don't have to get up for another hour. So don't get up."

"But—"

"I can fly. But there's no telling when the next time will be that it'll just be you and me alone in the same room. We may finish the assignment and you'll have to go off in one direction while I go in another."

"Possibly."

"Then stay in bed with me. I don't think I'm done with you yet."

"Are you sure? It's going to be tough walking with your toes all curled up."

"Walking was going to be an issue anyway," I snickered against his mouth. "And I've missed feeling like this."

"Horny?"

I caught his bottom lip between my teeth and gently tugged. "This close to you. Like there's nothing else we have to do. And for an hour there isn't."

"You'll hate me by the time we get to Langley," he said, his lips on my throat.

"Worth the risk?"

"You're worth every risk," he sighed.

Two hours later we were standing on the tarmac waiting for Alex Barstow; I was tired but not yet fuzzy, thanks to copious amounts of coffee Ron kept shoving at me. Doug arrived a few minutes after we did and Chip followed; he took one look at us and laughed knowingly, but with one hard look from Ron stopped short of saying anything.

Instead he said, "It's after five. Why are we not getting on the plane?"

"We're waiting," Ron replied. He nodded toward the gate and the car approaching it. "As soon as he's ready, we'll leave."

"We're flying with the SG?"

"I knew that," Doug offered.

"So did I," I added.

"Wonderful," Chip muttered.

We'd all met Alex Barstow, though it was in passing and I don't think any of us, other than Ron, had actually spoken to him. I'd certainly never been this close to him, and had never realized what a formidable presence he was.

Ron greeted him with a handshake, ignoring the scowl that crossed Barstow's face. When they turned to the rest of us, it felt like a lead weight had dropped into my stomach. He briefly looked at Chip and at Doug, but it was me he settled on, and as he stepped closer his steel gray eyes seemed to be boring into me.

"No," he said roughly. "You're grounded." He turned to Ron, ignoring me, and added, "Unacceptable. I expect my pilot to be ready to fly and she clearly is not."

"She can fly," Ron said.

"Not my plane, not right now. You don't look any better, I might add. What the hell? Your job is to assure—"

"Don't tread into something that is none of your business," Ron interrupted.

"The condition of my pilot is my business, and I have no doubt you're responsible for her being in no shape to get into that cockpit.

Find me another pilot, and do it now." He turned away, pointed at Chip and then Doug and said, "You, in the plane. You, stay or go. You're not needed."

Ron sighed angrily. "Do you want—?"

"No." He turned to me. "Go home and sleep it off."

"I'm not drunk."

Ron was shaking his head, warning me to stop. "Doug, will you drive her home?"

"Yeah, sure."

Barstow was at the foot of the stairs to the plane. "I need a pilot, Gallery."

Ron spun, his entire body clenched like a muscle. "Alex, you're perfectly capable of going inside and using the damned comm system to have another pilot woken up and sent out."

"I wouldn't have to if you'd made sure—"

"That's none of your fucking business."

"Judging from how you both look, I'd say 'fucking' was the operative word."

"Die in a fire, Barstow."

Chip and Doug stared at Ron, mouths gaped open. Chip was simply impressed, but to Doug it was proof; Ron was a hell of a lot higher up the chain of command than he'd ever let on to. He turned his back on the Secretary General and looked at me, both anger and sorrow radiating off of him. "I'm sorry," he said, just loud enough for me to hear. "He's an ass and he knows it."

"I'm tired and he knows it."

"I'm sorry about that, too. Well, not *for* that…"

"I know what you're sorry about. How pissed off will he be if you give me a kiss before you leave?"

"Don't know, don't give a damn."

I reached out for him, my hands on his face, and kissed him deeply; if it embarrassed Doug, I didn't care. If it ticked off the SG, Ron obviously had no problem telling him to mind his own business. In colorful language, even. Chip would only be amused.

"If you get a chance, call me when you get there," I said when we finally came up for air.

"If I can't, I'll make sure Chip does. Just to touch base."

We'd never called to touch base before and I didn't honestly expect he would this time, but in that moment, neither of us was ready to let go. We'd connected, even if it was through sex, and I didn't want him getting on that plane without me.

From the look in his eyes I was sure he didn't want to go; whatever had propelled me out of the tub and into bed with him was something he wanted to examine and replicate. With that last kiss before he boarded the plane, the last glance, I could see it right there: *please be here when I get back; don't let that be it.*

He was headed up the steps and I turned to leave with Doug when I heard him. "Hey, Marge."

"Hey, Horatio."

"I love you."

My toes curled, just a little. "I love you, too."

I stood there until he was inside and undoubtedly arguing with Alex Barstow over the appropriateness of keeping his pilot up all night.

"That was too sweet," Doug said after a moment, pulling me away. "Really. On a scale of one to ten, it was nearly vomitus."

"Oh come on." I jabbed at him with my elbow. "That was nothing. You should have heard what I was calling him at midnight."

"Oh, Horatio!" he teased, his voice two octaves higher. "Take me, Horatio! Make me scream and call me Marge!"

"Shut up!" I was laughing, but still trying to smack him. "I had a good night, so sue me."

"So good it got you booted off an assignment and garnered me some time off, too. Good job."

"I'm here to serve," I told him, waiting for him to unlock his car. "But you? You're now here to take me to breakfast. I'm starving."

"Yeah, I wonder why that is."

"Significant exercise."

"Well, yeah, if it took you all night."

"Jealous?"

"Are you kidding? I don't think I've met someone yet that I'd want to stay up all night with."

"Not even the one that broke your heart a couple of years ago?"

He started the car and put in it reverse, glancing at me as he looked over his shoulder to pull out of the parking space. "Not even. And she didn't break my heart. It just wasn't working."

"We need to find you someone," I decided. "Maybe Chip's fiancée has a friend she can introduce you to."

"God."

"Hey, you never know, she might know the perfect person."

"There's not enough penicillin in the world."

"Listen to you, being all judgmental."

"Pot, meet kettle. I'll find the right person someday. After I get out from under the agency thumb."

"You keep saying that," I said. "Yet you're still here, still plugging away at the clinic between assignments. Your time is up, isn't it?"

"Not quite, but yours is," he countered. "You've been able to walk away for years, but you're still here."

"My original reason for quitting is marrying the town skank," I reminded him. "And at least if I hang in there I see my husband once in a while. What the hell is going on? We've had, what, five assignments as a team this past year?"

"Five or six. I don't really mind the down time for the most part. I'm getting a feel for what it's like to practice family medicine and seeing patients all day. I kind of like it, other than the mandatory annuals. Like, next week, if Ron can score us something, I would greatly appreciate it."

"Why next week?"

"They've scheduled half the women in the agency to get their annual exams. I'm sorry, but I don't relish the idea of giving Linda Jackson a pelvic. I don't want to see any part of a woman who reminds me of my grandmother naked in any way, shape, or form. That's just...wrong."

"Oh hell." I turned in my seat, leaning against the car door, hands gripping my seat belt. "*You're* running the clinic next week?"

"Delay yours for a week."

"I put it off last time I had an appointment. They're not going to let me reschedule."

He pulled into the parking lot at Denny's and cut the engine, leaving his hand on the keys for a moment before sighing. "I'm not doing your exam, plain and simple. I can be professional, but…the level of awkwardness, I'm not going there."

"Oh, you can see Linda Jackson in all her glory, but not me. I'm in better shape, bud. You won't be digging through my wrinkles to find a way in."

"Oh, my God."

"Well. Am I right, or am I right?"

He unbuckled and got out of the car, leaning against it after he closed the door. "I shouldn't do yours, and let's leave it at that. Now can we drop it, and go in and get breakfast?"

I was already headed for the door. "I think I'm in the mood for a Grand Slam," I said looking at him over my shoulder.

"I'm not surprised," he grumbled. "Not surprised at all."

~

Twelve hours later we were back at the bar, seated in the back booth where we could see everyone who came in, for no other reason than we wanted a chance to meet Brenda Webb. Over breakfast we'd decided that we really were being mean; just because she looked the part, that didn't mean she really was the skank I'd proclaimed her to be. Chip wasn't going to make an effort to introduce us, so it seemed reasonable that we take it upon ourselves to spring ourselves on her when it was least expected.

We almost gave up; we had no way of knowing if she ever hung around when Chip wasn't there or not, and the crowd was growing faster than we expected. I was tired and sure that Doug that had better things to do, and was about to tell him we should just bag the whole idea when he spotted her pushing her way to an empty stool at the bar.

My initial impulse about her didn't change on a second look. I couldn't even explain it coherently; it was more than the way she dressed and the way she spiked her hair up; it was the air around her, the vibe that was rolling in waves from her. We watched as she ordered a drink, and Doug mumbled, "Didn't Chip say she was only nineteen?"

"He did." I slid to the end of the booth bench and pushed myself up. "We want to get to know her, right? I think I'll invite her to come sit with us a while."

"Don't get pushy," he said.

"Me? Pushy?"

I had to wedge myself past a tall brute of a man to get to the bar, and had to brace myself against it to keep from being pushed uncomfortably into it. As soon as Teddy realized I was there he came over, and I nodded toward Brenda and said, "You know she's not legal."

Brenda poked at my arm with a sharp finger. "What the fuck? Who the hell are you and why would you give a damn?"

"She's drinking iced tea," Teddy said, and then to Brenda, "Be nice to her. She can hurt you."

"So?"

"What could you possibly want, sitting in a bar when you can't even get so much as a beer?" I asked.

"I'm waiting for someone," she snapped.

He hadn't told her he was leaving, I realized, feeling a bit sorry for her. I thought he'd gotten past that, and that he'd learned that leaving a note or making a phone call extended to women other than me.

"Chip's not coming tonight," I said, and hoped it sounded nicer than I had let on so far.

"You know Chip?" She turned on her seat, now a little interested in what I might have to say.

I pointed over to the booth where Doug was waiting. "Why don't you join us? It's a lot more comfortable over there."

Irritation flitted across her face, and then, "Nothing personal, but why would I?"

"I'm Chip's stepmother," I explained. "Come on, we don't bite."

From the look on her face I was sure that Chip had told her as little about us as we'd heard about her. After a few minutes we determined that she knew Chip's mother had died, but she had no idea he had any other family left. She knew Doug's name, but only in an abstract, he's-Chip's-friend way.

I should have been hurt, but I wasn't. Here was the girl he was saying he was going to spend the rest of his life with, and he hadn't told her much, either. He was good at dividing his life, so it didn't surprise me. Eventually he would have casually mentioned to her that he was still somewhat close to his father, friends with his wife, and that Doug wasn't just a friend, but his best friend.

I counted on Chip just being an ass, and that he wouldn't have run off and married her without telling anyone.

"He does things in his own time," Doug told her. "If he didn't tell you about us, it's not personal. He's just…"

"A dick sometimes," she finished for him. "I know that. He was an even bigger dick in high school but not so much now. But he's still a fucking dick sometimes."

I couldn't help but laugh.

"It would have been nice if he'd told me about you, though," she added. "I mean, family is a fucking big deal. You know, if you speak to them and shit."

"We're close enough," I assured her.

"I can't get too fucking mad, you know, because I haven't let him meet my family, either. Not that he'd want to. They're fucking freaks. I don't speak to them a lot. Maybe a couple times a year."

And the apple doesn't fall from the tree.

I mentally slapped myself for thinking that the second it popped into my brain; she was different, surely, and my opinion hadn't changed yet, but it was still unkind, and other than the barrage of f-bombs, she hadn't been anything but nice about being dragged over to sit and talk to complete strangers.

"Couple times a year?" Doug seized on that. "You're only nineteen?"

"Yeah, well, I kinda dropped out when I was like fifteen and my dad, he was like, get the fuck out, so I got the fuck out."

"When you were fifteen?" The picture of Chip at fifteen, standing in a hotel room soaking wet and shivering because he was cold, while he tried desperately to keep me from walking out on his father, popped into my head. He'd had crap heaped upon him, but none of the people doing that would have even considered pushing him out the front door then. He kept running from them, but they always managed to bring him back.

Skank was beginning to fade from my brain. She was abandoned and wounded, and she was what she was because no one had treasured her enough to protect her.

"I got it figured out pretty quick," she said. "You know, sleeping on friends' floors and shit until I could get something regular."

"How the hell do you get something regular when you're fifteen?" Doug asked.

She lifted her shoulders in a light shrug. "You do what you gotta do."

"I'm not sure I want to know what you have to do," I muttered.

"Or who," Doug offered.

That made her laugh, and she sounded like any other teenage girl; for half a second, I thought I could see what appealed to Chip. She was rough around the edges, sure, but her laugh was wonderful, and it made me think more of her might be.

Since she seemed to have relaxed a little, I decided to push a little bit. "So what is it you're doing now? What kind of regular is getting you through day to day?"

Another shrug. "I'm in between gigs right now."

Relying on Chip, I thought, but before I could ask she added, almost in a panic, "But don't tell Chip that. He doesn't know I'm not doing anything right now."

"He won't be ticked off," Doug said.

"Yeah, but it's not his problem, you know? I wanna find something solid so he doesn't think I'm, like, leeching."

"You're marrying him; I don't think he'd see it as leeching."

"Yeah, but I got enough shit behind me and I oughta, you know, do something."

"Fair enough," I said.

"Can I ask you something?" Doug reached across the table for her wrist, gently pulling her hand across the table so that he could see her arm. "Does he know about this?"

She tried to pull her arm back, but he didn't let go. "Fuck off."

"Not trying to judge. And none of the marks look fresh. But does he know?"

This time she pulled hard. "He fucking knows. He says it's my own business."

I expected her to jump up and bolt; I would have in her position, but she sat back, defiantly crossing her arms across her chest.

"He can afford to support a wife, but he can't afford to support a drug habit," Doug said evenly. "We're just trying to look out for him, Brenda. And if you marry him, you'll have to get used to it, because we'll probably look after you, too."

"We're kind of nosey," I added.

"No fucking shit," she muttered. "What do you mean 'if' I marry him?"

"Figure of speech," Doug said. "Though I have to wonder why you're marrying him. Guy doesn't even tell his family he's got a girlfriend and then they stumble onto that info by accident? I'd be pissed."

"He probably has reasons."

"And you're okay with that?"

She had Chip's shrugging habit, and it was beginning to make me want to start shaking her.

"Why are you marrying him?" I asked, wanting to cut through the bullshit. "And don't shrug again for God's sake."

She started to, but stopped herself. "He's a good fuck, you know? Really good. And he gets me. Doesn't expect me to change."

"You're marrying him because he's a good lay?" Doug sputtered.

"No, he's *really* good. And we get along."

"And what about you?" I asked. "Do you expect him to change?"

"Why would he? I mean, once we have kids, fuck yeah I expect him to change a little. Like, it would have been nice if he'd told me he wasn't working tonight, but he'll probably show up later. I can deal."

"He's not showing up tonight," I said. "He's out of town with his dad. They'll be gone for a few days."

"Okay. Are we done here? Because this is like the fucking Swiss Inquisition and I don't speak Spanish."

"Just wanted to meet you," I said as she got up. "I know Chip's dad wants to, as well."

"Spiffy. We'll do cocktails or whatever the fuck normal people do." She started to step away but then turned back. "Thanks, you know. I mean, for wanting to meet me. You're pretty cool even if you are nosey as shit."

Doug waited until she had elbowed her way toward the door before he let the derisive snort out. "I didn't know they spoke Spanish in Switzerland."

"Oh, be nice. I think she was trying hard."

"Fucking hard."

"Stop."

"Don't think you can save her," he warned. "I can see it in your head now. You can't save her, and Chip can't save her. Just stay out of their way, because he's building a house of cards and that girl is the breeze that will blow it all the hell."

"If I try to save anyone, it'll be Chip. I think she might be nice enough, but she's a—"

"Thirty car pileup on the Interstate," he said, saving me from saying anything worse. "And you can't save Chip, either. Let him make his mistakes, and focus on your own life."

"And what's that supposed to mean?"

He took his time in answering, weighing, I think, whether he should tell me what was on his mind, or tell me what I wanted to hear.

I wasn't sure when it happened, but Doug was no longer just Chip's best friend, he was mine, and I think he knew it. And he saw more in my life than I did sometimes, and was learning to not pull punches about it.

"Your all-nighter," he finally said. "Was that about trying to stop shutting Ron out?"

"He's my husband, Doug."

"No kidding. Your husband, with whom intimacy has been sorely lacking, and about which you've said lately wasn't bothering you."

"So I had an itch to scratch."

"Yeah. I don't think so."

"You're a horrible girlfriend. You're supposed to just agree with me when I bitch about my marriage, and be thrilled for me when I grind his ass into the mattress."

"If you meant it, I am thrilled for you."

"Doug. I stayed up all damned night talking to him."

"About anything important?"

"It's all important," I said. "You know I love him, right?"

He nodded. "I also know you have too many moments when you think marrying him was a mistake. And I admire the fact that you didn't walk away when you had that epiphany and have really tried to make it work."

"But?" I pressed.

"But you have to mean it. It's not his fault he has the workload he does right now and you knew going in he would never choose anything else over it. You stayed with him knowing it. So mean it if you're going to keep him up all night with pillow talk and whatever else you were doing to him."

"He's more than willing to scratch when I itch, you know."

"That doesn't mean the man wants to be used or that it's fair to pull him close and make him think you're in tune with him, and then push him away. I like Ron. Just play fair."

I leaned in close to Doug, close enough that if he'd been a little bit drunk he could have kissed me. "I love him. I don't always like him, but I love him, and if I have an itch, I'd be an idiot to not ask him to scratch it. And it goes both ways. We don't have to always hear the same tune in order to dance with each other."

"Still."

"Don't think we haven't talked about it. He's noticed I'm not always completely into it. He knows there's something not quite right. But we talk."

"Good," he whispered, looking a little uncomfortable with how close I'd gotten.

Before he started to squirm, I pulled back and started to get up. "All right, I really do want to get home. There's a slim chance he'll call tonight, and even if he doesn't, I'm dead tired and just want to go to bed."

I also didn't want to let him dig any deeper.

There was a deeper itch developing, and if I stayed and had anything to drink, I was afraid I'm be looking for someone else to scratch it.

What bothered me was that he knew it.

~

The bar had regulars; I sat in my usual spot in the back booth where I could watch people coming and going, and after three nights running I realized I was seeing the same faces every night. Some drank alone, but most met up with friends, cramming into booths and milling around barstools; when all the available seating was taken the hostess was guiding the customers spilling out onto the floor into the dining area to the booths near the dance floor.

There was no live music that night, but the ceiling-mounted speakers pulsated with throbbing rock, and people were dancing, inebriated grinding that was marginally better than the spastic movements of the typical white-guy-overbite dancers that were usually there.

I hadn't seen Brenda since Doug and I had cornered her; she was either avoiding the place because she was afraid we'd be there, or she didn't see a point as long as Chip was gone. I was prepared to be on my best behavior and intended to resist every impulse I had to keep grilling her, but I wasn't sure how long I could keep it up and decided it was better that she wasn't there.

Doug, on the other hand, showed up every night. We sat in the booth and had dinner together while we made fun of the drunken hookups stumbling out the door, and we avoided talking about Ron or about Doug's lack of a love life, thought I never restrained myself from pointing out single women with whom he surely had a chance.

Ron had never called—I hadn't honestly expected him to—but I was grateful Doug never mentioned it. The night he and Chip left I lay in bed, even as tired as I was, and knew I was half hoping the phone would ring. I could still smell Ron on the sheets and on his pillow, and wanted only to hear his voice for a minute, long enough to say hello, long enough to tell him to come home safe.

By morning, I was over it. If he had time to call, he wouldn't think about doing it; if he had time, he would be using it to grab a shower and to rest. I knew that. I wanted that; he didn't need the distraction of trying to find a phone just to make me feel better.

On the fifth night I sat in the bar alone, waiting for Doug, watching rain-soaked people dart in from the parking lot. I could hear the rain pounding on the roof and was glad I'd gotten there ahead of it, and half hoped that Doug had sense to not be driving in it.

That was only half hope, though. The other half hoped he was insane and would be there soon.

There was breathing room in the bar because of the weather; I noted a few regulars, but most of the bar stools were empty and only a few of the booths were taken. The volume of the music was turned down so that people could hear each other, and the dance floor was empty. Waitresses were carting pots of coffee towards customers instead of beer mugs, and I wondered briefly how bad the tips would be because of it. I was as guilty as everyone else; all I wanted was something hot to drink and had refreshed the same cup of coffee half a dozen times.

I made a mental note to tip high; as often as I was there, it seemed the sensible thing to do.

I considered getting up and going home; neither Doug nor I had specifically said we'd be there, and the only thing holding me back was the roar against the roof and a crack of thunder that made me jump when the front door opened.

Might as well stay put until it lets up. Either Doug will be here or he won't, and there's no point in trying to drive through this.

I startled at the snap of fingers just two inches from my face and was about to cut loose with a string of expletives when he laughed.

Not who I expected.

"Where the hell were you?" Chip asked, amused. Water dripped from the tips of his hair and he was shivering. "I thought you'd seen me when I came in, but then I realized you were off in your own little world and figured I'd better come over here before you got lost there."

"Very funny." I knew he wasn't going to sit as wet as he was, so I got up and kissed him on the cheek. "You're soaked."

"Observant, you are. Come on, my office is quieter and warmer."

I followed him, but before he could close the office door I hesitated and said, "Wait. If you're here, then I should get home."

"Ah, maybe not." He reached into his jacket and pulled out a battered red rose and handed it to me. "Regrets from Ron. He's in

Chile, but expects to be home in a couple of days."

The petals on the rose were so wet they were more water than flower, the stem was soft and drooping, and it was so absurd looking that it made me laugh. "How far did you carry this?"

"From Rio. Ron picked it up before he took off and asked me to give it to you, and to say he was sorry he didn't call."

"I didn't really expect him to," I said almost absently as I sat on Chip's giant sofa. "But this was sweet."

He was pulling his jacket off, grimacing at the water that ran down his fingers. He dropped it onto the hearth and then kicked off his shoes. "Is it going to bother you if I change clothes?"

"You keep clean clothes here?"

"Of course I do." He pulled his t-shirt over his head and had his hand on his belt buckle. "Well? I'm not modest but I don't want to embarrass you."

"I won't look."

"Don't care if you do," he said as he dropped his pants.

I kept my eyes glued to the floor while he changed.

Mostly, anyway.

"Any idea what he's doing in Chile?" I asked as he shoved his legs into dry jeans. When I heard him zip up, I leaned back on the sofa and looked at him.

"No idea. I heard him say something to the SG about a coup but I think it had already happened. There was also talk about tracking money that had changed hands. But I really don't know."

"I'm surprised you overheard that much."

He sat next to me, our shoulders touching. "I don't think they intended for me to hear. Did you know Ron speaks fluent Russian?"

"I did know that."

"How the hell?"

"The same way you've learned Portuguese and Spanish. He also speaks German, French, Spanish and Pothead."

"Pothead," he snorted.

"I'm guessing. How do you know any Russian?"

"There was this girl," he started. "Anyway, he wanted me to be sure to tell you he was sorry, because he said he'd call and didn't. And there may have been something about Alex Barstow's tiny penis and giant ego, but I had kind of tuned him out by then."

"And you? Do I get to know what you were doing?"

"Delivery boy. I took a package from the SG to a fat, sweaty Swiss guy about a hundred miles out of Rio, and got to ride a really sweet bike while I was doing it. That thing was slick as shit and faster than anything I've ever been on. Tried to get them to let me bring it home, but no..."

"Good. But that was it? No one taking shots, no one died?"

"I delivered a package, and I got to ride a really sweet bike," he repeated.

"Fine."

"What'd you do to keep yourself occupied?"

"Ate here a lot, sat in the bar with Doug and made fun of your customers. Missed my husband."

"Hm. That last part doesn't sound like you."

"Fine. I tried to tell myself I was missing my husband. I'm just a little too used to not seeing him much. But I did have fun making fun of your customers, and we did have a nice little chat with your fiancée."

I expected him to heave an irritated sigh, but instead he seemed intrigued. "And?"

"And...other than having a mouth on her and an obvious drug problem, and more baggage than American Airlines, she seems nice enough. At least she was willing to have a conversation. And you should have told her you were going somewhere."

"Why? That just would have meant dodging questions."

"Chip. Don't think you can marry her and keep taking off without some kind of explanation. You'll have to figure something out. But this time we told her you'd gone somewhere with your dad. You can fudge the details on your own."

He leaned over and kissed me on the cheek. "Thanks. I'll call her after I've checked in on stuff here."

"Chip, she's got so many issues..."

"I know. I'm not trying to change her, Kris. I have issues, too, and I don't intend to change me, either."

Where to start?

Was it even my business?

I decided it was.

"Something for you to chew on," I said. "When I met your father he was very up front about his job and how committed he was to it, and where I would be in relation to it. I thought I was fine with that, and I had no intention of trying to change him."

"And you haven't," he said.

"I know. But I really want to. Almost from the beginning, I've wanted to throttle him into changing his priority order. I mean, when I realized just how serious he was..." I felt my breath hitch, and swallowed hard, trying to not give into it. "I fight that feeling all the time, but the worst part is that the longer it goes on, the less I care."

"You're not happy." It was both a question and a supposition. "And you don't think I can make Brenda happy."

"Not if you don't put her first," I said quietly.

"She's not really the domestic type, you know. I think we're both the type that want to come and go as we please. If you and Ron were both more alike—"

"If you marry her," I said evenly, "she'll want to be first in your life, no matter what. Take my word on this; no matter what she says now, she'll want that. She'll need that. If she doesn't get it..."

"She'll leave?" He turned on the sofa to see me better. "Are you thinking about leaving Ron? Because I never would have guessed it from the way you were hanging on to each other at the SG's plane."

"I'm not leaving him. I'm trying very hard to not leave him."

"But you're not happy."

"Not always. But I love him and I know he loves me, and he's always been honest with me. He's been the best husband he knows how to be. So I owe him that, to keep trying anyway."

Very gently he asked, "But for how long?"

He should be upset, I thought. This was his father I was talking about; he should be angry at the idea that I'd ever even remotely thought about leaving him. "Until I can't take being left behind all the time."

"Does he know?"

"He knows I'm not entirely thrilled with life right now."

"But does he know how close to being over it is?"

"I'm not leaving him," I said again. "Besides, how cold would that be? Walking out on my marriage when you're just walking into yours?"

"Don't put your life on hold because of me." He was looking right into my eyes, so serious. "I'm pretty sure you've been doing that for nearly five years."

"Chip."

"You wanted to leave then, before I even got to know you. We were in that hotel in San Francisco, and I practically begged you to not go. If I hadn't—"

I reached for his arm and tugged on it, trying to get him to sit back again. He went with it, sliding his arm behind me. "I have no regrets."

"But you would have walked away back then, wouldn't you?"

"I don't know. I would have left him for the weekend, at least. But for good, I don't know."

He leaned his head against mine. "I think you do know."

"Sometimes I think I do," I said. All the times I had defended my marriage to Doug, and the times I had admitted to him I stayed for Chip, those moments became gaping wounds seeping with guilt. "Other times…all I know is that I loved him then and I love him now, and I'm getting tired of saying it."

He lifted his head. "I don't think Ron gets tired of hearing it."

I couldn't explain it to him, not without also explaining the inordinate amount of time I was also spending with Doug.

"I'm not ready to give up," I told him, hoping he would let it go.

"All right. But if you ever do—I'll still be here."

"Good." I pushed myself up off the couch. "I'm going home. You go call your girlfriend, and don't forget you were off doing whatever with your dad, wherever it was you were doing it. Just let me know if I need to back you up on anything."

"Thanks. And hey, before you go."

I turned at the door.

"I know I can't count on Ron, but will you be there when I get married?"

He was fifteen again, standing there shivering. I walked back and bent over to kiss him. "You know I will. But dammit, think about what you're doing. Don't promise her anything you can't give her, and make sure she's all right with what you're offering. And I mean really all right."

He said he would, and in that moment I think he meant it.

Three days later everything went to hell.

~

Forty-eight more hours of rain; I stayed home as much as I could, checking into work by phone, and I worked hard at avoiding Doug and Chip. I watched TV, trying to figure out a string of popular soap operas that seemed more implausible than my own life, and I read the newspaper in between bouts of trying to slog my way through a novel Ron had been picking at for as long as I'd known him.

Doing nothing was making me more tired than if I'd had a full work schedule. If I'd flown from HQ to Washington I'd have had more energy than I did at the end of a day where all I did was sit and fidget, with occasional breaks to stare out at the rolling gray sky. I forced myself to stay up long enough to catch the beginning of the news—thinking that if something major were happening some-where in the world I'd have an idea of where Ron might really be—and then went to bed just to avoid the boredom.

Sometime around one in the morning I felt the bed heave with his weight and pushed myself through the thick fog of sleep. He was naked, cold, and his skin was still damp from the rain, and without being asked I pulled across the bed and wrapped myself around him, trying to help him warm up.

"I got your rose," I whispered, kissing him. "That was sweet."

"Just wanted you to know I was thinking about you. I wasn't thrilled about having to detour—"

"I knew it was a possibility."

He pulled me a little closer, stealing as much warmth as he could. "Day after tomorrow I'm back out again. But this should ease up soon. I don't think I'll be going out solo so much."

"Where to this time? Or can't you say?"

"I'll start out in South Korea. After that…"

"You're shivering." I threw the blankets back and ignored his sharp protest. "Come on. You need a hot shower. Instead of me warming you up, you're making me cold."

I was halfway out of the bed and he grabbed my hand, pulling me back, rolling until he was nearly on top of me. "We can warm each other up. Unless that was a hint, and I smell pretty bad."

"You smell," I said, touching a finger to his ear, tracing along the edge of it, still amused after all that time that he was bare millimeter away from having pointy ears, "like rain and Irish Spring soap, and it's not half bad."

His lips were on my neck, and his fingers traced slow lines over my shoulder and down my arm, then over to my ribs, teasing me. I lifted his hand and pulled his arm behind me, making him put his arms around me so that I could lie there against him, skin on skin, connected from our lips to our toes.

He twitched against me, hard already, his hands tangled in my hair while he kissed me softly and deeply, both of us so lost in the moment that we didn't hear the creak of the front door as it opened, didn't hear the lock click, and didn't realize for nearly an hour that a light had flicked on in the living room.

We noticed it at the same time. Now warmed, sweat slicked and half hanging off the bed, at the same time I asked him if he'd left a light on he quietly said he hadn't turned on any lights, and was carefully climbing out of the bed as he reached for the jeans he'd left on the floor. He whispered for me to stay there, but I didn't think an idiot was robbing us. I grabbed shorts and a sweatshirt and followed him out into the living room, where Chip was sitting on the sofa, staring into the fireplace.

As soon as Ron stepped out of the room, the tension coiled around him visibly relaxed, and he breathed out his son's name in a loud sigh.

Chip didn't look up.

He was in the middle of the sofa, hunched forward with his elbows on his knees and his chin resting on top of hands that were clenched together. His clothes were damp, hair messed up and wild, beginning to dry, and he just sat there, staring; Ron sat on the hearth in front of him, and he still didn't look up or even register that we were there.

It wasn't until I sat beside him, so close that our legs were touching and I could slide my hand across his back, that he blinked.

What radiated off him was pain and confusion; my first thought was that something had happened to his brother, because to shut him down like this, it would have to be big. But his eyes were clear, not red-rimmed with tears. If it had been his brother, he would have been crying.

Neither of us said anything to him, we waited until he was ready, a tense string of time that ticked mercilessly on the clock, the only noise in the room.

Finally, he sucked in a deep breath, and whispered, "She's dead."

Ron's eyebrows knotted together as he asked, "Who?" while at the same time I asked, "Brenda?"

Chip leaned back, managing a slight nod.

"She's only nineteen," I breathed out.

"Yeah, well."

"How?" Ron asked. "Nineteen year old girls don't just die."

Don't, I was thinking, but he wasn't looking at me and didn't see the glare.

"Overdose," Chip managed to get out. "I left her in my apartment and went to the restaurant for a couple of hours. When I got back…"

Ron rose from the hearth and headed for the bedroom without another word. Chip didn't seem to notice, but I was bordering on fury and if not for the fact that Chip was trying to burrow himself into the sofa cushions, I would have followed Ron with a barrage of expletives.

Your son needs you; what the hell are you doing?

Between the ticking of the clock Chip's breath moved audibly in and out; he was forcing himself to breathe normally, fighting to keep from hyperventilating.

In tears, I could deal with him; in a panic, I doubted it.

"What happened?" I asked Chip as gently as I could.

Before he could answer, Ron came out of the bedroom, dressed, his keys in one hand and shoes in the other. "Where is she?" he asked sharply.

"Ron—"

"Chip," he said firmly, shoving his feet into the shoes. "Where? Which hospital?"

"North Bay," he finally replied.

"And the police?"

"They were there. Took a statement. Said someone would find her parents."

"All right." He tied his shoes and then looked at me, and I could see the fatigue pulling at him. "Keep him here. I don't care if you have to sit on him, but keep him here. Call Doug if you need to."

"Where are you going?"

He was at the door, yanking it open. "To cover his ass."

It banged closed behind him, and Chip barely blinked. I had no idea what I could do for him; this was a world away from the night when Nicky Lockhart had died. Then he curled into a tight ball and let loose tears of grief, but now he sat eerily still, clear eyed and staring straight ahead.

I wasn't sure he would even hear me if I said something to him.

I had to try. I had to pull him out of the hole he was crawling into, for myself as much as him. With a gentle squeeze to his neck I asked again, "What happened?"

The seconds that ticked away felt like they were pinging off my skin. He opened his mouth to speak, stopped, but then finally he said, "I'm not sure. We were talking about when to get married and where. We never came to an agreement, but I had to get to the restaurant and said I'd be back in three or four hours…"

"She was there when you went home?"

"On the floor," he whispered.

"Was she—?"

"She was already gone. I called an ambulance, but she was already gone. The needle…" He swallowed hard. "Still in her arm."

"God."

"I knew she had a drug problem, Kris, that wasn't a surprise. But how much did she take to die that fast? It was still in her arm."

From the sheer number of scars on her arm, I would have thought she knew well what she was doing.

"I didn't know where to go," he said after a measure of silence.

"I didn't want to go back to my apartment. The restaurant seemed wrong. I just wanted to go…home."

"I'm glad you did," I said gently.

"I didn't want to wake you up. And then—"

"Ah, sorry about that."

He managed a wan smile. "Would've been funny any other time."

"And you would have been out here making obnoxious noises."

"If I'd known Ron was home I would have gone to Doug's."

"Chip." I forced him to look at me. "You came to the right place. If we'd known you were out here…we wouldn't have left you sitting out here alone."

"Awkward. Oh! Oh! Oh! Oh…Hi, Chip!"

"Stop," I said. "Don't try to act like everything is normal right now. You get to be a downer and I get to fuss over you."

"You're going to try to feed me, aren't you?"

"Sooner or later. I don't really know what to do for you right now, to be honest. I didn't know Brenda well enough—"

"My fault," he muttered.

"Please don't."

"Why not?" He pulled back and scooted down the sofa, leaning against the arm and putting distance between us. "I didn't have a good reason to hide her from you. And I know that I did, I intentionally did not want any of you to meet her until it was too late to stop me from doing anything stupid."

He'd decided early on she was the one he would make an effort with. Yet he also knew it wasn't his brightest impulse and that we'd each have something to say about it. Ron would grunt his disapproval and I would try to make him wake up to the mess he was making out of his life. But he liked her; he liked her edge and her sense of not giving a damn what anyone thought about her. He liked that she didn't ask questions about where he was or who he was with, even when she had to know he was with another woman. He liked the way she was both completely independent and very much in need of his help.

He liked her.

As I listened to him, I guided him into the kitchen, as determined as he knew I'd be to get some food in him; he talked while I made pancakes, one of the few things I could be certain I wouldn't burn and he could choke down. I listened while he pushed the food around on his plate, bits and pieces of barely knowing her in high school but remembering how timid she'd been then, and how intrigued he'd been in how much she had changed by the time she found her way into the Charybdis' bar.

I listened, and heard more than what he was saying.

He never said that he loved her.

Out of everything, he never said that he loved her.

An hour after he'd snuck into the apartment, I gave him the break he desperately wanted; he managed to eat one pancake, which I suspected was the first food he'd had since lunch, so I kissed him on the forehead and told him to go to bed. He was starting to speak in monotone and looked trapped there in the kitchen with me, and I didn't have anything I could say to him that was going to help at all.

The only thing I could do was to make sure he had something dry to change into, and then wait quietly for Ron to come home.

The only thing that was going to save him from my wrath was the hope that Chip was drained enough to sleep; he'd walked out on his son at the time he was needed the most, and I wanted to hang him from the ceiling by his toes.

The first thing out of his mouth when he came home half an hour after Chip had gone to bed was, "Is he still here?" and before I could follow that with every pissed off thing I'd been thinking he said, "I'm sorry, but it couldn't wait. I had to make sure all the bases were covered to keep him from being arrested, and that the news wasn't slow enough that she would wind up on the front page of the local newspapers."

The wind sucked right out of my storm.

"I'm sorry she's dead, but I wasn't risking that he'd be blamed for it. And I didn't think it would be any good for him to see it played out in the news."

Part of me wondered if he'd manufactured that excuse for my benefit, but I could see it right there: it had to stay out of the news. Chip had to stay out of the news. The only publicity Ron wanted him to have was for the restaurant; his personal life had to be off limits, lest anyone try to dig deeper.

"You tried to make him eat, didn't you?" He sniffed at the air, and with a sly grin said, "Pancakes."

"There's still batter left, if you want some. I could only get him to eat one."

"In a minute." He held his arms out, beckoning me to step into them. "Please tell me he's all right."

"In shock, I think. We might want to try to keep him here for a while."

"I sent a team to clean up his apartment. There won't be a trace of anything."

I leaned back to look up at him. "Trace of what? It's not like someone shot her."

"Bodily fluids," he said simply. "I'm sure it wouldn't be pleasant for him to go back to. I thought it would help—"

"You thought right," I said. I lifted up on my toes and kissed him, then took his hand and led him into the kitchen. "I hope you're hungry."

He looked at the pitcher filled with pancake batter, and sighed. "You made enough for ten people."

"I made enough for Chip with an appetite," I said. "Just make me happy and eat two or three. I don't know what else I can do tonight other than shove food at you guys."

While he ate, I filled him in on the things Chip had told me, but I kept to myself the idea that in all of it, I never heard Chip profess any love for his fiancée. Even if he'd come straight out and said it, I didn't think he'd want me to repeat it.

When he finished, he put his dishes in the sink and grabbed my hand to keep me from turning around and washing them, and led me back into the bedroom. "We need to try to get some sleep," he said when I started to protest. "The dishes will be there in the morning."

"It is morning," I reminded him.

He pulled his clothes off and slid into bed next to me. "Morning, middle of the night, either way, we're going to be tired as hell when we get up in a few hours." He settled onto his back, reaching out to set his hand on my stomach. He wanted nothing more than contact, and I set my hand on his, keeping it there.

A few minutes later I whispered, "Hey, Horatio."

"Yeah, Marge?"

"Thanks for eating my pancakes."

He rolled over and placed a kiss near my ear. "Thanks for taking care of my son."

~

Brenda Webb's parents weren't interested in saying goodbye to their daughter; her funeral was small and sad in ways that had nothing to do with grief. It was held at her graveside a week after her death, and attended by only one person who cared about her and three who had barely known her. The minister muttered generic platitudes about a girl who was surely in God's hands, whose promise-soaked future had been snuffed out in a moment of all too human weakness; he asked us to pray with him, and asked us to keep praying for the wounded soul of Brenda Webber.

I reached out for Chip's hand to keep him from lunging at the minister as much as I did to reassure him we were still there.

He refused to leave until her casket had been lowered; Doug tried to pull him away and I begged him to not watch. Only Ron agreed with him; he clapped his son on the shoulder and told him we'd be waiting by the car, and to take as long as he needed.

We waited close to an hour for him, and as he made his way back to the car he intentionally wouldn't look at us; he watched his feet, stepped carefully over grave markers, and once in the car fell eerily quiet. I sat beside him and stole glances; he looked out the window and watched the world speed past, but he was dry eyed and resolutely, stubbornly silent.

Two days after Brenda died Ron left, leaving Chip and I to deal with the police and with Brenda's father; when it was clear that her family truly did not care and were more upset with having their lives intruded upon than they were that their daughter had died, Chip took control of the arrangements. He bought a cemetery plot and paid for a grave marker, and spent an hour with the paperwork, staring blankly, until he decided he could only place upon it her name and the dates of her birth and death.

When he wasn't dealing with the details of laying Brenda to

rest he sat on the sofa staring at the fireplace, or sat in his office staring at the wall. On Doug's advice I gave him long stretches of time to be alone, time to deal with his grief, but I didn't think it made a difference. He was shutting down, and nothing I did or said was helping.

The morning of her funeral Ron came home; it was the timing of coincidence rather than an overwhelming desire to be there for his son, though he was grateful he'd made it in time. He stood next to Chip through the short service, his hand on Chip's shoulder, offering whatever comfort Chip could take from that.

After the ride home from the funeral Chip climbed out of the back seat of Ron's car, thanked us for all being there, kissed me on the cheek, and asked Doug to take him back to his own apartment. I wanted to stop him; he needed someone around, someone to remind him that yes, he had to eat even if he didn't feel like it, and someone to shove him toward bed at night even if he just wanted to stay rooted in his spot staring at the fireplace.

Ron took my hand, a clear message to just let Chip go.

"Give him some space," Ron said as Doug drove off. "He has wounds he needs to lick, and he doesn't need an audience while he does it."

I gave him the rest of the day but tried to call him in the evening to see if he wanted me to bring food over, but he wasn't answering his phone; I called the restaurant, but he wasn't there either.

Two days later, with him not answering his phone or showing up at work, I went to his apartment. I rang the bell three times and was about to let myself in when he finally opened the door; he was unshaven and rumpled looking, wearing clothes that looked like he'd pulled them out of a laundry basket, and exhaustion rolled off him in waves.

"I'm not going away," I said, pushing my way past him. I expected the apartment to be in its usual state of entropy, but it was spotless. The bed was folded away, the general clutter that he usually kept piled up on the kitchen counters was gone, there were no piles of dirty laundry stacked in corners.

The balcony door was open, letting fresh air spill in.

If he was cleaning, he was feeling miserable.

"I'm all right," he said.

"You look like hell. But that's fine; I just wanted to see for myself. You're not answering your phone and not going to work."

"Ted said he'd be fine holding down the fort for a while."

"That's what you have him for." He wasn't going to be hospitable, so I planted myself on his sofa bed and tossed my purse onto the end table. "You have to start answering your phone, though. You didn't, so now you have to suffer through me being here and being nosey."

With an exaggerated sigh, he dropped onto the other end of the sofa. "You'd be just as nosey on the phone."

"But you can hang up on me on the phone. Now, you're stuck."

"I could get up and leave," he pointed out.

I had no doubt that if I said the wrong thing that he would get up and storm out, leaving me to either sit there and stew while I waited for him to return—which could take anywhere from an hour to a day—or lock up on my way out. He wasn't in the mood to banter; I wasn't sure he was even in the mood to talk, so I decided I'd pester him for five minutes, offer to grocery shop or whatever else he needed, and then leave him alone.

"So you don't worry, I'm not just sitting in here hiding," he said after a moment of awkward quiet. "I'm doing things."

"Cleaning, it seems."

"Semi-annual event. No, I meant I'm getting out. I went over to Doug's to watch a ball game last night."

During which neither of them likely said a word other than to ask or answer the important questions: want another beer? Onions on the pizza? Pretzels or Cheetos?

That's probably what Chip needed, but still—I wanted to make sure he was actually all right.

"Who won?" I asked.

He answered with a shrug.

"That's fine, at least you got out. Any chance I can get you to come over for dinner tonight?"

He answered with a sideways glance that dripped with *Your cooking? Are you freaking serious?*

"I'll order in."

"We could do that here."

I wanted him to get out and he knew it; I was ready to argue the point—it might be nice if he saw his father and I expected Ron to actually be home—but the phone rang. He looked at it but didn't move, and on the second ring I said, "If you don't answer that, I will."

He rolled his eyes but got up and answered the phone. He barely did more than grunt, and just before he hung up he sighed hard and his shoulders slumped forward, clearly irritated.

"That was Dan," he said. "His office, half an hour."

"Just you?"

"All of us. We have an assignment."

Muttering expletives under my breath, I closed his balcony door and locked it while he went into the bathroom, and I double checked his kitchen to make sure he wasn't leaving something turned on or plugged in, and then steered him towards my car once we were out the door.

He was silent during the twenty-minute ride to headquarters and barely acknowledged Dan and Doug once we were in Dan's office. While we waited for Ron Chip pulled a folding metal chair out of the corner and opened it, setting it next to Dan's ancient file cabinet, and he sat next to it, leaning his head against the cold metal, eyes closed.

When Ron came in he handed a manila envelope to Dan. "Back to Chile," he said. "We have the SG's plane and the time out is estimated at seven to ten days."

"All of us?" Doug asked.

Dan and Ron both looked at him, both somewhat annoyed. "What else?" Dan asked.

Doug gestured to Chip with his thumb. "He's not ready to go anywhere."

I followed everyone's gaze to Chip, who hadn't moved and looked like he'd fallen asleep. "He's right," I said quietly. "We need to leave him behind."

Ron shook his head. "We'll need him."

Doug was on his feet hands planted on Dan's desk. "You either cross him off the orders, or I'll do it."

"Do you need to be reminded of the order of operations, Doug? Sit down and shut up."

"Not a chance. He's in no shape to be any use to us. Hell, he could get us killed. And do *you* need to be reminded that I have the authority to medically de-authorize anyone in this agency? I will if I have to."

Dan got to his feet and leaned across the desk, mirroring Doug's stance. "Don't push me on this. He goes. Period."

Let them piss on each other, I thought. I turned to Ron instead. "He can barely think straight, Ron. It's too soon."

"It's been over a week. He can grieve his ass off, but he can get his shit together long enough to get the job done."

"He can't even pull it together long enough to *shower*. He's not eating. I doubt he's sleeping. He's a walking hazard."

"And I promise you I'll go from here to the clinic and start the paperwork," Doug threatened. "He's not going."

Chip sighed hard, and without opening his eyes said, "I'm fine."

"Bullshit." I stepped over to him and grabbed his face by his chin, forcing him to open his eyes. "Who won the game last night, Chip?"

"Don't really care."

"When was the last time you ate anything?"

"Don't know. Don't really care."

"And sleep?"

"If you would all shut the fuck up, I could sleep now."

I let him go, and turned to face Dan and Ron. "He is *not* all right."

"He can sleep on the plane," Ron said.

"Get out," I snapped, pointing to Dan. And to Doug I said, "Take Chip to the clinic and do whatever you have to."

"This is my office," Dan protested, but when Doug grabbed Chip by the arm and pulled him out, he snatched the manila envelope off his desk and stomped out, following them.

I slammed the door behind him and spun on my heel hard; Ron was sitting against the desk, arms folded at his chest, and those green eyes were hard and angry.

"Your *son*," I hissed. "He is your *son*."

"And he has a job to do."

"Like this? You expect him to be able to function when his heart is shattered? He can barely think straight. How the hell do you expect him to be able to do any kind of job, especially one that requires him to concentrate?"

"I expect him to suck it up, Kris. I expect you to suck it up, too."

"We're headed into a country that just went through a coup, Ron. If he can't focus, he'll get himself killed."

He wouldn't budge. "Then I suggest he focuses."

"Get someone else."

"Why? He speaks the language, Kris. He has all the specific training we'll need. Language, driving and riding skills, he can fight, he can reason his way through his assigned tasks, and he can protect his team members. We need him, and we don't have the luxury of enough time to trust anyone else."

"That," I said, jumping on his line of thinking. "He can't reason his way through anything. He's so damned depressed that he might walk into something thinking that he wants to die."

He nodded, just barely, and I thought I had him.

"Don't you get it?" he finally said. "That's why Chip is as valuable as he is. He doesn't care if he lives or dies, he never has. It gives him the balls to do most of what he does. He takes needed risks where other people hesitate. It's why we need him."

"Oh, my God, Ron. He's—"

"My son," he finished for me. "You're my wife. But that has never stopped me from putting you in precarious positions before."

"Because I was mentally there."

"Right now, in this building, you are both members of this team, and we've been handed an assignment. I expect you both to follow orders, and I expect there to be no further questions or protests. That's it, Kris. This is not up for debate."

"Doug will board him out of the job before he'll let Chip go."

His jaw clenched and nostrils flared as he tried to get a grip on his anger. "Getting this job done is more important than babying Chip's broken heart. I trust him to be able to do his job, but Kris, don't make me think for one moment that I can't trust you to do yours."

He pushed off the desk and opened the door; Dan was on the other side, fist held up as if he'd intended to knock. And right behind him was Alex Barstow, hands stuffed into his pockets as he waited for Dan.

"Doug signed the paperwork," Dan told Ron. "We go without him."

"I believe we're going without Kris as well," Ron said evenly, almost formally, most definitely angrily.

"Don't walk out that door," I said to Ron.

He turned towards me. "And what would you have me do? I have an assignment."

With a quick glance at the SG, I said quietly, only for Ron, "Stand up for your son. Stand up for me."

"Kris."

"Don't you dare walk out that door, Ron."

Dan was walking down the hall, and Alex Barstow turned to go after him with one more look at us; Ron watched them go, and for just a moment I thought he was going to do the right thing; for that heartbeat of a moment, I thought he was going to stay.

Instead he turned, and without another word to me, walked out the door.

PART THREE

"That was it, I think." Ron leaned back on the bed, propped up on pillows. "It took you over a year after that to actually leave me, but when I left Dan's office and followed Alex, you were done. I'd picked the job over you one time too many. And I knew it; I knew as soon as I turned around that you'd never forgive me for it."

My heart had broken that day; that was as much as I was certain of. As clear as I'd been about his dedication to his job, on the day when he so obviously chose an assignment over both his wife and his son—the son who was spiraling into depression so deep that it would take him nearly a year to come out of it—our marriage fractured beyond anything I thought we could repair.

"I stopped feeling so guilty about all those stolen lunches with Doug."

"I knew about that," he admitted. "I was fairly sure there was nothing more than that going on, but…"

"It was still cheating," I whispered.

"No. You may have wanted to sleep with him, but you didn't. You were still sleeping with me, more or less."

"Less and less."

"It started to suck, to be honest. And the last time—"

I sat up. "Wait. You remember the last time?"

"Of course I do. After months of hit and miss and pretty horrible sex, we had one night of some serious passion."

"Passion," I snickered. "God, you have gotten formal."

"Fine. We fucked like horny little rabbits hell bent on repopulating the world. It was as good as sex had been at the very beginning.

The point is that I had a feeling you were saying goodbye, but you didn't really know how to leave."

I needed a push. Torn between staying or going, it would have taken only a small push in either direction. I didn't want anything from Doug other than sex, and that was a line he wasn't willing to cross. I kept thinking there was something I might want from Ron, something that would pull me back into our marriage, but I didn't know what it was until the day Chip married Terry.

Or I thought I knew what it was.

"You wanted the choice to have a child," Ron said when the words, 'a baby' rolled off my tongue. "You wanted me to choose family, and with Chip grown, the only way that would happen was if we created one of our own. For that, you would have stayed. Only I'd made the choice years before I even knew you. I regretted that, by the way."

"Seriously?"

He nodded. "I didn't realize how much until it was too late, but when it occurred to me that the decision I'd made when I was single meant you would never have the choice to be a mother as long as we were married…yes, I regretted it. I watched Chip drive off with Terry and it hit me. You didn't have a choice, and I would have loved to have had a child with you."

"You had a vasectomy."

The look of surprise on his face made me want to laugh. "I thought that was a given."

"And the job? If you hadn't been snipped and if I'd ever gotten pregnant…?"

His smile faded a little, and a wisp of sadness crossed his face. "Do you really want to know? You will someday, but now?"

"I need to know."

"In spite of what you thought, I made the choice between family and job when Chip got sucked into it. The day he sat in Alex's office with his hands cuffed and they worked him backwards and forwards, ignoring the truth of how old he really was and dangling a metric ton of money in front of him—I chose then. I wasn't going to stop until I figured out how to get you both out of it without any loose ends."

"Wait. If anything, you burrowed deeper into the job. And you insisted on Chip—"

"I wanted him to hate it, Kris. I wanted him to hate it so much that he would beg to be let out of his contract, and I had hoped that by the time he did I'd have something on Alex Barstow to make it happen. If I could do that, I could get you out, too."

"All I needed to do was quit, Ron."

"Theoretically." He reached up and touched a finger to my face, letting it slide softly across my cheek. "How long did it take Chip to quit completely, even after they let him go? There were always strings attached. I wanted your strings to be severed, and for you to be free from it, because I knew that somehow the agency wasn't everything it was supposed to be."

"Why didn't you tell me?"

"Because I didn't know how long it would take, and what you didn't know, you wouldn't be able to tell anyone else. All those solo assignments, most of them were smoke and mirrors that Dan helped me create. I was tracking down information on Alex with the hope that I'd be able to use it to cut everyone loose."

"Why Alex? I mean, we all know what he really was, but then we had no clue."

"I had my first clue on our first assignment together. The Russian pilot. He was defecting to get to family, and in the hangar when he was trying to explain how hard that plane would be for you to fly, he mentioned 'Uncle Alex.' Nowhere in the information that we had on him was there a mention of an Uncle Alex. He tried to cover it with sputtering 'Uncle Sam' after, but I didn't buy it. And getting him out was too damned easy. It sent my suspicions up, and they stayed up."

"You knew he was a mole."

"I had a feeling he was not who he said he was. And to be honest, I didn't care, but I had a feeling it was something I'd be able to use. Later, after Chip killed Cooper in London—what Donnigan and I stumbled onto was information Justin Ray had been collecting on Barstow. He was on the same trail I was; he suspected Alex was passing information to his Soviet counterparts. If Brenda Webb hadn't died and Chip hadn't fallen into such a deep depression, I

might have been able to get the final proof I needed, but after that…
when I walked out on you in Dan's office, when I was willing to so
visibly put my job ahead of my wife, Alex knew something was off.
It didn't take him long to figure out how to use it all against me."

I saw it all laid out then, the lack of work for nearly a year
while Chip recovered, our team then being dissolved, my contract
being terminated, and Chip being let go while getting to keep the
restaurant.

Dan Martin helped him.

Dan Martin was killed in his office.

Barstow knew then.

"You traded his secret to get us out," I realized, letting it spill
out as the thought formed. "I knew you'd taken the Maverick position to get Chip out, but…"

"It was part of the package. I kept my mouth shut, I took the
job, and in exchange they would close the books on you. Chip…I
couldn't get a completely clean break for him, but getting him the
restaurant and a strong hope that he'd never be put in the same position again? If getting you both a chance at normal happy lives was
possible, I was taking it. Alex knew I'd probably last two years at
best. And I suspect he knew that the one name on that hit list that
would trip me up was the one I would read as being yours."

Near tears, I managed to ask him, "He knew you still loved me
that much?"

"A better man would have made sure *you* knew how loved
you were. Still, it worked out. You got out and had a good life with
Doug, and Chip had the life I always wanted for him. I never did
tell you that setting him up with Terry was the right thing, after all."

"I could have had that life with you," I murmured. "Dammit,
Ron, I married you first, and if I had known…"

He reached out, sliding across the bed to put his arms around
me. "It wouldn't have been as good of a life, Kris. I never would
have gotten away from the agency. I couldn't have given you the
baby you wanted and adoption would have been off the table. I think
I knew, even when I was trying to juggle everything, that I'd lose
you in the end."

"But that's so sad. And it wasn't fair to me, to take my choices
away."

"I had to. If I had told you what I was doing and why, you would have chosen me. You would have honored our vows...and you would have been miserable. I wouldn't have wanted that for either of us. And you would have become my widow, because one way or the other my time was up."

"Still..."

"Spider," he said. "Steven Mark Stone. Don't tell me he's not worth everything, even losing me."

"Oh my God, don't go there."

I felt his lips at my temple, a warm, familiar kiss. "I'm sorry, but it is what it is. And if someone had been able to paint a vivid picture for me when I was still alive, and it showed me that by opting out you would have a happy marriage and an amazingly wonderful son, I wouldn't have hesitated. I got what I wished for, Kris, and it makes me truly, deeply happy."

~

"Do you know that Chip will come here first?" I asked Ron. We were back outside, sitting on the beach, and I was marveling at how warm it felt to sit there in the sun, yet at how cool the sand was between my toes; I wondered, too, if Ron felt the same things I did. He loved heat; the ideal for him would be for the sand to warm his feet, but I had no idea how much of what surrounded us was under his control.

"It's a feeling," he answered. "You know that gut feeling you get when something is a little off or when you know something you would otherwise question is right? This is that, amplified. I feel that when either Terry or Chip passes on, this is where they'll come."

"And you'll be waiting."

"In a sense. I want to see Chip, and I know that I'll be able to find him here without any real effort."

"And if he pops up somewhere else?"

"I'll know. But here is where he'll want to meet me."

"You feel that."

"I do."

"And how hard will it be if he pops up somewhere else and doesn't think to want to see you for a very long time?"

He tilted his head just a little, amused. "Linear thinking, Kris."

I couldn't get past it; an hour was still an hour to me, even if I had only been there for a moment. Ron might have grasped that the hours spent with me were only sheer heartbeats in my mortal existence, but I wasn't there yet. I sensed that I wouldn't be, not until my heart really did stop beating.

I wondered if I would wind up like poor Rusty, feeling the stretch of every minute while he waited for his beloved master.

And then I wondered if that ever happened.

"Does anyone ever get here and get stuck in the whole time thing? Does anyone ever not get to where you are, understanding how time doesn't work?"

"Most people don't get it at first," he said. "But again, it's not painful, Kris. You won't be weighed down by all the things that make living through time difficult."

"Difficult."

"The loneliness. Grief over your lost life. Embarrassment over the things you've said or done. When you die, you might feel time ticking away, but it won't be a burden. I promise you that."

"If none of this is linear, then you know when I'll die, don't you? When Chip will die. Doug, Terry, our kids...? Hell, have we already died and been here?"

"You're going to sprain a brain cell or two," he warned lightly. "Stop thinking so hard."

"Oh, like you wouldn't analyze this up one wall and down another if you were in my position."

"Angel, if our positions were reversed, I would be driving you bat shit crazy with all my questions. I know that."

"I wish you had lived," I said suddenly.

"I did live, Kris. The fact that I'm here now with you—"

"No, I mean I wish you hadn't died, Ron. I wish you'd gotten the long and happy life you deserved."

"I got what I deserved," he mused. "Some people would think that because of what I'd done, I didn't deserve what time I had."

"But you were a good man."

"I shuffled on the edge of being a good man. I was one who did terrible things on the whims of terrible people."

"Chip killed him, you know. He broke Barstow's neck."

"I know. Alex doesn't hold that against him, either."

Of course he didn't. Alex Barstow was probably lounging on some tropical beach enjoying the hell he had apparently escaped.

"He was surprised," Ron added. "He certainly didn't expect to die when he did or how he did. He was actually quite amused to be holding onto Chip in one moment and sitting in a Russian bar the next. He had a certain sense of pride, that Chip had learned well, and that his loyalties were fundamentally sound."

"I suspect he wasn't half as surprised as the rest of us were when we found out that he'd been a damned mole all that time."

"He served his country well," Ron said, almost snorting with amusement.

"You know, I think Chip would actually be relieved to hear that Barstow isn't tap dancing in some inner circle of hell. He felt bad about the whole thing, for God's sake."

"Deep down, Chip is the better man," Ron said.

"And going after Barstow? That damn near blew his marriage apart."

"The job can do that. It could have destroyed yours, if you had let it," Ron pointed out.

"Oh hell, that was a weak moment for them, Ron. It hurt for a little bit, but in the end..."

"You felt like you deserved it."

"I did! Ron, when you and I were married—"

"You don't have to confess anything, Kris. It doesn't matter."

"But it does to *me*."

"You didn't sleep with Doug while we were still living together."

"But I would have, Ron. The fact that I didn't—that was all on Doug. You were a good man, a good husband, and I didn't work hard enough at honoring that."

"To what end? If we want to be bluntly honest about our marriage? We weren't open enough with our expectations, and you were so much younger than I... I think I knew then that if Doug hadn't been so"—he fumbled for the right words—"green, you probably would have taken note of him a lot sooner than you did."

"Green. You mean virginal, don't you?"

He laughed right along with me.

"Doug was a little immature when he joined the team. That's why he and Chip became such fast friends. They were about at the same level back then. Chip afforded him the means to get all the stupid teenage things he'd never had a chance to do out of the way, and when he finally grew up…"

"There I was," I sighed.

"There you were. And there you were supposed to be."

"That hardly seems fair to you."

"I had some wonderful years loving you, Kris. I wouldn't change that."

"But the way you describe everything makes it sound like you were a placeholder, Ron, and after Pat…that hardly seems fair."

"My relationship with Pat was what it was. I wouldn't change that, either."

"But Chip—"

"Blood doesn't run thicker than water. It just runs, heartbeat after heartbeat. I know that Chip wasn't my biological son, but from the moment I knew about him until the moment I died, I believed that he was, and that was a gift."

"And here I thought you considered him to be a pain in your ass."

"He was," Ron chuckled. "He was a huge pain when he was a teenager. But he loved me, I loved him, and his existence gave me a sense of purpose. Without that, I suspect I would have jumped into the darker agency pools years earlier than I did, and without the reasons that I had. I wouldn't have been able to swim, Kris. I would have drowned before I was thirty five years old."

"He was something to live for."

"He was a reason to be."

"Chip's youngest son, Kevin…sometimes he looks at his son and says that Michael is his reason for doing. And he says it with such purpose, like nothing else in life matters."

"Kevin," Ron said thoughtfully, "was born grounded."

"You know them, don't you? All the kids?"

"I know them. I love them. I treasure that Chip had the honor of being their father. For that matter, I feel the same way about your son, Kris. He's an amazing person. He could have taken his lack of hearing and turned it into a true handicap, but he didn't. And he owes his parents for growing up believing everything about him was perfectly normal, even when the rest of the world said otherwise."

I started to argue that Spider was normal, but then what Ron was saying penetrated my defenses.

"I feel guilty sometimes that he was our only child," I said quietly. "Doug wanted more, I know he did."

"Doug wanted you, period."

"Another son or a daughter would have made him happy."

"But no happier than he already was."

"Still."

"Trust me on this," he said, eyes twinkling with amusement. "I know things."

"You know that I have had a very good life."

"Your life has been filled with as much love as I could have wished for you."

"And if it ends now, I think I'll be all right with that."

"But."

"But, Doug. He would be broken."

"It would hurt him, yes. But it won't break him, Kris. He has Chip and Terry and that entire brood supporting him."

"He's always said he wanted to die first. And he meant it, Ron; it wasn't like one of those I-love-you-more games people play. I think he knows how much he can take, and me dying before him..."

"It will hurt," he said again. "But you don't have to die right now, Kris. Once you figure out why you're here with me, you can decide. Here or there."

I leaned into him, my head resting on his shoulder, and we stared out at the ocean, watching as waves lapped up just short of where our feet were.

~

I needed to move. I wanted to walk along the beach, where I could feel the breeze on my skin and taste the salty air. We walked towards Chip's beach house; it was oddly comforting knowing it was there, even in Ron's version of heaven.

Chip would be touched to know that Ron wanted to be that close.

Because it felt right, I reached for his hand as we traipsed through the sand. He let me wind my fingers through his almost possessively, as if I were warning anyone who happened to pass us that he was mine. It was ridiculous and I knew it, but I needed to feel that and was glad he was willing to indulge me.

"Chip and the agency," I prodded. "You wanted him out, I get that. But why did you stick him into so many dangerous situations? Right from the start you were laying his life on the line."

"I know. His first assignment, when I sent him up that building? I was hoping that it would scare the living shit out of him and make him rethink the whole concept of being this badass little operative. I knew he could get up and in, but I wanted him to be terrified. In-stead, he blew the damned building up like it was a matter of course. I hadn't counted on his cockiness to outweigh his common sense."

"He says he had a death wish."

"It was more that he had an absence of the fear of death. Hell, when he was fourteen he climbed into a drainage pipe on a rainy day just to explore the damn thing and got a quarter mile into it when it started to fill…he barely made it out. And when he was eighteen, right after Nicky Lockhart died? He took one of the agency's bikes down Rockville Road at over a hundred miles an hour. The only thing that stopped him was a random thought that if he wrecked, he might take someone else out with him. He was willing to take the risk, but not willing to inflict it on someone else. I know he wanted to live, but he wasn't afraid of dying."

"He hurt deeply when other people died," I reminded him. "When Nicky died…Ron, he cried so hard. He knew it was coming but it still sucker punched him."

"And yet it was Chip that made it easier for Nicky to let go. Everyone else bent over backwards to deny that he was going to die, and worked overtime to make him think he was going to be all right. But Chip didn't brush it off, and when Chip told him that his grandparents would be here waiting for him, and that he would get to play baseball and grow up, and that it was all right to be afraid… Someone needed to tell that little boy that being scared was fine and normal, and someone needed to tell him he would still be able to grow up."

I stopped and turned to face him. "Did he?"

"When Chip gets here, Nicky will be waiting for him as the little boy he knew. But once Chip is ready? He'll get to meet the man Nicky would have been."

"Oh my God." I clasped my hand to my mouth as the realization hit me. "Nicky. Chip named his firstborn Nicholas. We called him Nicky for years. I wonder if that was intentional."

Ron nodded.

"Why didn't I remember? I sat there and listened to him tell Nicky Lockhart that his name was tattooed on his heart forever. When his Nick was born, it never occurred to me."

"It only matters that Chip knew what he was doing, and that Terry wanted to honor that. And since the decision was private? There you go."

Chip would have assumed I'd remembered. I should have.

"Funny if you think about it," Ron said as we started walking again. "All the years I was sneaking around, trying to find a way to get him out or to make him beg out, and all you had to do was throw him together with your cousin and he wanted out of the job on his own."

"Well, I'd like to say I wish we'd introduced them sooner, but he was such a prick before then, and she was way too young."

"It happened at the right time."

"You know, there was a moment when we went with Chip to see Nicky in the hospital the first time. I saw you following him and had this thought, that he was the other half of your heartbeat. Even though I kept questioning the way you were raising him—I saw how you looked at him, and I couldn't help thinking that."

"But you were wrong," he said. "I married the other half of my heart."

"Only if your heart was prone to arrhythmia."

"You still can't grasp it. It's perfectly normal that you were who I was supposed to love, and it's perfectly normal that Doug was who you were supposed to love."

"No, I don't get it. I keep thinking that if we'd tried harder..."

"And then you feel guilty because if we had, then there would be no you and Doug, and certainly no Spider."

"I can't imagine—"

"Then don't."

"You're still an annoying ass, Ron. I'm glad that hasn't changed."

We'd walked all the way to the jetty, half-arguing, half-teasing, still musing out loud over Ron's assishness and my mouthy self. I'd hated the fighting when we were married, but I missed the not-so-serious bickering. When we weren't in heated disagreement over Chip, our arguments were rarely serious and almost always ended in laughter or sex, or both.

I couldn't get past the conflict of how much I missed him and wanted to be there with him, and how much I thought I would miss Doug and want to be home.

"No one ever said one to a customer when it comes to relationships," Ron said. "I loved women before you, it's just that I was never *in* love. After…"

"Who knows what would have happened if you'd had more time?"

I got it; he wouldn't have had much time no matter what. But it might have been enough time to find his soul mate, if he had one. Or even enough time to find someone who made him deliriously happy, someone who could soothe the hurt over the things that had gone wrong in his life.

"There's something I promised to show you but never did," Ron said as we approached the jetty. "If I have a regret, that's it. Not making the time for this that I said I would." He nodded in the general direction of the beach just past where we could see. "I'd really like you to see it for the first time with me."

"Over the jetty?" I asked.

"More or less."

We climbed over the jutting rocks, and as we neared the top the sunlight began to fade; when I stepped off the last rock onto the sand it was twilight, and the air around us had noticeably cooled.

The parking lot I had expected was gone; instead we were at Crissy Field, the beach stretched out before us, and just ahead there was a blanket spread out on the sand. Still holding my hand, Ron headed for it, and by the time we reached it, we were surrounded by night.

"Flat on your back," he said as he stretched out. When I hesitated, he grinned and added, "Trust me."

Laying there, looking up, the sky was perfect black with pinpoints of light scattered as far as I could see. I wondered what else was up there—if this was heaven then was this all for show, or was there more he couldn't or would show me?—and was going to ask, but the thought was stopped on the tip of my tongue when I heard soft humming.

It was an airy sound, so soft that at first I wasn't sure where it was coming from, but then the warm red glow began to form overhead, and with it streaks of blue and purple. The lights unfolded delicately, a sheer satin sheet being tossed open and set across a bed of inky black.

The hum grew louder and the lights pulsated, stretching across the sky, feeling so close that I could reach out and touch them, yet so far that I could barely comprehend how far they reached. It was a ballet of lights, the story written for only Ron and me, the sweetness of music that only we could hear; I found myself holding my breath and reaching for his hand, blinking past the tears that had started to spill from the corners of my eyes.

"Don't ever try to tell me there's not a God," I whispered.

"I should have taken you to Alaska the moment I knew this was something I wanted to share with you. Before you met Chip, before we started dealing with real life. If I have any regrets, this would be it, that I didn't make sure I would be the one to show you the northern lights. Who knows what this would have meant for us?"

"This is the first time," I assured him. "Now I know why you said you were afraid that you'd go back and never leave."

"I was tempted for a while. Just abandon the job and go hide for as long as possible, and hope that someday I would be able to go home."

"Why didn't you?"

"They would have found me no matter what. And I didn't know what that would mean for you and Chip...I couldn't be sure the agency would stay out of your lives, and I really worried they would invoke Chip's contract. So I kept working."

"And you wanted to live," I whispered.

"I wanted to live," he said softly. "Even when I couldn't bear the idea, I wanted to live. I just..." He turned his head and looked at me. "I would do it again, Kris. If I were back in the same place, seeing your name, I would do it again. Because not living? So much better than thinking the world was going to lose you."

"If it had been my name on that list, you realize the next RM would have come after me, and I'd had been dead either way."

"That was off my radar until I was already dead. All I knew then was that I had your name on a list, and I looked for every way out until I could only see the one way. I knew it was the coward's way out, but I didn't care. I couldn't exist in a world where your life had been snuffed out for no good reason."

"And now you know that Barstow put that name on your list to trip you up."

"I suspect it. We've never actually discussed it, and I'm not a mind reader."

"As long as you don't defend him over it."

"I'm not. But in the grand scheme of things, he never did anything worse than the things I did. We were both doing what we thought was right, even the things we knew were horrible."

"I wish you had run, Ron. Even if it only got you a few more years. You could have run to Alaska and seen this over and over. And now..."

"Now? If I want this kind of communion, I can have it. But trust me, this is so much sweeter with you here. This is peace."

Asking me to stay? He couldn't just come out and ask, but could he hint?

The temptation was strong.

He was only in my life for six years. Six years that defined who I was and who I would become, who would matter to me the most. Six years that left an indelible mark; for the next thirty I thought of him often, I tended his grave, and often felt pangs of bittersweet longing when I saw his son.

It didn't matter that Chip was not Ron's; even in my heart, he always would be.

I didn't leave him for Doug; I had wanted Doug even as I was on my way out the door; yet I hadn't loved Doug then. I left in anger and in disappointment, and none of it was his fault.

We laid there in silence for a long time, bathed in the glow of the northern lights, wrapped in the moment, and trapped by years of simply not having known the whole truth. I reached for his hand again, intentionally soaking in his touch, marveling at how perfectly my hand fit with his.

"I did love you, Ron. I know I keep saying it, but I need to."

"I know."

"And I think I know why I'm here."

~

We went back to the pond. The lights above thinned and the hum dimmed, and as we got up the sky began to lighten. We left the blanket where it was, turned around, and walked right onto the path that wound around the duck pond.

The sun was bright and the temperature warm; the water still moved in the gentlest of breezes, the light reflecting in ripples across the pond.

I wasn't sure why I wanted to be there until we were.

"That last time I saw you was right here," I reminded him. "I sat on that bench and watched you dump your popcorn into the water, and I could feel pain pouring off you, but there was nothing I could say that was going to make it any better. You got into your car and drove away... The last thing I saw before you left was you sitting there with your head rested on the steering wheel, like you were fighting hard to keep from just banging your head into it as hard as you could."

"I think I wanted to."

"And then the whispers began about what you were doing for the agency and how good you were at it. I hated that, I hated knowing you had gone down that road and I couldn't believe that you of all people—"

"That I could kill other people for a living?"

"It wasn't *you*, Ron. I knew that you'd had to save your own skin before, but the idea that you were hunting people down? That just wasn't you; it wasn't any part of who you were. And then you ate your own gun, and I knew it. I'd broken you. You'd been so wounded by Pat, and then I took your heart and promised you I'd take care of it, and I broke you. I broke you."

A very gentle smile played at the corners of his mouth and he reached up to brush a tear from my cheek with his thumb.

"I broke you," I cried, "and I'm sorry. I am so sorry."

"You didn't break me, Kris."

"If I'd had more of the person I wanted to be in me, I would have taken better care of your feelings. I would have made sure that you were all right and that you knew no matter what, I honestly, genuinely loved you. You'd still be alive, you'd be playing with your great-grandkids, and you'd have gotten to see Chip turn into the man you wanted him to become. And he did, he became such a good man."

"I saw that as it happened."

"But you would have been *there*, Ron. In the flesh. Chip's kids would have grown up with you as their grandfather, and they would have been better for it."

"They did just fine, you know that."

"But it would have been *better*. You would have gotten away from the agency, you would have found someone who deserved your love and your attention, and instead of being here..."

"I would still be here," he said quietly.

"No, you'd be alive."

"Kris." His hands were cupping my face; his eyes clear where mine were filled with tears. "I'm not here because you didn't love me well enough. I knew you loved me. I knew you were better off with Doug. I didn't become the agency's kill boy because of you."

"Chip and I—"

"Essentially, you were my reasons. I wanted to protect you and I'd have done anything to make sure of that. But I made my own decisions, and it was no one's doing other than my own. My mortal timeline was over. If I hadn't ended my own life, it would have ended some other way. You have nothing to be sorry for."

"But I broke you," I cried, still certain of it.

"No, you didn't. I swear that you didn't. If you've been carrying this around as guilt for the last thirty-plus years, I am so sorry. I agreed to do the job to protect you both, but I didn't kill myself because you'd broken me, Kris. I killed myself because I couldn't bear to be the person to end your life. It really is that simple. But if I hadn't, I would have still wound up dead, because it was time."

"I didn't even know—"

"You didn't know how guilty you felt until you reached a point where you needed forgiveness. There's nothing to forgive, which is why you wanted me here. You needed me to forgive you, but you don't need to carry the blame for anything I ever did, or anything I became."

"Ron."

"If what you honestly need is forgiveness, you have it. I forgive you for all the horribly burned dinners I had to choke down to avoid hurting your feelings. I forgive you for dying your hair a streaked bleached blonde when I begged you not to. I forgive you for faking an orgasm or two, even when you knew that's the last thing I wanted you to do. I forgive you for ruining the most expensive suit I would ever own because you really didn't know it wasn't supposed to be thrown in the washing machine with my dirty jeans. I forgive it all, Kris."

"I never faked anything," I tried to say, wanting to laugh at the absurdity of what he was saying to me.

"Oh yeah, you did. I can even tell you when and where, if you want me to."

"No." Now I had to fight the laughter that was warring with my tears. "My God, Ron, I loved you, and I still do."

"I know."

"How can you forgive me any of it?"

"Can you forgive me for my part in everything? Because it took both of us to screw it up."

"You didn't do anything…"

"Neither did you. But can you forgive me for the stupid things I surely did? Because I know I faked it once or twice, too."

"Oh my God, you did not!"

"I got tired. I was older than you, you know."

I fell against him, laughing, and tried to absorb the near electricity that glowed off of him when he put his arms around me.

"Are we connected?" I asked.

"We are," he sighed. "But not the way you mean. You're still my Marge and I'll always be your Horatio, but the man who is still sitting at your bedside, pleading with you to open your eyes? You're far more connected to him. You always will be."

"I thought you weren't supposed to tell me that."

"You won't remember," he whispered.

"If I choose to live, I won't remember any of this?"

He arms went a little tighter. "You can't, Kris."

"Then how can I go back, Ron? How can I decide that? I love Doug but I know he'll be here sooner or later, right? I can turn around and he'll be right there..."

"I know."

"This is when I have to decide, isn't it?"

"It is." He let go, and gestured towards the water, leaning over the rocks that lined the pond to look into the water. "Look."

I leaned over next to him; the woman reflected back at me was my thirty year old self, not the sixty five year old woman who fought arthritis and sagging skin in her own personal war with time. If I stayed, I would remain thin and young for as long as I wanted to, and I could wait for Doug right there.

If I stayed, I would have Ron for company when he wanted; we could see the people I missed. I could find my mother and father. I could find Dan Martin and tease him about his stuffed shirt. I could find Nicky Lockhart, and see the man he would have grown to be.

"Kris," Ron whispered into my ear, "in less than a year Spider and Eileen are going to have a baby girl. And a couple of years later, another. If you choose to live, you'll be there long enough to give those baby girls memories of the grandmother who doted on them, baked them cookies and babysat every chance she had. If you live, you'll be something real to them, not just someone in the stories that Mom and Dad tell, not just the person Grandpa misses more than anything."

"But still."

He reached for me, one hand holding onto mine, his other hand going to my face, and he leaned in slowly, testing, before he kissed me.

"I will love you forever, and miss you in every moment that your heart beats."

He took half a step back, letting go of my hand. He slid his hand up my arm, warm and electric, and when I felt it move to my back I realized his composure had cracked, and tears had welled up in his eyes, spilling onto his cheeks.

"Kris," he breathed, and with my name I felt his hand shove me towards the water, where I would sink like a stone. "Go home."

PART FOUR

I leaned back with my eyes closed, soaking in the warmth of the sun, digging my toes into the sand, relishing every sliver of coolness that wrapped around them. The sound of waves lapping onto the beach was quiet music, the honking of seagulls overhead a drumbeat that was just a little bit out of synch with the melody that was playing out around me.

It was wonderful, and I wanted to take in every bit of it.

"I can't tell Doug any of this. I can't explain how it felt without hurting him. I can't even think about it without feeling guilty."

"You can't be faulted for a complicated dream," Terry pointed out. "He's just grateful you've recovered. I think at this point you could tell him you wanted to pick some random boy toy from the bar at the Charybdis for a night of kinky fun and he'd be fine with it."

I opened one eye. "I might do that, just to see the look on his face."

We were sitting on the beach just outside of the house at Bodega Bay; Chip was crouched in an old lawn chair, leaning forward with his elbows on his knees, having barely said a word through the entire time I poured out the things that I had been pondering for over six months. Terry was in a lounge chair next to me, slathering on sunscreen; I needed to tell them everything I remembered, every detail that I wasn't supposed to still have dancing in my brain. I wanted them to know why I felt so pressed to spend a few days at their beach house, why a weekend away with Doug wasn't enough.

It had to be here, and I needed them.

It had to be just up from where I could still picture Ron's winter cottage on the beach.

Doug was in the house with Spider, watching a baseball game; I knew Chip wanted to be in there with them, but he grasped that I needed to get something out of my system, all the things that had been frustrating me so openly that he worried it was an effect of the stroke.

I cried easily, something I had never done before; I backed down from arguments with Doug, even the insignificant ones. I was quieter; I wasn't the mouthy thing Ron remembered me being and the one they were all used to. Chip noticed and worried, so when I asked him and Terry to sit with me on the beach, he didn't think twice. He simply grabbed the rickety, webbed lawn chair off the deck and carried it to the sand.

And he listened; the few times I had tried to explain to Doug that while I didn't seem to suffer any physical effects from the stroke, there were definitely deep emotional ones, his gut reaction was to simply nod and say, "Of course," and then try to paint a picture for me, one with complicated brushstrokes of medical-speak that left me tired.

I didn't need a lesson in anatomy to know my own brain had attacked me. I didn't need to be reassured that what I felt was normal. I only needed to be able to feel it without feeling as if I needed permission.

Most of all, I couldn't tell him that I missed my dead ex-husband more than I ever had.

"This is horrible," Terry said, "but I'd actually forgotten we'd named Nick after that little boy."

"I didn't," Chip said quietly.

"God, I'm sorry…"

He waved it off. "You never met him, Terry. It's all right. But he pops into my head once in a while and I wonder what he would have become. He'd be over forty now and would probably have a family of his own. I think about him, about my brother. I think about Dan and my parents. Ron. Too many dead people in my brain."

"And Brenda?" Terry asked.

He nodded. "I've never come to terms with that, Terry. If not for what a complete prick I was, she might still be alive." When Terry started to protest, he shook his head. "I know we've been over it and I know you think if she had lived you and I might not be together, but I suspect Kris would have found a way to hook us up one way or another. But the truth is that I treated that girl so horribly... I'm culpable. I'm most of the reason she's dead, so no, I haven't come to terms with it, and I doubt I ever will. I don't think I should."

"We all did things we'll never come to terms with," I said before she could try to argue with him. "The things we did because of the job? I'm not sure we can really justify it all."

Terry held the bottle of sunscreen out to Chip, and when he screwed his face up she pushed out of the chair. "I can't take another cancer scare with you, mister. You're going to wear it, and you're going to wear it thick."

For all of his facial protesting—an all too phony grimace and knotted eyebrows—he leaned into her hands as she rubbed the lotion onto his back. "That weekend in San Francisco," he ventured. "When we were showing you around, right after you met me. If I hadn't practically begged you to give Ron a chance, would you have really walked out on him?"

"Seeing that scar on your chest was a wakeup call. It was the first real hint I had that he wasn't just serious that his job came first, but dead serious. I couldn't fathom how he could leave his son..."

"Sometimes I still can't," Terry muttered. She was working the sunscreen into his shoulders, squirting more onto his chest, fingers brushing over his scar. "He should have grabbed you and run that night."

"But at least now we can be pretty sure Grant wasn't really lashing out at me," Chip said, craning his head back to look at her. "I just happened to get in the way of what would have been a very bloody suicide."

Less bloody than Ron's had been.

Just for a moment, I wondered how Chip's life would have unfolded if Grant had succeeded before Chip walked in on him. He would have lost both parents in one day, and Ron would have had no choice but to take custody of him.

Would that have been enough to get him to quit?

And if he had, I would have never met him. Never met Chip.

My stomach did a slow flip; no Ron, no Chip, and probably no Doug because the team never would have formed. No Spider, no Eileen and future grandkids.

If I hadn't bent to the pleas of a fifteen-year-old boy, where would we all be now?

Completely unselfconsciously, Terry was rubbing the lotion onto Chip's stomach, oblivious to the way he was now watching her face. "Did your grandfather really act like that when Ron took you to meet him?" she asked him. "Called you a bastard?"

Chip's eyebrows knotted together as he reached back into his memory. "Yeah, he was a real piece of work. Ron's mother was cordial but cold as hell, but his father was an ass. And they were never my grandparents, not even when I thought they were. I'm not even sure Ron ever mentioned them to me again after that."

"I still can't picture him as a priest," Terry said with a bit of a laugh. "He struck me as being a little too badass."

"He could be," I said. "But he could also be so warm and gentle...he was always open about how he felt and even when I was mad as hell, I knew that he loved me. I hate that I shoved all that out of my head for so long."

"You visit the man's grave on his birthday every year," Chip pointed out. "I suspect you're there on the anniversary of his death and most holidays, too. I don't think you forgot the good in him."

"Doug doesn't know about that," I started. "I mean, he knows about Christmas, but—"

"Bullshit. He knows."

"Fine. But he doesn't need to know about this. It's still so... overwhelming. I don't know what to make of it and I'm sure it would hurt him."

"Doug's not going to get bent over a dream," Terry said again, snapping the bottle closed. She tossed it onto the sand, stole a kiss from Chip, and sat back down.

Chip folded his arms, and was looking at me with a seriousness that might have made me laugh any other time; he was begging to be made fun of.

"What?" I asked.

He hesitated, as if he wasn't sure he should say anything.

"Chip," I said. "What?"

"What if it wasn't a dream?" He took a deep breath before going on, so much like Ron used to that it stabbed at me. "You're presuming that all of that was only going on in your head, but what if it wasn't?"

Terry reached out with her leg, touching her foot to his. "Come on, Irish. You're not suggesting she really was bouncing around some Northern California slice of heaven, are you?"

"I'm not discounting the possibility."

"I'm not sure that jibes with your Catholic self," Terry teased.

Chip leaned forward again, looking right at me. No matter what the truth was, those green eyes always reminded me of Ron's, and now they were making me ache. "I would say it was all just a complicated dream to divert you away from the things that were happening to you during and after the stroke if not for two things. That little bit about me crawling into the drainage pipe and barely getting out? I never told Ron about it. I never told anyone. I was too afraid of the shit storm I'd get caught up in if I did. Ron and Grant had both just lost my mother, and if I'd told them how close I'd come to killing myself—pissed off wouldn't have covered it. So I kept it to myself. How could he tell you about it if he never knew? It certainly wasn't some factoid buried in the back of your brain."

"You must have said something—maybe to Doug?"

"I don't think so."

"He never told me, either," Terry said. "What the hell were you thinking, Chip? A drainage pipe?"

"Who knows? I don't think I was using my entire brain for any part of my life then. The point is that I never told Ron. And the time I took the bike down Rockville Road. He had no way of knowing that. I never said anything and until you mentioned it, I'd forgotten about it. You shouldn't know about that if that was just a dream."

"But if that wasn't a dream…"

"Then you spent some quality time with someone you love, and you made peace with your feelings about him. You were able to forgive each other. There's not a damned thing wrong with that."

"It has to be a dream, Chip. I didn't make peace about my feelings. I didn't choose life and I didn't choose Doug. I didn't…"

"You didn't get a chance to choose. Ron made the decision for you. You had the chance to ask forgiveness from him, and he wasn't going to let the warm fuzzies keep you from living out the rest of your life. With Doug. Because Ron knew you belonged with him."

"Then I could have waited for him there."

Exasperated, he exhaled sharply and rose from the chair. "Walk with me," he said, reaching out to help me up. "Do you mind, Ter? I'd like to talk to her alone."

I think Terry did mind, but she waved us off.

Holding my hand, his fingers laced between mine so much like the way Ron always had, he headed in the direction of where I pictured Ron's cabin. He walked slowly, knowing I would have trouble keeping up if he didn't; the stroke may not have robbed me of anything, but age certainly had.

When we were out of Terry's earshot he asked, "Do you really think you would choose to die instead of coming back to see your grandkids? Or that you'd have taken what would amount to a blip of time with Ron over what might be ten or fifteen years with Doug?"

"Does it matter?"

"You don't want to admit it could be anything but a dream."

I wasn't sure how I could make him understand; I desperately wanted to believe it wasn't a dream. I wanted more than anything to know that I'd spent that time with Ron, and that when I did die he'd be waiting there for me.

Ron had seen Chip grow into a man, at least. He'd seen his grandkids born and watched them grow; he knew them as well as any of us did, and he loved them as much as we did. If he could see all that and feel all that, and didn't feel as if he was missing something, then I could still see my son become a father, and I would be able to watch as his daughters grew into women.

I also hoped that none of it had happened; I hated the idea that there was even a wisp of a chance that I would have opted to leave my husband and family behind.

There I had love; here I had love. And I wasn't certain which I would have chosen.

"It doesn't matter what it was," I finally said. "What matters is that I remembered why I married Ron in the first place, and that even when we were fighting, I still loved him."

"You knew that."

"But I've felt guilty about it for thirty years, Chip. I keep shoving it down my throat like stolen cookies. If Doug knew, he'd feel second best, and that's not fair."

"All right, fine. So you don't tell Doug. But you can't deny some pretty stark things—he told you things he didn't know about when he was alive."

"He also said I wouldn't remember."

"He didn't count on how damned stubborn you are."

He stopped and turned back to look at Terry, and I felt a shiver run through me; we were standing in the spot where Ron and I had lounged on the sand, looking out at the ocean. Behind us, the house that stood in place of Ron's cabin. When he looked back at me, he asked softly, "Right here, right?"

How could you know that?

"You hesitated," he said before I could think of anything to say. "I looked at Terry, and you very slightly twitched in the direction of that house. This is where he hangs out, isn't it?"

"You have no doubt, do you?"

"How could I?"

"Chip—"

His face softened, and his mouth turned up in slight smile. "Kris. Since the day he died, I've worried that he was burning in some horrible circle of hell, even when I knew deep down he was a decent person. But now? I know he's fine. I know why he did the things he did, and I know he was a far better father than I ever gave him credit for. I knew he loved me, but"—he swallowed hard—"he *loved* me. And make no mistake, it doesn't matter who the semen donor was, Ron was my dad. Not just my father. He was my *dad*. I wasn't just an inconvenient obstacle in his life."

"You thought that?" I set my hand on his chest, fingers resting where his scar was thickest. "Of course you did. If only he'd let us know what he was doing."

"He couldn't. If he had, I would have screwed it up by saying or doing something stupid, and you would have stayed with him. And he knew, Kris, he knew you needed out. Maybe it wasn't right there in the front of his brain, but he fostered the distance between you and once you were with Doug…he walked away completely."

"He loved us both," I murmured.

He sniffed, and I looked up at his face; his eyes were filled with tears and he was struggling with them. "He's not in hell, Kris. He's not—" He blinked and let the tears spill over. "Holy fuck, this is selfish. But if he's not—"

"Neither will we be."

"How many people did I kill? Yet I told him I thought he was nothing more than a murderer. I didn't even try to get him to talk about what he was doing. I just shut him down and told him I thought he was a murderer."

Even so, when Ron killed himself, Chip wanted to clear his name; he wanted the whispers in the agency halls to stop, for the gossip mill to grind to an embarrassing halt. He wanted the people who were whispering the worst about the agency's rumored assassin to decide that he hadn't take a coward's way out; there had to be something no one knew. Something to lend a little honor to having been found in a toilet stall with his brains splattered on the wall.

As quickly as he jumped into it, he stopped.

I wanted to know what he'd really found.

Why did he stop looking for answers?

With a deep, shaky breath, he told me. "I saw the list, Kris. I saw the names of the people he hunted down and they things they did. And trust me, he was picking off some horrible people. But then I got to the last name on that list"—he swallowed hard—"I didn't see what he did at first. I saw the list of crimes the person was accused of, and I couldn't think of a single reason why he had hesitated finishing the job.

"But then I showed it to Doug, and he saw the same thing Ron did. He saw your name, and he freaked out. He never looked beyond the name to the details; he saw your name, and the world just… stopped. That's when I knew why Ron had done it. He couldn't get past it being your name on his list. He couldn't live with it."

"But you never told anyone."

"I left it alone. Gut feeling told me I should, and Doug didn't disagree. And Doug never told you any of it, did he?"

"No. No, he didn't."

"And yet you know."

I reached up and brushed tears off his face. "He knew you loved him, Chip. He never doubted it."

"I really did have a dad," he whispered.

"You were luckier than we realized. You had two, and they both loved you. They'll both be waiting for you, along with your mother. I didn't see her, but I know how much she must want to get her arms around you."

He sniffed hard, still not able to stop the tears.

"I still remember the fifteen year old who admitted he missed her. You couldn't cry in front of me then."

"I would have, if you'd waited ten minutes," he said softly. "You were the only one who ever really listened when I talked about her, Kris. I missed her horribly."

"Still do."

He nodded. "I miss Ron, too. And if there's a chance that I'll get to see him again, it *can't* have been just a dream."

"I know."

"But?"

"But...I think I wanted to stay there with him, Chip. I wasn't ready to choose and I honestly don't know what I would have done if he hadn't pushed me. He spelled out everything I would give up if I stayed there, and still..."

"Not just staying there. Don't sugar-coat it. If you had *died*. No one is ready for that." When I took a hesitant step back, he added, "Not even you are, Kris. You have so many things to look forward to. And now you have the chance to make sure that the people you love understand exactly how much. Everything you've ever wanted to tell Doug—you know you have the time to not just say it, but show him."

He looked over my head, to where Terry was still sitting.

"I'd give anything to know how much more time I might have with her."

"You weren't listening, werc you?"

"I was. And I heard quite clearly that when I die, I will probably feel every moment of time that passes before she joins me. And I imagine that heaven or not, it will be quite painful."

"I don't think it will be. I think it will pass more like a little kid knowing Christmas is coming. You'll be excited, but deep down you won't want it to come too soon. You'll miss her, but you'll want her to go on living."

It hit me then.

"He wants me to live," I whispered. "He knows I'm coming back. He can wait."

"Christmas," Chip said.

"But he also said he wasn't the love of my life. How can he want so much for me and be excited to see me again if I'm not?"

"Well hell, if I die before you do, I'll be excited to see you again on the other side. Maybe not with all the happy horny thoughts Ron is sure to have—"

"Oh my God!"

"Well." He shrugged. "I have had some pretty conflicted and messed up feelings about you in the past. For all I know we get there and the taboos fall away."

"And that's been the wall in your way? That it would have been taboo?"

"When I met you," he said carefully, "the only way I knew how to deal with women was through sex. And that was with women I barely gave a second thought to. Then there you were, incredibly beautiful, paying attention to me that wasn't laced with all these disappointed expectations...I didn't know how to separate loving someone from being in love with someone, and I especially didn't understand how feeling like that didn't have to have anything to do with sex. It took some time."

"Doug tried to tell me."

"Doug helped me wade through a lot of it. You can love someone like crazy and not want to do them. Who knew?"

"Will be you honest with me about something? If you know the answer, you'll tell me?"

He nodded.

"Does Doug feel like I settled? Like my marriage was falling apart and he was just there and then knocked me up, not that I was deeply in love with him?"

"I was there, Kris. You obviously loved him."

"I know that. I want to know what he felt at the beginning. Because when we started out I honestly didn't consider being with him forever until I got pregnant. So I wonder, does he feel like I settled?"

"Did you settle?"

"Chip."

"It's a legitimate question, Kris. But no, he's never made me think he feels like that. But I wonder…if you hadn't gotten pregnant when you did, would you have married him? Or would you have given Ron another chance?"

"Not knowing why he was doing what he was? No, I wouldn't have."

"And Doug? Do you think you would have eventually married him, baby or not?"

"Spider sped things along, but I would have married Doug eventually."

"Then why would he feel like you settled?"

"I just want to be sure."

"You love him, he knows that. You trust him?"

"What? Of course I do."

"Then tell him, Kris. Tell him about Ron, tell him about everything he said to you and all the things he showed you. Tell him that you could have stayed there and existed completely happy and out of pain, and then tell him that you came home."

~

I hadn't been to Crissy Field in years. I wanted to go back to the beach, to find a bench where we could sit and where we would have the Golden Gate Bridge in full view. I told Doug it was just a place I wanted to revisit, but deep down I knew I would sit there on a bench and look for an excited yet incredibly patient golden retriever.

That would be a sign, I told myself. Proof.

It was late when we got there, twilight already beginning to give way to night, and the breeze that picked up across the bay was cold and wet.

I didn't care. I just wanted to sit there with my husband and watch the waves lap up onto the sand, and look at the bridge lit up against the night sky.

Doug didn't think it mattered if I'd had an extensive dream or a true out of body experience; whether everything took place in my head or I'd actually spent time with my dead ex-husband, he believed that the ultimate choice had been mine.

"So Ron pushed you into the water before you made a final decision. The simple truth is that if you had wanted to die, you would have died. You're not done here, Kris."

He understood that I was torn and wasn't hurt by the idea that I'd been tempted to just let go and spend the rest of his life with Ron.

"You'd be waiting for me. If that means you also spend some time test riding Ron, fine."

"Seriously."

He leaned back on the bench, his arm behind me. With a light laugh, he said, "Say it was going to be another ten years before I died. I grieve hard for a few years and then some nasty little redhead catches my eye. Would you be pissed off if I caved into temptation?"

"No. Of course not. But I know you; you don't go for nasty, you'd be checking out the nice little old ladies who can cook."

"Hey, this is my fantasy. Let me have it."

"Fine. While I'm off doing bouncy things with my ex-husband, you can find yourself a nasty redhead."

He scooted just a bit closer, pulling his arm a bit tighter around my shoulders. "It had to be a dream, though," he said quietly. "I know Chip wants it to have really happened, but from where I sit—it has to have been a dream."

"God, don't give me the entire medical rundown."

"It has nothing to do with medical facts. It has everything to do with the thought that you're going to die first."

"We don't know that."

"Ron told you that if you lived, you'd be real to our grandkids and not just the person Grandpa misses more than anything. That insinuates that I'll be left behind. So it has to be a dream, because you can't die first."

"But if I do," I pointed out, "you at least know that I'm having a pretty good time and that sooner or later you'll be there with me."

"But I don't want to be *here* without you. And I know that's selfish, because if by some wild stroke—no pun intended—you really did find your way to heaven for a while, then you were out of pain and happy."

"I'm happy now," I told him, resting my hand on his leg, giving it a gentle squeeze. "I'm not sure I've ever been happier."

"But?"

"But...I'm also not afraid of what happens if I have another stroke and if it kills me. And just in case, you need to really think about life without me. Stop backing away from the idea and whining about wanting to be the one who dies first. It might very well be me, and it'll be all right."

"Well, yeah, for you. You get to go to the beach and play with Ron. I'll be at home seeing you everywhere and missing the hell out of you."

"Okay, so you die first. Is it more acceptable that I'm left behind missing you and seeing you everywhere?"

"Yes, it is," he said with a twist of a laugh.

"Fine. We'll pick a day, go for a ride heading toward Tahoe, miss a curve, and tumble off a mountain. We can die together."

"Damn, you're mean."

"And you love that." I snuggled in closer, feeling the bite of the cold seeping through my coat, and I tried to absorb a little of the warmth he radiated. "We have to be honest with ourselves, Doug. No matter who goes first, the truth is that we have a whole lot more years behind us than we do ahead. We're not even middle aged anymore. We're old."

"It could still be ten or twenty more, you know."

"And it could be five or six. I'm not even talking about the chances of a swan dive off one of the Sierra Mountains. I could have another stroke or a heart attack. I'm in horrible shape, Doug. You were smart enough to keep working out, and I just..."

"You just decided to dive into the whole housewife and mother thing, and you didn't take time for yourself. That's as much my fault as it is yours."

"You didn't exactly tie me to the stove, you know."

"No, but I also didn't exactly push you into doing the things you loved. You left the agency and married me, and then what? We had Spider and you pushed back all the things you used to do. When was the last time you flew an airplane, Kris?"

I know I'd flown after we married, but I had to reach back to remember when the last flight was. And when I remembered, the sadness that pulled through me was bittersweet. "When my dad died," I said. "I flew his ashes up for one last time and we scattered them. God, that was a beautiful day. It was cold and clear, and when we pulled up over the bay the sun was just starting to go down...all I could see was red and gold, and the water below. I remember thinking he would have loved it, nothing but the ocean stretched ahead and the sun setting almost perfectly."

"And instead of keeping his plane, which is what he wanted, you sold it."

"I didn't think I could ever fly it again," I said. "That last flight was for him, and it would never be the same."

"But you didn't have to stop flying. We could have gotten you another plane."

I didn't know how to explain it to him; I flew because of my father, and when he was gone, so was my reason for loving it as much as I had. It didn't appeal to me anymore.

"I didn't give up the things I loved, Doug. I just found other things I loved more. You. Spider. And unfortunately, baking."

That made him laugh, and he leaned over, melting a warm kiss against my lips. "Do you remember when Nick was kidnapped, the night we brought him home? I couldn't figure out what the hell to feed a nine month old, and you went straight for the pancakes. I always thought it was because you knew he could chew them, not that it was the only thing you could cook without charring the hell out of it."

"I got better."

"Yes, you learned to make a grilled cheese sandwich."

"Shut up," I snickered.

He got up, holding out a hand to help me up. "Come on, you're starting to shiver. We don't have to go home, but we need to at least get in the car and run the heater."

"Better idea," I said. "Let's get a room downtown and stay overnight. We can spend the night pretending we aren't older than dirt, and tomorrow we can wander around Union Square whining about how sore we are, and then have lunch somewhere."

"Looking for the giant piece of chocolate cake you didn't get in the afterlife?"

"Something like that."

He stopped and leaned against the car door, pulling me against him. "Dream or not, you know why it doesn't bother me? Because you put me first, Kris. You've always put me first. And I remember how horrible it was for you thinking you were third on Ron's list."

I started to protest, but he was shaking his head. "So now you know that you weren't, but at the time you felt like it. And for all these years, you've made sure I always knew where I was on your list. Whatever else comes after this doesn't matter, because when it did, you put me first."

I didn't know what to say to him. I held on tighter, resting my head on his shoulder, hoping that I had longer than I suspected before I really had to let go.

He turned the car heater on high and while we waited for it to warm up we looked out the windshield at the Golden Gate Bridge; it was the long way home, but that was the direction we would head tomorrow, and Doug would drive, just so I could look at the it the entire time we were on it.

Maybe he was right; regardless of how I'd woken up from the stroke, I chose him.

I kept watching the bridge as he pulled out of the parking slot, the lights of cars streaming across it, the glow of light radiating upward. And just above it, stretching over the water off Crissy Field, for just a moment, I was sure I saw a soft blanket of red light unfurl and then thin, disappearing like fog.

www.ingramcontent.com/pod-product-compliance
Lightning Source LLC
Chambersburg PA
CBHW050539260626
47157CB00002B/359